THE SHELL

THE RAYMOUTH SAGA / BOOK 1

J R CLEMONS

VERSION 1

ISBN 979-8-9876839-0-3 *(paperback)*

ISBN 979-8-9876839-1-0 *(ebook)*

A man will come to change the fate of the clans and the kingdoms.
He will come from an unimaginable distance and live his life in the life of another.
The clans will rise with him and a daughter.
He will be a warrior, a hero, and a legend.
Good will flow from him for a thousand years.

Prophecy of the Ancients

HIGH KINGDOM

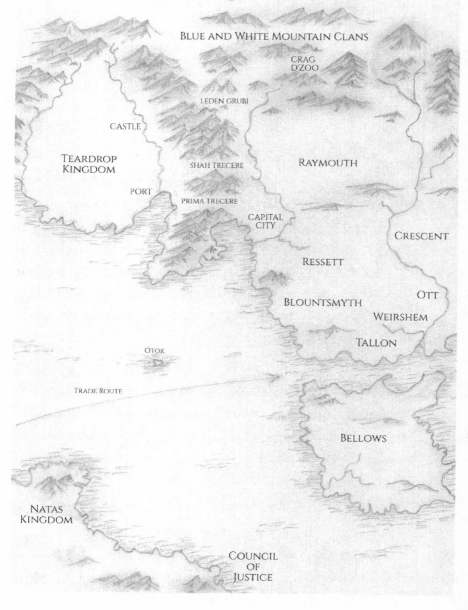

BLUE AND WHITE MOUNTAIN CLANS

CRAG
D'ZOO

LEDEN GRUBI

CASTLE

TEARDROP
KINGDOM

SHAH TRECERE

RAYMOUTH

PORT

PRIMA TRECERE

CAPITAL
CITY

CRESCENT

RESSETT

OTT

BLOUNTSMYTH

WEIRSHEM

TALLON

OTOK

TRADE ROUTE

BELLOWS

NATAS
KINGDOM

COUNCIL
OF
JUSTICE

Chapter One

The Shell

The last warm days of summer escorted the Royal Courier as he made his way to the Teardrop Castle. Upon arrival, he was directed to the study of Chancellor Geoffrey Goldblatt. Although the title *Chancellor* no longer technically applied, having held the position for twenty years made it part of his identity. In fact, all who knew him called him *Chancellor*.

"Enter," Chancellor Goldblatt said in response to the knock on his door.

A young officer of the Royal Guard moved forward to stand at attention before the Chancellor's desk. "I have been instructed to deliver this to you personally," he said as he presented a plain envelope.

"Thank you," Goldblatt said. "You have had a long journey. Go to the kitchen and ask the cook, Nelly, to give you something to eat. It will take me a while to read the letter. Were you instructed to wait for my reply?"

"Yes, sir," the lieutenant responded.

Wait for my answer. Goldblatt thought. *They are expecting a quick reply—a matter of urgency?*

"After you eat, find the Captain of the Guard and he will get you accommodations for this evening. I will have my response ready by the morning," the Chancellor said. "Oh yes, the captain can also tell you the best place in the village to get a pint of ale."

A broad smile crossed the young lieutenant's face. "Thank you, sir."

An ordinary person would have just opened the envelope, but Geoffrey Goldblatt was not ordinary. He was a renowned scholar with a keen eye for detail. Letters from the Capital City were rare, and those delivered by a Royal Courier even more so. As he studied the envelope, Goldblatt reminded himself the manner of delivery is itself a message. The young man was a lieutenant in the Royal Guard, not the sort who normally delivered simple letters. It was clear whatever the letter contained required competency and confidentiality. A young, aspiring lieutenant assured both.

The plain envelope, with just his name on the outside, was an attempt to make the matter appear to be ordinary. The handwriting placing the name *Geoffrey Goldblatt* on the outside was from a skilled person. *It must be from the current chancellor, who had written at the request of a member of the royal family. But which one?*

Goldblatt opened the letter and found another envelope inside, this one of finer paper, but with less experienced handwriting. The inscription read: *The Honorable Geoffrey Goldblatt, Administrator of the Teardrop Kingdom, and ex-Chancellor of the High Kingdom.* Rather than being glued as the first, this one bore the red signet seal of the king.

Whatever motivated this letter is significant. King Michael has not communicated with me in nearly eight years. In addition, the titles are telling. 'Administrator of the Teardrop Kingdom' was a subtle message that King Michael had granted my current position. The reference to 'ex-Chancellor' was a reminder of King Michael's ability to remove positions from anyone he chose.

The late Great King Mikael selected Goldblatt as the youngest chancellor in history. This brought him into direct contact with Prince Michael, the first-born son of the Inland Queen. The two should have been friends. They were approximately the same age, with Goldblatt being slightly younger. Both were deeply immersed in the kingdom's politics and the king constantly consulted them. Goldblatt was never a threat to

Prince Michael. However, his sophisticated knowledge of diplomacy and scholastic skills made Michael insecure. In addition, Michael felt, more often than not, the king took Goldblatt's advice over his.

Years later, when Michael assumed the throne, it was this insecurity and envy which drove Geoffrey Goldblatt out as chancellor. The Queen Mother, who understood the amount of respect the Great King Mikael had for Goldblatt, interceded to ensure Michael did not foolishly punish Goldblatt.

This presented a dilemma for the new king. He wanted Goldblatt away from the Capital City so as not to be compared, yet he wanted to accede to the requests of his mother.

The solution, which seemed perfect, was to appoint Geoffrey Goldblatt as Administrator to the armpit of all the associated kingdoms—the Teardrop Kingdom. It had gained its name partly because of its shape and partly because nothing good ever happened there, thus the Kingdom of Tears. It had only two redeeming qualities: it was the ancestral castle of the Great King Mikael, and it was far from the Capital City.

Geoffrey Goldblatt did not find this position to be a demotion. It removed him from the day-to-day clamor of the Capital City and gave him an opportunity to spend time with his books and his correspondence. During his tenure as Administrator, he continued to maintain contacts with every major power within the known world. In many ways, he was as well-informed now as he was the last day he had served as chancellor. The only difference was no one was coming to his door asking for advice. So, Goldblatt remained happy in the quiet solitude of the Teardrop Kingdom.

Finally, Goldblatt broke the seal. Inside was a handwritten note from the king.

My old friend, Geoffrey:
I am not sure whether you are aware, we entered into

a marriage contract between the High Kingdom and the Kingdom of King Natas for the marriage of his first-born daughter, the Princess Tarareese, to Prince Merryk, a first-born son of the High Kingdom.

The marriage counselor who drafted the document was personally selected by the Provost. King Natas believes the groom should have been Prince Merreg. I have it on good authority he intends to approach the Provost to revoke the contract of marriage based upon an alleged error in the names. I am confident the Council will affirm the original contract as signed by all and confirmed by the Provost himself.

As a father, I am very proud of both my sons. Although, I have found the actions of my younger son, Prince Merryk, are often disappointing. He is, candidly, not filled with the social graces or the normal pursuits one would find in a man of a royal family. I am concerned if he remains in the capital until the wedding, they might make a case he lacks the mental capacity to marry, which would render the marriage contract void.

We have already spent the first half of the dowry to order two new warships, and we have pledged the second half to complete the ships. A loss of this revenue for the High Kingdom would be quite devastating.

I would ask you to take young Prince Merryk under your wing. Let him stay in the Teardrop Kingdom through the marriage ceremony. I am confident being away from the Capital City will remove pressures on him. Perhaps this will allow you to instruct him, in what I am sorry to say, will be basic social skills and communication. My old friend, I believe this is the best solution.

I know I could command you to do this, but I am sure it is unnecessary. I believe your love for our kingdom will allow you to help, if not for me, for my father. You may send a simple reply with the messenger. I will have my brother, the Lord Commander, deliver Prince Merryk within a fortnight.

I hope you are doing well, and I thank you for your help.

Michael

Geoffrey noted the addition of the article '*a*' in front of *first-born son*. This confirmed the rumors about confusion, intended or unintended, over who was, in fact, the first-born son of King Michael. If someone did not understand the unique nature of succession in the High Kingdom, one would not recognize the possibility of two first-born sons.

The peril was obvious to Goldblatt. Losing the ships would severely weaken the kingdom's defense. A weakened defense was exactly what King Natas would want.

Goldblatt knew the story of Prince Merryk, and it was a sad tale. He was the first-born son of the Inland Queen Amanda, and joined the household with his older brother, Merreg, the first-born son of the Outland Queen Rebecca. Merreg, three years senior to Merryk, had grown quickly to be large and strong. Together with his twin cousins, sons of the Lord Commander, they had made Merryk's life miserable. The three older, stronger boys had delighted in tormenting young Merryk.

At the earliest ages, Queen Amanda had blunted part of the bullying. As Merryk got older, King Michael demanded he spend more time with men and less with women, which opened him to a never-ending flow of harassment and ridicule. The abuse affected not only the young man academically and socially, but also physically.

From birth, he had been a long gangly child with spindly arms and legs. Awkward by nature, he was prone to falling over his own feet, making him even more susceptible to tripping by his brother and cousins. All the abuse took a toll. Young Merryk had become hunched over, in an attempt to become invisible.

The last time Goldblatt saw him, he was about ten or eleven, and had developed a stutter. Goldblatt could already see Merryk withdrawing, and it evoked sympathy. The Chancellor guessed the prince must now be eighteen or close to nineteen.

The politics of the situation were intriguing. The Council of Justice handled the negotiations and drafting of all marriage contracts between royal families. The Provost and his counselors had an impeccable reputation for accuracy. This accuracy had prevented many disputes and was the basis for a steep fee based upon the size of the dowry. They permitted only the signatures of the parties on the final documents of marriage. Questioning the document was highly unusual. Revoking one for an error would impact all future agreements and fees.

Goldblatt surmised the current problem came to light when a date for the wedding was raised. King Natas had signed an agreement to marry his first-born daughter to the first-born son of King Michael. Merreg was the oldest son and assumed to be the first-born son. By tradition, the wedding would occur after the groom's twenty-first birthday, which for Merreg would have been within the year. When a date two or three years out was presented, King Natas discovered what could best be described as a scrivener's error. The name 'Michael Merryk Raymouth,' the younger first-born son rather than the expected older first-born 'Michael Merreg Raymouth' was on the signed and approved document.

Of course, Goldblatt would take the assignment. He would have taken the young man even without the current problem. His heart had gone out to him when he last saw him. Removing him from the abuse of his relatives might give Merryk an opportunity to grow and become more like a normal member of the royal family. He had no delusions about getting a scholar or someone impressive. He expected only a gangly, broken young man, a mere shell.

The next morning, after a quick visit into the village and a pint or two of ale, the young lieutenant returned to the Capital City with a simple envelope addressed to the king with the message:

> *Ex-Chancellor Goldblatt would most assuredly be honored to have Prince Merryk join him in the Teardrop Kingdom.*

CHAPTER TWO

RAYMOND

The digital display on Raymond's new car flashed 'Annabelle.' *Where is the answer button?* Raymond diverted his eyes from the road long enough to locate the point on the steering wheel. *This car has too many buttons. I need to read the manual.* "Hello."

"Where are you? Have you left yet?" Annabelle replied.

"I left Skamania about fifteen minutes ago. It is raining in sheets, which makes it seem even darker."

"How did things go?

"About as well as I could expect, if you can imagine twenty civil engineers talking about multi-state water management."

"Exciting, just like my day in a room of quarreling lawyers."

"How about you go to the condo, and I will pick up two steaks on the way?" Raymond suggested.

"Sounds great. Just be careful. This is the time of night when the deer come out."

"Don't worry, they designed this new car to practically drive itself. Oh Crap!"

There was a sound of skidding tires, followed by silence.

"Raymond! Raymond! Raymond!"

Blackness surrounded Raymond. *Where am I? What happened?* He shouts. His words fall like a stone dropped into a bottomless pit with no reply or acknowledgment. Darkness is described as the absence of light, but what surrounded Raymond had a texture, a sober thickness not dependent upon light for definition. It was 'black.'

Where am I? he cried again. Nothing!

What happened? He thought. *I am all alone with this blackness. What can I remember, the last thing?* The only response was the same: Nothing!

How long this blackness surrounded him, he did not know.

There was a flash. A sudden glimmer of white light bouncing toward him, first as a pinpoint, then turning into a beam.

"It's okay. We found you," said the man attached to the light. Raymond saw the large brim of the hat on a deputy looking at him. "There's been an accident. You're injured. Don't worry, help is on the way."

Blackness returned.

It's impossible to tell how often a human mind can repeat a single thought, but Raymond's attention to 'there was an accident' and 'help is on the way' consumed him. He reviewed each word in precise detail, clinging to each intonation, trying to squeeze more information out of his brain. Nothing else came. He remained engulfed in the same deep blackness. Raymond thought, *I may be in some personal hell, trapped here forever, going over and over the same thoughts, never changing! I don't know what to do!* This time he received a response, not from the blackness but from within himself. ***Panic kills, focus and live.***

After an unknown period, there came another flash, not of light, although it included light. It was a flash of feeling. Raymond felt the sudden attachment to every cell in his body. A sudden flood of sensation reconnected to each of his senses.

I can feel! I can feel everything! He exclaimed within his head. He realized during all his time in the blackness, he had not been aware of his body. *I feel cold, wet, and my head really hurts. There is light, but my vision is blurry.*

Then voices: Voice One, "I thought you said he was dead. He is still breathing. He looks bad. We should just kill him."

Voice Two, dark and ominous, "Only if you want to travel with his rotting body all the way back to the Capital City. I have seen this kind of injury. He will be lucky if he lasts a couple of days. We will take him to the castle and let time kill him!"

The last statement was more of a command, and less of a comment. Raymond felt rough hands grab him by the shoulders and lift him up.

Raymond returned to the blackness. Once more alone, his mind had more to review. *The deputy said, 'help is on the way.' The comments from the last two voices didn't indicate help at all. In fact, they were quite the opposite. How can both be true? One must be false, but which one? Either 'help is on the way' or 'let time kill him.' I prefer help is coming.* He reviewed the two new voices exactly as he had done the deputy's. Raymond could not shake the harsh insensitivity of the second voice. He also had the distinct impression his head hurt.

Slowly, he became aware of his surroundings, not preceded by a flashing light or by a bolt of sensation, but more of an awakening from the grayness of sleep. Again, he heard voices, but different voices. The first voice was older and kinder than the dark voice.

"If he does not wake up within the next day, I am afraid he never will, or worse, he will awake and be nothing like himself."

A thinner, softer male voice replied, "Chancellor, he needs a chance. He is a prince, grandson of Great King Mikael. He is so young and frail. There must be something we can do?"

"Unfortunately, Smallfolks, only time will determine the outcome," the older voice said. "The first thing we need to determine is if he even knows who he is."

Raymond slipped back into the darkness. His immediate thought, *this darkness is not as black! I still can feel my body and the surroundings.* Raymond's consciousness reached out, like the tentacles of a sea beast extending into an unfamiliar environment, tentative at first and then growing more confident.

I must be in a medical facility. My head is pounding. Why haven't they given me pain medication? If the last voices were my doctors, they don't have very good bedside manners. 'May not wake up' is not what I need to hear. Maybe they thought I was so far gone I could not hear them. I can tell them I am not who they think I am, if I wake up!

Raymond's mind continued to search the surrounding room. *If I am in a medical facility, there should be sounds or smells I can identify. I don't hear a monitor's constant 'beep, beep, beep.' I would have expected a monitor with a head injury. I can smell, but it smells nothing like a hospital. I smell an open fire, but hospitals don't have fireplaces burning actual wood. I don't even have one of those in my condo. I have a nice ornamental one which would never smell of wood. Everything also has an odor of dust and old furniture, like grandma's house. Maybe I'm here until they can transport me.*

Other comments confused him. *I am in my mid-forties. How can they possibly think I am young? Frail is not a word that has described me since I was a child, if ever. Why do they keep calling me 'prince?'* The more

Raymond thought, the more questions he had, including the one which would not go away: *Where am I?*

The words of the ominous voice made Raymond cautious to speak. Raymond lay quietly, allowing the surrounding people to reveal more about themselves. He had become particularly attuned to the movements and mutterings of the small voice he had heard in the last conversation. *I think the man called him Smallfolks. That's a strange name, but if it is good enough for them, it will be good enough for me.*

Smallfolks was constantly in the room: adding more wood to the fireplace, gently determining if Raymond was still breathing, and being sure the rough blankets had not fallen. Smallfolks seemed truly concerned for his health. The man's unique habit of wandering around muttering intrigued Raymond. *Muttering is a word we rarely use. It always describes the odd habit of talking to yourself.* A mental smile crossed Raymond's mind. *Yes, just like I am talking to myself now.*

The mutterings of Smallfolks were confusing. "No accident! Might as well just left him on the steps. Never trusted the uncle. No regard for a family member. No accident! He will get better." Listening, Raymond drifted off to sleep. He identified it as sleep, not blackness or darkness, because when he woke up, he was in the same place.

Awakening, two events affected him. The first was the pounding in his head. *Something has happened to my head. My guess is I have a concussion, but how did I get a concussion?* He thought back to the statement from the deputy. *I was in an accident. I hit my head. Yes, that makes sense,* he said to himself. *But what about the ominous voice? This does not match with 'Help is on the way.' I still don't understand.*

The second event was a need to go to the bathroom. He had attempted to move when no one was around and found it impossible. If he was going to go to the bathroom, he would need help. Raymond thought, *I have no choice. I must speak.*

He managed to first move a few fingers on each hand and then made an indistinct rumbling sound in his throat. *My throat is dry,* he said to himself. *I need water.* He made another moaning sound. Instantly, Smallfolks came to his side. Raymond had not opened his eyes, relying on his senses of smell and hearing to identify his surroundings. Now he attempted to open his eyes over the protests of his pounding head.

In front of him was a small man, commensurate with the voice he had heard, older than he had imagined, with long gray hair and a genuine look of concern upon his face.

"Where am I?" he said, but the words failed as they fell out of his dry throat.

Smallfolks immediately grabbed a cup of water and pressed it to Raymond's lips. Raymond gratefully sipped the water. It helped clear his throat. He tried again, "Where am I?"

The man replied, "You are safe, My Prince! You are safe! Do you know who you are?"

"Raymond," he tried to say as clearly as possible.

Smallfolk's face broke into a broad grin. "Yes, My Prince, you are a Raymouth. Prince Merryk Raymouth."

Raymond wanted to correct him, but the man seemed so delighted by the fact he had said his name, it did not seem like the right time. The water had helped the dryness in Raymond's throat, but had done nothing to deal with the other issue. With his head still pounding, it took effort to convey his need to relieve himself.

Raymond hoped he could stand and walk to the restroom. Instead, the old man brought him a rough bucket with a lid and helped Raymond sit up. Although humiliating to have a stranger assist him, he appreciated the help. Lying back down, Raymond drifted into sleep.

CHAPTER THREE

AWAKE

A hand touched Raymond's shoulder, as Smallfolks gently shook him awake. Raymond's head continued to pound, only slightly less than before. His eyes opened to the image of Smallfolks standing over him. The man was aptly named. He was diminutive, being no more than four and a half feet high. He wore the same rough tunic as yesterday. His eyes had the same color of gray as his long but neat beard.

"You need to eat something now, My Prince. Nelly has brought soup from the kitchen," Smallfolks said, pointing in the direction of the door where a middle-aged woman stood in a large white apron holding a tray.

Nelly looked like a cook. She had a bit of flour dusting the side of her hair and spots on her otherwise clean apron, showing something splattered during cooking. Although unkind to say, she was the stereotypical cook, a little plump but with a large warm smile. Her black hair was tied in a knot on the top of her head. With the mention of her name, Nelly moved across the room, setting the tray on a table next to the bed.

Raymond needed the help of both Smallfolks and Nelly to sit up. Responding to the surging in his head, Raymond had to close his eyes several times as he adjusted to being vertical.

Nelly beamed at Raymond and said, "We are all glad to see you awake, My Prince. We were worried." Completing her task, she moved toward the door.

On the tray was a large bowl of steaming broth with a few pieces of meat and some vegetables. On the side was a piece of freshly baked bread with a bit of butter. Although Raymond preferred to grab the spoon himself, his efforts failed. *I guess this is to be expected with a head injury,* he thought.

Smallfolks said, "Do not worry. I will take care of it for you." Smallfolks began slowly feeding soup to Raymond.

"Young master, tomorrow Chancellor Goldblatt would like to speak with you. He is concerned about your well-being. He, however, thought it best to limit the number of people you see until you feel better. You are new here, and we want you to feel this is your home," Smallfolks said with great sympathy and a large smile.

Raymond accepted the food and the conversation with little return contribution. Raymond thought. *There are many things which make little sense. How did I get here and where is here? Chancellor Goldblatt must be the other voice I heard with Smallfolks.* His head was thinking clearer than it had in the past days, but several questions swirled into his brain. *When are the real medical people coming? What about the man with the dark voice? What do I need to do to get an aspirin?*

There was a kind and considerate nature surrounding Smallfolks and Nelly. They both appeared tied close to this place. The cloak of night hid the surrounding room in darkness and other than the sparkling and crackling of the fire, he couldn't tell much about his surroundings. Of one thing he was sure, the warmth of the fire and the kindness of both Smallfolks and Nelly seemed to go together.

"It is time for a rest," Smallfolks said as he picked up the tray. "Tomorrow morning, the Chancellor will visit. Now get some sleep, young master. I will be close all night long if you need anything; merely speak out." Smallfolks helped Raymond back down to the pillow. His head continued to pound as he drifted to sleep. This time, for the best of reasons, he was tired.

———— ❈ ————

Raymond turned his head slightly to watch the sunlight creep into the room, reclaiming each item hidden by the previous night. The first thing he noticed were walls made of large blocks of stone. Arches spanned both the window and the door, showing they were structural, holding up whatever was above. *How do I know this?* he asked himself. He lay in a large bed on one side of the room with the window to the left of the foot and the door and the fireplace to the right. Across from the end of the bed stood a chest of drawers made of heavy wood. A piece of carpet hung on the wall behind the chest. *No, tapestry. The theme is about deer and hunters.* Raymond said to himself. *The bowl and spoon from last night were roughly hewn wood. The sole source of heat is the fireplace, and I have seen nothing requiring electricity. This must be a retro hunting lodge.*

Smallfolks quietly appeared in the room. "Good morning, My Prince. Are you feeling better today? Yes? Are you hungry? Nelly has prepared some boiled eggs, fresh bread, and honey. Can you eat?"

In a raspy voice, Raymond responded, "Yes, thank you. But I will need some help to sit up."

"No problem," replied Smallfolks, who immediately added pillows behind him. Moving to a sitting position today hurt less than last night, but still resulted in the increased pulsing in his head. Raymond closed his eyes for a moment to let it subside. When he opened his eyes, there was Nelly with the promised meal.

"Time to eat up now," said Nelly in her kind and gentle voice. "When you get stronger, I can cook almost anything you want," she said cheerfully, then turned for the door.

After breakfast, Raymond drifted to sleep, still upright until roused by Smallfolks.

"My Prince," Smallfolks said, "I would like to introduce Chancellor Geoffrey Goldblatt." The Chancellor stepped forward to the edge of the bed, drew up a chair, and sat down.

"Do you remember me, young prince?" Goldblatt said. "I met you years ago when I was in service to your grandfather. You have gotten taller." Disguising his true feelings, Goldblatt thought, *This boy is the shell I anticipated. Little to him; a strong wind would blow him over. No wonder he had trouble on such a large horse.*

"Do you remember me?" he asked again.

Raymond thought. *The best way to avoid being caught lying is to tell the truth, or at least as much of it as you can. This man is more important than either Smallfolks or Nelly. I will answer his questions as best I can, accurately and carefully.* Raymond answered truthfully, "No sir, I don't."

The Chancellor asked, "Do you know your name?"

Raymond replied as he had before, "Raymond."

"Yes," replied the Chancellor out loud, but to himself. *The pronunciation is not quite right, but it could be related to his head injury. He had problems with his speech in the past.*

"What do you remember about how you were hurt?" he asked.

Raymond again thought the truth the best answer. His mind had a sudden flash of the memory. He had taken a corner too fast on a wet road and went off the edge. "I remember some kind of accident. I hurt my head," he said to Goldblatt. Something stopped Raymond from completing the description. The Chancellor seemed satisfied with the accident and head comment. *Until I better understand exactly what is going on here,* he thought, *I will tell a limited version of the truth.*

"Yes, exactly what your uncle said," the Chancellor replied. "Do you remember your uncle?"

Raymond didn't have to hedge his reply. "No sir, I don't."

"Just as well," said the Chancellor. "Enough for today, young master. I will leave you now. We can talk again later." The Chancellor stood and moved toward the door. "Please rest if possible. Perhaps later today, you should try to stand."

"Very well, sir," replied Raymond. "Before you leave, can you tell me where I am?"

"Of course, you were unconscious when they brought you in. You are in the castle of the Teardrop Kingdom. Your father, King Michael, sent you here to stay for a while."

Raymond accepted the answer without question, but his mind was reeling. *This makes little sense. I am in the castle in the Teardrop Kingdom—sent by my father. What does any of this mean?*

Geoffrey Goldblatt moved toward the door with Smallfolks in tow. When they were outside, beyond earshot, the Chancellor said, "He remembers some things, but not as much as we could hope. His speech is very flat without an accent, and he is shortening some words. I think we need to be cautious about how much information we give him at one time. I would like for him to remember on his own. Be careful to answer his questions but do not overwhelm him with information or expect he will recall quickly. However, I am optimistic."

Smallfolks replied, "I will stay close as always and will answer the young master's questions. I will help him as best I can. We owe him, but even more so since he is a grandson of the Great King Mikael."

Chancellor Goldblatt reached down and put his hand on Smallfolks' shoulder. "I know how much the Great King meant to you, and to all of us," he said, patting Smallfolks and moved down the hall.

Later in the day, true to his word, Raymond attempted to stand with the help of Smallfolks. He was astonished his body had become so weak in just a few short days. *I've always been a robust man. My injuries must be more significant than I had thought. I will rehabilitate my body and regain my strength as quickly as possible.*

CHAPTER FOUR

DAYS

In the pre-light of dawn, Raymond lay on his back, looking at the ceiling. The only sounds outside his room were the wind pounding on the shutters and errant drafts wafting through unseen halls beyond his door. Within the room, the constant simmering and an occasional snap of fire had become a comforting staple. Everything was quiet and safe, but he could not shake the feeling something wasn't right!

With each passing day, the pounding in his head became more manageable. This morning, the pain was still there but controllable, unless he moved his head from side to side. The reduced pain had allowed his thoughts to become clearer.

He used the quiet before the rest of the world woke to review what he knew. *I remember my car on the road and the statements of a deputy sheriff. "There's been an accident. You're injured." I also remember, "Help is on the way." The comments from Chancellor Goldblatt and Smallfolks make sense. They are treating my injuries. The ominous voice must be a manifestation of my personal fear.* He chuckled to himself. *Seldom does the voice of fear sound like a beautiful woman. Yesterday, my feeble attempts to stand up can be explained by my body deteriorating while I was in an extended coma. This environment is one of minimal stimulus. It is a treatment allowing me to return slowly to the world. The fact Smallfolks continues to call me 'prince' is probably just a term like 'buddy.' It makes sense. I am in a facility designed*

to treat people in comas and assist them in returning to the actual world in
a slow and calculated manner.

A deep sigh of relief crossed his mind as he accepted these facts. *I am*
in a world I understand and will make my way through. Today, I will ask
Smallfolks the very simple question: "How long have I been here?" After
reaching his conclusions, Raymond slipped back to sleep.

The morning sun had fully invaded the room when Raymond reopened
his eyes. His head, though still throbbing, was better than earlier in the
day. He attempted to sit up, only to find his belief about reduced pain was
overly optimistic.

"Wait a moment, My Prince. Let me help you." Smallfolks, who was
never far away, moved to give Raymond help.

"I thought I was better," Raymond said to Smallfolks. "I thought I could
move on my own."

Smallfolks replied, "It has not been very long. You need to give yourself
time to heal."

"I think it's probably been longer than necessary. I must work on
regaining my strength," Raymond replied.

"I appreciate your ambition, My Prince, but you really need to go
slowly."

"Smallfolks, can I ask you a question? How long have I been here?"

Smallfolks stopped and got a look in his eyes like he was searching for an
answer. "Let me see. You arrived late in the evening. You were unconscious
for two additional nights before you opened your eyes on the third day.
You talked with Chancellor Goldblatt the day after, which was yesterday,
and today is the fifth day. Yes, yes, the fifth day. You have been here five
days."

Not the answer Raymond expected. He expected Smallfolks would tell
him he had been brought to the facility many months ago and had been
under his care since.

"Five days! It's not possible. I must have been here longer."

"Well, you slept a great deal," Smallfolks said, "but counting the night times, four night times, yes, today is the fifth day from when you arrived with your uncle and cousins."

"Arrived with my uncle and cousins? Smallfolks, I don't remember any of this! Can you help me?"

"Young master, Chancellor Goldblatt would like for you to remember these things on your own."

"Smallfolks, I am concerned if I must remember these things on my own, the Chancellor will grow tired of my progress and lock me away as insane."

Smallfolks laughed out loud. "You are really quite funny, young master. The Chancellor would never do such a thing. And our prison cell is attached to the kitchen. Nelly would love to have you down there with her. She would spoil you rotten. I can tell you, rotten indeed."

"Really, I don't think I can make the progress the Chancellor wants without having a little help. Perhaps if I ask questions and you give me answers, your answers will help jog my memory. Now, honestly, how long have I been here?"

Smallfolks shook his head and looked at Raymond. "My prince, this is the fifth day since you have arrived in the Teardrop Kingdom." A look of concern crossed Smallfolks' face.

"Okay, five days. Where was I before then?" Raymond kept searching his mind for a logical connection between the statements of Smallfolks and his rationalization of being in a coma.

"Before then," Smallfolks said, "you arrived by ship at the port and then came by horseback with your uncle and two cousins to the castle—a two-day journey.

These answers weren't moving Raymond in the right direction. "When I was waking up, I heard voices of two men. One was very distinctive; I would say dark. It said, *let time kill him*."

"The voice was your uncle. Voices do not get any darker than his." Immediately Smallfolks shifted into his mumble, "Knew it. Scum. It was the horse, they said. Never believed it."

"Smallfolks, you said you didn't think my injury was an accident."

"I speak, but most people do not listen to me. It is probably not a good thing to listen to me. I wander around saying what is on my mind, even though smarter folks would keep their mouth shut. Nevertheless, I will tell you because you asked. I do not believe it was an accident. What do you remember about your uncle?"

"This is the second time someone has asked me about my uncle. Chancellor Goldblatt asked yesterday, and when I told him 'nothing,' he said, 'just as well.' What did he mean, Smallfolks?"

"Smallfolks should keep his opinion to himself," muttered the little man.

Raymond insisted. "Please Smallfolks, I'll never work my way back to knowing if I can't rely on someone to help me."

"You can rely on me, young master. I will always do my best to tell you the truth. Now about your uncle, he is your father's half-brother. He is the firstborn son of the Outland Queen. Your father is the firstborn son of the Inland Queen. The very nature of our kingdom pits brother against brother. It was up to the Great King Mikael, your grandfather, to choose between brothers. He picked your father to become king over your uncle, who was not happy about the decision. Your uncle became the Lord Commander of the Royal Armies. He is brutal, perfect for the army."

"Brutal is an unusual word to use, Smallfolks."

"Yes, brutal, young prince. Your uncle does not care who gets hurt, so long as he completes his task. He came once to the Teardrop Kingdom looking to conscript men for the army. He took men away from their families while they worked in the fields. Did not let them say goodbye. One man resisted and your uncle slashed him down with a sword, left his body, and went to the next farm. The Lord Commander's greatest desire was for Great King Mikael to appoint him the successor. Wisely, Great King

Mikael knew a king needed more than a desire for power. He must also have compassion. Your uncle, the Lord Commander, has none."

"But why do you think my injury wasn't an accident?"

"Well, it is just a feeling. Actually, it is more than just a feeling. I find it interesting you were injured on the way here, and it occurred shortly before you made it to the castle. The way they treated you when they brought you in was more like they were delivering a chunk of meat than a member of their own family. Their concern appeared to be more about handing you off to someone and then demanding Nelly bring them something to eat. They left the next morning without even inquiring about your injuries. Last thing the Lord Commander said to the Chancellor, 'Notify the king when he is dead.' It was disgusting. Nothing like the way decent people would treat a family member. And then there are the circumstances under which you were sent here."

"What circumstances?" Raymond asked.

"Young prince, I am afraid I have said much more than I should today. Let us just say it looks like your uncle, in my opinion, may have intentionally harmed you. There are other good reasons, but those should come from Chancellor Goldblatt."

Raymond knew his questions had taken Smallfolks into an area he did not want to go. *This is a subject to revisit.* Smallfolks' information had given Raymond a great deal to ponder. He was unsettled by the prospect his formulated reality was massively incorrect. *If my view of the world is not correct, then, "Where am I?"*

"If I have been here five days, it is time for me to wash, get into some fresh clothes, and deal with this scruffy beard. When do you think the doctor will come check my head?"

Smallfolks seemed a little confused. "Chancellor Goldblatt and Nelly are learned enough to care for us. We have some midwives and other common healers, but they would not be appropriate for you."

Smallfolks' answers did not help Raymond understand anything more, nor had dropping the word "doctor" tricked Smallfolks into providing information. "Very well," Raymond said. "I need to change my bandage. Who will do it for me?"

"I will get Nelly. She is the one who put it on and she can help take it off. I will also check in the luggage you brought for some clean clothes."

"I need some hot water and some towels. Would a bath be possible?"

Smallfolks looked a little frightened. "A bath. We rarely do baths, Prince Merryk."

My formal name, Prince Merryk Raymouth, is something I must get used to.

Within a short period, Nelly returned to the room with Smallfolks. She was a little flustered, but moved to the side of Raymond's bed. "Good morning, Prince Merryk," she said. "I trust you slept well."

Raymond replied, "Quite well, Nelly. I'm feeling better this morning, at least if I don't turn my head too quickly. I feel almost human."

Nelly brought a bowl of warm water and some additional rags. She gently unwrapped the bandage from around Raymond's head. *If I had been in a coma for a long time, I wouldn't still have a bandage. Just one more inconsistency to sort out.*

Nelly let out a sigh of relief. "Well, Prince Merryk, it appears the bleeding has stopped and the stitches I added when you first came appear to have held. The swelling is down, but the hair is making it difficult for me to see."

Raymond's immediate response was, "Nelly, let's cut the hair off and move it away from the wound to make the area cleaner." Raymond moved his hand to his head. To his surprise, instead of finding his relatively short, cropped hair, he found long tangled locks. *Long hair would indicate a long time since someone had cut it.* Raymond looked at Nelly. "Nelly, I would like all my hair cut short, only this long." Raymond held up his thumb and first finger, showing a space of about an inch. "In the area around the wound, let's shave it so we can get to it easily and keep it clean."

Nelly looked flustered. "Young prince, that would be unusual. I should talk to the Chancellor." Immediately, she left the room. It was not long before she and Smallfolks returned, looking much relieved.

"The Chancellor has instructed us to do whatever you wish," Smallfolks said.

Nelly proceeded to cut Raymond's hair to within a couple of fingers all over his head. Then, with the help of Smallfolks, she shaved the area around the wound.

Raymond gently touched the shaved area and realized there were rough stitches holding together what felt like a fairly large gash running along the side of his head. "Well, it feels like a doozie," he said.

Nelly had a blank look.

Raymond rephrased his statement. "This feels like quite a wound, and it is really sore."

"To be expected," replied Nelly.

After Nelly had finished the new bandages, Raymond looked at Smallfolks and said, "Now, let's deal with this scruffy beard."

Smallfolks looked at him in disbelief and shook his head. "Are you sure you want me to remove your beard?"

"Yes," said Raymond. "Please, I will feel so much cleaner if I can feel my face."

"Very well." Smallfolks began removing the beard. When complete, Raymond let his hands roam over his bare cheeks and the top of his head.

He looked at both Nelly and Smallfolks and said, "I am feeling more like myself."

Smallfolks replied, "Very good, Prince Merryk, very good. I am hopeful you will not regret having removed your beard and hair."

"Well," Raymond said with a smile on his face. "Not to worry. Hair has a tendency to grow back."

Smallfolks chuckled, "Yes indeed, hair grows back."

"Now," Raymond said, "if I could have some warm water and soap, I will see if I can make the rest of me feel as good as my face." With the help of Smallfolks, Raymond took a sponge bath. Sometimes the movements of his body were more than he could handle, and the throbbing headache returned. As long as he kept his head relatively straight, he could continue. Smallfolks never left his side. Without his physical support, Raymond could not have completed his bath.

From Merryk's trunks, Smallfolks found a suitable pair of pants and a tunic top; both from a fabric much finer than Smallfolks'. Raymond thought. *These are a lot better than a hospital gown.*

"Young master, try to stand for a moment, to give us an opportunity to change the bed."

"I would appreciate that," Raymond said. "Please help me walk over to the window so I can look out."

"A good idea," Smallfolks replied. Smallfolks carefully assisted Raymond over to the window.

Raymond's attention focused on making his feet move. At the windowsill, he braced himself. "I should be fine now."

Smallfolks turned to get Nelly, who was waiting outside the door.

For the first time, Raymond raised his eyes to look out the window. He had been confident the primitive conditions in the room and the castle were tools used to keep stimulus to a minimum. In an instant, his theory crashed, leaving him only with the unsettling question. *Where am I?*

He was looking out a window at the top of an extensive structure inside a castle wall. On the other side of the castle wall was a village, the kind of village recreated for medieval fairs, with people dressed in traditional garb moving about with horses and oxen. Chickens and small children wandered freely. Smoke from open fires and blowing dust marked everything. Beyond the village was a second wall reminiscent of walled cities of an old-world country, a Roman built wall. Beyond the last wall lay a few houses, then a large alluvial plain, part of an ancient river system.

Raymond could not comprehend what his eyes were telling him. *This can't possibly be the outside world. It would be virtually impossible to extend the primitive conditions to all the surroundings.*

If I viewed this as part of a tour, I wouldn't believe the intricacies and accuracy. The people look like they are doing their daily tasks, not pretending for tourists. In fact, there weren't any visible signs of tourists, nor any modern roadway or system leading people into the village. Everything appeared to move in and out in carts pulled by oxen or horses. *Was it possible I might not be in a medical facility but really in the Teardrop Castle?* Raymond felt dizzy and closed his eyes.

Smallfolks grabbed his arm. "Are you all right, Prince Merryk?"

"I'm... I'm fine, Smallfolks." With a delay in his voice, "I need to lie down for a few moments."

"No problem at all, my lord. Let me have Nelly come and help us."

Although Raymond had moved with Smallfolks to the window, he now relied on the assistance of both Smallfolks and Nelly.

"I am afraid, young master, you may have overdone it," said Nelly with a voice of concern.

"No, Nelly, it was something I needed to do," Raymond said with hesitancy in his voice. "I think this was something I needed to do."

Nelly and Smallfolks looked at each other, worry crossing their faces. Chancellor Goldblatt had warned them to look for any inconsistencies in Raymond's activities or actions, specifically repeating phrases.

After getting back to his freshly made bed, Raymond asked to remain sitting up. Raymond asked, "Is there a mirror anywhere?"

"A mirror?" replied Smallfolks questioningly. "Why certainly, we can find a mirror."

"I would like to look at myself now that I'm all cleaned up."

Smallfolks smiled as he left. "Perhaps not a bad idea, My Prince."

Smallfolks returned with a square, more like a shiny metal surface than polished glass. Raymond raised the mirror to his face. For the first time since he had awakened, he felt panic. He expected his face would show the impact of his injury, but was certain his brown eyes and what his mother called "a strong square chin" would shine through. He gasped. His mind screamed like in the blackness. The mirror fell from his hands and tumbled to the floor. The face in the mirror was not his face. It was the face of a young man, sixteen to eighteen years old, displaying the gaunt and contracted look one might attribute to a prison camp escapee. Most startling, the eyes looking back at him were a deep blue!

"Prince Merryk, are you all right?" Smallfolks' voice was urgent. His hand settled on Raymond's shoulder to provide comfort.

Raymond slowly replied, "Yes, Smallfolks, I think. I am all right. Could I have the mirror again?"

Smallfolks retrieved it from the floor. The fall had cracked the wooden frame and creased the reflective surface from top to bottom down the center.

Raymond touched his face, now reflected on two sides, only to see each movement mirrored exactly. He took several deep breaths to calm himself. *How could this be my body? If it is, then I might be in the Teardrop Kingdom, sent by the king, who is a father I have never met. I now understand my lack of muscle. However, the total dissimilarity of the face in the mirror, the blue eyes, destroys every other part of my theory—every part.* There was a sudden surge of pounding in his head. Raymond felt terror welling up inside. Again, the voice from the blackness reached out. ***Panic kills, focus and live.*** He repeated the words, this time mouthing them out silently to himself, "Panic kills, focus and live." Raymond tried to remember where these words came from, but right now, he took another deep breath.

Smallfolks, who gently shook Raymond's shoulder, had viewed the whole flash of recognition or lack of recognition Raymond experienced, "Are you sure you are all right?"

"I think... I think I may very well have overdone it. Perhaps if I could rest for a few minutes. My head is pounding again."

"Most assuredly, young prince," Smallfolks hastened to help Merryk lie down. "I have to say, My Prince, when you looked in the mirror, you looked like you had seen a ghost."

Raymond replied flatly, "No, not a ghost, Smallfolks. Not a ghost."

CHAPTER FIVE

A SIMPLE LETTER

As Chancellor Geoffrey Goldblatt walked down the hall toward his study, he began formulating his letter to the king. He was dressed in his normal light tunic with dark pants, and a woolen sweater which hung to mid-thigh. The sweater was a going away gift from the Queen Mother, who had made it herself. The sweater held great sentimental value to Chancellor Goldblatt, reminding him of his deep support and loyalty to Great King Mikael and to his queen.

The letter should have been simple. However, the circumstances of young prince Merryk's arrival gave Goldblatt pause. The actions of the Lord Commander were confusing and the implications could be staggering. But he would not allow his mind to jump ahead to ask why. Experience had taught him this would result in missing something, so he slowed down. He knew the letter would need to cover two specific areas: first, the circumstances of the accident, and second, the status of the physical and mental health of the young prince. He must temper both to balance what he knew with what someone could reasonably report to the king. Above all, it must protect the prince.

It began a little over a week ago. Typical for early fall, the weather was unsettled, filled with the anticipation of a storm. The wind blew, but the promised rain had yet to appear. A little before dusk, the front doors of the main hall burst open and the Lord Commander and his two sons charged in. The sons held Prince Merryk under the arms, dragging him unceremoniously to the fireplace where they dropped him. A normal person would have summoned help for the prince. Instead, the Lord Commander bellowed for food and someone to take care of the horses.

On hearing the clamor, Smallfolks and I arrived to find a bloody and battered prince. Ignoring the Lord Commander, we gave our attention to the prince. With the help of other servants, they moved Prince Merryk to the room, prepared in anticipation of his arrival. Nelly, rather than assisting the injured prince, was compelled to stop and prepare food for the Lord Commander and his sons.

It did not take a master of deduction to conclude the Lord Commander did not care about Prince Merryk. This was not surprising since Prince Merryk was the son of an Inland Queen and the Lord Commander was the son of an Outland Queen. There was continual tension between the bloodlines. But not caring differed from intentionally harming.

Chancellor Goldblatt mentally reviewed his interaction with the Lord Commander. Questioning the Lord Commander was always a tricky matter and required choosing one's words carefully. He was a self-righteous man who did not like anyone scrutinizing his activities. Chancellor Goldblatt knew the Lord Commander held him in particular disdain for having frequently exposed him lying to Great King Mikael, his father. No other 'living' man could say he challenged the Lord Commander in such a manner.

"What happened?" asked Chancellor Goldblatt.

"There was an accident. The boy fell from his horse. He should not have picked the stallion," replied the Lord Commander.

Chancellor Goldblatt thought. *Pat answers. He shifts the blame to the horse and the prince. His responses are more measured than I would have expected. Why is the Lord Commander so patient in responding? His attitude toward me has always been confrontational. But now, even with the harshness of his tone, his answers seem calculated.*

The Chancellor turned to the two cousins, copies of their father. Both were slightly taller than normal men, strong in arm and leg. They wore the same riding armor as their father. All had heavy cloaks when they arrived, except Merryk, who had no armor and only a light cloak to keep him warm.

Both cousins responded on cue. "He accidentally fell from his horse."

They rehearsed their answers. It is clear the Lord Commander and the two cousins will provide no information. The conclusion, they want a simple report given to the king, but why?

The next indication something was amiss occurred the following morning when the Lord Commander hastily gathered his sons and headed back to the port.

"We need to get back to the Capital City before the fall storms arrive. Notify the king when the boy is dead." With that, they left.

His attitude of disdain against young Merryk was disconcerting. Goldblatt thought an uncle who had taken Prince Merreg, the king's other son, under his wing, would feel some sense of compassion toward this nephew. He showed none. The Lord Commander had not even asked how the boy was. He had assumed the prince would die.

Goldblatt continued to evaluate the physical evidence. First was the site of the injury. The boy's injury was on the side of his head, with the angle of the blow being slightly higher in the front and going lower to the back, just above his ear. Geoffrey Goldblatt had seen many head injuries from horses. If you were thrown backwards, the injury was in the back or even the top of the head, seldom the side. If a limb hits you, the injury normally occurs to the front of the head. Even if the limb was held by a preceding rider and released, it would have hit from the front. A wound on the side of the head, sloped as this one, is more indicative of a blow by an object being swung downward from the rear; an injury caused by a club or shaft, a man-made injury.

Then there is the horse. All the horses for the two-day journey were acquired at the port. The young prince rode a big, young black stallion—a beautiful animal, but barely broken. The other three picked older, more mature horses. Normally, the more experienced horseman would select an inexperienced horse. A look at Merryk confirmed he had neither the experience nor the strength to handle such an animal. The three other men were physically stronger and more capable of demanding the horse's compliance. Having him purportedly select this horse would make it reasonable to expect he would have trouble.

Finally, the injury to young Merryk occurred relatively close to the Teardrop Castle. A pragmatist would say an injury at this point in the journey would require the least amount of effort to get the body to the castle.

This physical evidence was circumstantial. It was possible to be thrown from your horse, hit your head on the side rather than the front or the back, and for a young naive prince to pick a large demanding horse. However, what tipped the scales in Chancellor Goldblatt's mind was the attitude. The lack of any respect or concern for an injured family member was number one on Goldblatt's list. The comment by the Lord Commander as he left the next morning was, "Notify the king when the boy is dead." Clearly, the Lord Commander expected Prince Merryk would not survive his injuries.

Finally, the comments the prince had shared with Smallfolks. The voices he heard, "He looks pretty bad. We should just kill him," and the dark voice said, "Let time kill him." These were statements of an intentional act rather than an accident. Perhaps Prince Merryk, after a head injury, was not a reliable source of information. However, everything taken together was more indicative of human action rather than an accidental injury.

Having reached his conclusion, Chancellor Goldblatt proceeded to the critical question. Why would the Lord Commander seek to harm Prince Merryk now? If the Lord Commander did not care for Prince Merryk, he had sufficient opportunities to harm him during the preceding eighteen years. But to injure him now, when the purpose for his removal from the Capital City was known to the Lord Commander, made no sense. The Lord Commander knew the importance of the new ships and the dowry. Had the Lord Commander successfully killed the prince, it would require the High Kingdom to repay the dowry. Why would the Lord Commander do this? What would he gain? Who else would benefit from the death of the boy?

The obvious beneficiary was King Natas. All accounts from Chancellor Goldblatt's correspondence indicated King Natas went into a rage when he found he had been, in his opinion, duped by King Michael. The result was a new chancellor for King Natas, the previous one having encountered a sudden, unfortunate, and fatal accident.

Geoffrey Goldblatt knew King Natas hated being made a fool. He would do whatever was necessary to save face and money. However, this did not explain why the Lord Commander, who had both money and power, would betray his kingdom to support King Natas. There was something more going on here than just the marriage between a boy and a girl. Chancellor Goldblatt did not have enough of the pieces to solve this puzzle. He would need more information.

For the first time in over a decade, Chancellor Goldblatt felt a sense of foreboding. The king and the kingdom may be in danger, but King Michael had chosen another to be his chancellor, and the responsibility lay with him. Right now, Goldblatt had a duty to protect Prince Merryk, grandson of Great King Mikael. This was his priority.

The Lord Commander would not be pleased to hear Prince Merryk was still alive. Whoever or whatever had motivated his actions would press for additional attacks if they thought Merryk would be fine.

Fortunately, the fall storms were about to begin. Starting in late fall and running into spring, the seas made the Teardrop's port practically unusable. Snow fell in the mountain passes, making land transfer between the Teardrop Kingdom and the Capital City difficult. This combination provided defense for the Teardrop in the past. Perhaps now they would protect the prince.

It is important I report accurately to the king his son is still alive, but I cannot overly state an optimistic outcome. It would be best if all thought Prince Merryk may currently be alive, but his condition is precarious. Even a short hesitancy in deciding to respond again may give the boy some additional time. The thing Prince Merryk needs now more than anything is an opportunity to heal and hopefully grow strong enough to defend himself.

Having completed his review of the situation, Chancellor Goldblatt sat down and drafted the letter to the king.

To your Royal Majesty, King Michael,

I am pleased to report your son is still alive. I am sure the nature of the incident has been reported to you by your brother, the Lord Commander. It occurred on the way to the Teardrop. Because of his injuries, the prince fell into a coma for three days. Since then, he is slowly recognizing his surroundings. His physical condition, however, is greatly diminished, making each day questionable.

Regarding his mental health, the noticeable symptom appears to be very flat speech. I use the word "flat" to describe a lack of intonation or accent expected of a person from the High Kingdom. Specifically, he shortens ordinary words and phrases, and his word selection appears to be random. The words apply, but not in the normal sense which you and I would use them.

I would like to report I am optimistic about the young prince's prognosis, but I do not want to put false hopes in the minds of either you or the queen. There will be many long months of recovery. I will continue to pursue our objective and do my best to make the prince a viable marriage partner.

This is the last letter I may get through before the winter seas inhibit our communication. I will, at the next available break, provide you with an update.

Most sincerely,
Geoffrey Goldblatt
Administrator of the Teardrop Kingdom

CHAPTER SIX

DOWN

Raymond's eyes drifted open. The preceding night had been like so many before, filled with fitful sleep, wakeful periods of confusion and doubt, followed by tormented dreams. He was still in the same large bed and the same stone room. The winds continued to rattle the shutters. The fire simmered and the smell of smoke lingered in the air. Nothing physically had changed in his environment. Though this world was filled with light, he could not find hope within it.

Although uncertain about this reality, he was certain about two things: the kindness of the people around him and the continued pain in his head.

"Are you feeling better today? How does your head feel? Are you hungry?" The questions never changed, but neither did Smallfolks' considerate nature focused on Raymond's well-being. He continued to be a wealth of information from family history to the weather, which, he said, was unseasonably good.

He had grown quite fond of Nelly, the doting cook who appeared each morning with her special smile and a tray of something she thought he would like. He had progressed from simple broth to oatmeal and well-cooked bacon.

Good thing I have always liked oatmeal. Like many random thoughts crossing his mind, it was not connected to any specific memory, but he knew it was true.

Chancellor Goldblatt checked on him daily. At the beginning, the visits were very brief but had extended with each passing day. His primary concern was always Raymond's health. The rest of the Chancellor's questions were carefully chosen, designed to jog his memory but not necessarily to provide a memory. Raymond's early decision to ask the same questions of Smallfolks had paid off.

In a short period, Raymond learned about Merryk's family. He now knew Merryk was the son of King Michael and Queen Amanda. He had an older brother, Merreg, the son of King Michael and Queen Rebecca. Queen Rebecca had died many years ago during the winter of a great sickness. Raymond concluded it must have been some kind of flu outbreak. He had one uncle, Lord Commander of the Army, and twin cousins. He had lived all of his life in the Capital City. This was his first trip to the Teardrop Kingdom. Raymond had not gotten Chancellor Goldblatt to talk about 'the circumstances' for his current trip as referenced by Smallfolks. The Chancellor merely said, "There will be time later."

Raymond's physical activities had started by standing each morning and walking with Smallfolks' help to the window. This expanded to three or four times a day. As he observed the people below, he became more acquainted with the village.

He chuckled to himself. *I remember when I thought this was a theme park. Now I see these people are doing normal things: cooking, washing, and trading. It's fun to watch the chickens and the children; both seem to have the same errant patterns. There is something simple and charming about the village.*

Every time he went to the window he scanned the sky, hoping to see a vapor trail across the blue, a sign his world was just over a hill. It was never there.

As the days went on, the length of his walks increased. He wandered around his room in circles, then asked to walk outside his room. The first time he stepped into the hall, the architectural design immediately intrigued him. He recognized its massive arches put together with dressed stone. It was Ashlar masonry, done by masons with real skill using little or no grout. *It is almost impossible to find people with this skill today.*

Each day made him a little stronger, but the pain in his head remained. It had become an intermittent, unwanted guest. It was frustrating because he never knew what would cause it. *I think I'm better, but when I wake up, it's there. If I move too fast, it's there. If I turn my head too quickly, it's there. This pain uses so much energy it is keeping me from understanding where I am.*

Raymond wished his mental condition reflected his physical progress. He spent many days in quiet and sullen thought, attempting to deny everything he saw was real. This became more difficult with each passing day. He then grew angry. He was angry for driving his car too fast. He was angry for not being able to physically move faster. He was angry about virtually everything. *The only good thing I can say is I haven't allowed my anger to reach out and affect Smallfolks, Nelly or the Chancellor. Though I think they have seen my frustration.*

How long this mental condition persisted, he did not know. He felt hopeless. He did not focus on the gains, but continued to respond to the pain. Raymond recognized this as an emotional, not an intellectual, issue. He tried to remember more about his previous life, but it didn't help.

Although Smallfolks, Nelly and the Chancellor are constantly willing to help me, I still feel alone. How do I explain I don't feel like I'm in the right body? I can't explain to them how their world seems foreign. I must have had periods in my life when I felt like this, alone and without direction, but I can't remember when. This loneliness seems as consuming as the continued pain.

Then one morning, things changed. *I don't know how long I've been here.* Raymond thought. *I'm stronger, but something is different today.* In an instant, it hit him. *I don't have any pain on the side of my head this morning, or was it there yesterday morning?* He stood up, *no pain.* He turned his head from side to side, *no pain*. He extended his arms and tilted his head back slightly. No *pain. I don't know when it went away, but it feels great!*

Raymond returned to his bed, lay back, and looked at the ceiling. It was still early. He heard the wind battering the shutters, the drafts running up and down well-known corridors. He could hear the crackle of the fire. A tinge of smoke hung in the air. Instead of being in a foreign environment, it felt like home. *I've been acting like a dolt the last few weeks. I have been feeling sorry for myself, feeling alone and depressed. This is not the person I am. It is not how I was raised, nor how I was trained. I can get through this, I can survive.* Perhaps the absence of pain was allowing him to effectively connect with his memories. The word 'survived' triggered something; the same internal voice he had heard in the blackness.

I must evaluate and gather my resources. Adapt and overcome because I have a duty to survive. This is my world. Raymond still couldn't identify where this came from, but he was sure of its wisdom.

Doubt crept in again. *Raymond, you are kidding yourself. You're in a weird situation. You are just deluding yourself. This cannot be real! Blue eyes?*

The struggle inside his head continued. *Maybe it isn't real, or maybe it is. Perhaps I'm crazy, in a coma, or this is some fancy dream. The truth is, **this** is the only reality I have. I need to deal with what is real to me right now. Real is a crackling fire, this body, three supportive people, and a castle made of old stone surrounded by a crumbling Roman-like wall. I will look for a way home, but until I find one, I must rely on myself and do whatever is necessary to adapt and overcome in this world.*

Immediately, Raymond understood a new thing. He was excited. *I have a purpose. I have a goal. I have a direction. I can make this work.*

He swung his feet off the edge of the bed, raised his hands over his head, and attempted to stretch himself up. He found resistance at every joint of his body. *Didn't this guy ever stand up straight?* He forced his body higher.

We will fix this soon, Merryk. He smiled as he tried on his new name for the first time.

Smallfolks entered the room, surprised to see Merryk standing by the side of his bed. "Are you all right this morning, sire?"

"Yes, I am perfectly okay. Smallfolks, I would like you to go to Nelly and find out what's for breakfast. Whatever it is, tell her to double it. I am starving this morning."

CHAPTER SEVEN

TOWER

M erryk turned from the window. "Smallfolks, how do you get to the top of the castle?"

"Oh, it is two flights of stairs up the old tower," Smallfolks replied.

"I want to see."

"But you are just walking alone. You have not tried stairs." His voice filled with concern, a standard for any new activity.

"Well, I can't stay on this floor forever, can I?"

"No, but—," Smallfolks was running out of reasons for him to stay put.

"You will be with me. If it gets to be too much, you can help me back." Merryk's confidence seemed to remove Smallfolks' doubts, at least momentarily.

"All right, but if you look weak, we will come right back." His statement was more of a question.

"Yes, absolutely. I need to see my world."

The flights turned into two, twenty-step vertical ascents in a tight circular stairwell.

I should have understood the tower was designed as a defensive structure, more than a quick path to the top. These steps are roughly hewn. The tower must be older than the rest of the castle. I can't let Smallfolks see me falter. If I am to return to my strength, I cannot fail.

After what seemed like forever, Smallfolks opened the door at the top, allowing the light to spill into the tower stairway.

I don't know which is worse, the trembling and burning of my legs or the full flame consuming my lungs. I must mask my agony from Smallfolks, who right now is neither impressed nor fooled. I know he would have run for help but was afraid if he left me, I would be a pile of broken bones at the base of the steps when he returned.

After finally making it to the roof and sitting for a quarter hour with his back against the turret wall, Merryk took a deep breath and looked at Smallfolks sitting beside him. "Well, that was fun."

Smallfolks was not finding any humor in the situation. "You have exerted yourself beyond reason," he said.

"To grow I must push, sometimes if only to find my limits."

"Well, you found them today." Again, a voice filled with frustration.

Merryk put his hand on Smallfolks' shoulder. "I don't say this often enough, but thank you. Thank you for working with me."

Smallfolks was surprised. It was his duty to serve the prince. To receive gratitude was beyond thought. "It is my pleasure to serve you as always, young master, at least most of the time." They both laughed.

"Better help me up so I can see. Now, tell me what I am looking at."

The prince was standing at the edge of a round tower approximately twenty feet across, surrounded by a waist-high turret wall. Smallfolks stepped up to the wall, pointed to the south, and began his narrative.

"Well, to the south is the view from your window. This is the face of the castle looking across the plain which floods most every spring. The land is filled with light forest. The port is a two-day ride with lots of little ups and downs along the way. This is how you came to the castle. From the port, it is a two or three-day sail around the peninsula to get to the Capital City."

He looked toward the east. "Here are the coastal mountains, fairly rough. They are difficult enough to cross when they are dry. However, when it snows, they become almost impassable. Crossing the mountains takes four or more hard days to get to the Capital City. Some say they have been able to make it in two days, but I think this is a boast. I have never been to the Capital City. Great King Mikael asked me to come with him, but I could not think of leaving. The outside world is too big for Smallfolks."

With no sense of regret, he turned to the north and continued. "Now, if you like snow, this is the way. These are enormous mountains, row after row of them, going all the way to the Great North, which is inhabited by savages. They used to raid our northern territory to kill and steal. Savages were the ones who killed my family. The clans hold the lands between us and the Great North. The Blue-and-White Mountain Clans stopped them from coming south."

"Why are they called the Blue-and-White Mountains?"

"Some mountains have snow on them year-round. They look like big loaves of white bread or fluffy clouds and at other times, if the sunlight is just right, they look deep blue, so the name. They are incredibly beautiful to visit.

"Do you know, the only reason the Blue-and-White Mountain Clans are part of the High Kingdom is because of your grandfather? When I was a boy, and he was just a prince, I went as his valet on a trip into the mountains, just the two of us. We should have had better sense. We came in direct contact with the Blue-and-White Mountain Clans, specifically a brash young Walter named Gaspar Zoo. The clans are ruled by a Council of Walters, their chiefs. Gaspar Zoo became a good friend of your grandfather's. Why, I never knew. Still, they joined the kingdom, and that is what matters. Your grandfather ultimately left to become king and Gaspar became Gaspar ZooWalt, the leader of the Council of Walters. He gained his position by stopping the attacks of savages from the Great North. Savages killed his son. I understood his need for revenge, but I never trusted him. He was too willing to place your grandfather in peril.

"Now to the West lie most of our farmlands and large swaths of grasslands encroached upon by trees. This is where we get the bulk of our food and wood. Then there is another range of mountains. I do not rightly know what is on the other side. My guess is more of the same.

"Well, that is pretty much it. Once Chancellor Goldblatt showed me one of his maps. We looked like a big teardrop, wider on the bottom than the top, surrounded by mountains all around. So, that is how we got our name."

With this brief narrative, Smallfolks had described his entire world. Other than the one trip to the Blue-and-White Mountains, Smallfolks had never left the Teardrop Kingdom. This was his home.

It had been two months, or two moons as Smallfolks counted, since Merryk first made his way to the top of the castle tower. As the weeks passed, Smallfolks allowed Merryk to make the trip alone, which he now did once or twice a day. The tower made a perfect place for him to start a regimen of morning exercises. Merryk, as Raymond now thought of himself, continued to work on his physical development. Still struggling to stand erect, he found it hard to believe how much damage a person could do to himself by hunching over. Merryk was making progress. *A few more months and I can stand straight with my shoulders back in a natural position.*

This morning, Merryk thought how different everything looked from the first trip. The wind had whipped the remaining leaves free from the trees' grip, leaving only bare fingers extending to the sky. A light coat of snow gave everything a clean look. Snow was now common. It fell at night, but by mid-day was melted by a bright sun. The days were shorter, the wind sharper, the temperature colder as the kingdom moved toward the heart of winter.

The village below had not yet awakened, though smoke was drifting from a few chimneys. The most notable change in recent days was the chickens no longer ran freely as in the fall. The children appeared to have followed the chickens' lead, both staying inside as much as they could. When the rooster crowed in the village below, Merryk knew it was time to descend the stairs to start his day. As he had done many times before, he went all the way to the bottom of the old circular tower and came out near a short corridor leading to Nelly's kitchen.

He was confident Nelly would already be preparing her bread. According to Smallfolks, Nelly was following in her mother's footsteps. Nelly was born within the walls and now seemed woven into its fabric, a part of the strength of the stone. Merryk was certain the castle would not function without her.

Smiling to himself, he remembered his first visit to the kitchen. It was also the first time Merryk had eluded the all-seeing eyes of Smallfolks to venture out on his own.

———————⬥———————

Merryk knew the stairwell at the opposite end of the corridor from the old tower was wide and much more easily navigated. The problem was getting to it meant passing the room Smallfolks occupied. Smallfolks had an uncanny ability to hear the softest of footsteps. His only other choice was to take the old tower and go down. Merryk did not have a good idea where the tower would end, but was determined to find out. As he moved down the stairs, the aroma of warm bread baking in the oven filled the tower shaft. At the bottom, he came to a hallway leading to a well-lit kitchen where Nelly and several other women were scurrying to prepare breakfast.

"Good morning, Nelly," Merryk said with a chipper voice.

"Prince Merryk, what are you doing here?" she said in surprise.

"I thought I would do a little exploring this morning."

"Does Smallfolks know where you are?"

"I think I might have escaped Smallfolks this morning. I am sure he thinks I am asleep in my room."

"He will not be happy to find you have gone about the castle without him knowing your exact whereabouts," she said in a scolding tone.

"I just wanted to see what you do," he said with his best disarming smile.

She was flustered and had difficulty getting back to her normal routine. She seemed to have forgotten her exact place in the bread recipe, adding a second, unnecessary cup of flour. Merryk's presence equally confused the other women in the kitchen.

"You cannot just be here in the kitchen with us," said Nelly. "This is not a proper place for a member of the royal family."

One of the other women under her breath said, "Or a man."

"That's ridiculous, Nelly. It's just a kitchen."

"Yes," Nelly said in deference, "but there are some places you can go that you should not go."

Merryk laughed at her, "I just think you are afraid I will see the secrets to your cooking."

"There are no secrets to my cooking: just practice, endurance, and time," she said nervously. "How is it you always get me so confused?"

"Well, I don't mean to," Merryk replied with the same disarming smile.

"Okay, if you must be here, you must be out of the way."

Then Nelly did what Merryk was sure she would have done with any other small child who entered her kitchen. She found a stool, moved it to the side, and told him to sit.

"What's for breakfast?" Merryk asked from his stool in the corner.

Nelly replied, "It will be your normal breakfast: eggs, bacon or sausage, and freshly baked bread with milk and honey, unless you make me mix up the recipe again."

As Merryk sat, he observed Nelly was an amazingly well-organized woman. She directed the list of tasks: from starting the fires and baking the bread to preparing the individual dishes for Chancellor Goldblatt and himself. She executed them all with the mastery of a drill sergeant.

The visit had been memorable because for the first time Merryk had seen the under workings of the castle. As a twenty-first century man, he did not understand why his presence in the kitchen was an issue. *There is much I need to understand about the roles of men and women.*

An additional truth hung in Merryk's mind. He enjoyed being in the kitchen. The smell of bread, the warmth of the ovens, and the clank of the pans all reminded him of his mother working in their farmhouse on the Palouse. The visits were a connection to his "old" life. Raymond was adjusting to being Merryk, but he did not want to get lost.

CHAPTER EIGHT

CHAIR

Chancellor Goldblatt stood at his study window, looking out toward the northern mountains. Goldblatt never tired of the view. The mountains lay like saw teeth across the horizon. This time of year, they were covered in snow and gleamed pristine white. Today a bright sun allowed never-ending and ever-changing shadows to cross them. Sometimes in the evening, when the mountains caught the light of the setting sun, they would go from white to red and all the colors in between. The scene was a vision of great beauty. The practical side of Goldblatt noticed there were no brown spots on any of the mountains. A large snowfall in the north meant flooding in the springtime.

Goldblatt's thoughts were interrupted when two guardsmen entered his study carrying a leather wingback chair. The chair was oversized and stood several inches above the other furniture in Goldblatt's study. However, it did not seem to be new or foreign to the room. In fact, it looked as though it had been there longer than the book-laden shelves surrounding the walls.

Smallfolks entered as the two guardsmen headed out the door.

"I see you have returned Great King Mikael's chair. I think that is where it sat before," he said.

Goldblatt replied, "Yes, I thought it would be appropriate for Prince Merryk. He seems to outgrow things quickly."

Smallfolks chuckled, "If he keeps growing, even that chair may not be big enough for him."

Goldblatt replied, "He is just going through a growth spurt. I think nutritious food, exercise and less stress are allowing him to develop as a man."

"I am concerned he is pushing himself too hard. It has only been three months. I found him on the floor yesterday, pushing his head up and bending his back in the opposite direction of what is natural."

"He is just focused on getting his back straight."

"What bothers me is he had tears of pain in his eyes."

"I believe the prince can measure how much he can endure."

"I am concerned. When he is not working on your books, he is constantly moving, never resting. I am having great difficulty keeping him safe. Did Nelly talk to you about his trip to the kitchen?"

"Yes," Goldblatt said. "He was probably just hungry. She says he is hungry all the time."

"I have given up on getting him to grow his beard. I stopped shaving him, but he now shaves himself. He is constantly washing himself and his hair. He will get sick, I tell you."

Goldblatt chuckled, "I am not sure anybody ever died because they were clean."

Smallfolks was troubled. "Well, it cannot help."

Chancellor Goldblatt thought for a moment, "I have read of head injuries where people act out different things, but as they heal, they go away. Maybe the shaving, bathing, and visiting the kitchen are all related to his injuries, things that will improve."

"I hope so," Smallfolks replied. "Changing the subject, how are his studies going?"

"At first he struggled. He had so many questions. I could not make any progress in his education. Then one day, it was as though Merryk realized the problem. He was trying to question me at the same time I was trying to question him. The interesting thing is, he came up with a solution. We began each day with me asking him a series of questions on a subject. We would start at the lowest level and continue until we got to material he did not know. This allowed me to know where to direct his studies. At the end of the day, he could ask me questions."

"How did it work out?"

"Very well. Merryk is a surprising student. Very curious, focused, and far more educated than I had believed. The prince has an aptitude for numbers, passable in several languages, but tragic in geography and modern history. Although he knows small bits of ancient history. What is most confusing to me, his areas of weakness—geography and history—are the ones in which he is most interested."

Smallfolks looked back to the Chancellor. "You used the right word, 'focused.' Prince Merryk is very focused on everything he does. But what are we going to do about him wandering around?"

The Chancellor paused. "We may be making a mistake by trying to restrain him. He grows stronger each day. I cannot expect you to follow him around. Now it is winter, I am confident no one will come to the Teardrop without our knowledge. We should encourage him to explore the castle grounds on his own."

Smallfolks frowned. "Are you sure?"

"Yes, I am. I think he will be safe enough. But just in case, I will ask Yonn to keep an eye on him. If we can confine him to inside the main castle wall, he will have a few more months to grow and get stronger."

"In two months, he should be an inch or two taller and two or three stone heavier."

The Chancellor chuckled, "Yes, he is growing up."

His attachment to Prince Merryk surprised the Chancellor. Merryk looked so much like a younger version of his grandfather, Great King Mikael. He felt a sense of pride watching Merryk go from a scrawny, unsure boy to a determined young man, a man of whom the royal family could be proud. However, he knew he must carefully guard his opinion of Prince Merryk. There were others watching the prince's progress from afar, and they would not be pleased with his development. Winter protected the prince's life, but it also denied Chancellor Goldblatt access to his many contacts. Ultimately, guarding Prince Merryk would require knowing what forces had driven the attempt on his life. Only knowledge could defend his charge.

CHAPTER NINE

NEW FREEDOM

Smallfolks entered Prince Merryk's room and found him sitting at a small table near the window. The table was strategically placed to maximize the light and was covered with books from the Chancellor's study, some in the common language and others in Latin and Greek.

"Good afternoon, Prince Merryk." Smallfolks took a deep breath and delivered a practiced statement. "I have spoken with Chancellor Goldblatt and he believes you need more freedom to move about the castle." Smallfolks hesitated before continuing, concerned how his next statement would be accepted. "There, however, need to be some limits. First, stay within the castle walls, and second, you need to let me know when you are leaving and when you return. Please understand this is not to receive my permission, but to inform me so we can find you if needed." Smallfolks was uncomfortable giving this message to a member of the royal family.

Merryk gave Smallfolks a large smile, "Thank you Smallfolks for asking the Chancellor. I appreciate being given the opportunity and I know how difficult it has been for you. I have not been the best patient. I have caused you worry, and I know my trip to the kitchen down the back stairwell was particularly concerning. Please accept my apology. I was acting like a child rather than giving you the respect you rightly deserve."

Prince Merryk's response totally surprised Smallfolks.

"Master, you have no obligation to apologize to me."

"Smallfolks, any man who cannot recognize his error and apologize for the damage it may have caused is not yet a man. You have been nothing but kind and I, in evading you, have undermined your ability to provide support."

Smallfolks looked at the prince, "I just want to be sure you are safe."

"Smallfolks, I will be safe and careful. Now, if it's all right with you, I would like to walk around the castle grounds."

Smallfolks replied, "Remember, you may go wherever you want. You need not ask my permission."

Merryk again smiled at the old man, patted him gently on the shoulder and said, "May I go anyway?"

Smallfolks nodded.

Merryk didn't waste any time. He grabbed his coat, headed out of his room, down the broad stairs, through the Great Hall and out the front doors of the main castle building. These were the same doors he had been dragged through by his cousins and uncle three months earlier.

The typical winter afternoon was a patchwork quilt of gray and white clouds layered over each other, filtering the winter sun. The air was cool, crisp, and invigorating. Merryk exhaled and watched the steam from his breath float away. He was thankful for the warm coat Smallfolks had provided. He made his way across the courtyard and up a stairwell to the top of the castle wall. Merryk had seen the wall many times from the tower. Now, standing on top gave him a different view of the wide floodplain which lay in front of the castle. He decided he would turn right and walk along the top of the castle wall.

The view reminded him of touring the Tower of London's ramparts. This wall did not overlook a river like the Thames, but merely the flat landscape tilting down into the plain in front of the castle. The topography upon which the castle sat was more elevated inside the walls than London's tower, more like the castle at the head of the Loch Ness or Edinburgh Castle in Scotland.

The other thing he noticed was the castle's general condition. They had built the castle over multiple years, perhaps centuries. Some stonework was soft and irregular; other sections were defined and solid. It seemed to have gone through recurring periods of decline followed by repair. Hydrostatic pressure had pushed portions of the wall out from the bottom. Other portions had lost the mortar and slid. Both problems were simple to fix. He thought, *once an engineer, always an engineer*. He could not stop himself from making a mental list of needed repairs.

Obviously, the castle was designed for a significant number of people, far more than the current occupants. As he moved along the wall, he noticed there were rooms and complete buildings abandoned.

He increased his pace and soon found himself at the back of the castle, looking toward the northern mountains. It was then he caught sight of the stables.

His mind drifted back to when he had been a boy on the farm in the Palouse. His parents were mostly dry-land farmers, wheat primarily, but also soybeans and hay when irrigation was available. They had a small barn, nothing like the stables he was approaching. He enjoyed spending time there as a young boy, jumping into the hay and helping his father and older brother feed the animals. He specifically remembered two horses, along with a cow and the chickens. He chuckled. *Why do I always remember the chickens?*

He worked his way down from the top of the wall and across a broad exercise yard into the stables. The stable was well organized, with many stalls, but few horses. In a large stall near the end, he found a large black stallion. *This must be the horse blamed for my injury.*

"Well, hello boy," he said in a soft, soothing voice. "How are you doing? I understand everyone thinks you are dangerous. You and I know that's not true."

The horse responded to the sound of Merryk's voice, moving toward the front of the stall, closer to Merryk.

"I bet it has been lonely with everybody keeping their distance. Kind of unfair, don't you think?" his voice maintaining a smooth tone.

The horse's eyes focused on Merryk. Merryk moved to the front, and the horse also moved closer, reflecting an instant connection between the two. Merryk kept speaking in a low, soft voice, finally reaching across the stall gate to pat the side of the stallion's neck. Rubbing the spot behind his ears, the horse twitched a little and shook his head, but immediately returned for more. Soon the horse was standing with his head over the edge of the stall, allowing Merryk to stroke its neck. *This is an animal who enjoys the attention of humans, not a vicious creature.*

"Well, you and I need to be friends," Merryk said to the horse. "I have very few, other than Smallfolks, Nelly and the Chancellor."

The stallion shook his head, seeming to understand everything Merryk had said.

There was a sound behind Merryk. "You need to be careful," the voice admonished. "That horse is dangerous."

The horse rocked his head and moved away from the edge of the stall toward the back corner.

Merryk turned around and looked at a young man standing behind him. He was taller than most men Merryk had encountered, about five feet-seven inches in height, relatively slender but muscular. On his guardsman's jacket was the insignia of the Captain of the Guard.

Upon seeing Merryk turn, he immediately replied, "I am sorry, Your Highness. I did not recognize you. We do not have many people wandering around the castle these days, and finding you here is a surprise."

"You must be Yonn Gryson, Captain of the Guard," Merryk said. "Smallfolks has mentioned you."

"Yes, I am," he corrected quickly, "Yes, Your Highness."

"Yonn, what is the horse's name?"

"We do not know. It is your horse."

"I will have to give a name some thought."

"Yes, Your Highness."

"Yonn, you and I appear to be the two youngest people in this castle. When we are together, I would like it if you called me Merryk."

Yonn looked concerned. "Your Highness, I am not sure it is appropriate. I will misspeak from time to time."

"Yonn, if it happens, don't be concerned. Now, I would be very interested in learning how a man of your age has reached the rank of captain."

"I am twenty-four years old," he said defensively.

"No offense intended. I meant, compared to everyone else, we are very young. But I can see now you are, in fact, quite elderly." Merryk replied with a broad grin.

Both men laughed.

Merryk sat down on a bale of hay. Yonn followed but did not sit until Merryk motioned for him to do so.

"I would like to hear the story of how you became Captain of the Guard."

"Well," Yonn said. "I have your uncle to thank. Like most of the people in the Teardrop, I was born here. My father was in charge of the stables. When your grandfather was here, the stables were filled with horses and men. After your grandfather died, your uncle came to collect men and horses for the army. He took my father away, leaving me in charge of the stables. I was only fourteen. Like so many men of the Teardrop, my father went away and never came back." Sadness was in Yonn's eyes as the memory of his father washed across his mind.

"Sorry," Merryk's voice filled with sympathy. "I cannot imagine the loss of a father at such an early age." Memories of his own father filled Merryk.

"Some years later, Chancellor Goldblatt got word the Lord Commander was coming back. By then, I was old enough to be taken into the army. You may have noticed the other guardsmen are older, retired, or surviving members of the army. Hearing your uncle was coming again for another gathering, Hugo, the swordmaster, went to Chancellor Goldblatt and asked if there was a way to save me. The Chancellor concluded if they appointed me captain, I would already be in service to the throne and they could not conscript me. Your uncle was not pleased, but arguing with Chancellor Goldblatt over the law was a battle he did not want to wage. As a result, I got to be Yonn Gryson, Captain of the Guard, though people seldom use my last name."

"How often does the Lord Commander come?"

"Every three or four years, but it seems more often. Our young men just get started and before they can have families and jobs, they are taken away. Most never come back." Sadness again covered Yonn's face.

"Is there nothing the Chancellor can do to protect them?"

"No. Other kingdoms can provide money, and if they can send money, they are not required to send troops. The Teardrop does not have money, so we have to pay in blood and tears—again, our name."

"There must be something we can do. I will speak to Chancellor Goldblatt."

"As far as I know, we have only two choices, money, or men. We do not have money." His voice filled with grim acceptance.

"Money can be generated or raised."

"If you do, you will be the first to generate tears of joy for a change."

Merryk made a mental note. *I need to understand why my uncle needs so many men. If the Teardrop needs money, perhaps I can think of things easy to make, profitable to sell. With money, we may avoid conscription.*

"Well, I better get back to the castle. It is getting close to dinner time. I don't want Nelly to think I no longer like her food."

Yonn chuckled. "It is easy to like Nelly's food. She is a superb cook."

"I think so too," Merryk replied. "I look forward to talking more."

Yonn looked at him with a smile. "As you said, there are not very many of our age in the castle, so I am sure you will see me again."

Merryk smiled and returned to the castle.

Yonn reminds me of my younger self, except he had to grow up fast without a father. I am blessed to have a loving family. Correcting himself, *I was blessed.*

That evening, after dinner, Chancellor Goldblatt asked Merryk if he would join him. A bright fire illuminated the study with a golden glow. Merryk settled in his grandfather's chair, and the Chancellor took his favorite chair across from Merryk.

"There is no simple way to have this conversation," Chancellor Goldblatt started. "Merryk, I am sure you know your accident was not an accident."

"Yes sir, I do. Smallfolks said as much but would never answer specific questions."

"We have been worried about more than your health. We have also been concerned about your safety. We are in the middle of winter, which, I hope you now know, provides protection. No one can easily come to the Teardrop this time of year. The snows hinder them on land and the seas are rough. If any strangers were to come to the Teardrop, we would know immediately. This means you can have more latitude to walk around the castle grounds, but we still have other concerns. In all honesty, Prince Merryk, your memories are still flawed. Technical material is well memorized and recalled on demand, but in some ways, young master, you lack a normal understanding of things that are risky."

"What do you mean?" Merryk asked.

"For example, today in the stable, you did not recognize the horse as dangerous."

"But I don't think the horse is dangerous at all. I think he was falsely blamed."

"A very positive attitude, but the animal has been so violent. The farrier had to cover its head with a cloth to attend its hooves. He has bitten more than one person. It is my understanding you had his head over the top of the stall, stroking the side of his neck. That could have been very dangerous for you."

"I've been around horses before, and he seemed to respond to my voice."

"Well, in any event," replied Goldblatt, "that is not exactly the point. You did not recognize or understand the potential danger. If you do not mind, as you wander around, I would like you to keep Yonn close."

Merryk looked at the Chancellor with a large grin, "So my newfound freedom is from Smallfolks but not freedom from Yonn."

The Chancellor returned his smile, "Yes, true, but your safety will always be my primary concern."

Merryk accepted the situation quickly. "As you choose. I like Yonn. He had to grow up fast, just like I am now."

Anticipating the next question, "Prince Merryk, I know you want to know *why* your uncle would attack you. I do not have an answer. I will continue to investigate the reasons but cannot do so until the winter breaks. I sent inquires before the seas closed the port. I promise to tell you all I know when information arrives. Until then, please, be patient and alert."

Merryk recognized this was all he would get from the Chancellor. "Very well, I know you will keep me informed."

"One more thing," continued the Chancellor, "Smallfolks told me you apologized for evading him the other day."

"Yes."

"You understand this is not appropriate for a member of the royal family. Royals have no obligation to apologize for their actions."

Merryk's face and tone turned serious. "Every man has a responsibility, regardless of birth, to acknowledge their mistakes. We all make them, Chancellor, and failing to acknowledge them only makes us weaker. I guess you still have a great deal to teach me about being royal. But I assure you, despite your best efforts, I will still take responsibility for the impact of my actions on others."

"Very well, I just wanted to advise you. It would seem strange to others."

"What is more important is it does not seem strange to me."

As Merryk left the room Chancellor Goldblatt shook his head and thought, *there are things about this young man that are exceptional and strange.*

CHAPTER TEN

MAVERICK

The darkness of winter was losing its battle with the light by a minute or two each day. The air was still chilly, but lacked its frosty bite. Merryk crossed the exercise yard, heading to the stables. He walked through the large doors, moved down the row of stalls, and whistled softly. Immediately, he received a reply whinny from the black stallion. Selecting the name for the horse was remarkably easy. The horse had a mind of his own and did not fit the normal standards. Maverick was the only choice.

Merryk asked, "How are you today?" as he scratched behind the stallion's ears. "Have they been treating you well?" The horse appeared to be keenly interested in each thing Merryk said.

"Talking to your horse again, I see," Yonn said, as he came through the stable door and joined Merryk.

"It would amaze you what Maverick knows. You should talk to your horse. You might learn something."

"The only thing my horse cares about is food and mares."

"Just like you," Merryk replied to Yonn. Both of them burst out laughing.

Yonn had an infectious sense of humor. Shortly after meeting him, Merryk realized he had missed laughter. Yonn provided a great deal, and the two had grown close.

It also turned out Yonn was a bit of a rogue. He told Merryk, "Having the Lord Commander take our men is a problem, but it can be a blessing."

"How so?" Merryk asked.

"There are lots of young widows and women whose husbands are away," he said with a mischievous smile.

Merryk looked back at Maverick. "Would you like to go outside?" The horse literally moved his head up and down.

"I believe the horse understands every word you say."

"I think he pays attention to everything and is an excellent judge of character."

"Today he proved himself to be a trickster."

"How so?" Merryk asked.

"The farrier came earlier. The last time he had to cover Maverick's head to work on his hooves. This time, instead of leaving the stall in fear, he left laughing. It appears every time the farrier laid down a tool, Maverick moved it. When the farrier looked for it, Maverick stared off into the other corner of the stall as though he had nothing to do with the disappearing implement."

"That's my boy," Merryk responded. "Let's go outside."

The horse again nodded. Merryk took a loop of rope and threw it over the head of the stallion, opened the gate, and walked outside.

Yonn said, "I remember the first time you led Maverick out with a simple rope. We all thought we would chase the stallion around the castle for hours. Instead, he simply followed you."

"What I remember is letting him loose into the open field and watching him kick up his heels and run in the snow."

They made their way to the exercise field, which lay inside the castle walls, opened the gate, and removed the rope. The stallion immediately shook his head and ran into the center of the field. Again, kicking his heels through the snow and running and jumping, enjoying his newfound freedom. In a short period, the horse lay down in the snow and rolled around on his back. Merryk sat on the top of a fence post to watch. Rays of sunshine momentarily illuminated the field like little spotlights breaking the gray of the winter's day.

Yonn broke the silence. "I think this winter is ending."

"It is about time. I could use some warm weather," Merryk replied. "I feel like Maverick. I need more exercise."

"I do not know how you can say that. Every time I am around, you seem to be doing some kind of exercise."

"Which reminds me," Merryk interrupted. "I'd like for you to stand behind me while I use the yoke again."

"All right." said Yonn.

Merryk had found an old oxen yoke and attached buckets to each end, then added oats to each bucket for weight. He would lie on a low bench and push it upward. Yonn stood at Merryk's head to ensure the contraption did not fall on the prince. Merryk even convinced Yonn to use the yoke. The two of them traded-off, giving the other an opportunity to do what the prince called, 'bench presses.' Merryk hung from the long trusses in the center of the stable to straighten his back and do pull-ups.

"My back is not as straight as it needs to be," Merryk said to Yonn.

"It is not because you have not tried. Compared to when you first came, I am amazed how straight you stand."

"Well, maybe another two or three months and my back will be completely straight." Merryk's voice filled with determination.

Merryk let out a whistle and the black stallion crossed the field to the gate. The prince opened the gate and placed the loop loosely around the horse's neck.

"I do not believe you need the rope any longer," Yonn said, as the three of them walked back to the stable. The horse seemed to enjoy the camaraderie. How Merryk had developed such a relationship with the horse, Yonn did not know. Although raised in the stables with his father, a master at caring for horses, he had never seen this kind of relationship. The two of them seemed to know each other's thoughts and responded to each other instinctively.

Yonn had asked Merryk how this bond developed. Merryk only replied, "I think it comes from how we came to be here, both injured, he by reputation and me physically. The experience somehow tied us together."

"Yonn, I will ask the Chancellor to allow us to leave the castle. Springtime is coming and I want an understanding of the topography of the land."

"The what?" Yonn said.

"The levels of the land. I need to understand the highs and lows of the land around the castle. I can't determine them from inside the walls."

"Why would you need to know levels?" Yonn asked.

"I want to determine if there is something we can do to avoid the floods of springtime."

"You are working on a way to avoid the floods?"

"Yes," Merryk replied.

Merryk continually surprised Yonn. The way Merryk looked at the castle and the people within it differed from anyone he had ever met.

"You know, I will go wherever you go."

Merryk chuckled, "I hope you don't mean that literally. One day I might jump off a cliff."

"If it seemed appropriate, I would follow." Yonn thought for a moment, and then offered, "If there is something you could do about the floods, it would make a big difference. At times, it has shut us off from any outside contact for twenty or more days."

Merryk replied, "For centuries, people have controlled water. I'm confident there is a way to do so here. Also, I think storing some water behind the castle might be a good way to give us irrigation in the summer. I've heard Smallfolks say we have way too much water in the spring and not nearly enough in the summer. Perhaps there is a way to even it out."

Yonn looked at Merryk. "You are indeed an ambitious young man," he said in both jest and admiration.

"And you, my friend, would benefit from a little more ambition of your own."

"I am considered quite ambitious. Just ask the local ladies." Again, laughter filled the air as the two men left the stable and returned to the castle.

Across the sea, in the warm castle of King Natas, Princess Tarareese and Contessa Yvette D'Campin, her lady-in-waiting, walked down a broad hall toward the sun terrace. Around a corner came Princess Mandaline. "I understand father has found another groom for you," she said, her voice dripping with sarcasm. "This time, instead of an old, fat belly king, you get to marry a scarecrow, a bent simpleton prince. And what is even better, you will not be married until next year. By then, you will be so old, I doubt you will ever have children. I wonder if this groom will die before he marries you like the last one."

"Why are you so mean and nasty?" Princess Tarareese demanded of her younger sister.

"I am just glad I am not father's favorite. Mother told me I will get someone tall and handsome."

"I hope you get someone to match your naturally sweet disposition," Tarareese said with biting sarcasm and controlled rage.

Fearing the outbreak of a full brawl, Contessa Yvette gently guided Princess Tarareese away from her sister.

"Why did you let her rile you? You never have before."

"Because this time, I am afraid she is right!"

Chapter Eleven

WATER

"Hydrology is the science of the movement and distribution of water." This is the definition Raymond learned in his college hydrology class. The instructor also said, "You never really appreciate the power of water until you see a flood with your own eyes." The torrent surrounding the Teardrop Castle could easily have been the inspiration for the statement. From an engineering standpoint, water was just a scientific topic. But Raymond always thought of it in personal terms, the same way a firefighter talks of the fire demons lurking inside a burning building. Raymond saw the water as filled with determination and strength; a formidable force determined by the path of least resistance to return to the sea.

These mystical qualities motivated Raymond to lead the water management department in his engineering firm. He had stood many times on the bank of the Columbia River and wondered what the untamed river had looked like as it rushed over long-gone Celilo Falls and filled with unrestrained spring flood water. He knew the small river surrounding the castle was nothing like the Columbia. He had spent ten years of his life working on the management of the Columbia River, and now here he was in another place and time, watching a wild river needing to be tamed.

Merryk's internal reverie was broken when Smallfolks and Chancellor Goldblatt made their way to the top of the old tower. Both men were breathless as they stepped out of the long climb, the Chancellor more so than Smallfolks.

"I had forgotten how steep those stairs are. There is a reason I do not come up here often." the Chancellor said with a gasp as he gathered more air in his lungs.

"I thought coming up here would allow you to see what I have in mind. As they say, 'a picture is worth a thousand words,'" replied Prince Merryk.

"I have never heard that before," the Chancellor remarked.

"I think it just means it is easier to explain something if you're looking at it rather than just hearing the words."

"Very well," the Chancellor said.

Prince Merryk continued, "Today we are looking at the full flood for this year. I have been watching the flow over the past few days and it appears to be steady, indicating this level is the high flood mark."

All three men turned their eyes southward toward the flat plain which lay in front of the castle. Normally, the plain was a gentle basin of grassland, surrounded on the left by the rise of forested mountains and on the right by a slender ridge of raised land called 'the Finger.' Today, a muddy brown lake of churning water had replaced this pastoral scene. Merryk turned to the two men. "The plain has a simple problem. Water flows in faster than it flows out. Chancellor, if you look to the right, you can see the Finger extends from the back of the plain down to the choke point where the water struggles to get out."

"Yes," the Chancellor said. "I can see the blockage."

"We have two potential solutions to this problem: reduce the inflow of the water or speed the exit. Speeding the exit won't stop the flooding, it will only manage it. To stop the flooding, we need to stop the inflow. Perhaps it is not initially obvious, but there are three ways the water moves down from the mountains to the choke point."

"Three ways. I thought water came only from the right side and the left side of the castle." the Chancellor questioned.

"I am not talking about how the plain floods, but how the water gets past the castle on its way to the sea." Pointing to the Finger on the right side of the castle, Merryk said. "If you look on the other side of the Finger, you'll see water running down the outside, isolating it with water on both sides. This creates the third way.

"The closest opening on the right-hand side of the castle is approximately twenty feet wide, and its bottom is currently twelve to fourteen feet below the surface of the water."

"How are you able to determine that?" the Chancellor asked.

"Before the floods, Yonn and I did some measuring. I asked Yonn to step off the width. He also measured that rock sticking from the wall, about a foot over the flow, at about fifteen feet high. The right channel is approximately ten to twelve feet over its normal low stage at the end of the winter. He also made marks vertically on the face of the Finger in fifty-foot intervals, so I could get an indication of how fast the water was moving."

Chancellor asked, "Why would you need to know the speed of the water?"

Merryk replied, "With the height of the water, the width of the gap, and the time to cover the distance, I can calculate the rate of flow. This will give us a better estimation of the amount of water we are trying to stop and what kind of structure we would need to do it. I will get the exact measurements when the water subsides."

"Where did you get this idea?" the Chancellor asked.

Merryk thought for a moment, not wanting to say, "Hydrology 207 at the University," instead, "I think it was from one of your books on ancient engineering."

Chancellor replied, "I have been through those books, and I do not remember any specific discussion about the rate of flow."

"Well, it must have been a reasonable inference from the information."

Chancellor Goldblatt just shook his head. "Your reasonable inferences are only obvious to you."

Merryk then pointed to the far side of the Finger. "On the other side is a gap thirty-five feet wide. Yonn said it only carries water when the level exceeds six feet. It is not nearly as deep as the main channel on the right side of the castle. So, it does not carry water at any other time of the year. If I had to guess, I would say it is the old riverbed. The river used to run on the other side before breaking into the floodplain in front of the castle."

Smallfolks, who had been looking at the flood but not engaging in the discussion, interrupted, "When I was first brought to the castle by your grandfather, there was an old steward. He must have been sixty or seventy years old. He told me his grandfather had said at one time all the water ran on the other side of the Finger. His grandfather told him one night there was a big shaking of the earth. Big chunks of the main wall fell, and a lot of the old wall crumbled. Afterward, the water ran on this side of the Finger rather than on the other side. I never thought much of it. You cannot trust the stories of old men." Suddenly recognizing the irony of his statement, he added with a quirky smile, "except mine, of course."

Merryk smiled. "Smallfolks, that makes sense. It suggests a hundred, to maybe a hundred and fifty years ago, there was an earthquake which shook the earth and broke the rocks to create a new passage for the water on this side of the Finger. This would mean the natural way for the river is on the other side. If we could steer the river from where it is now, back to the old riverbed, we could reduce or remove the flooding."

"Are you going to move our river?" Chancellor Goldblatt asked skeptically.

"Given it is the old riverbed, I am not sure we're really moving the river, but simply reminding it where it is supposed to be."

The Chancellor chuckled, "This is not the way a normal man would think about this problem."

Merryk ignored the comment and returned to his proposal. "What I would like to do, when the water recedes, is block both the right and the left channels on the sides of the castle. This will bring the water up behind the castle until it reaches a level where it will run across the old riverbed rather than on the inside. We can make this year a test. If it works, then we can take it up higher next year, so most, if not all, of the water goes to the old stream bed."

The Chancellor looked at the streaming water. "What you are saying is, back the water up behind the castle to force the water to go down the old streambed?"

"Yes sir, exactly. We will also create a lake. A lake we can use, with careful management, to provide water in consistent amounts year-round, giving us the opportunity for better irrigation from here to the port. This is your idea, Smallfolks; a way to take care of too much water in the spring and not enough in the summer. We will need to study the impact on people upstream as the lake expands."

The pragmatic Chancellor Goldblatt inquired, "How do you propose doing this, Merryk?"

Merryk did not pause. "To determine whether this will work, simple log cofferdams on both sides of the castle should be sufficient. Also, we will make a few changes on the old riverbed to ensure when the water flows through, it stays in the course we intend. If this works, we will move the bulk of the water to the right-hand side of the Finger. When we understand the correct height, we will need to create a stone dam for a more permanent solution."

"How soon would you start?"

Merryk answered, "When the water is back down to the lowest level. My guess is mid-fall. It would be almost impossible to do a cofferdam now. The pressure of the water would be far too great. Although, we can start gathering the materials right away."

"Well, it sounds like an ambitious but reasonable project," the Chancellor added. "You must remember, it is your opinion that matters. You have the final say."

"I know. This is my decision and if it doesn't work, I am the only one who can be blamed," he added with a smile.

Chancellor Goldblatt chuckled, "A Royal Prince can never be blamed."

Merryk paused. "I am still not accustomed to that concept."

CHAPTER TWELVE

FATHER AUBRY

The changing of the seasons meant the calming of the seas and the opening of communication between the Teardrop Kingdom and the outside world. Just as the warming of the air signaled spring, so did the appearance of Willem, the gray-haired courier with a large brown satchel over his shoulder. The rough leather of the bag matched the weathered face of its carrier. Both had seen many long days traversing between the Teardrop Castle and various points throughout the kingdom.

"Sorry I am running a little late, Chancellor." His voice reflected a friendship born from years of contact. "Normally you are the only one getting letters from abroad, but today I had two extras," he volunteered. "The first was a letter from a cousin to the smithy in the small village just south of the castle. The second was a beautiful envelope directed to Father Aubry, which bore the seal of the Provost. It was a pretty document, a blue wax seal, and a nice ribbon. I have never seen a letter from the Provost. Father Aubry seemed quite surprised. Was not expecting it, I guess."

"I am sure there has to be communication within the church from time to time," Chancellor Goldblatt replied. Immediately, his thoughts drifted. *Why would the Provost suddenly, after the arrival of Prince Merryk, contact Father Aubry? In all the time I have been in the Teardrop, I have never heard of a communication from the Provost directly to Father Aubry.*

"Just put the letters down on the table, as always. Go find Nelly. Tell her I said to get you a good lunch before you continue your rounds."

"Thank you, Chancellor. I sincerely appreciate it. Food is a little hard to get this time of year this far out." Then the man turned and left the Chancellor's study.

There was a significant pile of correspondence on the table. Chancellor Goldblatt felt mixed emotions. *Perhaps there is something within one of these letters which will give me a clue as to the actions of the Lord Commander. However, my immediate problem is Father Aubry. I know nothing good can come of a letter from the Provost.*

Later that afternoon, Smallfolks knocked on the Chancellor's office door.

"Yes?" The Chancellor responded.

"We have a guest," Smallfolks replied. "Father Aubry wishes to speak with you."

"Very interesting." The Chancellor's thoughts were different. *Given the man has talked to me perhaps five times in the last ten years, this is not a coincidence, but tied to the letter.*

Smallfolks said, "I thought it was interesting too. He has shown no interest in what was happening inside the castle until he received a letter from the Provost."

"You knew about the letter from the Provost?"

"Why, of course," said Smallfolks. "The courier could not help but talk about a fancy seal on a letter with a ribbon. He told Nelly, and Nelly told me. I wanted to be sure he had told you, but I forget this is a tiny place. What should I do with Father Aubry?"

"Please bring him in."

A few moments later, Smallfolks returned with the father. The poverty of the Teardrop Kingdom was reflected in his attire. It was battered and dingy. The black robe showed dust at the bottom and on the seams of each wrinkled crease. The Chancellor did not move from behind his desk nor stand as the priest entered the room. He merely motioned for the cleric to sit in the chair near the desk. *It is important the man knows this is my territory and abides by my rules when he is here.*

"Good afternoon, Father Aubry," he said coolly and firmly. "To what do we owe the honor of your visit?"

Father Aubry sat down on the edge of the chair and looked straight into the eyes of Chancellor Goldblatt. The mutual animosity was clearly reflected not only in tone but in their physical postures.

"I will come right to the point. The Provost has sent me to inquire as to the condition of Prince Merryk Raymouth."

"Why would the Provost want to know about the condition of Prince Merryk?"

"It is not my place to question the reasons for inquiry by the Provost. It is merely your duty to provide me with the information I need to reply." His voice projected the smugness of self-importance.

Goldblatt pushed back in his chair and slightly turned his head. "I have no duty whatsoever to you or the Provost to provide anything."

"Nevertheless, I have been asked to inquire as to the condition of Prince Merryk."

"The prince is well, thank you."

"The Provost wants me to speak with the prince, personally," Father Aubry said emphatically, as his throat tightened in frustration.

Without raising his voice but directing it toward the door, the Chancellor said, "Smallfolks."

Immediately the door opened and Smallfolks appeared. "Yes, Chancellor."

"Do you know where Prince Merryk is?"

"He and Captain Yonn are currently outside of the castle walls."

"Well, there you have it," Chancellor Goldblatt said. "He is not here."

"I would like to arrange a time to meet with him tomorrow." Father Aubry demanded, with emphasis on the word 'tomorrow.'

The Chancellor did not waver in tone or expression. "I will check with His Highness, the Royal Prince, and if he agrees, we will arrange an opportunity for you to speak with him. I will send notice to you later."

"Until tomorrow morning." Father Aubry stood. His voice implied the assumption they would honor his demand.

"Just to be clear, Father Aubry. If the prince agrees to meet with you, he will tell you when you may meet. We will send notice to you later."

"Very well," Father Aubry defiantly rose from the chair, turned, and brushed past Smallfolks out of the room.

"What was that all about?" Smallfolks asked.

"Just another danger for the prince and another piece of a puzzle," replied Goldblatt.

CHAPTER THIRTEEN

QUESTIONS

Early the next morning after breakfast, Chancellor Goldblatt came to find Prince Merryk, who was finishing his daily visit to Maverick.

"We need to talk. There have been some developments," the Chancellor's voice was filled with unusual anxiety.

Merryk sensed an awkward silence as the two walked toward Goldblatt's study. Upon entering, each moved to what had become their customary places with Merryk in his grandfather's chair and Goldblatt to his favorite over-stuffed one. After settling, Prince Merryk asked, "Chancellor, there is something bothering you. What is going on?"

"The weather has changed. As it becomes warmer, the seas calm and we receive correspondence. Unfortunately, the correspondence does not come just to us. It also comes to others within the Teardrop Kingdom."

"I would have expected correspondence between other people."

"But not to others from abroad, specifically regarding you."

"To others regarding me, personally?"

"Yes, we received a visit yesterday afternoon from Father Aubry."

"Father Aubry is the local priest?"

"Yes, he had been in the Teardrop for probably seven or eight years before I arrived. The two of us have had a very difficult relationship. He did not recognize I represented the Crown and had ultimate control over the kingdom. He believed the Provost was over even the king, and he, as the representative of the Provost, had the authority."

Merryk chuckled to himself. *The Chancellor doesn't like anyone to question his authority.* "So why did he visit us yesterday?"

"The Provost had instructed him to speak with you."

"As I recall," Merryk replied, "the Provost is the head of a group of men called 'The Council of Justice.' They have control over all local religious leaders, but no authority over anything else. Wouldn't it be all right to talk with the priest?"

"Actually, I was afraid this would be your response. It is not prudent, because the request came specifically from the Provost."

"What is the issue?" Merryk asked. "Why would the Provost want anyone to talk to me?"

"The Provost and the Council of Justice are not only responsible for the religious order, they also draft marriage contracts between royal families."

"Marriage contracts? I still don't see what this has to do with me."

"They sent you to the Teardrop Kingdom because of a marriage contract."

"Would this be the special circumstances Smallfolks mentioned months ago?"

The Chancellor nodded his head. "We have chosen not to discuss this with you, to give you time to heal, time to remember who you are, and to regain your strength. But you were sent to the Teardrop because there was an error in the marriage contract between the kingdom of King Natas and your father, King Michael. Not understanding our two queens system, the marriage counselor sent from the Provost to negotiate the contract, assumed you were the firstborn in time and not the firstborn of the Inland Queen. My belief is the fact Prince Merreg's mother, Queen Rebecca, having passed away, led him to believe your mother was the only queen. As a result, he inadvertently put your name in the marriage contract rather than your brother's. No one discovered the error until after the contract was signed and ratified."

"Why is this the first time I have heard about this?"

"I am sure you were told of the marriage before you came, but I believe this is a memory you lost because of the accident."

"I have no desire to marry, and certainly not in an arranged marriage."

"Regardless of your desires, the contract has been executed. Now the issue is bigger than your marriage."

Merryk interrupted, "Getting married is big to me."

"The issue is the return of the dowry and the Council's fee. The Provost and the Council of Justice receive a percentage of the dowry. The dowry in your case was, by far, the most significant in many years."

"I still don't understand why they can't simply change what appears to be a scrivener's error."

"Your practicality makes sense. However, the reputation of the Provost for accuracy of the marriage contracts is the basis for such substantial fees. If the Provost had to admit a mistake in the marriage contract, he would not be entitled to the sizable fees, not only in this instance, but in the future. This is, frankly, a matter of pride and economics."

"I can appreciate the confusion in the contract, but why would I need to be sent to the Teardrop Kingdom?"

Uncharacteristically, Goldblatt hesitated before he spoke. "It is difficult for me to say, because you have been a surprise. We were expecting to receive a broken young man—a shell. The official commentary is you are mentally slow, socially inept, and politely phrased, awkward. The general descriptions are you are a simpleton, a physically twisted and bent man, a scarecrow, and unsuited to wed. Many feel you are mentally incompetent. Your father sent you here to avoid public scrutiny."

Merryk's face registered surprise. "I was sent here in order not to be declared mentally incompetent?"

"Yes," said Chancellor Goldblatt bluntly.

Merryk paused for a moment, got up from his chair, and walked over to the window facing the northern mountains. "Chancellor, I know a man can never see himself the way other people see him. Please tell me, is this how you see me? Am I a simpleton, twisted and bent, and incompetent?"

"No! That is my point," Chancellor Goldblatt said emphatically. "You are a surprising young man, completely the opposite of these descriptions. In fact, I would say you are the best student I have ever had. Your comprehension of numbers and science is far beyond mine. Your current plan to evaluate the floodplain and the potential solutions is inspired. I do not know how any man could be considered a simpleton with such thoughts."

"So, my father sent me here to avoid being declared incompetent."

"Also, to protect the kingdom from returning the spent dowry," Chancellor Goldblatt reverted to his analytical tone. "Legally, to void the contract as written, you would need to be mentally incompetent or dead. Both circumstances would require the return of the dowry, but not the fee. The fee would have been earned when the contract was signed, and only subsequent events affected its completion. All of this explains the actions of the Provost, but what I still cannot fathom is the action of your uncle."

Merryk paused. "I am recognizing the complexities. If I am dead or declared incompetent, the marriage contract would be void, allowing the Provost to save face and his fee."

"Yes, you understand completely," said Chancellor Goldblatt.

"Which brings us to a meeting with Father Aubry," Merryk began his own summation. "The priest received a letter yesterday from the Provost instructing him to determine if I am mentally competent. I could sit down and have a discussion with him."

"In a normal world, it would make sense, except we have the fact your uncle tried to kill you. The expectation you are incompetent has been a deterrent to further actions against your life."

Merryk interrupted, "If I have a meeting with Father Aubry and demonstrate a level of competency, the report to the Provost would be good, but I would place my life in greater danger."

"Exactly," the Chancellor said. "How this is handled directly affects your life. Therefore, you must decide."

"Today brings three revelations," Merryk said. "First, they sent me here to avoid being declared incompetent; second, it is clear my uncle intended to kill me; and third, I am pledged to be married."

"I hope you can appreciate our desire to keep you safe and to not overburden you. Based upon what we had been told, it was possible you would not have understood. How wrong we were. Merryk, I respect your intellectual capacity and have no doubt about your ability. But I need to help you learn to think as a member of the royal family."

"How does this differ from normal logic?"

"First, your logic is not particularly normal. You seem to weigh factors by your own standards. Your desire to apologize to people and your unwillingness to accept your nobility, all these things, are unusual for a person of royal birth."

"Are not these the actions all human beings should exhibit?"

"This is exactly the kind of discussion, my young prince, which shows you are not incompetent. I want to be for you what I was to your grandfather, an advisor. If you will allow me, I can help you."

Merryk responded, "I don't understand how this differs from the relationship we have now."

The Chancellor looked at him and smiled with a deep sense of appreciation. "That, Prince Merryk, is one of the unique things about you. You treat people with the expectation they are your equal. This is not the royal way. It makes you quite unusual. If you will think of me as your chancellor, the way your grandfather did, I can help by providing information and analysis to aid your decisions. Under normal circumstances, I would not expect one of your age to understand, but again, you have demonstrated a remarkable ability."

With a new sense of determination in his voice, Merryk looked at the Chancellor. "First things first, what should we do about our friend Father Aubry?"

"Initially, we must recognize he is not our friend."

Merryk replied, "As I interpret it, his intention is to validate my incompetence."

"I believe that is correct. In this circumstance," the Chancellor offered, "we need to use his assumptions against him."

Merryk said, "For example, he assumes I am frail, twisted and bent over. If we do the interview from a chair, leaning forward, he could not observe my physical condition."

Chancellor Goldblatt interjected, "It leaves your physical condition in question. I will report to your father you have made some improvement but still have a long way to go. This message will also reach others. It is clear my correspondence to the king is not completely confidential."

"This would," Merryk added, "show I am still feeble and perhaps still susceptible to death."

The Chancellor said with pride, "Now you are thinking the way a royal would. Second, we need to answer the Father's questions in a way to leave questions."

Merryk paused. "The priest needs to leave believing I may be incompetent, but without enough information to confirm or deny it."

"Absolutely," the Chancellor responded. "His report back to the Provost needs to be equivocal, at best."

Merryk looked out the window pensively. "If I make an effort to not answer the questions quickly, but appear to be pondering each word, it would strengthen the theory I am slow-witted. I also believe you should be in the room and interject often as though you are protecting me from wrong answers, hiding my true condition."

"Agreed. I also should be seen as deliberately delaying your meeting. This will continue the conflict I have with Father Aubry."

"Why is that important?" Merryk asked.

"For the last forty years, there has been a power struggle between the church and the state."

"Not unusual. I believe it has happened many times over the centuries."

"Yes," the Chancellor said, "but this has become especially contentious. The Provost has demanded all tithing be sent directly to the Council of Justice rather than being left in the country churches. As a result, vast sums of money have passed to the Council. They have used the money to build a sizable military they call the Army of Justice. Although the army has not engaged in any actual combat in over twenty years, it continues to grow. It is extremely well-equipped. Although mostly ceremonial, its threat has become the biggest lever the Provost has for soliciting funds. Any money left over is being used to build a massive cathedral for the Provost and the Council of Justice. As their power grows, they have reached into the relationships between kingdoms." Goldblatt added. "Eventually, someone will need to challenge them to restore balance."

"Very well," replied Prince Merryk. "Since he wants an immediate meeting, set something up four or five days from now, in the afternoon."

Chancellor Goldblatt thought for a moment. "We have a small throne room used only for monthly adjudications. It has a raised dais where you can sit when he arrives."

"Sounds regal!" said Prince Merryk with a smirk.

Chancellor Goldblatt grinned back, "I am confident, my young prince, you are more than capable of handling a raised dais."

Sensing the conclusion of their discussion, Merryk turned and looked sternly at Chancellor Goldblatt. "After we deal with Father Aubry, you and I need to have a discussion about this marriage contract."

Chancellor Goldblatt looked at Merryk, chuckled, and said, "Very well, after we are done with the priest, and after I have read my correspondence, we can talk."

CHAPTER FOURTEEN

LETTER TO KING MICHAEL

K ing Michael and Queen Amanda sat at the head of the long dining table. They had finished their morning breakfast when a steward delivered a letter to the king. The envelope was marked "Confidential" and bore the seal of Geoffrey Goldblatt.

"A letter from Goldblatt," the king announced.

Queen Amanda set aside her knitting and focused intently on her husband. "What does it say?" her voice filled with anxiety.

"Just a moment," King Michael said as he broke the seal, unfolded the note, and read aloud.

To your Royal Majesty, King Michael:

The status of your son has changed since the incident and our last communication. Prince Merryk has stabilized and made consistent strides in improving his physical condition, increasing in both strength and weight. His speech is still flat, and I do not believe he will ever return to a normal speech pattern. He has for some time walked about the castle and shown an interest in his horse. We continue to carefully monitor his activities. Overall, there is still much room for improvement.

Prince Merryk has been a good student. However, there are subjects which I no longer attempt to teach him. The focus of my instruction is on helping him understand relationships. The prince does not have a complete grasp of personal roles and responsibilities. Occasionally, his conduct is not consistent with the expectation of a member of the royal family. We are discussing these areas and making progress.

Separately, as you anticipated, others are interested in Prince Merryk's condition. The Provost instructed the local priest to interview Prince Merryk to determine his competency. I have handled the interview, but I am certain the reply will not fully satisfy all questions.

If they press you, I suggest you show a willingness to accept the Council's request to interview the prince. This will give them pause. It says we are confident in the prince's competency. Perhaps a bluff, but an interview requested by the Council would mean they are uncertain. Seeds of uncertainty and weakness are not worth whatever problems this may cause with King Natas. As you know, infallibility of their decisions is the cornerstone of their power. Perhaps I overstep. Your current chancellor may be better able to advise you on this matter.

Our aim, and my task, is to ensure Prince Merryk is a viable, competent groom. You may be certain I have no intention of failing in this endeavor.

Most sincerely,
Geoffrey Goldblatt
Administrator of the Teardrop Kingdom.

"Thank goodness he is better," responded Queen Amanda as her eyes glanced heavenward. "I must let the Lord Commander know right away. He has been most anxious about Merryk's condition."

"How is that possible? I have never known my brother to be anxious about anyone other than himself."

"Michael, you are too critical of your brother. Every time we have talked since the accident, he has asked if we have word of Merryk's condition."

"It is strange he never seemed to care for the boy before."

"Merryk is family! Look at the way he takes care of Prince Merreg. He has acted more like a father to him than you. Why would he not be concerned about Merryk?"

Because Merryk is an inland prince and you are his mother. King Michael kept these thoughts to himself, knowing they would deeply hurt Queen Amanda.

Queen Amanda continued, "I think he feels responsible for the accident."

"My brother does not feel responsible for anything, especially injury to others."

Queen Amanda stood and turned toward the door. "Nevertheless, I will tell him Merryk is doing better."

After she left, King Michael thought. *Amanda, you see the good in everyone, even when it is not there. That is one of the reasons I love you. It makes you a loving wife, but perhaps a naive Queen.*

King Michael returned his attention to the note in his hand. *Why do I feel this letter is saying more? What did you always tell me, old friend?*

"Look for the message in the message." What am I missing? The boy is better, but not great. The Provost looking to disqualify him as a groom was to be expected. You have me looking for ghosts, Geoffrey. His eyes scanned the letter line by line. *'Incident.' Why not call it what it was, an accident? No, you say incident, not accident.*

A sudden realization flashed across his mind. *The incident was not an accident! This could explain my brother's sudden interest in Merryk, but why would he want to hurt the boy? Simpleton Merryk is not a threat to anyone. I need to give this some thought. However, this is exactly what you would want me to know and knew could not be written.*

You may not have forgotten my actions against you, but I had forgotten the depth of your skill and intuition. My old friend, your advice was always sound, and right now, Merryk could not be in better hands.

CHAPTER FIFTEEN

LETTER TO THE PROVOST

S unlight filtered through the stained-glass windows into the Provost's study. The walls and the high ceilings were covered with polished wood, which reflected a deep natural texture. Intricately carved moldings surrounded the room and the windows. Books covered one wall from floor to ceiling. The focus of the room was an oversized desk which sat on a low dais. The whole design ensured the occupant of the desk was always looking down on those in front.

Secretary Bernard never grew tired of this room, though he had entered it every day for over twenty years. His immediate attention was directed to the desk, occupied by a thin man dressed to complement the richness of the room. His clothing was of crisp linen accented with delicate gold thread embroidery and immaculately tailored to fit him perfectly. He had a long face, framed by a carefully trimmed beard. His eyes had a sharp, critical glint. He was the Provost and without doubt; he was in charge.

Secretary Bernard moved to the front of the desk. "We received this from Father Aubry. Because of its sensitivity, I brought it to you directly, unopened. I did not want to take the chance the information would inadvertently be released."

"I appreciate your discretion, as always," responded the Provost. He took the letter from the hand of the secretary. "I hope this makes our decision easier," the Provost said as he broke open a simple wax seal.

To the Provost of the Council of Justice,
Your Excellency,

In the matter of Prince Merryk, your servant went to the Teardrop castle to see the prince as instructed. I met with Administrator Geoffrey Goldblatt, who is a most disagreeable man. Although I requested an immediate meeting in your name, he found multiple reasons to delay the event until nearly a week later. Rather than extending the common courtesy of a meeting in an informal setting, Goldblatt directed me to the Administration Hall, where I found Prince Merryk seated on a raised dais. They gave me a chair in front of him like a common criminal. Administrator Goldblatt never left the room.

My first impression of young Merryk was of a bare-faced boy, even though he is a man of nineteen. His general physical condition appeared as weak or feeble, which would be consistent with recovering from a serious accident. During our brief discussion, he held himself in a bent over position with his hands on his knees. Reports of the prince being stooped or bent forward would seem supported by his sitting posture. It was impossible to determine Prince Merryk's exact physical condition. He did not stand or walk in my presence.

I had prepared a series of questions to help determine Prince

Merryk's mental condition, but found my inquiries either answered or interrupted by Administrator Goldblatt. Prince Merryk often turned to Goldblatt for confirmation or help in answering questions. I received correct answers to all the questions, but it was not possible to determine if the answers were Prince Merryk's or those of the Administrator.

Overall, Prince Merryk's speech was slow and had a lack of accent. All the words were correct, but without the intonation of a High Kingdom native. Perhaps this was caused by the accident, but it is also what one could expect from a mentally impaired person.

Prince Merryk was very polite and gentle in his responses, in contrast to Administrator Goldblatt, who maintained an aggressive posture throughout the interview. Nothing I saw would dispel prior reports of his mental condition. I can only believe the current injuries furthered any previous difficulties. If he were leaning toward incompetency, his injuries would only have moved him closer.

Had the interview been in a different setting, without the Administrator, I would be better able to provide an assessment of Prince Merryk's true mental status. Should your Eminence need anything further, I am at your disposal.

Sincerely, Your Humble Servant
Father Aubry

When he had finished reading the letter, the Provost pushed it across the desk to his secretary.

"Not exactly what we had hoped." Secretary Bernard said after completing his review. "At best, this is inconclusive."

"Who is this Administrator Goldblatt?" inquired the Provost.

"You would remember him better as Chancellor Geoffrey Goldblatt, Chancellor to Great King Mikael of the High Kingdom."

"The one who seemed to continually resist us?"

"Yes, most disagreeable, but very competent."

"His presence in the Teardrop adds a level of complexity I had not expected," replied the Provost. "We cannot declare the boy incompetent with this kind of information. I had prayed for an explicit statement from Father Aubry."

"You could request an interview with the boy personally. They could not challenge your opinion," suggested the secretary.

"No, my position must stay as an impartial judge, not as a fact finder. Everyone must have the ability to appeal to me for relief. Also, it might show an inappropriate relationship with King Natas. We need to act to keep our position of strength and as the ultimate arbitrator. I truly do not care if we ruffle King Natas a little, and I do not want him to believe we will do anything he asks. However, we must appear to have done all we can, so his contributions continue," he added with a small smirk.

"What do you suggest?"

"We need a more reliable source of information than Father Aubry. We need an unanticipated visit by someone with sufficient authority that Goldblatt will not attempt to derail their efforts."

"If I may suggest, I would be an excellent candidate to do an interview with Prince Merryk," the secretary offered. "I could go immediately to the Teardrop Kingdom, traveling with no trappings of office, and arrive at the doorsteps of the castle unsuspected and unannounced."

"An excellent idea," the Provost responded. "Your authority could not be doubted and your opinion would be second only to mine. If you determine he is incompetent, it is the end of the matter. If the boy is competent, it will be decided quietly and quickly, with no sign of indecisiveness. Also, because of your position, it will show to King Natas we had done everything we could to prove the boy incompetent."

"As you wish, your Eminence, I will make preparations to leave immediately."

Chapter Sixteen

GOLDBLATT'S CORRESPONDENCE

S everal days had passed since the interview by Father Aubry and Goldblatt had completed reading his correspondence. True to his promise, Chancellor Goldblatt asked Merryk to join him in his study to review what he had discovered.

"The situation is far more complicated than I had thought," Goldblatt told Merryk. "The pressures being placed on King Michael are coming from multiple sources. Initially, King Michael had entered the marriage agreement at the insistence of the Lord Commander and his current chancellor to gain funds to build two new ships, and to reduce tensions between the kingdoms. The first half of the dowry should have been enough with expected revenues to ensure the completion of the vessels. However, for several conflicting reasons, the revenue has not been forthcoming. As a result, your father had to borrow additional money to complete the vessels. It now appears the repayment of this loan would be in jeopardy without the completion of your marriage."

"How can the dowry for one wedding be so significant?" Merryk asked.

"The dowry is large for two reasons. First, with your brother as groom, it is for a royal wedding where the bride would most likely become queen, and second, because Princess Tarareese is older than a normal bride, therefore less desirable, which made the dowry higher."

"How old is she?" Merryk asked with a note of concern in his voice.

Almost apologetically, the Chancellor responded, "She will be twenty-three at the time of the marriage, but do not let that worry you right now."

"She doesn't sound very old to me," Merryk said. *I blew by my twenties a couple of decades ago. She's just a child.*

"Nevertheless, her advanced age meant the dowry was higher."

"With your father's revenues delayed, he must have another source to repay the loans. It also appears the lender required the new ships as collateral, a fact not disclosed to the king until after the loan had been made. My sources indicate the lender is King Natas, although your father may not know."

Merryk thought for a moment. "In other words, he leveraged his revenue by pledging the new ships as collateral for the loan, and now the revenue is in danger. His backup plan is the wedding dowry. If it doesn't occur, not only will he owe the dowry, but he also loses the ships."

"Precisely, my prince," Goldblatt said, smiling to himself. "King Michael is getting terrible advice, or worse yet, someone is directing the advice he is getting from the Lord Commander and his chancellor. Several sources say there has been a narrowing of advisors with access to your father. The current chancellor has selectively excluded anyone who has a different opinion than himself or the Lord Commander. I am sure you can see the difficulty."

"Yes," Merryk said, "people are directing him into an ever-increasing position of peril."

"Utilization of financial pressure has been a keystone of King Natas' plans to expand his kingdom. I believe he originally started this practice during the first betrothal of Princess Tarareese."

"How exactly?"

"Shortly before her seventeenth birthday, negotiations began for her to marry King Hauge. He was forty years her senior. King Hauge's kingdom lay on the southern edge of King Natas' and was a natural for expansion. King Natas believed having his daughter as the queen would give him an opportunity to gain inside information about King Hauge. The negotiations took longer than expected and were not completed until after Princess Tarareese's eighteenth birthday. Before the wedding could be scheduled, King Hauge became ill and asked the wedding be delayed until he was better. Unfortunately, King Hauge did not get better and died."

"The good news for King Natas was he had provided funds while King Hauge was ill to support Hauge's Kingdom. After King Hauge died, King Natas demanded immediate repayment of all loans. The weak successor to King Hauge could not fulfill the commitments and had to agree to several treaties, transferring the authority of the kingdom to King Natas. As a result, Natas gained what he had wanted, and he still had Princess Tarareese."

"Natas plays a long game," Merryk inserted.

"The problem, she was quickly approaching twenty. He needed to find another kingdom where he could use her as leverage. In a very bold move, he focused on the High Kingdom because of its location. Geographically, the passageway between the High Kingdom's outer islands and the mainland sits in the middle of the primary shipping lanes between the east and the west. Travel through this passage removes three or more days of sailing. Your grandfather placed a toll on the ships passing through the Inland Passage. This is extremely profitable for the High Kingdom and the toll is structured, so it is cheaper to pay than it is to waste the days at sea."

"This is quite a clever tariff structure. I did not know my grandfather had these skills." "Well, technically, it was put in place when I was Chancellor and advisor to High King Mikael."

Merryk chuckled to himself.

"But I digress," Goldblatt continued. "The nature of your father's problem has been exacerbated by the delay in revenues. This is the time of year when revenues rise. A shortfall now is most unusual."

"It is obvious King Natas has a great deal to gain. He would not only reclaim the dowry but also the ships," Merryk concluded.

"Informants within your father's castle said your brother, your uncle, and the current chancellor have engaged in a multitude of communications with the court of King Natas. Chancellor Bates identified the dispatches as necessary to confirm the upcoming wedding. The brief portions which have been intercepted show they are focused on the loan and bloodline."

"You have excellent sources of information," Merryk said to the Chancellor.

"It takes decades," Chancellor Goldblatt replied, "to establish reliable sources, particularly within closed systems."

"I have thought extensively, but I am still confused by what your uncle gains in this process. In one communication, the Lord Commander specifically talked about the importance of bloodline in the development of noble families. Your uncle is the son of an Outland Queen. Maybe he possesses the bloodline of King Natas, and perhaps Merreg's mother did as well. A wedding between Prince Merreg and the princess could further strengthen the bloodline. All of this is just a guess."

"Historically, the concept of bloodlines and creation of a 'super race of nobles' are just ways to disguise the desire to gain power over others. It always leads to widespread bloodshed and misery," Merryk added with a tone of disgust.

"Your understanding of history always surprises me."

"If my name in the marriage contract was an error, how would things have worked if the agreement was correct?"

"Merreg would have married Tarareese. The dowry would have been paid and your father would get the ships," Goldblatt concluded.

"This seems too simple of an outcome. Something more must be going on," Merryk pondered, "particularly if it involves my uncle."

"You are now thinking like a royal," Chancellor Goldblatt said. "I will continue to seek information for you. Right now, you know all I do."

"I gather from this discussion my preference not to marry is out of the question?"

"Should you refuse to marry the princess, your father's entire kingdom would be at risk."

"If I am to be married, can you tell me something more than her age? What is the princess like?"

"Shortly after you arrived, I made inquiries about Princess Tarareese. The formal presentation described the princess as possessing all the attributes one would expect—grace and beauty."

"Are grace and beauty the only attributes valued in a bride?"

"Truth be told, even they are rarely required. It is only important the woman be of noble birth, young, and capable of bearing children. All else is unnecessary."

"No more than a productive post?"

"Harsh, but true." Goldblatt continued, "Those who have seen her give a more complete picture. Remember, King Natas is an immensely proud man. Everything which bears his name must be the very best. Nothing can be second rate."

"It is said he selected his wife the way he selects stock for his stables—bloodline is everything. Queen Stephanie is a woman of exquisite beauty and keen intellect. She is wise enough to negotiate through his fits of rage and continue to be married to King Natas. Some suggest she gives him advice, although this has never been seen in public. A woman giving advice to a man like King Natas would show weakness. The one thing King Natas can never show is weakness. The Princess Tarareese is said to possess her mother's skills, plus those of Natas.

"The princess is, by all accounts, strikingly beautiful, like her mother. She has blonde hair and deep blue eyes. Other than her age, her one significant flaw is her height. She is tall, standing at perhaps five foot eight; two or more inches over an average man and six or eight inches over the average woman. Her height makes her quite intimidating. They described her as having a regal bearing, and it is said she literally flows into rooms.

"King Natas raised her to be a queen. Without sons, he considered his daughters his most valuable tools to expand his kingdom. She is skilled in multiple languages and has been instructed in history, geography, and economics by the finest teachers available. Although, I turned down requests to be her teacher." Goldblatt added, as an aside.

"Tarareese is an expert in horsemanship. Her father gave her a white mare said to be the finest in the stable. The two have been inseparable. Her love of horses ties her to her father. Except for power, it is said the closest thing to King Natas' heart is his horses. It is believed if Natas had to choose between his family and a horse, the horse would win.

"The only person close to her is Contessa Yvette D'Campin, her lady-in-waiting, who possesses none of the graces of the princess. The Contessa balances Tarareese's formality."

"The princesses' relationship with her father is unusual. King Natas gave her all the trappings of a queen with the anticipation she would be absolutely loyal to him. With her as your wife, you must be aware of this relationship.

"In short, she may be one of the best educated women in the world. I have described what she is. However, I do not know if her personal story is as glorious as her skills or if she is happy."

"Thank you, Chancellor. You have given me much to think about." Merryk moved to leave the study, then turning back. "They will not stop, will they? My uncle tried to kill me, and the Provost has sent people to declare me incompetent. We need to assume this is not the end."

"In this instance, I do not believe you will be safe until you marry. As a member of the royal family, you will never be completely safe."

"My father's problems could be bigger than two ships and a loan. I need to prepare."

"What did you have in mind?" Goldblatt asked.

"Yonn mentioned he has a swordmaster. Could you ask if he will take on one more student?"

Goldblatt thought. *Merryk still does not understand what it means to be a prince.* "Your Highness, the swordmaster is your man. Of course, he will train you."

Chapter Seventeen

TWO CASES

This is not what I expected, Merryk thought as he entered the Administration Hall. His last recollection of this room was his visit with Father Aubry. Then, the room appeared to be a large, cavernous space. However, today it was crammed full with people of all sizes and shapes, filling every nook and cranny. Their sounds and chatter overfilled the room.

"I thought you said this would be a simple day?" Merryk whispered in an aside to Chancellor Goldblatt as they entered the room. "Why are so many people here?"

Goldblatt replied, "They want to see the prince."

"Great, no pressure."

"Do not worry. There is nothing you cannot handle, and I will be right beside you."

I believe the Chancellor knew this would happen when he said, "I must start some royal duties."

The entire chaotic condition continued until Yonn, Captain of the Guard, announced Prince Merryk and Chancellor Goldblatt in a loud booming voice, whereupon the room fell into silence. Merryk moved to his chair at the center of the dais with Goldblatt on his right. Chancellor Goldblatt looked across the room and said, "I would like to call the first case—Farmer Johnson versus Farmer Jones."

Two men moved to a small table which sat in front of the dais. Merryk thought, *This is nothing like a TV show.*

After they were seated, Chancellor Goldblatt again looked at Captain Yonn. "What is the nature of this dispute?"

Yonn replied, "Farmer Jones wanted to sell a cow at what he called 'a good price.' Farmer Johnson bought the cow but claims the cow is sick and will not give milk. Now Farmer Johnson wants his money back."

Goldblatt then looked at Farmer Johnson. "Please describe what happened."

Farmer Johnson stood. "Your Highness, I was talking to Farmer Jones at the local inn one evening about two weeks ago. Farmer Jones said he had a milk cow he would like to sell at a good price. I told him it sounded good, but I would like to look at the cow. Farmer Jones said okay, but I must come and look at the cow before noon the next day or he would look for another buyer. I went and looked at the cow. It looked okay, so I gave him the price he asked and took the cow home. I had expected it might take a couple of days for the cow to adjust and give milk. However, the cow has yet to give milk. Farmer Jones sold me a dry milk cow and now I want my money back." With the summary complete, he sat down.

Goldblatt looked toward Farmer Jones. Farmer Jones stood. "Your Highness, I was at the local inn and met Farmer Johnson. I told him I had a cow for sale at a good price. Farmer Johnson never asked about milk. He came the next day and looked at the cow. After he had looked at it, he paid me and took the cow. As far as I am concerned, this is a completed deal, and I owe no money back."

A roomful of eyes shifted to Prince Merryk. Now he was expected to ask questions. Prince Merryk looked at Farmer Johnson. "Mr. Johnson, did you look at the cow?"

"Yes."

"Did you specifically ask Farmer Jones about the milk?"

"No," replied Farmer Johnson, "but it is not a milk cow if it is not giving milk. Farmer Jones made me decide quickly, and as a result I could not determine whether she gave milk."

"Mr. Johnson, have you ever purchased cows before?" the prince asked.

"Yes," replied Farmer Johnson. "I have purchased a lot of cows."

"How did you know this was a good price?"

Farmer Johnson replied, "Because I have purchased other cows and I knew what the prices were for milk cows."

The prince then turned his attention to Farmer Jones. "Mr. Jones, did you know the cow wasn't giving milk?"

"Yes," replied Farmer Jones. "I did."

"Why didn't you tell Farmer Johnson?"

"I did not tell him because he did not ask. That was the reason it was a good price."

Prince Merryk then looked across the assembly of people. "Is there someone here who knows the value of cows?"

Several people raised their hand. Merryk picked one gentleman and asked him to come forward. "Was the price offered by Farmer Jones for the cow a good deal?"

"Yes, My Lord, it was a good deal for a milk cow, but it would not have been a good deal for just a cow. My Lord, the price was lower than a milk cow would have been worth, but higher than just a cow."

"Very well, thank you," the prince said, dismissing the independent witness.

Goldblatt looked toward Merryk. It was very clear, now he must now pronounce a decision. He looked at both farmers and began. "Farmer Johnson wanted to get a deal. He knew the price of the cow was low, but all evidence shows he did not ask why. In addition, this was not the first cow Farmer Johnson had ever purchased, and he was a knowledgeable buyer. Farmer Johnson asserts Farmer Jones required him to decide quickly and therefore prevented him from determining whether the cow gave milk.

However, Farmer Jones did not coerce Farmer Johnson into buying the cow. He could have inspected it, simply said, 'no,' and walked away.

"On the other hand, Farmer Jones knew of the problem and testified he lowered the price, taking this into consideration. He also offered the opportunity for inspection. Although he did not tell Farmer Johnson of the problem, he never lied because he wasn't asked. Had the seller hid the condition of the cow or lied about the production of milk when asked, then the decision might be different. It is my ruling this was a fairly bargained deal between two experienced traders and there will be no repayment. My advice, Farmer Johnson, is next time to ask and remember, if it seems too good to be true, it probably isn't."

There was murmuring in the room, but generally a nodding of heads in agreement with the prince's decision. He turned and looked at Goldblatt, who also nodded, indicating he had done the right thing.

Chancellor Goldblatt then called the second case. Four young boys were brought into the courtroom. They looked to range in age from eleven to about fourteen, all scrawny and disheveled. After they sat down, Captain Yonn, as the prosecutor, presented the charges. "Your Highness, we arrested these four individuals for theft of apples and a squash. All four have readily admitted their theft. After being caught by the owner, they waited until the guardsman came to take them into custody. This arrest occurred just two days after being released for a previous theft. They have been in the lockup for the last two weeks, awaiting this trial."

At this point in time, Chancellor Goldblatt added, "We have a constant problem with petty crimes, mostly theft, and most committed by bandits of this age. Our solution has been to keep them locked up."

Merryk asked, "Who are these boys, and where are their parents?"

Goldblatt answered by naming each boy and then added, "They are orphans or children of widowed mothers."

Merryk thought to himself. *This is another problem created by the Lord Commander.* "Keeping them locked up may be the best way to keep them from committing additional crimes, but I do not think it moves them toward becoming valuable citizens. I believe we should find things for them to do, labor they can provide while locked up."

Goldblatt looked at Merryk, "Whatever you think best, Your Highness."

Merryk looked at the four young boys. "Do you have anything to say for yourselves?" All four shook their heads, no. Merryk then pronounced sentence. "I will modify your confinement. You will perform hard labor during the daytime for three weeks plus one week working with the farmer from whom you stole, to help prepare his soil for this year's crops."

One boy interrupted, "Do we still get to come back each night to our cell?"

"Yes," said Prince Merryk.

"Before dinner?"

"Yes," said Merryk.

"All right," the oldest boy said, and all four nodded in agreement.

Merryk hid his amusement and looked as stern as possible. "You understand it does not matter if you are 'all right' with your sentence. Also, I want you to understand unless you change your ways, you will be the first given to the Lord Commander when he comes again." A ripple of concern moved through the entire audience. To be turned over to the Lord Commander was the threat of a death sentence.

Unimpressed by the peril, one boy replied, "But until then we can stay in the Teardrop?"

"Yes, you can," a perplexed Prince Merryk replied.

Goldblatt looked at the prince, "What do you have in mind for labor?"

"We need repairs on the castle walls. Before we can start, we need to clean and stack all the fallen bricks and stones. Also, we have a problem with rats in the stable."

Merryk thought. *Why are these young boys so willing to be punished?*

CHAPTER EIGHTEEN

KING'S LETTER

C hancellor Goldblatt entered his study to find Willem, the Teardrop courier, had dutifully delivered the monthly correspondence. Willem had dropped the letters on the table by the door. Goldblatt assumed he had gone to the kitchen, as he always did, for a bite of food and to share recent gossip with Nelly and Smallfolks.

The letters presented an opportunity for Goldblatt to sharpen his analytical skills. He liked to arrange the letters on the table in order of priority, based on the sender. This morning, however, his normal practice was disrupted by one particular envelope.

This envelope was unmarked, except for his name 'Chancellor Geoffrey Goldblatt.' It was the same paper used for King Michael's initial request. The seal was plain. Nothing about the exterior of the letter gave any indication of importance. Chancellor Goldblatt remembered the last time such an envelope had arrived by Royal Courier. This time, it came in the standard post. Initially, he believed it was from someone different, but a careful review of the handwriting convinced him the skilled hand of the current chancellor drafted it.

The absence of special delivery could have two meanings. It was either an ordinary message, or it was important, but the sender did not want to attract attention to its delivery. If it was from the king, he would believe any of his correspondence was important. He would have had it delivered by

Royal Courier unless the king was attempting to downplay the significance of the letter.

Goldblatt pushed aside all the other letters and focused his attention only on the one. He broke the seal and found, on finer paper, a note addressed to 'Chancellor Geoffrey Goldblatt' in a different hand. He turned the note over and there was the king's seal. Goldblatt broke the seal and read the letter.

Chancellor Goldblatt,

Queen Amanda and I cannot thank you enough for your care of our son. It heartens us to hear he is doing better. Since the **incident,** *I have been making* **inquiries** *into the potential causes of Merryk's speech problem. As yet, I have not found any obvious solutions. I am sure you are also researching the problem. Should you discover a solution, I know you will advise me immediately, as I will you.*

Many are concerned *about Merryk's health. In fact, the Lord Commander has repeatedly contacted Queen Amanda, seeking any new information on Merryk's status.* **She has kept him informed.**

Neither the Provost nor the Council have contacted us. The visit by your local priest will not be the end of this matter. The Provost likes surprises, and I know you will be ready for any such event. I trust your judgment in this matter.

Thank you again for all you are doing. There are **few I trust** *to care for my son. Also, you understand the importance of this* *wedding.* **Together***, we will find the right solution* **for the kingdom***.*

Michael

Geoffrey Goldblatt's mind searched the letter for hidden messages. He had known King Michael for almost thirty years, and his handwriting had always been smooth and flowing. This letter, however, had some heaviness around particular words. Goldblatt thought. *It is almost as though he put extra pressure on some words so they might appear to be slightly darker than the rest of the text.*

The first word to catch his attention, not only in his initial reading but also from the darker text, was the word **incident**. Goldblatt smiled to himself. *The king has gotten my message. He now knows the attack on Prince Merryk was not an accident.*

Second, there was pressure on the words **making inquiries**. The Chancellor concluded this meant the king was making independent inquiries about the attack on Prince Merryk.

It surprised Chancellor Goldblatt to learn **many are concerned**, and **she has kept him informed,** referred to Queen Amanda herself. *In effect, the Lord Commander is using Merryk's own mother against him. A clever ploy.*

The next section catching Goldblatt's eye was the phrase **few I trust**. Goldblatt knew the king would have correctly phrased it as **few I would trust**. Failure to use the word "would" and the subsequent darker pressure showed the king was now wary of those around him.

The highlighted **together** gave Geoffrey Goldblatt a sense of vindication. *Perhaps King Michael has concluded I am not a threat and, in fact, can be a valuable asset.*

The last phrase highlighted was **for the kingdom**. Had the letter been totally about Merryk, it would have been **for my son**. **For the kingdom** indicates the threat King Michael perceives extends far beyond his son. Only a sense of foreboding would explain the king's willingness to accept quickly that Merryk's injuries were part of an attack and a plan.

Chancellor Goldblatt raised his eyes from the note as Merryk entered the room. "I am glad you are here. I have just received a letter from your father. As you are aware, I have been attempting to warn him about the attack on you. His letter, though couched in terms of your health, shows he has received my message."

Goldblatt pushed the letter across the desk to Prince Merryk. Merryk picked up the letter, walked over toward the window, and read it. "Is my father healthy?" Prince Merryk asked.

"Why would you ask that question?"

"Well, there are portions of the letter which seem written with more intensity than others. It is the style of writing I would expect of someone ill or unsteady."

"Your intuition is good, young prince. The differences in text highlight specific words and make up a second message within the first one."

Merryk's attention returned to the document. "Is there anyone he can trust?"

"Few."

"Is there anything we can do?" Prince Merryk asked the Chancellor.

"Well, the only thing we can do is try to discover the underlying motive for your uncle's attack and ensure your wedding goes off without difficulty.

"The king is a resourceful man. Now forewarned, I am sure he will take precautions for his personal protection, as we need to protect you."

Merryk looked back at the Chancellor. "I am working with the swordmaster and increasing my capacity to defend myself."

"Merryk, protecting you will require more than increasing your skill with a sword. The challenges from the Provost and King Natas will come from a variety of sources. We must prepare for whatever form they take."

CHAPTER NINETEEN

FATHER BERNARD

"I love this kind of day," Yonn said. "It gives me hope warmer days are coming."

"I can't believe it's almost mid-summer," replied Merryk, as the two men rode out of the forest onto the main road connecting the port city to the castle.

"This morning it was a little crisp and filled with sounds of the forest, but this time of afternoon is great," Yonn said.

Sporadic streams of people occupied the main road. Traders, visitors, and common folk moved up and down the road daily. Merryk and Yonn blended in. Both had worn ordinary clothing on their daily trips. "We don't want to stand out," Merryk had said. Although Yonn was sure a barefaced giant, like Merryk, and a handsome man, like himself, could not help but be noticed. It appeared to work. People in the village seemed willing to ignore them, except the ladies, for whom Yonn always had a ready smile. Yonn knew the Chancellor had talked with the village leaders and asked them to give Merryk some room and to keep an eye out for him. If anything would have given them away, it would be their horses, particularly the large black stallion, which seemed to fit Merryk perfectly. To help complete the disguise, Merryk had asked Yonn to call him "Raymond."

As they moved toward the castle, they overcame an older priest walking beside his horse.

"Good afternoon, Father," Merryk said.

"Good afternoon, my son," the priest replied with a gasp of breath.

"You look tired."

"Yes, I had forgotten how strenuous riding a horse can be."

"Where are you headed?"

"I am on my way to visit Father Aubry, but I need to stop by the castle to see Administrator Goldblatt."

"Everyone here calls him Chancellor," Merryk offered. "I think it is out of respect for when he served for Great King Mikael." Merryk's eyes strayed to the fine leather bags the horse carried. *This man is not what he seems.* "We are headed that way. Perhaps you would like to ride with us. It will help the time go faster and perhaps divert your mind from the pain of the saddle."

"Yes, the time would pass faster, but I am not sure about the pain," the priest said with a small chuckle. "I am Father Bernard."

"Some people call me Raymond, and this is Yonn," replied Merryk.

Yonn acknowledged the father with a grunt. Traveling with a priest would not enhance his appeal to the ladies.

"What do other people call you?"

Yonn replied for the prince, "Depends upon the establishment." All three laughed.

"What brings the two of you out this warm afternoon?" queried Father Bernard.

"We were visiting a woodsman's home about jobs. It is just off the road," Merryk explained.

"Honest work is good for the soul," replied the priest.

"Also the pouch," Yonn inserted. Again, they all chuckled.

The road meandered its way along the side of the river toward the castle. "I'm glad to see the water is down," Merryk said.

Yonn added, "In the springtime, Father, this becomes a torrent, and the area in front of the castle floods, cutting it off from everything. Raymond has a plan to stop this from happening."

"More of a dream, but if we could figure out how to direct the water elsewhere and to store it behind the castle, it would make a big difference to the people," Merryk added.

"Ambitious plan for one so young," replied Father Bernard.

"Even a minor success would help reduce the burden of the spring floods."

The three had moved over a small hill and now looked across the floodplain.

"There it is," Yonn said, pointing to the castle.

The field in front of them was recovering from the spring flood, covered now with a sea of wildflowers. The area was abuzz with bees moving from plant to plant.

"This is beautiful," responded Father Bernard. "So many wildflowers, I have seen nothing like it. What of those boxes?"

"Another one of Raymond's ideas. He wants to trick the bees into using them instead of random trees," Yonn said.

"It's more like giving them an alternative, making it easier for people to harvest the honey," Raymond replied.

"Very interesting idea. Is it working?" The priest asked.

"Appears to be. We won't know for sure for a few more weeks," Merryk said.

Father Bernard used this encounter to gain additional information. "Do you know Prince Merryk?"

"Yes," responded Yonn.

"What kind of man is he?" the priest asked.

"Very much like me," replied Merryk.

"I hope not. That would make my job difficult."

"Why difficult?" asked Merryk.

"Well, there are expectations about the prince you would dispel."

Merryk frowned. "My experience suggests it is best not to jump to conclusions."

"Very true," acknowledged Father Bernard.

The rest of the journey was uneventful. Soon, all three were standing in front of the Great Hall.

"Why don't you let us take your horse and get it some water and oats." Merryk offered.

"Thank you, my son. You have been most helpful."

Smallfolks had been expecting Merryk and Yonn. Hearing the horses, he came out the front door. "Smallfolks, this is Father Bernard. He is here to see Chancellor Goldblatt. Can you take care of him?"

"Yes, your—"

Merryk interrupted Smallfolks' response. "We will be in the stable if you need us. Goodbye, Father Bernard. I hope I will see you again."

"I do too, Raymond," replied the priest.

Father Bernard followed Smallfolks into the Great Hall. As soon as the large doors shut, the priest's voice changed from casual to formal. "Please advise Administrator Goldblatt, Father Bernard, Secretary to his Eminence the Provost, wishes to see him immediately."

A normal man would have been intimidated by the change in tone and the flash of title, but Smallfolks, who had been around people of power his entire life, simply replied, "I will see if the Chancellor is available. Please follow me." Without stopping for a reply, Smallfolks turned and moved toward a small sitting room off the Great Hall. At the door, he said, "You may wait here." Smallfolks then turned and disappeared down the hall.

Father Bernard, Secretary to the Provost, expected a different response, more haste and deference. He received neither from Smallfolks. In a time longer than the priest expected, Smallfolks returned. "Chancellor Goldblatt will see you now. Please follow me." Again, Smallfolks moved forward at a slow, measured pace, leading Father Bernard to Chancellor Goldblatt's study.

Goldblatt rose from his desk as Father Bernard entered the study and came forward to greet him. "To what do we owe this honor?" Goldblatt asked as he extended his hand to Father Bernard.

"I am here to interview Prince Merryk."

"Very well. Smallfolks, can you please ask the prince if he would like to join us?" The casual response from Chancellor Goldblatt surprised Father Bernard. Rather than allowing an awkward silence, Goldblatt began. "How was your trip?"

"Always longer than expected," replied the priest. "I met two delightful young men on the road this afternoon. One was engaging and articulate. I had not expected such an interesting conversation."

Further discussion was interrupted as the study door opened. "Father Bernard, I had not expected seeing you again so soon."

"You two have met?" asked Chancellor Goldblatt.

"This afternoon on the road," stated Prince Merryk. "We both hid our actual identities: he as Secretary to the Provost and I as prince. I think we both understand how titles change a person's responses and their expectations."

"I could not agree more, Prince Merryk," Father Bernard added, trying to disguise his complete surprise.

"Chancellor Goldblatt, can you see if Nelly has any tea, or would you prefer sherry, Father Bernard?"

"Tea would be fine."

Goldblatt left the room in search of the tea.

"This will give us a few minutes to talk alone," Merryk stated as both men settled into the comfort of the study.

The conversation lasted for over two hours. Father Bernard began with his general questions. Name your father and living relatives, give a family history, then shifted to geography and history. Merryk answered all questions. Some questions on history he didn't know and replied accordingly. The conversation drifted from the daily to the practical to the philosophical. Somewhere in the process, it shifted from an inquiry into a dialogue, often punctuated by laughter.

"My goodness, the time has flown," Father Bernard stated. "I have only one more question. Are you a good man?"

Merryk smiled. "A question of moral competency. The answer should be simple, but as you know, it is not. Everyone believes they are good. They can point to someone they believe themselves to be better than. The thief believes himself better than the murderer, but this is a comparison of one man against another. Goodness is not to be measured by man's standard. The apostle, when asked the same question, replied, 'I do not do that which I know I should, and I do that which I know that I should not. I am a wretched man.' He understood by the standard of God all men fail."

"Very true," nodded Father Bernard.

"I have one last question for you. Have I dispelled your expectations of me?" Merryk asked.

"Yes, Prince Merryk. Absolutely. In fact, I find it unfortunate you are to marry. You could have contributed greatly to the order. It would surprise you the number of men of noble families who are part of the clergy. The Provost himself is of a noble family."

"I don't know if I would be a good priest, but I know much needs to be done for the people. If I can do that, it will be enough," Merryk replied.

Chancellor Goldblatt returned to the study, as if on cue. "Chancellor, can you see to Father Bernard's needs?"

"Yes, Your Highness."

Father Bernard took the outstretched hand of the prince. "Thank you, Your Highness. This has been a most enjoyable day." He then bowed and left the room.

"I am sorry we did not have an opportunity to talk," Chancellor Goldblatt said as they moved down the hall.

"Prince Merryk mentioned during our discussion the two of us, in his opinion, could have been friends had we not been on opposite sides of what he called the classic 'church-state' conflict."

"Yes, the prince has an interesting way with words," Chancellor Goldblatt replied. "But I do not think being on opposite sides of an issue should prevent our ability to communicate with each other."

Father Bernard nodded in recognition of the value of informal contacts. "I agree. Perhaps we can exchange letters from time to time."

The message from the Provost to King Natas was simple and clear.

> *After due inquiry, including an extensive interview by my personal secretary, we have concluded Prince Merryk has recovered from his accident, is of sound mind, and more than competent to be a groom. We appreciate your inquiry, but now consider the matter to be closed.*
>
> *Most sincerely,*
> *Provost of the Council of Justice*

Chapter Twenty
THE ANSWER

The summer days had not yet extended light into the late evening, but the fullness of the moon illuminated everything around the castle. Merryk stood, as he often did on nights like this, at the top of the old tower, looking at the scenery. There was something comforting about being above everything. It gave him perspective.

He was about to leave the tower for the evening when he looked down along the side of the wall. There, just outside the holding cells, were several figures. From this height, he counted eight or ten small people against the wall. They appeared to be talking with those inside the cells. *The people on the outside are smaller than the captives on the inside. They appear to be a mix of small boys and an assortment of girls of multiple ages.* Merryk watched the exchange taking place between those within and those without. It suddenly occurred to him. *The boys on the inside are handing food through the window to those on the outside. This must be why they were willing to be punished.*

This surprised Merryk. After the hearing, he had not considered why the boys had engaged in petty theft. *Their confinement was a source of food for other small children.*

Merryk went to the front guard tower and instructed the guardsman to approach the children from one direction while he approached from the other. As Merryk had expected, the children attempted to run, but the placement of the guard prevented escape. Soon he rounded up ten culprits and moved them into the Great Hall. He surveyed the children who stood before him. Fear was reflected in the eyes of the children. This was not a circumstance they had expected.

In a very stern voice, Merryk said, "I will ask you some questions. I expect your answers to be truthful. I do not want to ask the questions twice."

One little boy, no more than six, replied, "Then can we go?"

It occurred to Merryk his sternness was lost upon these children. They were all small, alone, and very frightened.

One girl, perhaps the oldest at twelve, was particularly agitated. "We cannot stay here. We have to go. We have to go get Maizie."

The prince replied, "You have no choice. You will stay here until I figure out what is going on."

"No sir, please, you do not understand. Maizie is all alone." Now her voice teetered in panic.

"Calm down. What is your name?" Merryk asked the young girl. "Tell me the problem."

"My name is Jane. The little one, Maizie, is just a little over two. She was asleep when we left. She is all alone in the barn. The farmer told us if he caught us there again, he would kill us." Pointing to one boy, "He already hit Billy with a stick. See, he still has the mark on the side of his face and his arm where the switch hit him. If he finds Maizie, he will hurt her for sure. Please, please, let us go!"

"Where is the barn?" Merryk asked.

"Just on the edge of town," she tearfully replied.

"If the man had threatened you, why did you hide there?"

"It was the closest place we could hide and still be able to get food each night."

The entire situation made Merryk sad. *These children are the direct result of the Lord Commander taking away the men. The children are left either as orphans or with a single mom who isn't able to take care of them.*

Alerted by his guardsman, Yonn entered the Great Hall. "Yonn," Merryk said. "I need Maverick and I need you to come with me."

"Yes, your Highness."

After acquiring the horses, the two, with Jane sitting behind Yonn, headed out of the castle. "Show us where to go," Prince Merryk said to Jane.

"This way," she pointed out the castle gate.

The three moved past the south section of town and the old wall to a farmhouse with a barn lying off to the side on the piece of land called 'the Finger.'

People arriving in the night at the farmer's house was never good news. When he heard horses, he concluded marauders had come intending to steal. He hurried out to the barn and immediately demanded, "Who is there?"

"I am Prince Merryk."

"Sure, and I am the king of the Seven Seas," the man replied.

"It doesn't matter who I am. I am retrieving someone from your barn."

"You will get nothing from my barn," the farmer answered angrily.

Merryk stepped down from his horse and moved toward the farmer, who was holding an old shovel. "I would suggest you not attempt to use that," Merryk said. The man moved forward. In a single motion, Merryk tore the shovel from his hand and threw it against the wall. Grabbing the man by his collar with his other hand, he lifted him off the ground.

"You go sit over there until I say you can move." With a push of his hand, he threw the farmer against the wall. The man was clearly frightened. He sat by the side of his barn quietly, quivering.

Moonlight flooded the barn as Merryk opened the doors. In the most soothing tone possible, he said, "Maizie. Maizie, where are you?" There was shuffling off to the side, but no answer. Merryk looked at Jane. "Can you call her?"

"Maizie, this is Jane. Maizie, you need to come. They are here to help us." Although a side-wise glance at Merryk showed she was not entirely sure.

"Yes," Prince Merryk said. "We are here to help you. Now come out, Maizie. Let's go meet the others." From under the wheel of a cart came a small child, barely able to walk. Jane's voice had been enough to coax her from her hiding place. Merryk dropped to his knee and looked at Maizie. "Hello, Maizie. My name is Merryk," he said with the biggest smile he could muster.

She nodded with a small smile, but her eyes told the truth. She was frightened.

"How would you like to go for a ride with me on my horse? His name is Maverick?" The little girl shook her head no.

Jane looked at her and said, "Maizie, it is okay. They will take us back to the castle."

Maizie extended her arms and wrapped them tightly around Merryk's neck. Merryk thought. *There's something about the way a small child attaches to you. It always feels filled with trust. My guess is it has been a long time since an adult hugged you back.* Merryk and the small child mounted Maverick. He looked at the farmer who was still sitting against the barn. "Tomorrow, in the light of day, I will come back, and you and I will talk about what has been going on here."

Upon arrival at the Great Hall, he found Nelly had already taken charge. All the children were sitting at places around the table with clean hands and faces. They were eating bowls of steaming soup with buttered bread.

Nelly asked, "Where are we going to put these children tonight?"

The prince said, "Let us get some blankets, stoke the fire, and let them sleep in front of the hearth tonight?"

Yonn replied, "Your Highness, I am not sure having these urchins in the castle is a good idea. They will wander around and get into mischief."

Merryk looked at the group in his *new* stern voice. "There will be no mischief, will there?"

All the children simultaneously shook their heads from side to side.
A weak whisper at the end of the table asked, "What is mischief?"

CHAPTER TWENTY-ONE

CHILDREN

"What are we going to do about the children?" Chancellor Goldblatt asked. "There is no one to watch or care for them." The Chancellor, Nelly, Yonn, and Smallfolks had joined Merryk in the study to discuss the small children.

"We cannot send them back out on their own again," stated Nelly.

Yonn suggested, "Perhaps we could pay people to take them."

"If we pay, people will take them for the money, not because they wish to care for them," Chancellor Goldblatt replied. "They will use the bigger boys for labor. The little ones no one will take because of the burden. And, the girls would not be safe if we sent them out."

"I have a particular interest in the outcome of this discussion," Smallfolks said. "I would like to remind you all, were it not for the generosity of Great King Mikael, I would not be here today. I do not know what my life would have been like if the prince left me alone after he found me."

"I appreciate your passion," replied Yonn. "These children have no one to care for them. They are orphans or survivors from families with overwhelmed single mothers. Is this the church's responsibility?"

Goldblatt replied, "In a perfect world perhaps, but this is not a perfect world. Father Aubry does not have money to restore his own church, much less care for small children. The Provost and the Council of Justice take every penny for the Army of Justice and the new cathedral. There is nothing in their hearts directed at a group of small children. All of this being said, I still do not know how we will care for them."

Merryk, who had sat quietly throughout this discussion, spoke for the first time. "Perhaps we don't need to take care of them. Perhaps all we need to do is find the place where they can be safe and help them learn to take care of themselves. Already we have seen they are very resourceful. The older boys were willing to take punishment to provide food for the others. This kind of determination and commitment will allow them to succeed."

Chancellor Goldblatt looked at the prince. "Ultimately, Your Highness, this is your decision."

All eyes turned to Merryk. "This morning, I was out wandering through the abandoned buildings on the outer edge of the castle wall. There's an old building which looks like an abandoned barracks."

Nelly responded, "I know the place. It is a real mess. I believe no one has used it in forty or fifty years. The last time I looked, it had a kitchen and at least two working fireplaces."

"I think we should inspect it to see if it might become a permanent place for the children. If so, we can have the older boys, as part of their punishment, help the little ones clean the building," Merryk suggested.

Nelly replied, "The oldest girl, Jane, seems to be their leader. I think she has been doing the cooking. Working with me, I think she could take care of the children. I would help them organize if she is willing."

Smallfolks piped up, "I would be more than willing to help direct their cleaning efforts and the removal of the debris from the barracks."

Yonn joined the discussion. "The guardsmen and I can help move the heavier things."

Merryk looked around the group. "All right, first we must talk with the children. If they do not agree, then we are wasting our time. If they agree, then we need to evaluate the building and create a list of what we need to make it habitable. Each of you, get me a list of supplies you need. We can send Yonn to the village to gather them. Until we settle the children, we will meet every morning to review our progress. Does anyone have questions?"

All shook their heads no.

Goldblatt thought to himself. *Another surprise, Merryk is taking the lead and organizing the effort. He has more skill than just intellect. Also, more compassion than one would expect of a royal.*

As they moved toward the door Smallfolks touched Prince Merryk on the arm. "Thank you, Your Highness. You are more like your grandfather than you know."

They found the children in the Great Hall, near the warmth of the fireplace and close to the food table. The older boys had joined the smaller ones. Women from the kitchen had delivered breakfast—oatmeal, bacon, and bread. The children had huddled together, some of them still wrapped in the unaccustomed warmth of the blankets. As soon as Merryk entered the room, the little one, Maizie, grabbed her blanket and ran to him. Merryk picked her up, and she wrapped her arms tightly around his neck. Moving to the center of the children, Merryk sat down on the floor.

"We need to talk," he said to the children as they gathered closer. "I have been speaking with Chancellor Goldblatt and the others about how to help you. You can't stay outside like before. It is not safe. We know you are all strong and capable of taking care of yourselves. If we could find a permanent safe place for you, would you be willing to work to make it into a home? It will be a place inside the castle wall. It will have guards, not to keep you in, but to protect you from people like the farmer. Are you all willing to work for a place like this?"

They all nodded 'yes.' All except Jane, whose face reflected skepticism.

Merryk caught the look in her eye. "Jane, do you have questions?"

Jane, who had been silent, other than last night's insistence on finding Maizie, now looked directly at Prince Merryk. "We had promises before. Father Aubry promised he would take care of us. The boys will tell you, all he did was hurt us."

"I assure you that will not happen here."

"We can take care of ourselves."

"I know, Jane, but what I'm offering is a place that is dry, warm and safe. Also, it's an opportunity for you to work and learn how to provide for yourselves."

After a moment of silence, Jane hesitantly replied, "Could we see this place?"

"Absolutely," Merryk said, "but before we leave, there is one more thing. This castle is our home. If you share it with us, by being within the walls, there will be rules. Nelly, Smallfolks, Yonn, the Chancellor, and I will, from time to time, ask you to help with things. Also, we cannot have theft of any kind. This would be your home. If you steal, you would be taking from your own home. Do you understand?"

The older boys, Jane, and a few of the others, acknowledged affirmatively. The little ones looked around and saw the nods of the others and agreed. Maizie simply squeezed Prince Merryk's neck tighter.

"All right, let us go look at this new place and see what we have to do to make it into a home."

The children started to gather up their meager possessions. "You won't need to take all your things. Everything will be here when you get back, I promise. You will be here in the Great Hall for a few days until we get your place ready. No one will bother your things."

They looked at Jane, who nodded her head in agreement.

As they moved toward the door, Nelly reached out to the prince. "Give me the little one. She seems to have fallen asleep." Maizie was comfortably pressed against the prince's chest, blanket in hand, and sound asleep.

"Okay, but if she awakes, bring her to the group. I don't want her to be frightened."

CHAPTER TWENTY-TWO

TASKS

The longer days of summer afforded Chancellor Goldblatt the opportunity to enjoy the terrace which lay outside his study. Many years ago, they had planted a small tree. Over the years, it had grown to provide shade for a bench which sat beneath it. Chancellor Goldblatt liked to take his afternoon tea on the bench to enjoy the quiet and warmth of a summer's breeze. This afternoon, he had just settled and was waiting for Nelly to bring his tea. Nelly appeared like clockwork. Unfortunately, behind Nelly came Smallfolks, clearly with something on his mind. The Chancellor shook his head. *This may not be the quiet afternoon I had hoped.*

Without waiting to be asked, Smallfolks began. "I am worried about Prince Merryk."

"You are always worried about Prince Merryk," the Chancellor replied.

"Now more than before, even when he tells me where he is going, I cannot keep up with him. Instead of one place, it is three or four: the swordmaster, the barn with his horse, his shop, or with the children. I have no idea where he is going when he and Yonn leave the castle grounds. If keeping track of the prince was not enough, there are the children. One of them keeps following me around. The other day the boy asked what he had to do to be like me when he grew up."

Nelly chuckled. "You volunteered to help, and the boy admires you."

Smallfolks scoffed, "He is crazy to ask what he can do to be like me. Why would anybody want to be like me? It is not just me. You have seen it too, Nelly. Jane is at your side from morning to night."

Nelly replied, "Yes, she is becoming an excellent cook and baker. Jane makes the children's breakfast and lunch and helps each night with dinner. It will not be long before she can take care of all the children's needs."

Chancellor Goldblatt, who had sat quietly during this exchange, responded, "This self-sufficiency is exactly what the prince had intended."

Smallfolks continued, "But there is more. Prince Merryk hired the old stonemason. The man must be a hundred. I do not know what the prince expects he will do. The man is so old he cannot even lift a stone. One of the older boys attached themselves to him."

Goldblatt replied, "I understand from the mason the young man is an excellent worker. The old man may have a weak back, but he has a strong mind and is willing to share his experience. The boy has a strong back and is eager to learn. Prince Merryk said it was an excellent opportunity for us to save the knowledge trapped in the old stonemason."

Nelly inserted. "The children are all responding fantastically. Do not forget Billy, he is a genius in catching rats. He got all the rats out of the old barracks and then cleared out the barn. Now he is going through the castle. Soon there will be no rats. Never thought I would live in this castle without rats."

Chancellor Goldblatt added, "Prince Merryk insists the rats are a real danger, something about sickness and history being changed." Goldblatt continued, "Smallfolks, you are not the only one having difficulty keeping up with the prince and you are seeing only part of the picture. Prince Merryk has been working with the local blacksmith and other craftsmen. The blacksmith has one son left who was too young at the last collection by the Lord Commander. He now would be one of the first taken away, particularly as a blacksmith. Prince Merryk went to him and asked the blacksmith for help on a project. I believe it all started with the garden."

Nelly inserted, "Oh yes, it is a beautiful garden. Prince Merryk turned the soil over so quickly, and the children are taking care of it all by themselves. The little ones love to watch things grow. There will be a good crop of root vegetables, which would not have been possible without the deep soil plowed by the prince."

Chancellor Goldblatt added, "Yes, Prince Merryk designed the plow. Most ingenious, it quickly turns the sod. All the old plows just dug a trench, but he makes it possible to take virgin grass land and make it ready to seed. Merryk says the current plow is just a 'prototype.' He said the only problem was we needed 'draft horses,' not oxen. I am not even sure I know what a *draft horse* means.

"He made a deal with the blacksmith to make a hotter forge, one to create stronger steel and plates of steel. When done, Prince Merryk will show him how to make the plow in exchange for the blacksmith taking one boy as an apprentice. He also advanced money to the blacksmith for supplies for the forge. The blacksmith will pay a ten percent tax to the king, and a ten percent royalty to Prince Merryk. It is an excellent deal for everyone. Prince Merryk will also protect his son if the Lord Commander comes back."

Smallfolks shifted subjects. "Have you seen what he calls 'his shop'? It is filled with contraptions. I asked the other day what he was working on. He said something about survey tools for the cofferdam. And how many white bee boxes has he made?"

"Yes," Goldblatt said. "Merryk is paying a reward to anyone who finds bees in the forest. Then, he and one of the boys have been collecting the queen bees to put in the white boxes and placing the boxes in the fields around the castle."

Chancellor Goldblatt interjected, "This year he wants to do a 'proof of concept' to see if he can collect sufficient honey and beeswax to generate cash."

"This is my concern," Smallfolks stated. "Royals are not supposed to work like this or this hard. Have you seen all he does? He carries block and stone, takes care of his horse, works in his shop, and spends untold time with those children. I do not know when he sleeps. All of this is stranger than when he was sick. He will really hurt himself."

Chancellor chuckled, "Hard work will not hurt him any more than being clean. He can become an idle royal later. Right now, everyone in the village is growing to respect him."

"As they should, he is royal and their prince."

Chancellor Goldblatt replied, "Prince Merryk does not want that kind of respect Smallfolks. He wants the kind which is earned."

"Well, Smallfolks, just so you can start to worry about something real, he wants to go to the port to talk with the shipwright and hire some additional men to work on his cofferdams."

"But it may not be safe."

"I will stall him, but he cannot stay in the castle walls forever. We must let him explore, even if it is unsafe. I will send Yonn and the swordmaster with Merryk. He should be safe enough."

Chapter Twenty-Three

SALT

Leaving the main gate, Merryk made his way to the blacksmith's shop. He enjoyed this path because it led him through the heart of the village and gave him the opportunity to interact with the people. Coming around the corner into the village square, Merryk saw an elderly woman sitting on a step. Tears were running down her face as she tightly gripped a small cup.

Merryk recognized her as one of the many older widows of the kingdom. "What's wrong?" he asked as he sat beside her.

"I cannot buy salt," she said between sobs. "The new salt dealer will not sell less than a pound and raised the price to seven-pence per pound."

"What was the old price?"

"I could buy a cup for a pence. It is all I can afford. I need just a pinch each day for my biscuits," again more sobs.

"Where's the salt merchant?"

"He is unloading casks for the Blue-and-White Mountain Clans near the blacksmith."

"Why don't you sit here in the shade until I get back? I will try not to be too long."

"Yes, Your Highness."

The salt merchant was a short but burly man, with shaggy hair on his chin and head. Merryk stood watching the casks being taken from the wagon and set on the ground. He saw one man standing apart but closely watching the process. Making his way toward this man, Merryk twice bumped his foot into separate casks. The man watching the unloading wore the cross sash, designating him as a member of the Blue-and-White Mountain Clans.

"Hello, my name is Merryk. What brings you to the village?"

"Good morning, Your Highness," the man said as he made a short bow. "I know who you are. I am Jamaal ZooWalter, son of Gaspar ZooWalt. I have come to the village to buy salt."

"How much are you buying?"

"Forty casks—2,000 pounds. But right now, I am watching our friendly vendor. He is an agent of King Natas and cannot be trusted."

Merryk watched for a few more minutes and then, excusing himself, said, "I will be right back."

Walking toward the salt merchant, the plainly dressed Merryk asked, "What's the price of salt?"

"It depends on how much you want. A full fifty-pound cask is two hundred pence; anything less is seven-pence a pound."

"How much did you bring?"

"Sixty casks. Forty are already sold to the mountain people."

"How do you plan to sell the balance?"

"Just sit here until they are gone."

"So, your time has no value, and whatever you may get for the balance will be reduced by your expenses. You do understand, with the increased price, there will be many more small quantities. It might take three or four weeks."

"I hope not."

"What if you sell me the remaining casks at one hundred and fifty pence, and you can go home this afternoon?" After a little more haggling, the salt merchant finally agreed. "Very well, twenty casks at one hundred and fifty pence; 3,000 pence."

"One hundred and fifty pence for a full cask." Merryk took the man's hand, shaking on his deal. "The money and the scale will be right here."

"What scale?" the merchant replied.

"Some of these casks seem lighter than others," Merryk answered. "We will open one and be sure it is full and compare it to the others. Any not full, we will fill with salt from another cask. "

"I never agreed to that."

"Good morning, Your Highness," Captain Yonn said. "The money and the yoke, as you requested."

Seeing the Captain of the Guard and two guardsmen brought the salt merchant up short. "I mean, Your Highness, that will be fine."

The process Merryk outlined revealed a twenty percent reduction in the actual amount of salt.

"The salt must have settled," the merchant offered in defense.

"Salt is sold by the weight, not by volume. It could settle but would still weigh the same. These casks did not weigh the same." Merryk paid the merchant for the remaining sixteen casks.

Jamaal had watched the prince weigh each cask. "Prince Merryk, would you mind if I borrowed your scale?"

"I thought you might want to use it," Merryk said with a smile. "I will have my guardsmen stay to gather the scale and to ensure it is used fairly. Oh yes, when you end up short, I will sell you enough to load your horses at your agreed price. It would be unfortunate to travel so far and go back with only a partial load."

"Thank you, Your Highness. It would have been frustrating to learn later of the shortage."

Merryk stayed with the salt long enough to sell four casks in small batches to the locals, who were delighted to pay four rather than seven-pence a pound.

"Jamaal, if you have time and could stop by the castle, I would like to talk with you."

"Yes, Prince Merryk, I will come after I finish here. We do not have to leave until the morning."

Prince Merryk nodded. "Until later."

Prince Merryk moved to one cask. Opening it, he scooped a pound or more into a small bag. "I need to drop this off on the way to the castle," Merryk said to Yonn.

The widow was exactly where Prince Merryk had left her. "Please take this salt. When this is gone, come to the castle guardhouse. They will always find salt for you."

She thanked the prince and offered him the pence. Prince Merryk wrapped his hands around her hand and the offered coin, "It's at no charge."

Merryk found the Chancellor in his study.

"I brought back the money," Merryk said, laying the purse on the desk.

"You did not buy any salt?" Goldblatt asked.

"Yes, I have four casks minus a pound or so."

"How much did they charge this year?"

"Our salt was free, or at least it came out as free, after a little trading."

Merryk turned to leave the room. Goldblatt shook his head from side to side and smiled. Before Merryk reached the door, he turned back to the Chancellor. "Goldblatt, why do we buy foreign salt when we have an ocean?"

Chapter Twenty-Four

TAX COLLECTOR

O nly small swirls of high clouds marred the bright blue of the morning sky. The outside air was filled with the warmth of a summer's day and the fragrance of wildflowers. The natural beauty of the Teardrop Kingdom always amazed Merryk. The snow had removed itself from the visible northern mountains, except for the tips of white on the far peaks of the Blue-and-White Mountains. *One day I need to venture north to meet more of our friends in the clans.*

Yonn lead his horse up next to Merryk's. "Good morning, are you ready to find timbers for the cofferdams?"

Merryk nodded as he tightened the cinch on Maverick's saddle. "Are you ready for a trip to the forest, my friend?" Merryk said to the great black stallion.

The horse responded by bobbing his head up and down.

"I do not know why you even have me go along," Yonn said in mock frustration. "You and the horse can talk all day without me."

"Stop complaining, Yonn, and lead the way," Merryk said with a broad smile. "Where are we going today?"

"We will go to the house of the woodsman's widow, Marta."

"Another widow. Is that how you met her?"

"I will admit, Marta is as beautiful as any in the entire kingdom, but her true charm comes from her personal strength and determination to raise her two sons on her own. She and the boys still gather wood in the forest and sell it to the people in the village. She lost her husband about three years ago when the Lord Commander came and took him. Later, she learned he had died in battle."

"As harsh as it sounds, I guess knowing may be better than guessing," Merryk said. "Although I'm sure it doesn't make it any easier for her and the boys to live alone."

After an hour of riding, Merryk and Yonn crossed into a small valley surrounded on three sides by forest. The spring flowers still painted bright patches of color on the meadow's green palette. At the head of the valley was a small house, actually more like a large hut, with a wisp of smoke rising from the chimney.

"Everyone says Marta knows the forest better than anyone. She will know where to find the best trees," Yonn said.

As they rode forward, Merryk said, "It looks like we aren't the only visitors today."

"Oh no, the Royal Tax Collector."

Merryk looked at Yonn. "Why didn't I know he was in the Teardrop?"

"Your Highness, he is carved from the same tree as your uncle. He does not believe he has to report to anyone."

Two horses were tied near the door of the hut. One man, a guard, was sitting against a tree. *The second rider, the tax collector, must be inside.* Merryk concluded.

"Good morning," said Merryk. "What brings you this way?"

The man stood. "We are here on behalf of the king. Go away."

Merryk and Yonn ignored his directions, dismounted from their horses, and moved forward.

Suddenly, a woman screamed, "No!" followed by the sound of a large crash from inside the hut.

"What is going on?" Merryk's voice filled with alarm.

"Go away. This is none of your business!" The guard reached for his sword.

Yonn drew his. "Sit down."

Merryk moved quickly to the hut and swung open the door. In front of him, a fat, middle-aged man with a trimmed rounded beard was tightly gripping the arm of a woman, whom Merryk presumed was Marta. She was desperately attempting to hold her torn blouse to her breasts and push him away. With an open hand, he hit the woman hard across the face. Merryk could see her eyes were already swelling from a previous blow.

"What are you doing?" Merryk shouted.

The man turned toward Merryk but did not release the woman's arm. "I am the Royal Tax Collector. No one may interfere with me while I am performing my duties," the man said with a pompous air.

"And your duties include attacking women?"

"This is none of your concern. Go away. I am collecting taxes for the king."

"I paid. I gave him my coins." She glared at the fat tax collector. "He put them in his purse, and said, 'I will keep these for myself.' Then he said he wanted something more." Tears and anger filled Marta's voice.

Merryk spoke, his tone measured and hard. "Let her go."

"I will warn you one more time. It is an offense punishable by death to interfere with me."

"I said, let go of her," Merryk's voice did not waver.

When he realized his threat was not working, the tax collector released the woman and pulled a small glittering dagger from his belt. Grinning, he moved toward Merryk.

Merryk parried the blade with his left hand, grabbing the man's wrist and twisting it until the knife fell. Then Merryk stepped forward and hit the collector solidly across the center of his face with his forearm. The loud crack of the man's nose was immediately followed by a spurt of blood shooting down his face.

Merryk grabbed the man by the collar, lifted him up, and threw him toward the door. The tax man didn't pass through the door but hit the frame with a resounding thump. Merryk grabbed the man again and gave him an added toss, this time cleanly through the door and out to the ground.

The man, lying on the ground with blood gushing down his face, was having difficulty breathing. Between gasps, he shouted, "You will pay for this. They will hang you. I am the Royal Tax Collector. No one can interfere with the tax collector during his official duties."

"You have said that before. Tomorrow is the monthly trial date at the castle. I think we should present this to the prince and allow him to decide."

"The prince," scoffed the tax collector, "is a sniveling imbecile, bent over and twisted. He will have no interest in protecting a woman, only his tax revenue."

The chill in Merryk's eyes reflected his anger. "I will be there tomorrow without fail. Now get on your horse and get out of here."

Yonn motioned to the guard, "Go, and help your master."

The guard got up, grabbed the tax collector, and the two of them moved to their horses. After they had mounted, the tax collector looked back one more time at Merryk. "I doubt you are brave enough to show up tomorrow. If you do, it will be to find a warrant issued by the Administrator sending you back to the Capital City to be hanged."

They turned and rode off down the road.

Marta came out of the hut, still clutching her torn blouse. She was shivering. Merryk stepped inside, grabbed a blanket, and threw it around her shoulders.

"It will be all right," Merryk tried his best calming voice.

"No, it will not be all right," Marta said. "He is the Royal Tax Collector. You interfered with him. You cannot show up tomorrow. They will hang you."

Merryk looked at her with a slight smile on his face. "I think everything will be just fine. But it is important you join us tomorrow. Can you be there?"

"Yes, I can, but you should leave the kingdom immediately."

Yonn looked at Marta. "Marta, please trust that everything will be fine."

Merryk and Yonn stayed at the hut until the two sons returned. Marta had regained her composure and was no longer shaking.

She is being strong for her sons. I see why Yonn likes this woman. She is tough and determined.

"Marta, I will send someone to guide you to the hearing tomorrow."

"Young sir, I truly appreciate what you have done for me, but please, run."

"It is critical you be there to testify against the tax collector."

"I believe nothing I say will be enough."

"We will see," Merryk replied.

Chapter Twenty-Five

TRIAL

S mallfolks burst into Merryk's room. "Your Highness, the entire castle village is buzzing. Someone attacked the Royal Tax Collector."

Merryk looked back at Smallfolks. "Yes, I know."

"This is an unbelievable circumstance. No one in the Teardrop's history has ever dared interfere with the tax collector."

"Perhaps it was time."

"Perhaps it was time! The king cannot have those who collect his taxes harmed. They must be protected."

Merryk continued to put on his tunic, a more formal tunic than normal. In addition, he added a medallion which bore the insignia of his position as prince.

"It is unusual for you to dress so formally. I guess finding out who assaulted the tax collector is of great importance."

"Yes, it is, Smallfolks. It is."

The first time Merryk had entered the throne room for trials, it was filled with people curious to see him. Today, it overflowed and rang with the chatter of anxious and fascinated people.

Guards had forced people away from the two tables in front of the dais. At one table, the Royal Tax Collector sat with his back straight and head held high. The other table was ominously empty. *They came to see who would dare attack a tax collector and how he will be punished.*

The doors to the room swung open. Captain Yonn, dressed in his finest official attire, stepped through the door. "His Royal Highness, Merryk Raymouth, firstborn prince of the Inland Queen and son to His Royal Majesty, King Michael Raymouth." The entire room bowed.

Prince Merryk, accompanied by Chancellor Goldblatt, moved to their chairs on the dais.

Merryk's eyes scanned the audience. Two guardsmen stood on either side of Marta at the edge of the crowd. When she caught sight of Merryk, her mouth opened in astonishment as she looked at the man who had saved her. Her eyes were swollen and bruised. The face of the tax collector was much worse. His nose had been reset and taped on both sides. His entire face was black, blue, and swollen. *I heard you were in the tavern boasting whoever attacked you would be on their way to the capital for hanging.*

Upon seeing Prince Merryk, the tax collector's eyes widened, and his entire body stiffened. Apprehension and uncertainty seemed to wash over him. He stood to speak. "Your Royal Highness, there is some kind of mistake."

"Did I give you permission to speak?" Merryk's voice was resolute.

The collector shook his head 'no' and sat down.

In a heartbeat, the tone of the room changed. Silence filled the room as a hundred people suddenly inhaled. Merryk could only assume the expectation of the crowd was the identification and punishment of miscreants who had attacked the Royal Tax Collector. They now perceived something else was about to happen. "Captain Yonn, announce the first case."

Yonn stepped forward, looking directly at the tax collector. "Sir, what is your given name?"

"Jarvis," replied the collector in a weak and tentative voice.

"Your Highness, Jarvis, the Royal Tax Collector, is charged with the crimes of abuse of office; violation of the king's trust; theft of the king's property; assault on and attempted rape of Marta, citizen of the Teardrop

Kingdom. In addition, I charge him with attacking a member of the royal family with a knife."

Murmurs spread throughout the crowd. This was nothing they had expected.

"Call your first witness," Prince Merryk said in a firm voice.

Yonn looked across the room, his eyes focused on Marta. "Marta, please come forward with the things I asked you to bring." Marta moved to the second table and stood. "Can you tell the prince your name?"

"I am Marta, the widow of the woodsman."

"Where do you live?"

"I live with my two sons in our hut north of the castle."

"In your own words, can you describe the events of yesterday?"

"Yes," Marta said, her voice a little shaky. "It was an ordinary day. My boys had left, as they do every morning, to gather wood for our next bundles for the village. They had not been gone long when there was a knock on the door. I opened the door to see the Royal Tax Collector. He looked at me and said, 'I am here to collect the taxes for the king.'

"I told him, 'Very well', and moved inside the door. He followed me without being invited. I went to my purse for the six coins I had saved for the purpose of paying my taxes. I gave him the coins. He took them from my hand, placed them in his own pouch and said, 'These are for me. The king will never know, and now I want something more.'"

Jarvis started to object, but a single look from Merryk silenced him.

Yonn said, "He wanted something more?"

"Yes, he wanted something else from me."

"What happened next?"

"He hit me across the face and grabbed the front of my blouse and pulled down hard, tearing it."

"Did you bring your blouse with you today?"

Marta held up the blouse, showing it had been violently torn.

"Please continue."

"He then grabbed me and pushed me against the side of the table, knocking over several chairs. I yelled, 'No!' He just laughed and hit me again. Then the door flew open and a young man, Prince Merryk, came in."

The room erupted in a sound of amazement. "Silence!" Merryk said, "Marta, please continue."

"The prince asked the tax collector what he was doing." Merryk listened as Marta repeated the events, including Jarvis pulling the knife and the prince throwing the tax collector out the door.

"Marta, did you bring the knife the tax collector pulled on the prince?"

Marta raised the jeweled dagger for all to see.

"Is there any question in your mind, Marta, the man sitting at the table and identified as Jarvis, the tax collector, is the man who assaulted you and pulled the blade on the prince?"

"None whatsoever."

"Thank you, Marta. That will be all for now. Please be seated."

"Jarvis, do you dispute anything Marta has said?"

"Yes, all of it. I was there collecting taxes for the king, which she did not pay. When she did not pay, I said to myself, 'Well, women can always pay, one way or another.'" A smug grin crossed his face, coupled with a slight chuckle.

"Are you laughing?" Harshness filled Prince Merryk's voice.

"No, Your Highness, I am not. I was just collecting the taxes for the king."

"So, you are telling this court you intended to collect taxes for my father one way or another?"

"Yes, Your Highness."

"How exactly, Jarvis, do you share that kind of collection with my father?"

A chuckle ran through the crowd, but no smile crossed the face of Jarvis. Just by looking, Merryk knew this day had not gone as Jarvis had expected.

"Do you deny you hit Marta?"

"No, I do not. But some women like it rough."

"Did she or did she not say 'no'?"

"I do not remember."

"I will remind you. I was outside, and I heard her say 'no'. I ask you again. Did she say '*no*?'"

"Yes, Your Highness. She said 'no.'"

"Where I come from, Jarvis, when a woman says 'no', she means 'no.'"

"Now, to the next matter. Did you or did you not pull a blade on me as I entered the hut?"

"Yes. But I did not know it was you."

"I thought you said, 'I was a sniveling imbecile, bent over and twisted,' suggesting you knew me. What difference would it have made if you knew it was me? You pulled a knife against the man coming to the defense of a woman you were attempting to rape." Merryk's tone did not vary. It was hard, abrupt, and commanding.

"Do you have anything else to say for yourself, Jarvis?"

Jarvis pulled himself up, gathering whatever dignity he had remaining. "Yes, I am the Royal Tax Collector. The king's law states no one may interfere with a tax collector while he is performing his duties." Jarvis put as much emphasis on "king's law," as possible.

Chancellor Goldblatt spoke for the first time, "The tax collector has correctly stated the law. There is only one issue to be decided. At the time of the incident, was Jarvis performing his official duties or engaged in personal pursuits?"

Merryk paused for a moment in thought. "Jarvis, stand. It is the determination of this tribunal that, at all times after Marta paid her taxes, you were engaged in personal folly and not the official duties of the king. I appreciate whether she paid her taxes could be disputed, although pocketing the king's taxes would be consistent with your other actions. Even if she did not pay the taxes, the law does not permit a Royal Tax

Collector to collect 'something for himself' instead of coin for the king. Your actions would have no value for the king. As a result, the king's law does not protect your activities in the hut.

"In addition, it is my judgment you have abused your office, and the trust given you as a tax collector. You have stolen from my father, the king, his rightful tax money. Therefore, in the name of my father, I am stripping you of all powers, duties, and privileges associated with the title Royal Tax Collector. I am ordering the guardsman to seize all taxes you have collected along with your personal purse. We will collect the balance of the taxes due for the Teardrop Kingdom and forward them to my father. I will advise my father we shall collect all future taxes in the Teardrop to insure this does not happen again.

"You now stand in front of me as an ordinary man charged with assault, attempted rape, and attack on a member of the royal family. All three crimes could be punishable by death."

Turning to Chancellor Goldblatt again, "Should we just hang him?"

Shock rippled through the room like electricity.

The Chancellor looked at Merryk with a slight smile. "I would suggest we not hang him, at least immediately. Your uncle, the Lord Commander, appointed him."

Merryk's eyes flashed as he looked back at the Chancellor. "Does the Lord Commander appoint all tax collectors?"

Goldblatt nodded his head 'yes.'

Merryk's attention returned to the man who stood in front of him. "I think I will take time to determine the appropriate penalty for your crimes. Until then, you are to be locked up."

The look on Marta's face was filled with a glow of appreciation. The look on Jarvis's face was the exact opposite, one of disbelief. "Guardsmen, remove this man from my presence."

The two men who escorted Marta stepped around Jarvis. They grabbed him by the arms and lifted him toward the door. Merryk looked across the silent crowd. "Captain Yonn, is there anything else we need to address today?"

"No, Your Highness, everything else can wait."

Marta's thoughts that day had run the full gamut. She woke up in the morning with apprehension about what might happen, which only grew as two guardsmen showed up with an extra horse, insisting she come with them. As she rode away, she was fearful she would never see her sons again. *It is never good to run afoul of powerful people, and the tax collector was powerful. The law protected him. Even though he was assaulting me, it will not be enough. Kings need taxes and giving extra leeway to a tax collector was a price they would accept.*

The shock of seeing Prince Merryk walk into the room was overwhelming. The young prince had been kind to her the day before; he had stayed with her until her boys had returned. He was sure she had something to eat, and he had sent men to ensure she could safely make it to the trial. The events at the trial were beyond any expectation. *I cannot believe Prince Merryk took my side over the Royal Tax Collector.*

The tax collector had said the prince was a sniveling fool, but there was nothing foolish about this young man. He was tall and strong and filled with a sense of justice.

Following the trial, the guardsman took her back to a small room where Prince Merryk was waiting by the door. "How are you today, Marta? I hope the swelling on your face goes down quickly."

"I am sure it will, Your Highness. I have no way to thank you."

Prince Merryk interrupted. "It is unnecessary. Let's sit for a moment and have a cup of tea."

She sat down at a small table across from the Royal Prince. "I cannot believe I am having tea with you, Your Highness?"

"Are you surprised princes drink tea?" he said with a smile and a chuckle.

They chatted about small things, and she talked about her boys. When she mentioned the loss of her husband, Prince Merryk seemed genuinely sorry. When it came time to go, Prince Merryk reached across the table and handed her a small purse filled with coins.

"Marta, please accept these coins as partial restitution for the damage and wrong done to you. I will do what I can to ensure this kind of incident never happens again."

Marta's eyes scanned the lean young man. *If only I were younger.*

Chapter Twenty-Six

TRAVEL

Captain Yonn was standing outside the door when Merryk exited.

"Chancellor Goldblatt would like to see you right away." Yonn's voice told Merryk it was important. "He has discovered something."

As the two moved down the hall, Merryk asked, "Have you secured the taxes?"

"Yes. At the beginning of the trial, we seized the taxes and they are inside the castle. I can tell you the guards were not pleased to have us remove them."

"I think we should keep an eye on the tax collector's guards. We should tell them they will need to escort the collector back to the Capital City. I want to know where they are at all times. I don't want one of them sneaking a message to the Lord Commander."

The two rounded a corner, went down the corridor, and up the stairs to Chancellor Goldblatt's study.

Merryk loved this room. The colors within the study always reflected the light and clouds outside. It seemed almost magical. Today it was gray, matching the brewing clouds. Merryk looked out the window as he entered. "It looks like we're in for a storm."

"Yes," said Chancellor Goldblatt as he slipped from behind his desk. "There will be a storm tonight, much like the one you created with the tax collector."

"It needed to be done."

"There is no question in my mind about that," replied the Chancellor. "Jarvis was a man who had grown accustomed to his power to the point of abusing it."

"Yonn said you've discovered something?"

"Yes," Chancellor Goldblatt said as he pointed to two large bound books which lay on a side table. "These are the tax records for the Teardrop Kingdom. They are duplicate books of tax collections. One book reflects the actual numbers and the second, half of each line item in the first, the amounts for the king."

"We knew Jarvis was a thief."

"This is not the act of a thief, Merryk. An ordinary thief would take the money and not record what he had stolen, only what he left. Jarvis has detailed individual collections and then entered them into the other book. The first book is an accounting for the person directing his actions."

"Do you think it's my uncle, the Lord Commander?"

"That would be my initial guess, but we do not have actual proof the extra money is going to him. If the Lord Commander is responsible, it would affect all taxes and tariffs, not just the Teardrop's. It could explain your father's shortfalls in revenue and the pressure on the dowry for your wedding.

"My current calculation is the amount of money collected so far is more than the whole reported for last year."

Merryk thought for a moment and then cast his gaze back toward the Chancellor. "I think we should get this money to my father quickly so it cannot be intercepted."

"Agreed. What do you have in mind?"

"We will hold the tax collector until just before the winter storms, and then I will send him to my father for sentencing. This will prevent my uncle from immediately appointing another tax collector. By then we will have collected the remaining taxes. This will also give my father time to look at other collections without giving away the inquiry."

"Getting the money inside the Capital City will be difficult without attracting the attention of the Lord Commander."

Merryk thought for a moment. "Perhaps if we were to send the swordmaster and five guardsmen, not with a chest but with saddlebags, and have them go in pairs into the capital. This should avoid attracting attention."

"I have a friend who can deliver a letter to the king, the old Chamberlain from your grandfather's reign. He can get to the king in total confidence without raising suspicion. I have known him for over thirty years. His every action is to support the king. There is no one more loyal than he."

"I can carry the funds to the ship. I've never been to the port, and this would be a good time for me to do so. I can use the opportunity to meet with the shipwright and also meet the harbormaster."

"The danger to you would be real. Many unknown people come and go in the port. We will not have any warning about who is a threat. I do not suppose I can discourage you from doing this?"

"I think it's time I move further than a day's ride from the castle."

"Very well. I will prepare letters for your father, the Lord Chamberlain, and the harbormaster."

As Merryk stepped outside the door, he found Yonn waiting. "We're going on a road trip."

"Road trip?"

"Yes, we are taking the tax money to the port."

"We? I am sure the Chancellor told you this is not a good idea."

"Yes, he said it was unsafe. Nevertheless, I need to move around the kingdom. I want you to find the swordmaster and ask him to pick five men he can trust to carry the taxes to the Capital City."

"A long trip with a large chest."

"No chest, we will use saddlebags and go in pairs rather than showing up as an armed group protecting a lockbox. We will leave in the morning. I want to use the opportunity to talk with the shipwright and meet the harbormaster."

When Merryk returned to his room, it did not surprise him to find Smallfolks packing for his journey. "Prince Merryk, I have laid out things for your journey. I would prefer you not go at all; it is not safe. But it will not matter, as you will go anyway."

"Yes, Smallfolks, I will."

"So, there are two things I have added."

"What are they?" Merryk asked as he moved forward, placing his hand on the shoulder of Smallfolks to comfort the old man.

"The first thing is a coat, or more correctly, a special coat, long enough to hang over your back, legs, and the back of your horse. Perfect for shielding wind, and when it rains, you can throw up the hood. It was your grandfather's. I have oiled it every year for the last thirty years." Merryk saw Smallfolks was very proud of the care he had given the black leather riding coat.

"Thank you, Smallfolks, but I'm not sure there will be rain."

"It always rains at the coast; that is the reason I stay here."

Smallfolks next laid a bundle of canvas upon the bed. "This, Prince Merryk, is special. This is your grandfather's sword. He packed it in this canvas when he headed for the Capital City. Your grandfather told me to keep the sword until I could give it to his grandson. When I asked him which one, he said I would know." Smallfolks' eyes became tearful as he handed the sword to Merryk.

Care of this sword was the last duty my grandfather gave Smallfolks. All these years he has been waiting to fulfill it.

The sword was two inches longer than a normal broadsword. It was a Crusader type with a large round knob on the hilt with a dark red letter "R" embossed on a bright blue background surrounded by a ring of gold.

As though sensing Merryk's thoughts, Smallfolks said, "This is the symbol of the Raymouth family for the Inland Queen. It matches your medallion, and it was the symbol of your grandfather."

"I'm surprised he didn't take the sword with him."

"He told me if he took the sword, he would fight, and as the new king, would put the kingdom in danger. He had men who could fight for him, and he needed to learn to rely on them."

"Wise." Merryk continued to hold the sword in his hand and swung it around to test its weight. "I'll take good care of these for you, Smallfolks, and return them right away."

"There is no need to return them. They are yours." Smallfolks' voice was a little gravely. "Your grandfather anticipated you would need them, and I have now given them to you." Smallfolks' face became more serious. "But I want you to know you need to be very careful. The port is dangerous. There will be many unknown people."

Merryk placed a hand on each of Smallfolks' shoulders, so he was looking straight into his eyes. "Smallfolks don't worry about the port. No one knows who I am or that I'm coming. Yonn and the swordmaster will be with me."

"I want you to promise you will be very careful," Smallfolks said.

"I will be careful, I promise."

Chapter Twenty-Seven

PORT

T he journey to the port took a day and a half. Prince Merryk, Yonn, the swordmaster, and the five handpicked guardsmen started early and made excellent progress. A warm early fall day had favored their journey. Prince Merryk decided they would spend the night under the stars rather than risk attention at one of the small inns. The evening was clear, a little crisp, but pleasant.

Starting early the next morning, they arrived at the port not long after breakfast. The morning wind was coming off the sea and reached inland to bring a taste of salt in the air. *You can always smell the ocean in the air before you can see it. Seagulls are always noisy, and more so, near men bringing fish in from the sea. We must be close. I have never been this far away from the castle. I can't tell the others, but this is a completely new adventure for me.*

A short distance before the port, they stopped by the river to break into three groups, each to enter the port separately. Water ran down the river, but nothing like the torrent earlier in the year. Now it was a gradual stream meandering its way to the sea.

Merryk, Yonn, and the swordmaster went first. As they approached the beach, they crossed a small delta and moved toward a large cluster of wooden shacks.

Merryk looked out beyond the shacks into the harbor. Harbor was probably not the best description. It was a small bay which lay to the side of where the river entered the sea. Several fingers of wooden docks extended from the beach. Each appeared to float up and down with the incoming waves. All the ships lay at anchor offshore.

I don't know what I thought I would find. Perhaps wharfs where ships could dock and unload directly. It appears a smaller boat ferries everything to the shore. As an engineer, I see an opportunity for significant improvement. Building more substantial docks would allow the ships to come to shore. This would increase operational efficiency by allowing ships to unload and load cargo far more quickly.

This day, there were a half dozen larger ships at anchor. Some were two-masted schooners and others sloops. There were many smaller boats, slightly more than rowboats with sails. The entire scene was bustling with people coming and going. A number were engaged in loading and unloading goods between the larger ships and the shore. Many small boats were pulled onto the beach unloading the morning catch. Merryk could see salmon and other deeper water fish. Nearby, there was a group of huts devoted to the sale of fish. Others acted as warehouses for the goods from the larger ships. It was a place of commerce.

Merryk turned to Yonn and the swordmaster. "I would like to remain as anonymous as possible. Yonn, I will let you take the lead in our discussions with the harbormaster."

"The harbormaster knows me. I come to the port several times a year to check on the ten guardsmen who patrol here. I know where he is."

The harbormaster's shed was off to the side of the largest of the finger docks. The door was propped open to allow sailors to come and go without obstruction. The harbormaster sat at his desk. The top of his head and the area around his mouth and chin were devoid of hair, but large puffs of peppery gray hair filled the sides of his head and his cheeks. Although older, his eyes were quick and observant, reflecting a sharp mind.

Yonn spoke, "Good morning, harbormaster."

"Good morning, Captain Yonn."

"Chancellor Goldblatt sent us." He handed the harbormaster the Chancellor's note. The harbormaster took the letter, grunted, and read it. After concluding, he looked up at the three men. He nodded to the swordmaster and Yonn, but his eyes lingered on Prince Merryk.

"I have been expecting you. I received word yesterday from the castle to hold a ship. It will leave with the evening tide. How do you want to handle your cargo?"

"Several others will come in the next few hours. I think they should go immediately to the ship," Yonn said with hesitancy as he glanced at Prince Merryk for confirmation.

"If you do that, it should not attract any attention," the harbormaster said directly to Merryk to support Yonn.

Merryk nodded in agreement.

"Very well, sirs. Is there anything else you may need?" There was a slight change in the harbormaster's demeanor. His gruff exterior appeared now to be cautious.

"We are looking for a shipwright. A man named Franco," Merryk spoke for the first time.

"Yes, Franco is as old as the sea. My guess is the man has been building ships since he was a boy, which is so long ago no one can remember, not even him," he said with a slight chuckle. "The old man considers himself a piece of the sea and takes great pride in the boats he makes."

"It's exactly what I had hoped. Can you advise Yonn and me how to find him?"

"He has a place a little way back up the river where, at high tide, he can pull boats for repair. My guess is, if he is not asleep, you will find him there this morning."

"Thank you. Just out of curiosity, how many ships are in port?"

The harbormaster's eyes filled with a sense of pride and without hesitation. "We currently have seven ships docked in the bay. I have been the harbormaster for the last fifteen years. I make it my personal duty to know how many ships are docked at all times."

Merryk looked back at him with a smile. "I am sure you do an excellent job, harbormaster. We thank you for your help. The swordmaster will stay with our cargo until the others arrive."

As Prince Merryk turned to leave, the harbormaster stood. "If there is anything I can do to help, please do not hesitate to ask."

-------※-------

The three moved onto the wooden sidewalk outside the office.

"He was polite," Merryk said to Yonn.

"Probably because Chancellor Goldblatt told him exactly who you are."

"I don't believe Goldblatt would have done that."

"With all respect, Your Highness, if you believe that, you are not as smart as I thought you were," Yonn said with a grin. "Goldblatt trusts him and would want him looking out for you."

"Swordmaster, stay with the cargo. Yonn and I will go find the shipwright."

"Be careful, I do not want you two getting into any trouble without me," the swordmaster said.

Merryk said to Yonn as they walked away, "I think he is more interested in not being left out of trouble than he is in protecting us from it."

Mounting their horses, the two men rode back up the river. The original path had deviated from the flow of the river to come from the hillside to the port. The path they now took was directly by the river and moved along a quarter of a mile upstream from the market huts. Along the way, they passed fishermen in small boats returning from the sea.

"I am confident nobody is paying any attention to us," the prince said. "This will make Chancellor Goldblatt and Smallfolks happy." Yonn said nothing, but merely smiled.

Soon they came to a structure different from the others. It appeared to be both on the shore and over the water. *This is the structure a shipwright would want. It's designed to allow people to bring their boats inside for repairs.*

Merryk and Yonn went inside to find the shipwright. The harbormaster saying the shipwright was old, was clearly an understatement. The man appeared to be as old as the stonemason who was directing the work on the castle. There was something special about the shipwright. Although old and slight of build, his hands and arms were exceptionally strong. They moved the tools of his trade with the grace and confidence of a master craftsman with years of experience.

He had seen them enter, but he did not stop his work. *It's always amazing to watch a true craftsman.* Merryk thought as the man continued to use his hammer and chisel to tailor each board to fit the end of the last. After a while, the man stopped and walked over to meet Yonn and Prince Merryk.

"How are you today, Captain Yonn?" he said, in recognition.

"Quite well, my friend. I would like to introduce you to my friend, Raymond," Yonn said, attempting to maintain Merryk's disguise.

"Nice to meet you," Merryk said.

"Have I met you before? You look familiar."

"No, I am sure we haven't."

"Where did you get that sword?"

"It was my grandfather's."

Not wanting to get sidetracked, Merryk turned to the reason for their visit. "We have a project which needs your help." Merryk reached inside his saddlebags to produce plans for the cofferdams, which he laid on a side table. He described the height and width of the space. "I have several questions about the best method for putting the wood together for the cofferdam."

The old man looked at Merryk with curiosity, said nothing, but continued to listen intently as Merryk described the details of the entire project.

"This is not what I do as a shipwright. I prepare things that float in water."

"Floating in water is all about displacement. Displacement is about dealing with the weight and force of the water pushed out of the way to allow the boat to float. Think of this as half of a boat. I need your help in building a structure to sustain the pressure and which will not leak too badly."

"You have an interesting way of looking at this problem. How are you going to secure the ends of the wood?" the shipwright asked, now intrigued by the project.

"We found a master stonemason."

"I have known him for over thirty years," the shipwright said. "There is no better man with stone. Why not just make the whole dam out of stone? He is more than capable."

"We need to determine whether this will work and determine how high it needs to be. After we know the answers to these questions, we will make it out of stone. But even then, we will need to keep the water away while we build."

The shipwright nodded, "I understand."

"Is there a way we could hire you and three or four men of your choosing to come to the castle within the next month to help us build the dams?"

The old man, who had gone along with the general disguise of Merryk, looked at Yonn with a smile. "I would be more than happy to come to the castle and help you with the cofferdams," the shipwright said.

"Thank you very much. I have brought a purse which you can use to hire the additional men. If you need more, the harbormaster will provide it. We've already identified the wood, and the stonemason will have the surfaces ready."

"Very well," the man said as he picked up the purse. "I will be there in two weeks."

"Thank you," Merryk said, shaking the shipwright's hand.

———❧———

"That went far better than I expected. I thought he would be reluctant to help a stranger."

Yonn chuckled, "I do not think you are actually a stranger, Your Highness. I think the old man was smart enough to know exactly whom he was talking to. He would have known your grandfather and his sword. Normally, he is the grumpiest of men, and he was more than polite to you."

"Well, perhaps, but hopefully, the rest of the port will not know who I am. I need to maintain a low profile. I promised I would not take any unnecessary chances."

CHAPTER TWENTY-EIGHT

PORT ATTACK

Yonn and Merryk made their way back toward the harbormaster's hut. The shorter days of fall brought an early dusk. When they arrived, the swordmaster rose from the wooden bench where he had been waiting.

"Did you find a place for us to spend the night?" Prince Merryk asked the swordmaster.

"Yes," he said. "It is a comfortable inn with rooms upstairs and a tavern below. Next door is a stable for the horses."

The inn was a short walk up a knoll to an overlook with a view of the water. Weathered plank siding, reflecting years of battering by coastal winds, covered the two-story structure. Light and voices streamed from the windows. An open door welcomed travelers. Merryk followed the others into the inn.

After they had secured their rooms, Yonn suggested, "We could get a pint before the swordmaster has to leave for the Capital City."

"Yes, but if you don't mind, I will check on Maverick. Then I will join you," Merryk replied.

"Very well, Your Highness," the swordmaster said. "Are you sure you do not want us to come with you?"

"No need, I will be right back," Merryk said as he returned to the dusk of early evening.

There was nothing special about the barn. It was neat and well kept, with the clean aroma of fresh hay. The stable boy had removed the saddles from all the horses, except Maverick.

"I will take care of the big black one myself," Merryk said.

The young man gathered the other saddles and put them along the side of the wall. When done, he asked, "Unless you need me, I will go have my supper."

"Go, we will be fine," Merryk said as he placed his saddle across the stall fence. From a pouch on the saddle, he took a small brush and returned to rub Maverick's side. "Well, this has been an interesting day."

Maverick whinnied.

"The shipwright will be the exact person to help us."

The horse appeared to listen to every word Merryk said. "You did an excellent job of getting me here."

Maverick became fidgety.

"Are you okay, old friend?" Merryk asked as he continued to brush the horse's chest. Normally, grooming and talking to Maverick calmed the great stallion. But this evening, he was becoming more agitated with each moment.

"My goodness, what is bothering you?" Merryk whispered.

Merryk suddenly became aware the barn seemed unusually quiet. He continued to run his hand along the stallion's neck. "I don't think we are alone." Merryk removed the bridle to allow the horse total freedom.

He had placed his grandfather's sword against the stall wall, out of ready reach. Merryk dropped the small brush, bent over to pick it up, but instead removed an eight-inch knife from his boot. Holding it in a reverse position to hide it against his forearm, he rose.

Maverick rocked his head to direct Merryk's attention to a man crossing the barn floor. He wore black clothing and a hood.

Suddenly, Maverick gave a rear kick, catching a second intruder who had approached from behind. The horse spun around. Rearing up, his hooves pounded the prone figure.

The hooded man moved toward Merryk with a dagger in his right hand. Merryk knew the natural reaction was to move away from the knife. Instead, he moved forward, closing the gap between them. Merryk blocked the dagger with his left hand and pushed the man's arm away, exposing the attacker's right side. Merryk slid his hidden blade under the assailant's arm. The blade cut deep into the side flesh and left Merryk behind his assailant. He then pulled the blade in a backward motion, thrusting into the kidneys.

A voice in his head yelled, ***Wounded men can still kill!*** Responding, without a second hesitation, he delivered the same blow to the other side. As he removed the knife, the man crumpled to the ground.

Merryk shifted the knife to his left hand. Grabbing his grandfather's sword in his right, he turned to the other assailant. Looking down, he saw the second man's head was indented. "You must have heard the same message," Merryk said to Maverick. Hoof marks showed the horse had stomped the man several times.

The horse nuzzled against Merryk.

"I'm okay. Are you?"

The horse bobbed his head. Merryk stayed close, running his arm around Maverick's neck to calm them both.

The swordmaster sipped his ale as he watched Captain Yonn strike up a lively conversation with the young barmaid. His thoughts were disrupted when the harbormaster hastily entered the tavern and came directly to him.

"Two outsiders have been asking about the prince. They arrived late today on a ship from the south. Neither asked for food or lodging, only where to find the prince. Three separate villagers came to tell me. The outsiders were seen minutes ago coming up the hill toward the inn."

The swordmaster jumped from his seat and ran to the barn. Yonn and the harbormaster followed. As the swordmaster entered the barn, he found Merryk. "We came to tell you two outsiders were asking about you." His words stopped when he saw the bodies lying on the ground. He moved first to look at the man who had been behind Maverick and then went to the man who had attacked Merryk.

"Prince Merryk, did these men try to rob you?" Yonn asked.

"A robber would have asked for my purse. They just attacked. No, this was something more."

"These men are 'Blackhats,' professional killers," the swordmaster said looking up from the body. "They bear the tattoo of the Clan of Killers. I have come across them before. They seldom fail."

Looking at the prince, "Did you hold the knife against your arm, like I told you *not* to do?"

The prince nodded.

The swordmaster smiled. *Prince Merryk handled himself like a seasoned warrior. The last thing his assailant experienced was surprise. We now know Merryk is not reluctant to protect himself.*

"We need to get rid of the bodies. I don't want whoever sent them to know they were unsuccessful," Merryk said.

"You go inside with Captain Yonn and have a pint of ale. We will take care of this," the harbormaster suggested.

Shortly, the swordmaster and the harbormaster entered the tavern. Merryk sat at a large table, nursing his ale while he waited for something to eat.

The harbormaster came forward. "Do not worry, Your Highness. No one will know they were here."

Merryk looked up in surprise. "You know who I am?"

"Yes," the harbormaster replied. "You are the tall, young man on the large black stallion who got rid of the bastard, Royal Tax Collector. There is not a soul in the entire Teardrop Kingdom who does not know you, Prince Merryk. We owe you a deep debt of gratitude."

CHAPTER TWENTY-NINE

PROPHECY

The flash of lightning illuminated the white peaks of the mountains, making them look like caps of waves on a troubled sea. Helga's eyes felt the light, but it was not what she saw. She stood at the window of the stone fortress. Her gaze was somewhere far away.

Even as a small child, she had visions. Early on, the visions were simple; she could identify the sex of an unborn baby. Later, they became more complex, like the warnings of attacks from the northern savages. Her visions had saved many of the clans from danger. However, new visions had increased in frequency in the last year, ever since she had felt a presence.

All in all, she did not feel special. She looked like any middle-aged woman, with graying hair bound in a bun. Every morning, she made bread, cooked her meals, and helped Gaspar with Oolada.

Gaspar, the only special man in her life, was not even her husband. He was a widower and the Walt of the Council of Walters. Most thought of Gaspar Zoo as a confident and determined leader, but she knew a different Gaspar. To her, although unafraid to take risks, he doubted himself more than he should. He asked good questions and listened to the answers. More than anything else, he loved his people and kept their well-being first in his mind.

Fate had pushed them together because of her ability to see danger and his duty to defend against it. After Gaspar's wife died, she stepped in to help with Oolada, Gaspar's granddaughter. Savages killed Oolada's mother and father, leaving her an orphan at age three. Oolada, now seventeen, had grown up playing happily at the feet of the most powerful man in the Blue-and-White Mountain Clans.

"What did you see?" the deep voice of Gaspar ZooWalt asked.

"They attacked him this evening."

"Where?"

"You know I cannot see that."

"Did he survive?"

"I believe so. The future does not appear to have changed. I do not feel any immediate danger. For certain, I know the two who attacked him are dead."

"So now he is a warrior."

Moving closer, Gaspar placed his arm around Helga's shoulders. "I am sorry to be so impatient. I wish we knew who he is, where he is, and when he will come. You know all of my questions."

Helga reached up and placed her hand on Gaspar's. "You know my visions do not tell me. If they did, I would tell you. All we can do is remember the ancient prophecy:

A man will come to change the fate of the clans and the kingdoms.

He will come from an unimaginable distance and live his life in the life of another.

The clans will rise with him and a daughter.

"Do not forget, he will be a warrior, a hero, and a legend," added Gasper.

Helga smiled. "Only a man would focus on the warrior."

CHAPTER THIRTY

CAPITAL CITY

The early morning summer sun cast light through the slender windows of the long dining hall. King Michael and Queen Amanda sat, as was their morning custom, eating breakfast and tending to small matters. For King Michael, this time had become a rare moment in the day when he could be away from people constantly seeking his attention. It also gave him the opportunity to talk with his wife. He sat quietly and read his correspondence while his wife knitted and chattered about gossip within the castle.

Breakfast over, Queen Amanda worked on another scarf. She was commenting about a relationship between an earl's daughter and a duke. As best King Michael could determine, it was some kind of scandal. However, it did not rise to the level of 'matter of state,' at least not yet, so he mentally filed it away.

The staff had delivered his morning correspondence, and he worked his way through from the top to bottom. When the Lord Chamberlain entered the room, it surprised King Michael. *The Lord Chamberlain seldom asks to speak to me and even less frequently enters the dining hall. I never really know when he will appear, but he always seems to arrive when needed. He was the Chamberlain when my father was crowned, and no one knows his age, but unquestionably he is old.*

The Lord Chamberlain approached the king, bowed politely. "May I speak with you, Your Majesty?"

The king nodded. *This man is the embodiment of formality.*

The Lord Chamberlain moved forward so none but the two of them could hear.

"Outside the room?"

"Yes."

"I will be back in a moment," King Michael said to Queen Amanda.

If it were not the Lord Chamberlain, I would not attend without summoning my personal guard. I have never known him to be involved in any castle intrigue, which is quite a record, given his years of service; there is no one more loyal.

King Michael followed the Chamberlain out a side door and around the corner to find a man nervously pacing. The king directed the Chamberlain to wait just out of earshot.

This man was cut of much rougher cloth than those who normally frequented the halls of the castle. He bowed politely. "Your Majesty, I am Hugo, swordmaster for the Teardrop Kingdom. I bring critical messages to deliver only to you." He handed over the notes.

The first was under the seal of Chancellor Geoffrey Goldblatt. The king quickly opened and read the note. "You have the taxes with you?"

"Yes, Your Majesty, six of us carried them from the Teardrop."

The king turned to the second note. Written on plain paper, it had been quickly folded and sealed with simple candle wax. It was quite ordinary, except for the seal. The seal was the family "R" inside a circle. *This was mine as Prince, now it is Merryk's ring.* Hastily, he tore open the seal.

Father:

Over Chancellor Goldblatt's strenuous objections, I

accompanied seven men to transport the taxes to the port. All went smoothly.

Before they boarded the ship, we discovered two men had newly arrived and were asking about me. The swordmaster later identified them as "Blackhats," professional killers.

I am fine. They are not. No one will know of their failure. Please take extra precautions, as will I.

Merryk
Also, please burn these notes.

Concern filled King Michael's face as he looked up from the note, "Is Prince Merryk safe?"

"Yes, Your Majesty."

"Thank you for protecting my son. Under the circumstances, it would be best if you returned to him as quickly as possible."

The swordmaster nodded, "With your permission, we plan to leave on the next tide."

"The Lord Chamberlain will show you where to put the taxes. I will have a note for you to return to Chancellor Goldblatt and the prince."

"Very well, your Majesty."

"What was that dear?" Queen Amanda asked as he reentered the dining hall.

"One more piece of a puzzle," the king replied. Stopping at the fireplace, he tossed two pieces of parchment into the flame and watched them curl, blacken, and crumble.

CHAPTER THIRTY-ONE

QUESTIONS

Two days after the attack, Merryk and Yonn returned to the castle. They made their way through the castle village as they had done many times. Prince Merryk looked at the people; they no longer ignored his presence. Many stopped to wave and smile; some even attempted a curtsy. The words of the harbormaster lingered in his head. '*Everyone knows who you are, Prince Merryk.*' *The truth is, no one knows who I am. I am a man pretending to be Prince Merryk, but there is no other Prince Merryk.* For the first time, he became keenly aware he was constantly being watched.

Passing through the castle gates, they came to the steps in front of the main hall. There, sitting by herself playing with her stick doll, was Maizie.

When she heard the horses, her eyes lit up, and she ran out to greet them. "Prince Merryk, you home." Merryk reached down from his horse and pulled her up to the saddle. She attached herself around his neck with a big hug. "I missed you. You were gone too long," she said in a tiny voice. Maizie immediately ran her hands over his unshaven face. "I knew you not be a boy forever."

Merryk said, "Don't worry about my whiskers. I'll get rid of them."

"No! Look good. Just not get long like Smallfolks," she said with a smile.

"Let's take Maverick to the stable," the prince said.

Inside the stables, Merryk placed Maizie on top of the stall while he and Yonn removed the saddles and bridles from their horses. Maverick moved over to where Maizie sat, allowing her to scratch the spot behind his ears. *She is one of the few people Maverick allows to get close. They are kindred spirits; both are rebels.*

Nelly and Jane brought a tray of warm cider. "We heard you had returned," Nelly said. "Maizie's been out on the steps for almost the entire day. She stormed the guard station early this morning, demanding they tell her when they saw you coming. The guard said she was quite intimidating for a three-year-old. I got her to break away for lunch, but she went right back and has been there ever since."

After they settled the horses and finished their cider, Jane said, "Maizie, we need to let Prince Merryk get in for dinner. It is also time for us to get cleaned up."

Merryk ruffled Maizie's hair. "I'll come and get you tomorrow. You and I will do something special."

"Good," she said gleefully, grabbing Jane's hand as the two headed out of the barn.

Merryk got ready for dinner and had extra time to talk to Smallfolks. "I'm unharmed."

"I told you to be careful."

Merryk took Smallfolks' concern in stride. Putting his arm around the older man, he said, "I told you, I'm fine. Don't worry so much."

Smallfolks responded by bowing his head. "It is hard, Your Highness."

After a dinner filled with good food and light conversation, Merryk followed Chancellor Goldblatt to his study. The two entered, shut the door, and moved to their respective places by the fireplace. Merryk settled into his grandfather's large chair. Chancellor Goldblatt stopped by a small sideboard to pour two glasses of sherry. He handed Merryk a glass and moved to his chair. "My reports say you had an interesting journey."

"Very interesting," Merryk replied. "I got to meet the harbormaster and the shipwright who has agreed to help us with the cofferdams."

"Not exactly what I meant."

"Before you start, neither Yonn nor the swordmaster did anything wrong. I chose to go by myself to check on Maverick."

"I have never understood your relationship with that horse, but now I thank God for it. What were you thinking? Your father will order my execution."

"No, I've already told him. I had come to the port over your objections. I sent him a note after we had discovered the two Blackhats. I warned him to be extra careful."

"Also, I thought you told me a prince could never be wrong."

"Now you learn to be royal," Goldblatt said with exasperation, but could not help breaking into a smile. "This is an excellent lesson for you. You are never completely safe."

"I understand," Merryk said. He then took a few moments to describe what had happened.

"You are lucky."

"Fortune favors the prepared, and I was well trained. I'm fine, but we still haven't figured out what is going on."

"While you were gone, I received an interesting piece of information. After Father Bernard's visit, King Natas' request to have you declared incompetent was summarily rejected. My sources indicate Natas was not happy. My guess is the attack at the port had nothing to do with the tax collector's trial. A frustrated King Natas, however, might well send assassins."

"This is my conclusion, as well."

Goldblatt continued, "We discovered the shorting of the taxes by accident. It makes more sense that the attack is related to your wedding. Two separate events, both tied to money, but not connected to each other. The Lord Commander might be behind the shorting of the taxes, but he could have been doing it for years. No, this has to do with your wedding."

"You are coming to the same conclusions as I did," Merryk replied. "I also wonder if this could relate to succession, but everyone believes my brother will be the next king. Also, who he marries won't affect his becoming king. What is it about *my* marriage to Princess Tarareese that is causing so much concern?"

Chancellor Goldblatt scratched his beard and sipped his sherry. "Perhaps we are underestimating the ego of King Natas. He does not like to lose and definitely does not like to lose money."

"But he had already planned to pay the dowry. Whether it is being paid for me or for Merreg, it is still the same amount. We are missing something."

Chancellor Goldblatt rose from his chair and went to the sideboard for the flask of sherry. He returned and filled both glasses. "Perhaps everything is about opportunity. Natas accepted Merreg as a future king and thought him worth the price. When the error occurred, it presented an opportunity to reduce the dowry. So, he worked with your uncle to impact the revenue and bought the king's loans to gain leverage. It is not about you at all. It is about the second half of the dowry and his ability to gain two new ships. Your death or incompetence would mean no wedding. King Natas would get his money back, two new ships, and still have his daughter for another marriage, even though she is now quite old."

Merryk replied, "This would explain everything except the Lord Commander. Why would he act to kill me on behalf of King Natas, particularly if he has a separate source of income?"

Merryk stood and walked over to gaze into the glowing flames of the fire. "Surely women can't be like bread, worthless after a few days."

"Her happiness is not a concern, just money and power."

Merryk's face reflected increased concern as he slipped deeper into thought.

"What is wrong, my prince?" Goldblatt asked.

"It is just Princess Tarareese. What can she possibly be thinking? All the information she has about me says I am an imbecile, stunted, and twisted. What kind of life can she possibly believe she will have? Is there a chance King Natas is doing all of this just to protect her?"

"Nothing I know about King Natas would support this idea. His priorities are power, money and horses, in that order. The happiness of anyone else does not make the list. If this was his aim, he would have allowed her to choose her own match, and that was never a choice. This is about power or money or both."

"Anyway, I can't imagine what is going on in her mind," Merryk said.

"Of one thing I am sure, you will be a surprise," Chancellor Goldblatt said with a broad smile.

Merryk continued to look at the fire for a moment. Finishing his sherry, he turned to Chancellor Goldblatt. "We still don't have enough information. There are too many questions. The only thing I can do is stay alive long enough to marry, then we can see how things evolve."

CHAPTER THIRTY-TWO
BIG DAY

Nelly was normally the first person up in the castle. She always enjoyed the quiet before everyone else rose. This was the time she worked with her bread and got her kitchen moving for the day. It was her time.

These thoughts filled her mind as she made her way toward the kitchen, her sanctuary. As she got close, she smelled smoke. *Someone has already started the fires.* Nelly entered the kitchen to find Merryk and Maizie. "What are the two of you doing in my kitchen so early?" she said in a scolding voice.

Prince Merryk replied, "Nelly, don't worry, we're working on an invention."

Maizie, who was sitting at the end of a counter with a large towel wrapped around her neck and honey dripping down her chin, responded, "New 'vention."

"What invention?" Nelly asked.

"The blacksmith and I've been working on larger sheets of metal. I had one poured for you. It has a groove around the end to catch any excess grease, so it won't fall off the edges into the fire. It will make an excellent griddle."

"What do I need a griddle for?"

"It's good for making French toast and frying bacon," Merryk said with his best disarming smile. "We couldn't make it in Jane's kitchen because we didn't have any old bread."

"What is French toast?" Nelly asked.

"French toast is day-old bread dipped in a combination of milk and eggs. We didn't have any eggs or bread."

Maizie shook her head from side to side and looked as serious as possible. "No eggs; no bread."

"Sit down and I'll show you," Merryk said as he continued to cook on the slab of metal which stood on four legs over the coals. He dipped the bread into the milk and eggs, letting it soak up a requisite amount, then lifted it onto the buttered grill. "I've cut these in squares, however, we can cut them in any shape you want or you can leave the crust on if you choose."

Nelly looked on with continued displeasure. She turned to Maizie.

"Mine is a star," Maizie said as the honey continued to drip from her chin.

Nelly responded, "Of course, yours is a star. The two of you do not belong in my kitchen, and you have used almost all of my honey."

Merryk replied, "Don't worry about honey. We have gallons. The first collection from our hives is better than I hoped for honey and wax. This will be a very successful venture."

"What venture?" Nelly asked.

"The making of candles and selling of honey," said Merryk.

Nelly continued to fuss around them until they finished breakfast. "All right, I want the two of you out of my kitchen."

Merryk took a damp cloth to wipe Maizie's face and then put her down on the ground. "I will clean this up, if you want?"

"You most certainly will not. This is my kitchen."

"All right, but remember, this will be a big day. We will block the water. So don't forget there will be extra people. We have men coming from the port, and then there are Marta's two sons, and the two farmers."

"Yes, Marta's two sons already eat enough for four people."

"Working with the lumber is a tough job. They burn a lot of energy. Nelly, please plan on bringing the lunch to us. We can't stop this day to come to you."

"Do not you worry about me," Nelly said with righteous indignation. "I know what I am supposed to do and where I am supposed to be. Not like you, who are not supposed to be in my kitchen. Now get along. The two of you are killing me."

They proceeded down the hallway when Maizie stopped, turned, and ran back to throw her arms around Nelly's legs. "No kill Nelly. Love Nelly." Maizie gave an extra squeeze. Then the three-year-old gleefully skipped her way down the hall to follow Prince Merryk.

Nelly stood for a moment, shaking her head as she looked over the damage done to her previously clean kitchen. Taking her fork, she took a bite of the remaining French toast. *Not bad.* Her thoughts continued to wander as she finished the piece. *I hope the princess can handle competition, because that little one will not give up the prince easily.*

CHAPTER THIRTY-THREE

STONE AND WOOD

W ord spread throughout the village–today was the day the first rows of wood would block the flow of the river. Smallfolks had joined Chancellor Goldblatt on top of the castle's back wall, where they hoped to have the best view of the activities.

"This appears to be total confusion," Smallfolks said as he looked out at all the people moving in different directions.

"On the contrary," Chancellor Goldblatt responded. "This is the best organized project I have ever seen. Prince Merryk has a detailed schedule of tasks for each person."

"I do not see how that is possible," Smallfolks said.

"This project has been under Merryk's guidance since the beginning. The day after he returned from the port, he went upriver to meet with Marta and her two sons. With their help, they picked the trees needed for the dams. Later, he met with the stonemason to direct the building of the crane to move the stone and logs."

"The next day, he and the blacksmith returned up the river with a new saw the two of them had been working on for some time. The blacksmith told me the saw was created because he could keep the metal hot longer. The prince had created a double bellows, one that constantly blows on the coals. With the help of the blacksmith's son, his apprentice, and Marta's two sons, they felled a tree. Using the saw, they quickly cut it into four pieces, then they dragged the logs into the river. Marta's sons ran along the edge of the river with long poles to keep them flowing downstream. By the next morning, all four logs were lying just behind the castle. Unbeknownst to me, Merryk had arranged with the shipwright to send two men early to help. Prince Merryk, Captain Yonn, Marta's sons, and the two men worked for the next week until all the wood necessary for the project was ready."

"There the prince goes again, doing things he should not do. Royals just do not do that kind of work."

Chancellor Goldblatt just shook his head at Smallfolks. "I do not think it should surprise us. This is just the way Prince Merryk works, and we just need to accept it."

Soon, Merryk called the crew together. From a distance Goldblatt heard him say, "All right men, we now need to focus on blocking the water. This will be the hardest part of our entire project. We need to hurry, but we need to move safely. I want to remind you we are moving very heavy pieces of wood and stone. Please pay close attention. I don't want anyone injured."

Goldblatt and Smallfolks watched as the project began. The stonemason's crane placed the first stone. The block obstructed the flow of the water but allowed for some water to pass beneath. "This will be filled in later, but now it keeps the water from building up too rapidly against the wooden dam," Goldblatt explained.

"Merryk had hoped the shipwright and the stonemason could stay away from the actual work, if possible, relying on the younger men. But the shipwright insisted he needed to be at the dropping of the first row of wood to deal with any problems."

Sure enough, as they put in the log, a minor problem occurred. The shipwright immediately pulled out his chisels and, within a matter of minutes, the piece of wood slid smoothly into the groove the mason had cut into the wall.

Smallfolks asked, "What are those bright flags they keep waving?"

"Merryk said it was part of the system used by the Romans to direct the person moving the crane. The shipwright can stand at the bottom and give instructions to the stonemason at the top on how to move the wood with the crane without having to yell.

"Smallfolks, what you cannot see is they have flattened the opposing sides of the wood and cut small grooves in them. As they drop the wood in place, the grooves interlock. Merryk told me it will not stop all the water, but it will reduce it. The shipwright thought it might completely stop the water, but that is probably more than we can hope."

Smallfolks asked, "Why are they working so hard to get in four rows?"

"The four rows are necessary to raise the water up high enough to divert it to the other side of the Finger. Merryk has stationed children on the other side to let him know when the water runs over the old riverbed."

The third row went in without incident. "With the dropping of each row, the water seems to rise slower," Chancellor Goldblatt noted. "There is very little water coming out between the logs. The shipwright must have been right."

Shortly after dropping the fourth row of logs into place, a cheer came up from the far side of the Finger. Chancellor Goldblatt turned to Smallfolks with a smile. "He did it! The water is now running through the old river channel."

"This has not happened in anyone's memory. They told me about it when I was a boy, but I never saw it," Smallfolks said.

Merryk waved to both the shipwright and the stonemason. "I think it is time for lunch."

The entire crew stopped and moved off to where Nelly had delivered lunch.

Merryk has been everywhere. He has been with the shipwright when they dropped the first wood. He was with the stonemason as they worked the crane. Chancellor Goldblatt looked at him with admiration. *Although this project is all his, down to the smallest detail, he is more than willing to allow others to take responsibility for its execution. The prince had used the phrase 'he did not intend to hire dogs and bark himself.'* Chancellor Goldblatt thought it was an unusual expression, but it showed Merryk's ability to delegate to those he perceived to be better able to complete tasks. *This young man constantly amazes me. Merryk's ability to organize, his willingness to rely on the strength of others, and not believe himself to be right just because he is royal makes him a unique man.*

Goldblatt's thoughts were interrupted when Merryk told the group to get back to work.

"We need to get the rows in place and get the braces behind them and hope we don't have rain," the prince said.

The shipwright added, "Yes, if we do not get it secure before the pressure of more water comes, it will take out the logs like they were tiny sticks. Only when we are finished and the braces in place, will we have some level of protection. Even then, I am uncertain if this wooden dam will hold back the spring flood."

Merryk turned to him, "We will watch the dam carefully during flood season and Chancellor Goldblatt and I will attempt to ensure no one is immediately downstream."

By the end of the first day, Chancellor Goldblatt and Smallfolks gave up watching the constant progress. The Chancellor noted before leaving, "They have already put up almost half of what they needed."

The second day did not have the excitement of the first. The crew continued to methodically add rows of lumber, higher and higher. By the end of the week, they finished the entire project.

To celebrate, Merryk asked Nelly to prepare a dinner for the final evening.

Chancellor Goldblatt was pleased Prince Merryk wanted to thank everyone involved. The prince invited not only the farmers who brought their oxen, but he invited the farmers' families. At the dinner, Goldblatt noticed Prince Merryk walked around the table and thanked each person individually. He gave special thanks to the shipwright and the stonemason, who he identified as living treasures.

When the dinner was about over, Prince Merryk stood for one last time and called, "Nelly, where are you?"

Nelly was still shuffling back and forth between the kitchen and the Great Hall. He requested she come forward and stand at the head of the table.

"Projects like this run on many skills, but it also runs on our bellies. During this last week, Nelly took great care of our bellies. I would like to thank her and all of those who work with her in the kitchen for feeding us so well this week and for our dinner this evening."

Nelly's response to the prince's attention was almost more than she could handle. Her cheeks became bright red, and Merryk reached over and gave her an enormous hug. *This is not what one expects from a royal.* Chancellor Goldblatt shook his head. *This young man constantly surprises me. I do, however, worry his failure to understand his actual position will cause trouble when the princess arrives.*

The next day, all those gathered for the project headed home. The shipwright and his men left early, and the stonemason and his apprentice returned to their tasks in the castle. All were well paid for their efforts and pleased with their accomplishment.

The two most surprised by the events of the day were Marta's sons. At age fifteen and sixteen, they had helped cut the trees and move the logs down the river. Merryk had intentionally added extra logs, and he had ordered them lifted into an open space behind the castle.

Before Marta's sons left, Prince Merryk had taken them aside. "If you choose, I will sell you these extra logs. Ten percent of what you cut will be for the castle. The remaining wood is for you to sell. You can use the new saw and cut the logs into sections and split the wood here, then deliver it to the village. This way you will not have to transport it by cart from the forest. Before you decide, I want you to ask your mother if this is acceptable, since it will take you away from her."

The boys looked at each other in disbelief. The oldest son looked at Prince Merryk, "Your Highness, the amount you gave us was already generous, but allowing us to cut wood here and then deliver it is beyond our hopes. I know mother will be concerned about us being gone, but if we could do it in batches rather than doing it all at one time, I am confident she will allow us to do so."

Prince Merryk replied, "You have my permission to do it over whatever period best suits your purposes. Also, I want you to tell your mother you will be under my protection, and you can stay in the castle. We will provide food and lodging."

"Again, Your Highness, thank you."

"You may also tell your mother she can join you if she wishes."

Chancellor Goldblatt had listened to the entire exchange between Merryk and the boys. *Marta is the first woman Merryk has paid any attention to. Perhaps it is just his feeling of a need to protect her, or maybe it is something more. Marta is old enough to be Merryk's mother. I must talk to Yonn about whether Prince Merryk has shown any attraction to any of the younger women in the Teardrop.*

Chapter Thirty-Four

THOUGHTS

C ool air and the light of a winter's dawn splashed against Merryk's face as he stood on the top of the old tower. When the weather permitted, he did his morning exercises here. This was a special place where he could be alone.

It has been almost a year since I first stood on the top of this tower. The village below the castle no longer looks like a medieval re-creation. I know most of the people by name. The blacksmith is already firing up the forge. Smoke is rising from homes as the women make the morning meal.

The snow is deeper this year than last, the winter colder. But everyone should stay warm thanks to the firewood provided by Marta's sons. Those who could pay for the wood did, and others who were struggling, received wood from the castle's share.

These people don't want great things; just to have some of life's harshness softened.

Last year, I was uncertain if this was real. Now, there is no question. In fact, seldom do I think about my life before, other than to recall information. I could spend my time thinking about my mother and father on the Palouse, or my condominium down by the river, but I don't. Perhaps I have given up on returning to my old world. But the truth is, I believe I can make a difference here. I believe what I told Father Bernard, "There are things that need to be done for the people." The dams offer the hope of no flooding, which would be an enormous improvement.

A shaft of light broke through the clouds to illuminate the tops of the mountains to the left of the castle. Merryk shifted his attention to the surroundings.

When I first arrived, all I could do was look out at the hills. Now, I have stood on many of them. My world is definitely larger than it was before, and even more dangerous than even I thought.

Last year, standing on the top of this tower, I was weak and skinny. Working and doing ordinary things with the mason and blacksmith has significantly increased my strength and good muscle weight. I have straightened my back. My daily tai chi has worked wonders at improving my flexibility and coordination.

This morning I only did half the normal exercises; I will get the balance this afternoon with the swordmaster. He is as tough as any sensei I have ever had, but my skills are improving.

My habits of cleanliness still frustrate Smallfolks. Although pleased I finally grew a beard, even if it is light, he agrees with Maizie. It shouldn't get too long. Smallfolks said, "I should have known it would take a woman to convince you to grow a beard." The truth is, my previous beard was more like the random whiskers of a child. A year of shaving let them mature.

I have a full day ahead: breakfast, meet with the blacksmith to discuss an idea for a new double-bladed axe, time with Maverick and the children, the lesson with the swordmaster, then, a quick bath and dinner. I look forward to this evening and my time with Goldblatt to discuss the history of the various kingdoms.

It won't be long before the princess arrives, only two or three months. I still cannot imagine what she must be expecting. She has been told I am a simpleton or an idiot. I know those adjectives don't apply. Goldblatt said I will surprise her.

What she sees when she gets here will only be part of the problem. I am twenty years her senior, but no one knows. Even when I look at myself in the mirror, I see a twenty-year-old man. How I look and how I feel are so different. I know this will affect my relationship with a woman, a wife.

There is no way I can avoid this wedding without causing tremendous disruption. The political and economic implications are too great. I just hope we have time to get to know each other before the wedding.

I wonder if the threats to my life will stop after the wedding. Nevertheless, the threat to my father will continue. As Goldblatt said, there are bigger things happening than just a wedding.

The sound of doors opening below distracted Merryk. Moving to the other side of the tower, he looked down on two older boys starting their day. One was on his way to the blacksmith and the other to hunt rats.

No more delays; I have a busy day.

Chapter Thirty-Five

MUST GO!

Princess Tarareese sat on the end of her bed, rereading a parchment note.

> *Dearest Princess Tarareese:*
>
> *I know you are probably overwhelmed with the preparations for your journey to the Teardrop Kingdom. Although your kingdom has a vast selection of shops, it occurred to me the one thing you may not have is an ample supply of furriers. Please accept this gift for you and your ladies. The Teardrop can be quite cold, and I know from personal experience nothing keeps you warm like fur. I have specifically included several seal coats. You will find seal fur is particularly good for traveling over icy waters.*
>
> *I remember my nervousness before my wedding to King Michael. My thoughts of marriage were a strange combination of excitement and fear. There was excitement about becoming a wife, and hopefully, a mother. But fear of all the unknowns. What would my husband be like? Would he accept me? What*

would the castle be like? Would I be happy? I mention all these things not to increase your anxiety, but to assure you, all women have these concerns. I hope knowing others have felt these things will give you some comfort.

My life with King Michael has been a remarkable journey. He has a kind heart. Our son, Merryk, shares this quality. I pray you will keep an open mind and heart as you meet him. May your journey be uneventful. I look forward to welcoming you in person to our family.

Queen Amanda

An open trunk at the foot of the bed revealed an assortment of furs. Several other trunks sat against the wall opposite the bed. Lost in thought, she looked past the trunks through double doors to a small walled garden outside her room. Even in the short days of winter, the bright sunlight filtered through the tree branches. A multitude of greens, represented by the different plants, shimmered as the light passed.

Yvette, Princess Tarareese's Lady-in-Waiting, bounced through the chamber door. Her zeal for life came with her as naturally as her auburn hair.

Today, she dressed appropriately for a contessa and lady-in-waiting. Normally, she preferred things with a lot more cleavage. She must have just seen her mother.

"What is all this?" Yvette asked.

"They came today," Princess Tarareese replied, handing the parchment letter to Yvette. Yvette looked down and began to read.

"This is nice and thoughtful," she said.

"She is a royal and a queen, and while the letter may be thoughtful, it was assuredly 'thought through.' One thing both father and mother have taught me, a royal always has a purpose in what they do." Princess Tarareese stated.

"What do you mean?"

"This note has clear messages. The wedding will happen. We expect you will be a mother. You can find something to like about my son. And we are not far away."

"I think she also said her son has a kind heart."

"She is his mother. What do you think she would say? My son is a twisted, simpleton fool."

"Of course not."

"The truth is, I have made no preparations. I thought father would stop this terrible union. When he gave me the letter this morning, he told me the marriage would go forward, and I needed to get ready to go." Mother told me I needed to be a princess and must remember my duty to the throne.

"Go?"

"Yes, go, Yvette! Go to the Teardrop Kingdom, where you need to wear fur, because it is cold as hell! Go to marry a simpleton with a good heart!" She couldn't keep the frustration from filling her voice as tears streamed down her face.

Yvette went over, sat down, and put her hand on Tara's shoulder. "We can pack today. I am with you, but I get one of these coats for sure."

"Why? Yvette, you do not have to go with me. This is my responsibility."

"It will please my family that I am going away. This morning, my mother told me she was relieved they will no longer hear about my latest indiscretions. Then she added, I may find a landed sheepherder to marry who will know nothing about my past." Yvette sighed. "No, Tara, there is nothing for me here. And besides, I cannot let you go alone."

"I will not be going alone. Nan is going with me."

"Nan. Great! Miss 'Sit up straight; keep your knees together.' What a splendid companion she will be. You will *die* unless I go with you."

"Yvette, you are always so extreme," Tara said as a smile joined the tears on her face. She grabbed a fur wrap and threw it at her.

Yvette grabbed the wrap and put it over her head and shoulders. As she unburied her head, she ran her fingers through the deep fur. "Ooh, this is nice."

Several days after the arrival of the furs, Queen Stephanie came to Tara's room. The room was in complete disarray, partially filled trunks and random clothes lay askew across the floor. With the help of Yvette and several attendants, preparation for Tara's departure was in full swing.

"I would like to speak with my daughter," Queen Stephanie said. "All of you leave us." After everyone had left the room, Tara's mother pushed aside some clothing and sat down on a chair. She motioned for Tara to sit near her on the sofa.

"Tara, you will leave soon to start your new life. I know the groom is not the type of man you would have picked. Do you remember the story of Princess Astera and the Kalahhay Kingdom?"

"Yes, of course," Tara replied. "After the contract of marriage was signed, the princess refused to marry, saying she did not love the groom. The result was a war which destroyed the kingdom."

"I do not know what your father will ask you to do, but remember, you are both a royal and a woman. You have a duty to fulfill the obligations of your station. After that, as a woman, you have a duty to your new husband, whoever he may be. If you cannot honor your husband or if you reject him, as Princess Astera did, you will put not only your life, but the lives of countless others at risk."

Tara nodded in understanding.

"Try to find something about your groom to respect."

"Do not you mean something to love?" Tara asked.

"Love is always the hope, but seldom the result. Royal marriages are always based on politics; the people are secondary. For the woman, it is a lifetime of duty. If she can grow to respect her husband, it will make this duty easier. With luck, her children can lessen this burden.

"My little one, my greatest prayer is you will be the exception, you will find a man to love who loves you. I also pray if that occurs, you are wise enough to accept it."

Chapter Thirty-Six

CARLTON

Lieutenant Carlton stood at the rail amidship on one of King Natas' newest warships, the RS *Broadsword*, watching it slide into port.

The roll of the sea, to which he had become accustomed, had given way to the sound of men and rowboats pulling the large vessel into its docking space. The incessant squawk of seagulls filled the air. The voyage had been what a sailor would call 'smooth sailing.'

We traveled the first full day along the southeast coast until we reached the point closest to the High Kingdom. The captain had explained the land shielded us from the bulk of the storms. We had caught a break in the storms for the longer crossing, with only a few large rolling waves. I was not prepared for the vastness of the ocean. It was marvelous to watch the golden globe of the sun drop into the sea and watch as the clouds spun and turned around like steam coming from a pot. Ships cover amazing distances in such a short time. Just four days ago, I was 700 miles away, and this morning I am here in the Capital City of the High Kingdom.

As an officer, they afforded me every courtesy, my own stateroom, and dinner every night with the captain and the other ship's officers.

The three men who came with me all have substantial combat experience. I had asked Colonel Lamaze about their willingness to take orders from a man ten years their junior. Colonel Lamaze assured me these men would do whatever I asked without question. Then he added, "A man named Jho will meet you at the port. He will have all your supplies."

The night before I left, Elise had met me briefly around the corner from her house. I can still see her light brown hair and gentle eyes.

"This is an important mission for both of us," Carlton said.

"I know it is, but something inside says, 'Do not go.'"

"I do not want to be away from you," he had said as he held her in his arms. "But you know what your father said. Unless I am a captain in the King's Dragoons, he will not consider consenting to our marriage. I have been assured this mission will give me the promotion we need. This will allow us to begin our life together."

Elise had tears running down her face. "I understand, but you will be so far away, and this is a dangerous time to travel on the sea."

"I have gone to war before, and you have waited. This is not any different. It is just a voyage across an ocean rather than land, like the last two campaigns."

Elise reached into her handbag and pulled out a small medallion attached to an intricate silver chain. "I had this made for you. I have put something special on it. You can read it later." She reached up and hooked the chain around his neck. "The chain will let you conceal it beneath your uniform, so you will not violate any dress code."

"Thank you, my love. I should not be gone very long, only two months. My mission is very short, very precise."

"Cannot you tell me more about it?" she asked. "No mission needs to be this secret."

My heart broke. I could not tell her what I must do. The burden would be too great for her to carry. This was my price to pay for our future. "I just cannot tell you."

The slap of the water burbled along the side of the big ship. Sailors yelled at each other and threw ropes toward the dock. The men in the rowboat stopped pulling as the ship had reached the assigned berth. Soon the gangplank dropped into place.

Lieutenant Carlton and the three men had put away their official regiment uniforms of the Dragoons and now wore the clothing of common travelers. They hid their weapons with their personal effects.

As they got off the gangplank, a relatively nondescript man stepped up to Lieutenant Carlton. "You Carlton?" the man asked.

"Yes, I am Carlton."

"A mutual friend sent me. You can call me 'Jho.' You are to come with me. I have made arrangements." Without waiting for a reply, Jho turned and walked down the pier.

Had this been a port in a lesser kingdom, their arrival might have attracted attention. However, at the great port of the Capital City of the High Kingdom, two dozen or more ships from all over the world were going in and out. People of all sizes and shapes, some carrying packages or bundles, others pulling carts of goods, filled the wharf. Passengers of high birth and low birth moved up and down the wharf to and from the ships. In this environment, the four men and their guide moved inconspicuously.

Jho took them along the side of the wharf. They had passed through two security gates, but no one paid any attention. It was Jho who broke the silence. "I have acquired horses and gear for our trip. We will leave immediately."

Around the corner were six horses, five with saddles, and one loaded with supplies. "I will not sugarcoat it. This will be a grueling journey. It is still early in the year, and we might encounter snow, but I think we will be fine. We should be able to make our goal within the six days."

Lieutenant Carlton knew this was an extreme mission. His instructions were explicit: 'kill whoever was inside the carriage.' Colonel Lamaze said, "You need to be prepared. They will be young women and perhaps a priest. This is an important mission, one critical for our kingdom. Do you understand, lieutenant?"

"Yes, sir. I understand completely."

"You also understand this is a matter of utmost secrecy?"

"Yes."

"We will attribute your attack to others. After the attack, drop the extra weapons we will give you. Leave and return with the guide back to the Capital City. When you arrive, the guide will contact us. We will give you the name of the ship to return home."

"Very well, sir. I understand."

"One more thing. Do you have any concerns about your ability to kill the people inside the carriage?"

Carlton thought for a moment about his answer, about Elise, about becoming a captain and a groom, and marrying the woman he loved. "I have no concern. I am a soldier. I will do what is necessary to complete my mission."

"Very well," Colonel Lamaze said. "Until I see you again, Godspeed."

The colonel turned to leave and then stopped. "One other thing, if we have not arrived or if you have not received word from us within seven days of your arrival in the Teardrop, then you are free to abandon your mission and go back to the Capital City."

"Abandon?"

"Yes, it would mean other factors have intervened and your efforts will no longer be necessary."

After mentally reviewing his instructions, Carlton settled back into his saddle, comfortably riding along the trail. *I feel so much better now on land, where I am in charge rather than being at the mercy of the sea. That was an interesting experience, but I am glad I am a soldier and not a sailor.*

There was a little snow at higher elevations, but mostly, the early warm weather had removed it from the road. It was still a hard four-day journey from the Capital City to the Teardrop Kingdom. Four days after they had arrived in the Teardrop Kingdom, a rider came up the road from the south, dressed in the uniform of the Royal Dragoons. Seeing him, Lieutenant Carlton thought. *Tomorrow will be a key day in my life. I will become a captain, and tomorrow, I will gain the right to marry Elise.*

Chapter Thirty-Seven

ROUGH SEAS

*O*nly *two more nights and a day. This afternoon, Captain Slater said we should be able to see land at dawn the day after tomorrow.*

At the start of the journey, there was a slight chill to the sea air, but it has rapidly turned into an icy slap. Each passing day proves how right Queen Amanda was—seal coats really are best for this wet, frigid air.

Princess Tara stood alone, holding tight to the rail *near* the bow of the ship. A splash of icy water in her face, early in the voyage, had taught Tara not to stand at the exact bow of the ship.

We have been at sea now for six days. One more full day of sailing and two nights, I can make that. I do not know what I expected this voyage to be like, but not the constant rolling and slapping of the hull we have experienced. I have not slept more than a few hours any night. My hope was the gentle rock of the ship would put me to sleep and help the journey fly. Instead, I count hours.

Captain Slater had warned, "You can return to the deck, princess, if you must. Please remember to hold tight. It is still fairly rough."

"I will be careful, but I must see the sky and feel the air," Princess Tara replied.

Despite the cold and slipperiness, being on deck is preferable to being confined in a cabin. In the early part of the journey, Yvette and Nan stood

with me, but now they have gone below-deck. Nan is suffering sea sickness, the
same fate as several of the soldiers.

Only the necessary deckhands are topside, and they all duck below at
any chance. I should become accustomed to being alone. Nan and Yvette
abandoned me when it got cold. Will they abandon me when we get to the
Teardrop Kingdom because it is too dirty, or dangerous, or just incredibly
boring?

The day before I left, father called me into his study.

"I am sorry to see you go," he said. *He did not say, "My heart is breaking*
to lose you." Because this is happening, I am being lost forever.

Without pausing, he started with instructions. "You should have no
difficulty in gaining control of the boy. From all reports, he is weak, both
physically and mentally. The administrator of the Teardrop will be your
major adversary. He is ex-Chancellor of the High Kingdom, a man named
Goldblatt. He is old and completely out of touch with the world.

"Remember, these people are not to be trusted. It was their failure to
honor our agreement that cheated you out of the opportunity to be a
queen. Never forget.

"Next, if you need to contact me, do so through Nan. She will get
the information to me. It is important you never communicate with me
directly.

"Now, I am sure your mother will send you letters, and you may answer
them. Include only a direct response to what she has said or asked.

Father moved from behind his desk to the chair next to me and placed his
hand on my shoulder. "I know you understand how important this match
is to our family. Once you gain control of the Teardrop Kingdom, we can
use it to impact the High Kingdom for ourselves. It should be easy to make
the prince fall in love with you. Once he loves you, he will do anything you
ask. I know you will do whatever is necessary as your duty to the throne,
for the honor of our family, and for our country."

I knew he meant to sacrifice your body as needed. I cannot help believing I am really nothing more than a broodmare. What about me finding someone to love? Why do not I get to choose? Mother told me I would always have my children to love, but is that enough? What if I never have children?

"Father, why cannot I bring Bella with me? She has been with me since she was a foal, and I will miss her deeply."

"The seas are too rough," father said. "Perhaps we will send her when the seas calm in midsummer."

"Why not wait and send me in midsummer?"

"No," father replied sternly. "You must go at the first opportunity."

Father was right about the rough seas. Two days ago, I thought they were even too rough for the captain, since he ordered us to stay in our quarters and off the deck.

Colonel Lamaze agreed. The crossing had been challenging. He is a seasoned soldier who has served my father for twenty years. Father said the colonel was a man who could be counted on for loyalty. He would get me safely to the Teardrop.

Another slap of wind and water jolted the entire ship, shaking Tara from her internal conversation.

When did I become so negative? But what can be positive about this entire situation? My future husband is a simpleton, twisted, an imbecile with a kind heart, who lives in a frigid kingdom away from all forms of civilization. I should just let the next big wave sweep me off the deck. No one would even know I was gone.

I could cry, but the tears would freeze to my face.

I can hear Yvette say, 'not a good look.'

How can she worry about how she looks even in the middle of an ocean? It is beyond me, though if there were men around, Yvette would be concerned about her looks.

I am glad she came with me, but her choices for a suitable husband will be slim. Maybe she will end up, as her mother suggested, with a landed sheepherder. She felt a smile cross her face. *Yvette is a good friend. I will not be alone.*

The ship's bell tolled. *I need to go back inside and get ready for dinner. Only two more nights and a day.*

Chapter Thirty-Eight

ARRIVAL

Traveling this time of year, Colonel Lamaze had known the high risk the ship and all aboard would not make it to the port in the Teardrop Kingdom. He was on the upper deck as dawn broke through the clouds. As the captain predicted, they sighted land.

The colonel's loyalty to King Natas was unquestionable. The king had given him exceedingly difficult and specific instructions, and he meant to fulfill them. He knew this would place his life in danger, but he had risked his life for King Natas many times.

The port of the Teardrop Kingdom was nothing like the port they had left. Natas' capital boasted genuine wharfs and berths where arriving ships could dock. The port appeared to be only a sheltered bay, with a few loading ramps extending into the sea. Support for ships of their size required a tender.

The colonel and a few of his men boarded a rowboat to come ashore. Waiting for them were the harbormaster and two local guardsmen.

"Welcome to the Teardrop Kingdom. What brings a royal vessel like yours to our port?" the harbormaster asked.

Colonel Lamaze stepped forward, taking immediate control. "We are on a diplomatic mission from King Natas to deliver his daughter, Princess Tarareese, to the Teardrop Castle.

"We would like to know where we can get lodging for this evening. We have three women and a priest needing special attention." Colonel Lamaze had almost forgotten about Father Xavier. The man had disappeared into his cabin the first day and only emerged this morning. King Natas insisted the priest who drafted the marriage contract conduct the marriage ceremony. *I guess he means to punish the man for his error.*

"We also need horses, a carriage to carry the princess and her entourage, and a wagon for the luggage."

"We can help with all those things," the harbormaster said.

Colonel Lamaze told his lieutenant to deal with the details.

I am happy to be back on land. I want to feel the saddle beneath me. The only thing I want rolling is the back of my horse and not the insistent churning of the sea.

The harbormaster looked at Colonel Lamaze. "I will send notice to the castle telling them of your arrival."

"That will not be necessary," Colonel Lamaze said. "I am sending a man forward today. He will go halfway to arrange accommodations for tomorrow night and then go on to the castle. We will break the trip into two partial days to make the trip easier for the women."

Earlier, when Colonel Lamaze told Princess Tarareese about splitting the trip, she had not received the decision well. "It is my preference we ride hard one day, spend a quick night, and be there the next morning," she said.

"Your Highness, if it were just you and the ladies, I would travel more quickly," Lamaze had replied. "But the priest is older, and the trip has already taken a toll. One hard day of riding, even in a carriage, may be more than the man can handle. I think it is best if we split it into two days, each day a reasonable journey. We will have you in the Teardrop Castle mid-afternoon, the day after tomorrow." After the discussion, the princess finally conceded.

The harbormaster was disinclined to take direction anyone other than Prince Merryk or Chancellor Goldblatt. His duty was to the Teardrop Kingdom and the prince. *I will send my man this afternoon, after I see how many people have arrived.*

Later that evening, the harbormaster made his way to one of the local taverns. Not the finer tavern which sat on the hill overlooking the port, but a sailor's tavern, a place where men from the sea came to tell tales of waves and whales. It was the place he liked best. No one entered, other than those who understood the call of the sea.

The harbormaster's eyes scanned the pub. It was a rustic place with rough-hewn wooden tables. The room was always a little dark, but the accumulation of people seemed to fill it with life. Many were locals. The only women present were not 'proper ladies.' At a table against the wall, finishing his evening meal and a pint of ale, sat the captain of the newly arrived ship.

"Captain Slater, I thought I might find you here," the harbormaster said, extending his hand.

"I am pleased to be here, I tell you," Slater replied.

"I have to admit, it surprised me to see a royal ship show up so early in the season."

"No more surprised than me," Slater responded. "The critical transport of passengers to the Teardrop Kingdom, they said."

"Still, a significant risk at this time of year."

"Yes, and I thought it even greater when I found out the passengers were the Princess Tarareese, her entourage, a priest from the Provost, and the colonel and his men. Also, I was surprised they picked me and my ship for this journey."

"Why so?" the harbormaster asked.

"Well, King Natas recently acquired three brand-new warships. One of them, the R.S. *Broadsword*, left four days before us, headed to the Capital City of the High Kingdom. The other two were still at anchor when we left. All three ships are better designed for this rough weather than my flat-bellied old bucket. We barely made it through the storms."

The harbormaster shook his head. "This time of the year can be very unforgiving, but why did you take the risk?"

Captain Slater waved his hand at the wench to bring two more ales. "It was one of those unusual situations where everyone seemed to understand the risk and would pay for it—double my normal fee and gave me half upfront. In addition, something which I have never heard of before, King Natas guaranteed, under any circumstances, to pay the second half to whoever I chose."

"Most unusual," the harbormaster said. "But I suppose with the Royal Princess on board, it makes sense."

"What would have made sense was putting the princess on one of the new ships."

The barmaid delivered the ales to the table. "Thanks for the drink. How long do you think you will be in port?"

"I hope until the weather gets better. Colonel Lamaze said it would be a minimum of three weeks. So, I am dropping anchor to stay on land for a spell.

"The part that is interesting," Slater added, "was one of my sailors overheard the colonel telling his lieutenant they would be gone for only a week."

"Wonder why the difference in time?" the harbormaster asked.

"You can never really trust soldiers," Captain Slater added as he took a sip of beer. "Or my sailor might have misunderstood."

CHAPTER THIRTY-NINE
ATTACK

C hancellor Goldblatt bolted out of his study into the hall.

"Smallfolks, where is Merryk?" Goldblatt yelled, charging down the corridor toward the Great Hall.

Smallfolks intercepted him midway. "Captain Yonn and Prince Merryk left after an early breakfast. The prince said he wanted to test his new ax, and they had found the perfect trees for the beams for a southern bridge—a new project."

Goldblatt shook his head as he continued walking toward the Great Hall. "This morning, Smallfolks, I am inclined to agree with you, the prince is too ambitious. When did they say they would return?"

"Yonn promised they would be back by midday. What is wrong?"

"I just received a note from the harbormaster. Princess Tarareese landed in the port two days ago and will be here this afternoon. We are not prepared." Frustration filled the Chancellor's voice.

"Go get Nelly. She will know what needs to be done. Also, find the swordmaster."

"I thought we had at least one or two months before her arrival," said Smallfolks.

"So did I. Something is not right, but I cannot put my finger on it. Where did they say they were going, exactly?" the Chancellor asked.

"Just south was all they said."

As was normal for mid-March, the weather around the castle was unsettled with occasional showers broken by bursts of sunlight, all harbingers of the coming spring rains. The morning air still held the sharpness of a winter chill. Yonn and Merryk made their way down the road in the port's direction.

About a quarter of a mile below the floodplain, they turned into the forest. Over a berm, just off the road, were the trees they had cut the day before for a new bridge. This time of the year, no one needed a bridge, but Merryk knew the spring floods would block the road.

Near noon, they had limbed about half of one tree. Yonn turned to Merryk. "We need to go. I promised the guardsmen I would be back by noon to review the plans for the princess's arrival."

Merryk stopped swinging his ax. "I want to stay and finish this tree. It won't take long. Why don't you go ahead without me?"

"You know, leaving you alone is never a good idea," Yonn said, only slightly in jest.

"Yonn, it is barely March. No one has entered the Teardrop in the last three months. We have been out here for two days and haven't seen or heard a soul. What peril can I discover—a bear rising early from his winter's sleep? I'll be all right for an hour."

"Against my better judgment, I get your point. Do not stay any longer than needed. If I did not have all the guardsmen waiting, I would not go back."

"Go ahead. I'll be right behind you."

Only the smack of Merryk's ax and the occasional sounds of small creatures scurrying about broke the silence of the forest. Merryk smiled as he recalled all the trial and error that had gone into developing the right combination of heat and metal to create the perfect ax. Between swings, something else caught Merryk's attention.

Strange, sounds like horses galloping along the road. And they are getting closer. As the sound continued to grow, Merryk moved to the top of the berm, which stood between him and the coast road. At once, he identified the source of the sounds. Four men on horseback were pursuing a carriage. A guard and a driver, both wearing the red and gray of a Natas Dragoon, sat atop the carriage. One of the four riders had moved to head off the team and was forcing it to stop right in front of an unseen Merryk. *Natas' Dragoons. This must be the princess, but she shouldn't be here yet!*

As the carriage came to an abrupt halt, a woman screamed from inside. One of the other men jumped from his horse to engage the lone guard, besting him quickly. He then grabbed the driver, pulling him from the coach and plunging him to the ground. The driver attempted to defend himself against the obviously more seasoned warrior.

The remaining two men dismounted their horses at a short distance from the coach and moved toward the fray.

An internal voice spoke to Merryk. A voice he had heard many times before, but for the first time, could identify. ***"Marine, it's time to do your job. Defend. Plan. Breathe. Execute."***

In an instant, he knew what he had to do. *This isn't much of a plan. All I have is an ax. Surprise is my only ally. I must keep this a one-on-one battle as long as I can. They are not expecting anyone, so here goes.*

Merryk took a deep breath and moved toward the group of two.

The two men were focused on the action taking place at the carriage. One moved slightly ahead of the other. Merryk took his double-bladed ax and raised it to shoulder level, turned it sideways, and with a thrusting motion, drove the top of the ax into the base of the lagging man's skull. The man's head snapped, breaking his neck. He fell face first to the ground.

The second man, hearing the crash of his comrade, turned to look over his right shoulder, only to see Merryk swing the ax at his head and neck. Merryk had kept the ax high, catching him in the side of the neck below his chin, almost decapitating him.

Merryk looked back at the carriage. The driver had lost his battle. The man on horseback holding the horses yelled, "Tueur la Filles! Tueur la Filles!"

Merryk recognized the language as Franck and knew it meant "Kill the Girls!"

The man on foot pivoted toward the carriage door.

He will reach the door before I can get to him. Throw the ax! Merryk let loose the ax which made a swirling sound as it moved through the air. The weapon caught the man as he approached the door. The impact threw him against the door, where he hung for a moment and then slid to the ground. Another scream came from the carriage.

Merryk's aim and luck had been better than he hoped. The double-bladed ax was impaled in the man's back. Merryk moved forward into the space between the door and the remaining attacker holding the carriage horses.

He is on a horse. I need a weapon. Merryk's eye caught sight of a broadsword lying on the ground. Picking up the weapon, he turned to face the last attacker.

The man jumped off his horse.

His first mistake. Merryk thought. *The horse was an enormous advantage.*

He pulled his broadsword and moved toward Merryk. It was clear the man had been well trained. He held the sword high, the way the swordmaster had taught Merryk. He also did not hesitate to advance. This was not his first battle.

Merryk watched the approaching man, knowing he had made a second mistake, assuming Merryk, who was dressed as a woodsman, was an unskilled swordsman. He had raised the sword higher above his head, a position of advantage.

Merryk cleared his mind and allowed the instructions from the swordmaster to flow through his actions.

The first clash of the blades caught the attacker off guard. Surprise flashed across his face. In an instant, he knew the defense was perfect and the strength of the man who delivered the blow was immense. Only four more strokes, with the last blow landing across the attacker's chest, and the battle was over. The man fell to the ground, helpless.

Merryk kicked his sword away. "Who are you? Who sent you?" The man did not speak. With his last strength, he reached to his neck and grabbed a medallion hanging on an intricate chain.

Merryk again heard the sounds of horses. This time, they were coming from the castle. He jerked the medallion and chain from the man's neck, thrusting it into his pocket.

Merryk pivoted to the carriage. He could see heads from inside watching through the windows. As he opened the carriage door, a young woman with long, blonde hair lashed out at him with a small dagger. Merryk seized her wrist and removed the dagger.

This courageous defender must be the princess.

Surveying the interior, Merryk asked, "Is everyone all right?"

The inside of the carriage was in turmoil, with books, small bottles, and blankets tossed everywhere. A priest and an older lady were huddled in the corner. Behind the blonde sat a ruffled, ashen faced auburn-haired woman. The interior smelled of stale perfume, sweat, and fear.

"I think everyone is all right," the princess said, her voice quivering.

"Where are your guards?" Merryk asked.

No answer.

"Where are your guards?"

The woman's eyes were wide open in fear. She was having difficulty answering questions. "I do not know. They all left and went to the castle."

Merryk handed her back the dagger. "A dagger is a thrusting weapon, not a slashing weapon. Keep this close, this may not be over. Listen. Do not trust anyone, except the prince's men. Do you understand?"

She nodded her head in agreement.

At that moment, Merryk reached up and gently swept the hair which had fallen across her forehead back over her ear. His hand lingered on the side of her face. Looking directly into her bright blue eyes, he softly said, "The horses are coming from the castle. Remember. Only trust the prince's men. You have been very brave. Everything will be okay." He then let his hand drop from her face and stepped away.

The sound of the horses coming down the road increased. *I see Yonn and our guardsmen in blue, followed by more dragoons. The princess will be safe. I need to go back into the forest. I want to watch her guards when they get here.* Pulling the ax from the back of the man by the coach, Merryk hurried over the berm and back to where Maverick was tied.

Maverick stomped his front feet in displeasure at being prevented from joining Merryk in the battle. Merryk patted Maverick on the side. "I'm all right. You and Smallfolks worry too much."

When Yonn returned to the castle, he found Chancellor Goldblatt waiting.

"The princess will be here this afternoon. We must find the prince at once," Goldblatt said. "I am concerned something is wrong."

"We will get the prince immediately."

Captain Yonn assembled four guardsmen and started down the road to get Merryk. Near the village, they encountered a colonel of the Royal Dragoons and his men.

"What brings you this way?" Yonn asked Colonel Lamaze.

"I am Colonel Lamaze. We are here on a mission from King Natas to deliver his daughter, Princess Tarareese, to the Teardrop Castle. We were riding ahead to advise the castle we were less than an hour away."

"I am Yonn, Captain of the Guard. The castle knows you are on the way. Why do not we ride back and escort the carriage together?"

Yonn thought. *Something is wrong. Unless there were more guards surrounding the carriage, they have left her unprotected. We need to find the princess quickly.* Without asking, he increased his pace to a canter.

They came over a small hill and in the middle of the road sat the carriage. It was not moving, and there was no driver in the seat. As Yonn got closer, he saw there were bodies on the ground.

"Something is wrong here," Yonn said to everyone.

He and his guardsmen increased their pace. Colonel Lamaze and his men seemed to hold back. Arriving at the carriage, Yonn found six bodies lying on the ground.

Going to the carriage door, he knocked. "I am Captain Yonn, commander of Prince Merryk's guard. I am going to open the door. Is everyone all right?"

A weak voice from the inside said, "We are fine, shaken, but fine."

Looking inside, Yonn asked, "What happened?"

"They attacked us," a blonde-haired woman replied.

"We will get you to safety," Yonn said. Handing his horse's reins to one of the other guardsmen, he jumped into the driver's seat. Without waiting for anyone to comment, he seized the reins of the carriage and drove toward the castle.

As the carriage moved away, Colonel Lamaze instructed six of his men to follow. "Stay close to the princess."

———— ❖ ————

The colonel, the lieutenant, and two of his other men remained to assess the scene. This was not what he had expected to find. His four handpicked men, including Lieutenant Carlton, all lay dead. *What could have happened?* There was no one else to be seen. "Search the surrounding area quickly," Colonel Lamaze ordered. The other men immediately spread out.

The colonel dismounted from his horse and walked over to look at Lieutenant Carlton. He was slashed violently across the chest, penetrating one of his lungs. He had bled to death. *Who could have done this to four of you?* He shook his head in disbelief. His eyes scanned the surrounding area, looking for a sign of anyone who could have been responsible.

If I am going to fix this mess, I need to be near the princess.

Colonel Lamaze called the lieutenant over to where only the two of them could hear. "Find the guide and get these bodies out of here. Leave nothing which could be traced. Bring the two dragoons from the carriage back to the castle. I am riding to the princess."

———— ❖ ————

Merryk watched the colonel. *His first response was to inspect the men on the ground, not go to the carriage to see if the princess was okay. Also, I am surprised he did not spend more time looking for items to identify the assailants. Perhaps the colonel didn't care about the princess, and he knew these men.*

Chapter Forty

AT THE CASTLE

The oak doors sprang open as Captain Yonn escorted Princess Tarareese, Yvette, Nan, and a beleaguered Father Xavier into the Great Hall. Smallfolks, Nelly, and the swordmaster greeted them.

"Nelly, please take the ladies into the anteroom and get them settled."

"Smallfolks, take the priest to his room and get him a cup of tea." Under his breath he added, "and, take a bottle of sherry with you."

"Swordmaster, I need you to find the Chancellor. Then secure the castle and double the guards. Everywhere there is a dragoon, I want an equal number of guardsmen."

"What is going on?" the Chancellor asked as he joined Yonn in the Great Hall.

"There has been an attack on the princess."

Goldblatt's face clouded with worry. "Where is Merryk?"

"He is not with us. He should be back soon."

"What happened?"

"At the moment it is unclear. We met Princess Tarareese's guards on our way to find Prince Merryk. They were on their way to the castle. As a group we returned to the princess and found the carriage in the middle of the road. Bodies littered the ground around the coach—two of King Natas' Dragoons and four or more others."

"What about Merryk?" Goldblatt demanded as concern filled his voice.

"As we neared the carriage, I saw him briefly, going over the berm. I am confident he is safe."

"Where are the princess's guards now?"

"Colonel Lamaze, their commander, and three others stayed to survey the scene. The rest returned with us to the castle and now the swordmaster is watching them."

"Watching them?"

"Yes. Just before the attack, all the princess's guards withdrew, except for one and the driver, leaving the princess unprotected. Until we know who is behind this attack, we need to be very careful.

"Also, before you say anything, I will go over a cliff with Merryk, but I will never leave him alone ever again. My guess is he will arrive by one of the side gates anytime. Maverick is with him and will get him home."

A matronly woman with a warm, friendly smile escorted the three women into a small anteroom off the Great Hall. She directed Princess Tara to a comfortable chair in front of a burning fireplace. "Your Highness, I am Nelly, the housekeeper. There is water for freshening up and a fire for warmth."

Although Tara had not thought of herself as being cold, the warmth of the fire seemed to soothe her body.

"I will be back with hot tea in a moment. Is there anything else you need?"

Before the princess could answer, Nan barked, "Just bring the tea, without delay."

Princess Tara stopped her, "Nan, I can speak for myself. Thank you, that would be nice." For the first time, she noticed the shaking in her hands and in her voice.

"Your Highness, I see you have a chill. Perhaps this throw will help." Nelly gave a small blanket to the princess and left the room.

Yvette, who had made it through the entire ordeal in relative silence, now collapsed into a chair next to Tara. "Wow, I have never been so frightened in my life. I did not think we would get out of there alive. Where did the woodsman come from? I assume he was a woodsman. What did he say to you? Why did the colonel leave? Was the woodsman handsome?"

Tara was lost in her own thoughts. Before she could respond to Yvette, she heard a knock on the door. Nan answered, "Enter."

Nan is being too assertive, Tara thought. *I need to rein her in before she poisons everyone around us.*

Nelly entered with the tray of hot tea. Following her was a meticulously groomed, gray-haired man. Tara also caught sight of two sets of guards outside the door—one set was her father's Dragoons, and the others wore the deep blue cloaks of the Teardrop Guardsmen.

The man introduced himself. "Your Highness, I am Geoffrey Goldblatt, Administrator of the Teardrop Kingdom. I wish we could have met under better circumstances."

"I understand everyone calls you Chancellor, in recognition of your service to Great King Mikael, the prince's grandfather." *This is the man my father warned me about. Father said he was old and out of touch, but my teachers identified him as a scholar and incessant letter writer; a man very much connected to the world.*

Goldblatt asked, "Princess Tarareese, could you tell me what happened on the road? It is important, so we may assess if the threat has passed. The more information we have, the better."

A focused and precise man, just as I expected.

Yvette spoke up. "They tried to kill us."

"He knows," said Tara. "What he needs are the details, not the emotion."

The princess took a sip of tea, trying to control her shaking, and began. "We started this morning, later than I had hoped, but things seemed to drag on. The trip to the castle offered one more day of staring out the window and idle talk."

What Yvette and I wanted to talk about was impossible with Nan and the priest in the carriage. I did not care about the landscapes. I wanted to talk about my apprehension in meeting the simpleton prince.

"When we were about an hour away, Colonel Lamaze stopped the carriage and said he would ride to the castle to tell you I was close. A short time later, I heard voices challenging the coach. The driver took off at a gallop. Through the rear window, I counted four men following us."

"What were they wearing?" Goldblatt asked.

"Just plain gray and brown clothing. It looked serviceable but did not have any distinctive marks or insignia.

"I saw one rider race past the carriage toward the lead horses. The carriage came to an abrupt stop, throwing everything forward."

"I screamed," Yvette added.

Tara ignored Yvette and continued. "Through the curtains on the side, I saw a second man catch the carriage and there was a clash of swords. I could not see exactly, but I assumed the dragoon was attempting to defend us but was defeated. The first man must have continued holding the horses. I did not see him until later.

"I heard the driver being pulled off the top of the carriage to the ground. There were more sword clashes, then silence. Then I heard some shouting. I am not sure what they said. *Yes, you do. They said, 'Kill the girls,' in my native language.*

"Through the side window, I saw a second attacker approach the coach door. Just before he got there, he lunged forward and smacked his face into the window. He then slowly slid to the ground."

"I screamed again," Yvette added.

"Only after the man fell did I see the woodsman. At least I think he was a woodsman. He was tall and dressed in very plain clothing. He was covered in sweat, like he had been working. His hair was unkempt and wild, and some had fallen forward, obscuring his face.

"Although the curtains partially blocked my view, I saw a man come from the front of the carriage toward the woodsman. The woodsman picked up a broadsword from the ground.

"The front man held his sword the way I have seen my father's soldiers do—high over his head. The woodsman did not seem afraid. He engaged the other man. In less than half a dozen strokes, the woodsman defeated him.

"The woodsman came to the door. He asked if we were unhurt and where my guards were? I heard horses approaching, but he said everything would be all right, and then he left as quickly as he had come. *He said much more, but I do not know if I can trust the Chancellor. Until I do, I will hide a few things.*

"Only after he left did I see the other men lying on the ground. The woodsman must have bested all four attackers."

"Is there anything specific about the woodsman you can remember other than tall and plainly dressed?"

"No, nothing I can remember." *I could tell you he was incredibly brave and had deep, magnificent blue eyes, a gentle touch, a voice that could calm a storm, and when his fingers slid from my face, I wanted to follow him anywhere he wanted to go. I should not even be sharing this with myself. I am about to marry another man!* "No, nothing else."

Goldblatt responded, "Your recollection is very specific. These details will be of great value. Does anybody else have anything to add?"

Both Nan and Yvette shook their heads no.

Princess Tarareese asked, "Where are Prince Merryk and the commander of my guard, Colonel Lamaze?"

"I do not know where Colonel Lamaze is, but the prince was away from the castle this morning when we got word of your arrival."

"You should have had notice of my arrival yesterday. The colonel sent a man ahead the day we landed."

"I am sorry, but we never received word from the colonel. We got a notice from the harbormaster this morning. As to your first question, I expect the prince at any time. In fact, if you will excuse me for a moment, I will check to see if he has returned."

CHAPTER FORTY-ONE

CHOICES

P rincess Tarareese returned the blanket to her lap and settled back into the chair in front of the warm fire. Again, the turmoil of her mind swept her away. *Yvette was right. Only a set of fortunate circumstances kept us alive. I can still hear the words, "Kill the Girls!" The brave actions of the woodsman saved us. It must have been the emotions of the moment which made me feel so instantly attracted to him. He appeared so suddenly and then left so quickly. My imagination must have created the connection. However, something real about him engendered trust. I would follow him anywhere.*

Tara, what are you thinking? Any moment your new husband, the simpleton prince, will appear and the woodsman will become just what he is, a dream. Women never get to choose. Even if I wanted a life filled with love in a simple hut, it is not possible. I am a woman and a princess. I have no choice.

A shiver rippled through her body. *I was shaking before, but now, I feel sick just sitting here waiting for the prince and knowing I am trapped forever. This is not how I imagined our meeting. Although I am not sure what I thought would occur. I need to remember the calm in the woodsman's voice. Tara, you must stop thinking about him!*

Chancellor Goldblatt returned and in a formal voice said, "Princess Tarareese." The princess did not immediately respond. Raising his voice, he repeated her name. "Princess Tarareese." Finally giving her attention, she turned her head to see three men had entered the room. "I would like to introduce to you His Royal Highness, Prince Michael Merryk Raymouth, firstborn son of the Inland Queen Amanda and King Michael Raymouth."

As she stood to greet the prince, the throw on her lap slid to the floor, catching her foot as she turned. She fell forward, directly into the arms of the tall, broad-shouldered man who stood before her.

"Oh! Don't worry, I've got you. But you need to sit back down."

Tara heard the voice. There was something about *that* voice—she had heard it before. Tara was tall for a woman. In fact, she was taller than most men, but to look at the face above, she had to tip her head back, way back. *Oh, he is tall! This cannot be the stunted prince.*

Merryk spoke again. "Please, you need to sit down. You are reacting to the excitement of the day. When this happens, adrenaline runs into your system. It makes you strong for a while, but it leaves your body feeling shaky. In fact, you may be in shock."

Tara eased back into the chair and Prince Merryk knelt in front of her. "Are you all right?" he said in *that* special calm voice.

Tara looked at the prince. *If I was not in shock before, I am now. I have seen these magnificent blue eyes before. This cannot be the woodsman.* Tara started to say, "But you are the woods—"

Prince Merryk interrupted her, speaking quietly, "Please let us keep this a secret until we can talk in private. I am still concerned about your safety. Our secret, understand?"

Tara nodded her head.

Chancellor Goldblatt looked at Yvette and said, "Your Highness, I would also like to introduce the Contessa Yvette D'Campin, Lady-in-Waiting to Princess Tarareese."

Prince Merryk stood politely, taking Yvette's hand. Everything Tara could not say or had only flashed through her mind was reflected in Yvette's face. Her mouth slackened open and her eyes widened as she looked at the young prince.

To take Yvette's hand, the prince had taken a step away from the princess.

I feel like I am being pulled to follow him. I do not want to sit in this chair. I want to be back against his chest, in his arms again. Tara, stop it!

The Chancellor continued his introductions, "I am sure you have all seen, if not met, Captain Yonn."

Yonn stepped forward, nodded to Princess Tarareese, and took Yvette's hand. In a flash, the surprise reflected on Yvette's face was replaced by captive attention for the young captain.

Prince Merryk moved to the chair beside Princess Tarareese. "You have had a challenging day."

Tara replied, "A challenging day is a broken carriage wheel. People were trying to kill us." *I must hide my surprise and fascination with this man. He is the one my father wants me to dominate.*

Prince Merryk added, "But they failed. You were lucky Captain Yonn was close."

"Although we appreciate the captain's aid," Tara replied, her eyes fixed on Prince Merryk, "it was not Captain Yonn who saved us, but a woodsman. He appeared out of nowhere, fought four men, and then disappeared."

"I will send my men to find and reward him," Merryk said.

"He should not be hard to find," Princess Tara said. *There is no question he is the woodsman, but how is that possible? A nobleman would want everyone to know of his valor. He specifically wants to hide it.*

Colonel Lamaze burst through the door unannounced. "Where is the princess?" he demanded. Seeing her, he moved in a straight line, only to find his path blocked by a broad-shouldered man.

"Out of my way," he said indignantly. "I am responsible for the princess's safety."

The young man did not move. "A responsibility you seem to have forgotten."

"Who are *you*?"

Goldblatt stepped forward. "Colonel, you are speaking to His Royal Highness Prince Merryk."

Surprise had marked Yvette's face, but Colonel Lamaze was completely taken aback.

Tara responded from behind Prince Merryk, "I am unharmed Colonel, but where have you been?"

Colonel Lamaze turned to face Captain Yonn. "For the last half-hour, I have been standing outside the front gate waiting for Captain Yonn to give me permission to enter. Let me be very clear, I am a colonel. I do not take orders or wait for approvals from a captain."

Merryk replied in an even voice, "Let me be clearer. You are a guest in this castle and Captain Yonn is responsible for security, something he takes seriously and does not quickly abandon. If rank alone is important to you, then I assure you we can rectify this. During your stay, General Yonn will be in charge of security. Colonel Lamaze, I expect you will follow the general's orders."

Tara smiled to herself. *Prince Merryk knows how to take control. He was not what Colonel Lamaze expected, either. The colonel does not know what to say.* Recognizing the awkwardness, Princess Tara said, "Colonel, we are guests and new here. I am sure you can work with General Yonn to meet our needs."

Following Tara's instruction to the colonel, Merryk turned his focus to the group. "Nelly has prepared an early dinner while they are finishing your rooms. If you will please follow me, I will show you the way to the dining room." Merryk offered his arm to the princess, who readily accepted it.

The small number of inhabitants of the castle seldom used the long table, although it could handle many guests. Tonight, they had arranged the plates at one end, with Merryk at the head of the table. Princess Tara and Contessa Yvette sat on his left side, directly facing Chancellor Goldblatt, General Yonn, and Colonel Lamaze, who sat on the right. They discussed the severity of the ocean crossing and other insignificant items, avoiding all discussion about the attack.

The meal was simple fare, both warm and filling, but not fancy. Princess Tara picked at her meal. Merryk assumed it was not from a lack of hunger, but because she was preoccupied.

At the end of the meal, Smallfolks advised Prince Merryk the rooms were prepared.

"I am told the rooms for the Princess Tara and the Contessa Yvette are ready. Nelly will escort the ladies to their rooms. They are on the same floor as mine. I will not be very far away. Colonel Lamaze, we have prepared a place for you with your men in the barracks."

The Colonel immediately responded, "I need to be close to Princess Tarareese."

Prince Merryk was unshaken. "Your men will be outside of her door, as will mine. So unless you intend to stand guard, there is no particular reason for you to be closer."

Tara watched Merryk. The softness in his eyes disappeared as he spoke to Colonel Lamaze. *He does not trust the colonel. Why?*

General Yonn added, "Two of your men and two of my men will be outside the door. In addition, we have four men on the floor and two more at each of the stairwells."

Princess Tara looked around. "With the prince near, I am sure I will be very safe." *The colonel does not understand how true this really is.* "Colonel Lamaze, there is no reason for your concern."

The princess and contessa stood and moved toward the door. Before leaving the room, Tara stopped and looked back at Prince Merryk. "A quick word, please."

Merryk moved from the table to where the princess stood.

In tones no one could hear but the two, Princess Tara asked, "I know we said we would talk later, but one thing. Why did you move the hair from my eyes?"

Merryk looked at her with a knowing smile. "I could say, so I could better see your eyes, or to give you something to think about rather than people trying to kill you."

Princess Tara defensively replied, "Well, that did not work."

Merryk's smile increased. "Obviously. Good night, Princess." he whispered as he bowed politely and stepped away.

Tara and Yvette followed the ever-present Nelly down the hall and up a broad stairwell. Two of Merryk's men were in front of the women. Behind them followed two of her father's Dragoons, then two more of Merryk's men. Along the way, Tara noticed more blue-cloaked guards.

Yvette looked around and under her breath said, "I do not know if we are guests here or prisoners."

"We were attacked today. They are just being careful."

Yvette then again whispered, "What do you think of the prince? He is nothing at all like they described him. He is so tall and handsome."

"Yvette, we can talk later, but not here."

"Fine, but I will still find the woodsman and give him a special reward for saving us."

"You will do no such thing. Prince Merryk will take care of it. You are to do nothing. Do you understand me? Nothing!"

"Yes, yes. Why are you so upset over a woodsman?"

"The prince will take care of it. That is all you need to know."

Yvette gave her friend a puzzled look. "This day has really upset you. Can I at least talk about General Yonn?"

"Not now."

They continued the balance of the trip in silence.

Two guardsmen entered the dining room. General Yonn turned to Colonel Lamaze. "My men will show you to the barracks."

Colonel Lamaze stiffened. His eyes swept the room, meeting Merryk's. For a moment his mouth opened, as if he were preparing to speak, but then he sighed. "Very well, until tomorrow." With a slight bow toward Merryk, he turned and followed the guardsmen.

"We need to be cautious. While we have guests, you will both have guards," Yonn bluntly told Merryk and Chancellor Goldblatt.

"That will not be necessary," Prince Merryk said.

"Please, Your Highness, no argument. I also assigned guards to Father Xavier. I do not want a missing priest stopping your wedding," he said with a slight chuckle as he stood and left the room.

"The attack has changed Yonn. He is taking his responsibility for security seriously." Chancellor Goldblatt said.

"Yes, the young rogue I met in the stable is gone. Yonn has shown initiative and left little doubt he deserves to command the guard," Merryk replied.

Chapter Forty-Two

ANSWERS AND QUESTIONS

Later in the evening, despite Yonn's wishes, Merryk convinced his two guards to stay at the base of the old tower while he went up to think. "I am forty feet in the air; no one will fly up. You can stay at the bottom of the stairs where it is warm. I will be fine."

The night had grown deeper as an icy wind swept away the low clouds, revealing the bright light of the stars. The absence of ambient light pollution seemed to amplify the stars of the Teardrop Kingdom. Somehow, the skies were fuller than he remembered from the twenty-first century.

His mind reviewed the day. *The biggest surprise today wasn't meeting the princess, but remembering I was a United States Marine. All the voices in my head now make sense. "Panic kills, focus and live." "Wounded men can still kill." What was the name of the drill instructor?* One small question triggered a flood of memories.

I became a Marine by accident. My grandfather and my father were both Army men. Grandfather fought in Korea and father in Vietnam. I always assumed I would join the Army. After my senior year in high school, the time appeared right. Summer had faded into fall, and the harvest was complete. My friends had already headed to college. Although I was admitted to several colleges, I felt my first responsibility was to my country and the Army.

It was early October. Stubbled fields where the combines had harvested wheat lined the road as I drove into town. Our small community had one recruitment office. It serviced the Army, Navy, Air Force, Marines, and Coast Guard. I was waiting outside the door when the first recruiter arrived. He was wearing the uniform of a United States Marine.

He looked at me with a warm smile. "Why are you here so early?"

"I'm here to join the Army. I want to follow my grandfather and father."

The Marine opened the door. "Have a seat. I'll put on some coffee. The Army recruiter will be here soon."

There were five desks, one for each of the armed services, an assortment of recruiting brochures, and posters spread across the wall. The room's purpose was to put people at ease, but it didn't make them comfortable.

I sat down on a metal folding chair and watched the sunlight coming through the windows. In this part of the country, all outside windows held some dust from the harvest. It filtered the light, giving it a slight golden hint. The room smelled of wheat and rich earth. As a farm boy, the smell and filtered light wasn't unusual. I sat quietly as the minutes passed, watching the dust motes float in the air and waiting for the Army recruiter.

After half an hour, the Marine recruiter got up from his desk to check on the coffee. "Like a cup?"

"Yes sir, I would."

He poured two cups and brought one to me.

"Why exactly did you say you want to be in the Army?"

"My grandfather fought in Korea and my father in Vietnam. I have grown up on their stories and feel a responsibility to serve."

The recruiter looked at me with a smile. "Why aren't you on your way to college?"

"I was admitted to several and intend to go, but first, I want to serve my country. It's like a family duty."

"Very well," the recruiter said as he returned to his desk.

After a while, I asked, "Would it be okay if I got another cup?"

"Sure, help yourself," the recruiter said as he continued to work on the papers covering his desk.

After getting another cup of coffee, I returned to my chair. Time dragged on.

Finally, the Marine recruiter came over to me. "I'm not sure what is holding up the Army recruiter. He is usually here by now. You strike me as a motivated and intelligent young man. We don't find that combination here often." I was sure he had used this speech before. "I would like to ask you one question. Do you know the most dangerous weapon in the U.S. arsenal?"

I replied, "It must be an aircraft carrier, stealth bomber, or intercontinental missile."

"No, the most dangerous weapon is a United States Marine with an M-16. They're the ones the government sends out first to hold one square yard at a time until the other services can get there. I think a man like you would want to be one of the most dangerous and the first to see the action."

Being the most dangerous weapon in the United States arsenal appealed to me. The recruiter then presented his spiel about the opportunities within the Marine Corps.

Ten days later, I boarded a bus headed from my small eastern Washington town to Camp Pendleton. I had no way of knowing it would mark the start of eight years of my life and two tours of duty abroad as a Marine.

A rush of feelings threatened to overwhelm Merryk, but he immediately suppressed them. *I didn't want to remember the horrors of war before, and I don't want to remember now. But if I am honest, my training as a Marine saved lives today. Being a Marine here may be more important than ever.*

Merryk's thoughts were interrupted as one of his guards, breathless from the climb, came out of the door of the tower. "Excuse me, Your Highness, Chancellor Goldblatt would like to speak with you in his study."

"Well, this has been an interesting day. Nothing like welcoming a future bride to the Teardrop to brighten the spirits," Chancellor Goldblatt said with a chuckle as he handed Merryk a glass of sherry.

Merryk exhaled and shook his head from side to side. "It could have been a tragedy. If I hadn't been where I was in the woods, at that point in time, the princess and all in the carriage would have died."

"What happened on the road?"

Merryk provided Chancellor Goldblatt with a summary of the events.

"What I found surprising was Colonel Lamaze didn't immediately check on the princess, but he went to the dead men. After Yonn had left, the colonel didn't search the assailants for clues as to their identity. He sent his men searching for who could have attacked them."

"Do you think he already knew them?"

"I am uncertain. I know one yelled, 'Kill the Girls' in Franck. Highwaymen might yell to search the carriage, but they knew who was inside before they attacked."

"I was thinking profit motivated the attack." Goldblatt said as he sipped his sherry. "But if that were the case, ordinary highwaymen would have targeted the following luggage cart, a much easier target. So theft does not appear to be the motive."

"This reduces the reasons for the attack to the choices of kidnapping or murder, whether for politics, or revenge," Merryk said.

"You heard them say 'kill,' which would preclude kidnapping," Goldblatt said. "I had not considered revenge. King Natas has many enemies."

"Killing for revenge or politics might make sense, except it doesn't explain the timing of the attack nor the actions of the colonel."

Goldblatt stroked his beard in thought. "Had the princess been killed within view of the castle, blame would have fallen on King Michael and you. This would allow King Natas to demand the return of the entire dowry. The only person to benefit would be King Natas. If it were for revenge, the killing could have taken place anywhere. However, only a few people knew she was coming, all associated with King Natas."

"King Natas might try to kill me, but his own daughter? This seems extreme, even for him."

"But we do not know why he has objected so strenuously to you when he willingly accepted Merreg, your brother."

"A third party seeking revenge might be the truth. Right now, I wonder why a professional soldier like the colonel, charged with protecting the princess, would leave her alone. His actions suggest he was expecting the attack. Whether he is working for a third party or King Natas, it doesn't matter. We cannot trust him."

"We also have the report from the harbormaster," Goldblatt said. "Three women, a priest, the colonel, and ten men got off the ship. Of the ten, two are now dead. The colonel and eight men are in the barracks. The colonel said he sent a man forward to tell us of their arrival, a man who never made it. His response to my inquiry was 'he must have been intercepted,' yet at this point in time, we can account for everyone."

"So, Colonel Lamaze lied about the man and abandoned the princess at the exact time of the attack. He is working for someone, Natas or another.

His intent was murder. The longer he stays within the castle, the longer the risk exists for the princess."

"And for you, my prince. The death of either of you would still create a whole range of tough choices for your father."

"We must get rid of the colonel," Merryk added.

"This may not be a problem. After dinner, I went to visit Father Xavier, the priest that came with the princess. He advised me they had given him sealed instructions to open upon arrival at the castle. They were from the Provost and directed him to conduct the marriage ceremony 'immediately.'"

"You mean soon?" Merryk asked.

"No, immediately. Father Xavier said the Provost was concerned the two-year delay in completing the agreement had unnaturally pressured all involved. The Provost also knew of the attempts on your life. The attack on the princess would only confirm his suspicions and resolve."

"I hoped the princess and I would have time before the wedding. I want to get to know her before she becomes my wife. Delay, however, could only increase the peril."

Chancellor Goldblatt shifted in his chair. "Do you really need a delay?"

"Chancellor, you know how I am struggling with the arranged marriage. I know I cannot avoid it, but I wanted to at least become friends."

"Merryk, I do not believe we can delay the wedding by more than two or three weeks."

Merryk moved from his chair to the fireplace. "I will speak with her tomorrow. I need to allow her to help make this decision. A delay threatens her life as much as mine."

"Speaking of the princess, what do you think of her?"

"She is young. On the road she showed great courage and composure."

"Young? She is twenty-four, older than you by four years and well past the normal age for a royal marriage. I find it interesting the first things you identify about her are courage and composure. These are not the first virtues a man would seek in a wife."

"As you have told me before, 'my logic is not normal.' She is also lovely."

"Lovely! She is beautiful. I do not know where I went wrong in your education," Chancellor Goldblatt said as he shook his head.

Merryk turned to leave the room, and then stopped and reached into his pocket. "Chancellor, I took this off one of the attackers. It is a simple medallion, but the chain is intricate. Perhaps we could determine where it was made. It might help us identify them." Merryk handed the chain and the medallion to the Chancellor.

CHAPTER FORTY-THREE

HOPES

Tara followed Nelly through the tall oak door to her new chambers. An oversized fireplace with tapestry-covered stone on both sides immediately drew her attention. In front of the crackling fire sat a sofa draped with a lamb's wool blanket, two comfortable chairs, and side tables. Behind the sofa was a large four-post bed covered with an overstuffed comforter and multiple pillows. A large window covered with floor-to-ceiling drapery dominated the other side of the room. The room sparkled with bright candlelight and had a slight fragrance of honey.

This room belonged to a woman. They filled it with warmth and comfort.

"The candles are made of beeswax, one of Prince Merryk's ideas. He says they burn hotter and do not have the smell and smoke of tallow." Nelly then pointed toward a smaller side room. The room was a dressing area with closets in the rear, a dressing table, and a mirror. In the center of the room sat a steaming hot bath.

"I hope everything is acceptable for the evening. If you need anything else, just let the guards know and they will find me."

"Thank you, Nelly. Everything looks fine, especially the bath," Princess Tara replied.

Before Tara could settle into the warm tub, Nan arrived and immediately complained about the rooms. "They must have something better," she said. "I am confident Prince Merryk's accommodations are much better.

I am three floors below. How am I going to provide you with immediate attention if I am so far away? I need to be on the same floor as you," Nan insisted.

"I am no longer five years old. I can take care of myself and besides, Yvette will be close."

"Yvette," scoffed Nan.

"Nan, I need you to remember we are new here. I want you to be more accommodating, less demanding. I think the rooms are fine."

Tara finally extracted herself from the conversation with Nan and slid into the tub of steaming water.

This feels wonderful. What a harrowing day. I was attacked for the first time in my life and met the woodsman-prince with the deep blue eyes. Nan's voice echoed in her head. *Yes, I know what my father would want, but not tonight. Tonight, I am just going to consider the possibilities. Maybe I do not get love in a rustic cottage, but perhaps I will find it in a rustic castle.* The thought was as soothing as the warm water.

Yvette joined Tara in her room for the evening, like they had done since they were ten. Whenever they had a difficult day or there was a thunderstorm, the two found comfort in being close.

Nelly had left carved goblets and wine for after the bath, with a note that read: *Perhaps this will help you sleep.*

They settled into the bed. Within moments, the wine and the day pushed Yvette into a deep sleep.

Tara remained awake. Lying on her back, she observed the beams, her mind roaming. The fireplace provided little bursts of light which revealed the curves, divots, and flaws of the beams. Somehow, the light seemed to enhance their character.

They are roughly hewn wood, probably oak, nothing like the polished surfaces of the beams in my father's castle. Everything there is polished and perfect but feels cold, which no amount of sparkling light overcomes. This castle has a different feel. It is not polished at all. It is rustic, but with a warmth which permeates the stone, wood, and people. Everyone has been welcoming. Nelly could not be more helpful, and Master Smallfolks has the demeanor of a friendly old uncle. Chancellor Goldblatt is articulate, focused, and extremely well-educated. He will be a worthy adversary or, hopefully, an amazing friend.

Then there is the prince. People amplify their strengths. However, Prince Merryk was presented to the world in the worst light. He is not stooped, but tall and straight. He is not a weakling, but strong and brave. He is not a simpleton, but articulate and thoughtful. The depth of his beautiful blue eyes screams intelligence. He is not socially awkward, but everything you would dream of as a perfect prince. Most charming of all, he is Merryk first, then a prince.

Father would be disturbed if he knew how I was thinking about this man. 'Man' is not the word I thought I would use to describe him, but he certainly is a man. Maybe, just maybe, I will get a chance at an actual life with a husband, children, and even love.

Of course, I must stay alive long enough to achieve it. The men who attacked spoke Franck. They came to kill me! Why? Why did it seem like the colonel abandoned me just before the attack? Is this why Merryk does not trust the colonel? But I am safe right now, and Merryk is just down the hall.

I wonder when I will see him again. The first thing in the morning would be my choice.

Tara drifted off, floating on her thoughts and hopes.

Chapter Forty-Four

DISCUSSION

After breakfast, Princess Tarareese heard a knock. Opening the door, the princess found Smallfolks with a note. The note read:

Good morning. I hope you slept well. It is important the two of us speak. Can you join me for a mid-morning walk around the castle grounds? Smallfolks will wait for your reply. M.

"Master Smallfolks, please tell Prince Merryk I would be pleased to join him this morning."

"Very well, Your Highness. Let the guards know when you are ready, and they will advise us. Also, bring a warm coat. It is cold this morning."

Nan never seemed to change. She always wore dark clothing with a high-necked white blouse and smelled of lilacs. She constantly wore her hair in a tight bun. If it had ever come loose, Tara had never seen it happen.

Nan used to smile. However, Tara had not seen her smile in many years. Nan was always instructing, or as Yvette called it, "lecturing." Nan had memorized all of Tara's father's rules and never allowed the girls to deviate from them. Yvette said if she ever bent a rule, she would literally break.

Having Nan come with me seems a strange choice. I do not need a nanny. Yvette, as my lady-in-waiting, is a sufficient companion. Father is probably expecting I will need Nan to help take care of my children. Children, what an interesting thought.

"What are you doing?" Nan asked as she entered the room.

"I am getting ready to go for a walk with Prince Merryk."

"I am not talking about your preparation. I am talking about your conduct toward this prince." The word 'prince,' had a distinctive snarl attached. "You seem smitten by him. Remember what your father told all of us? These people are not to be trusted. You cannot forget, it was their deceit that placed you in this godforsaken castle, when you should be in the Capital City waiting to become the queen."

"I am not smitten. He is just being gracious, and I am being polite."

"Polite! He was most likely responsible for the attack. If it were not for the help of a stranger, we would all be dead."

A smile crossed Tara's face. Merryk saved us, but you need not know.

"He has no reason to attack us," Tara replied.

"You are already defending him. Ask yourself, 'What would your father want you to do?' Do not get excited by his looks."

"I am not excited by his looks."

"I know you," Nan said. "Soon you will dress like Yvette to attract his attention."

"I will not."

As if answering a call, the door to the room popped open and Yvette swept in. "I found the blouse you wanted to borrow."

Princess Tarareese chose a full-length, silver fur coat from the selection Queen Amanda had sent, one which accentuated her blue eyes. She and Contessa Yvette made their way down the broad stairway to the main floor.

Waiting for them at the base of the stairs were Prince Merryk and General Yonn.

"Good morning," Prince Merryk said. A warm smile sprang to his face as he greeted Tara. "I trust both of you slept well. I hope everything is satisfactory."

"Nelly has done everything possible to make us feel at home."

"Shall we?" Merryk extended his arm to Princess Tara.

The group, with four guards, moved out of the Great Hall, across the courtyard, and up the stairs to the top of the castle wall. A blanket of fog lay across the valley in front of the castle and rolled up the sides of the surrounding hills. At the height of the castle wall, the fog broke, revealing a bright-blue spring morning. White puffs painted the crisp air as they exhaled.

Upon reaching the top, Merryk said, "I thought we might walk around the castle wall. The view from here is spectacular, and it is safe."

"You think there is still a risk?" Tara asked.

Merryk motioned to Yonn, who, along with Yvette and the two sets of guards, moved a discreet distance away, allowing Merryk and Tara to speak confidentially.

"I believe we are both still in peril." He looked around to be sure they were not being heard. "There have been two attacks on my life and two attempts to have me declared incompetent. Now, a direct attack on you. In the forest, I heard your attacker say they came to kill you."

"Yes, they yelled, 'Kill the girls' in Franck. I did not tell anyone before. I did not know who I could trust. I assume Franck is not a common language in the Teardrop?"

"Other than Chancellor Goldblatt and myself, I can't think of anyone who speaks the language."

"Wondering why anyone would want me dead, especially if they were from my homeland, kept me awake most of the night."

"I believe it has something to do with our marriage."

"Perhaps the deceit surrounding the agreement is the motivation," Tara said. *Oh no! That was a little too sharp, too confrontational.*

Merryk chuckled. "Although I like your answer, it seems too simple. I didn't draft the agreement, nor was it my idea to get married. I woke up one day, and was told, 'Oh, by the way, you are to be married.' I assure you, it was not my choice any more than I guess it was yours. Also, trickery in the agreement would be a reason to kill me, but not you."

Tara's brow tightened. *I do not enjoy being called simple, but he is right. It does not explain an attack on me.*

Merryk continued. "We have an additional issue. The Provost gave Father Xavier specific instructions to perform the ceremony 'immediately.' The Provost knew of the attacks on me. With an attack on you, delay becomes even less desirable. I hoped we would have more time before the wedding to become acquainted. It would be my choice to delay. However, I fear the longer we delay the wedding, the greater the risk."

"Why do you say that?" Tara asked.

"I think you may have brought the risk with you. Chancellor Goldblatt and I are having difficulty understanding why Colonel Lamaze left you alone."

"I also wondered where my guards were at the moment of the attack."

"There is more. We received word from the harbormaster. Ten soldiers arrived at the port. Two were killed at the carriage and eight are currently in the barracks. Colonel Lamaze said he sent a man forward with notice of your arrival. He never arrived. The colonel said he must have been killed, which means there were eleven soldiers, or he lied. Also, when the colonel returned to the carriage, he did not check to see if you were safe. After you left, he looked for me, the person who foiled the attack, and never searched the attackers for clues to their identity."

"Prince Merryk, these are significant charges. Colonel Lamaze has been in my father's service for many years. I will not readily believe he would seek to harm me."

"If not him, then someone else in your group is involved."

"Assuming I agree with your conclusions, what should we do?"

"I would prefer to wait a few weeks to get to know each other, but this keeps your life in peril. This is not a choice I can make for you."

"Nevertheless, it is your choice, not mine. You are the man."

"No, at the least this is *our* choice, but at the root, it is *your* choice. You get to choose."

"May I think about it?"

"But remember the peril."

The agitated voice of Colonel Lamaze interrupted their discussion. "Where is the princess?"

They turned to see the source of the clamor storming toward them.

"What do you think you are doing? Private meetings before marriage are not appropriate and not without my presence."

Merryk's voice turned steely. "I was not aware we needed your presence. Contessa Yvette and your guards were with us at all times. The princess's honor is intact."

Princess Tara turned to the colonel. "You would have been bored by our discussions. We were simply selecting the date for the wedding."

"You cannot do that until we advise your father of the attack and wait for his instructions."

Merryk responded, "You have King Natas' instructions. Deliver Princess Tarareese to the Teardrop Kingdom and stay until the marriage. You need no additional instructions."

Why is Colonel Lamaze stalling for time? Merryk's intuition may be accurate. Did I bring a risk with me? Merryk is so considerate and has such blue eyes. Do I really get to choose?

"I am considering several dates," Tara said. "I will advise you of my decision. Now, Colonel Lamaze, we will continue our walk. You may leave or walk quietly behind us."

Tara turned to Merryk. "Shall we?"

Chapter Forty-Five

DECISION

T ara returned to her room, threw her fur coat across the end of the bed, and went to warm herself in front of the fire.

Nan entered the room. "Where is Yvette?"

"She has gone to find Nelly to get an extra set of pillows," Tara replied.

"How was your walk with Prince Merryk?"

"Interesting," Tara said. "He wants me to delay the wedding date, so we have time to get to know each other. He thinks we are both in danger until the wedding. It is a dilemma: time to know each other, but at increased risk."

"Or he needs more time to plan his next attack."

"Nan, why would you say such a thing?"

"I need to remind you again, these people are not trustworthy. How would your father analyze this request?"

"I do not want father's bias to cloud my relationship with Prince Merryk. I wanted to give him a fair chance. I want to believe I can trust him."

"What does Colonel Lamaze think?"

"He wants to wait until he gets instructions from father. However, the contract will not change. There can be only one outcome, my wedding. Waiting will change nothing." Frustration crept into Tara's voice.

"I am confused. As the man, Prince Merryk can just tell you when you are to marry. Why did he even bother to ask?"

"He said it was my choice."

"Unlikely, but if it is your choice, then ask for something in exchange."

"Like what?"

Nan walked around the room while she thought. Finally, she replied, "Tell him you prefer to marry immediately, but ask him to promise not to be intimate without your permission, to wait until you are ready. You will then be in control. If he agrees, you can wait to be a husband and wife until you know whether you can trust him."

"This seems extreme."

"Only if you are smitten by him, which you say you are not. I can help provide proof of union for the wedding night. You deserve to know whether you can trust this man. Later, when you believe he is trustworthy, you can become husband and wife. In this way, you will choose and you will be safe."

Tara's eyes brightened as a smile appeared. "Prince Merryk said he wanted more time for us to get to know each other. This would give safety and the opportunity to become acquainted."

"This must be our secret," Nan added. "You cannot tell anyone, except Merryk. There is much depending on your wedding. If discovered as a fraud, there would be a great deal of trouble."

Tara turned and threw her arms around Nan in an enormous hug. "Thank you for being here to help me."

"I will always be here for you. Now, when do you want the wedding?" Nan said.

Tara did not answer, but grabbed her coat from the foot of the bed.

"Tara, where are you going?" Nan asked.

"To find Merryk," she said. Looking back over her shoulder, she saw a broad smile had covered Nan's face.

Stepping out the door to the hall, she moved to the closest Teardrop guard. "Please take me to Master Smallfolks," she said.

The guards turned and moved down the hall toward Smallfolks' room.

Finding Smallfolks, she said, "I need to find Prince Merryk."

"He is inspecting the cofferdams at the back of the castle," he replied.

Tara again turned to the Teardrop guard. "Do you know where this is?"

The guard nodded.

"Please, take me there."

One of Natas' Dragoons suggested, "We should wait for Colonel Lamaze."

Tara looked at him sternly and said, "Now, please."

Tara followed the guards along the top of the outer castle wall to its northernmost point. The closer she got to the back edge, the more she saw a lake churning with the early spring runoff.

At the end of the castle wall, she looked over the edge into a gorge blocked by a wooden dam. Near the bottom of the dam, forty feet below, Prince Merryk was inspecting each row of logs, one by one.

Now there is my woodsman, she thought as she looked at the plainly dressed prince.

"Merryk," she called.

Prince Merryk turned, looked up and waved. "Stay there. I will come up."

Minutes passed before the prince made his way from the bottom of the gorge back to the top of the castle wall.

"What is this?" Tara asked.

"Last fall we built this cofferdam to push the water to the other side of the bar of land we call the 'Finger,'" he said, pointing in its direction. "Every spring for at least the last fifty years, the water has flowed on this side and in front of the castle, flooding the plain, and trapping everyone inside. This year we are attempting to return the flow to its old path."

"You are moving a river?" she asked in a tone of amazement.

"More like putting it back where it belongs."

"Was this your idea?"

"Yes."

He is definitely not a simpleton.

Changing the subject, Tara turned to him. "I have an idea that may solve our dilemma."

Merryk looked around at the guards. "Gentlemen, if you could please give us a moment." The guards moved a discreet distance away.

Tara continued. "I agree, we need to marry to stop the threat and the sooner the better. However, we both would like to have more time to get to know each other before we become man and wife." Tara looked down, uncertain of how to proceed, and then focused on Merryk as she made the next statement. "I propose we marry quickly, but you promise we will not be intimate until I am ready."

"I would never seek to do anything that you did not want." Merryk let out a sigh of relief. "This would solve many problems. I agree."

He agreed quickly. Perhaps he does not want to marry me.

"To make everyone believe we consummated the marriage, we will need to provide proof. I can take care of providing the evidence," Tara said.

"You have given this significant thought. If we are discovered, I can only imagine the repercussions."

"No one will know, except you and me." *You are lying to him. No reason to tell him about Nan's involvement. What are you doing? You asked for time to determine if you can trust him and start off by lying to him. What about him trusting you?*

"You have my word of honor," Merryk said. "I will not touch you without your permission." He extended his hand to seal the bargain.

Tara took his hand to shake it. *How can a hand be so strong and yet so gentle at the same time? Maybe I do not want to wait to feel his touch.*

Tara abruptly let go of Merryk's hand, took a deep breath, and tried to hide the glowing blush flooding her face.

"Now, take me back to the castle. I have a wedding to plan," Tara said, grabbing Merryk by the arm.

CHAPTER FORTY-SIX

FRIENDS

Yvette moved down the hall toward Nelly's quarters. Rounding the corner, she was met by Colonel Lamaze and two of his guards.

"Yvette, I wanted to talk with you," Colonel Lamaze said. Then turning to the guards, "You may go ahead. I will be right behind you." Both guards continued down the hall.

"What can you possibly want to talk to me about?"

Colonel Lamaze gripped Yvette's arm and pushed her against the wall. "We both know what kind of woman you are. You are stuck in this castle with no real men. I need to be sure you take advantage of me before I leave," he said as his other hand moved down the throat line of her blouse.

Slapping his hand away, she said, "I am a lady, and you are old enough to be my father."

"You are no lady," snapped Colonel Lamaze.

From behind the colonel came the voice of General Yonn, "Lady Yvette, is there a problem?"

Colonel Lamaze turned to find Yonn and two Teardrop Guards just feet away. "This is none of your concern. Go away."

"I am not speaking to you, colonel. Lady Yvette, may I escort you to your destination?"

"Yes, thank you," Yvette replied, shaking free of Colonel Lamaze's grip.

Colonel Lamaze's hand moved to the pommel of his sword. General Yonn did likewise. The colonel's eyes scanned his opponents. The numbers were not in his favor. "You are not worth it," he said, looking at Yvette. "The two of you deserve each other, a pretend lady with a pretend general." He turned and stomped down the hall.

Yonn looked to his guards. "Be sure he gets back to the barracks."

The two guards nodded.

Yvette and Yonn walked in the opposite direction. "Thank you," she said.

"I am sorry he insulted you," Yonn said.

"In truth, I do not have the best reputation. It seems I have terrible judgment in men. In a new place, my mother thought I might find a landed sheepherder to marry, someone unaware of my indiscretions."

"Sorry, but we do not have many sheep," Yonn said as his face filled with his infectious smile.

"Just my luck," Yvette chuckled, as she reached out to slide her arm through Yonn's. "Maybe I will find a dashing general instead."

Yonn stopped and gently removed Yvette's arm and turned to face her. "I am afraid your poor judgment with men has struck again. I am only a castle rat. I was born to the stable master's wife, who died shortly after I was born. I was raised as a stable hand. When the Lord General came for men, the swordmaster went to Chancellor Goldblatt and asked I be made an officer, to avoid conscription. My reputation in our kingdom, filled with widows and lonely wives, is well known and not admirable. I am not the right choice for a contessa."

Yonn saw the surprise on Yvette's face, but continued, "You can do better. Contessa Yvette, you need to remember, no one here knows anything about your past indiscretions. In the Teardrop, you are the beautiful lady-in-waiting to Princess Tarareese. A lady beyond reproach, who is wise enough not to be romantically associated with the pretend General of the Guard."

"The man who saved us on the road, who is protecting us in the castle, and who came to the defense of my honor, is a genuine officer."

"Thank you, but we need to just be friends. Prince Merryk and Princess Tarareese will be married, and we will be together often. I cannot allow your ability to support the princess to be endangered. Anything beyond friendship could make your task difficult. My past would make others think poorly of you. I am sure you understand."

Yvette replied, "I understand, but it does not mean I like it."

Chapter Forty-Seven

ADVICE

Immediately after Tara had left the room, Nan followed her out the door to find Colonel Lamaze. Just outside the barracks, she met the colonel, accompanied by two Teardrop Guards.

"Colonel Lamaze, could we talk?" Nan asked.

The colonel stopped and turned to the guardsmen. "Could you give me a moment?" The guards moved out of earshot, but they did not leave.

"Princess Tarareese has just announced the wedding date."

"She cannot do that," he said.

"She can and has. I have spoken with her. She believes, accurately, the marriage contract is binding and any delays would be futile. She plans to marry on Saturday."

"Saturday is only three days away. I must change her mind."

"I believe that will be difficult. Young Prince Merryk has captured her attention. I am working on a plan, but I need your help."

"King Natas told me to support you in any way I can."

"We need to take the shine off this handsome prince to create doubt and uncertainty. Perhaps the contessa could help us?" Nan asked.

"I fear Contessa Yvette has already reverted to indiscretion. I saw her with the fake General Yonn. She will be of no help."

The colonel stroked the sides of his beard. After several moments of thought, he replied, "I have an idea."

———— ❧ ————

Princess Tara returned to her chambers with a bounce in her step and a broad smile on her face. "I am getting married," she announced to Yvette as she entered the room.

"Of course you are."

"No, I am getting married on Saturday."

"This Saturday!"

Tara nodded. "Merryk and I agreed not to wait. He thinks I am still in danger."

"He may be right." Yvette said as she rubbed her arm where Colonel Lamaze had gripped her just moments earlier in the hall.

"Why do you say that?" Tara asked.

"Not important," Yvette said. To change the subject, she scurried to get some paper. "We have much to do. Where should we start?"

Colonel Lamaze and Lieutenant Jordan interrupted their discussion.

"We need to speak with you," Colonel Lamaze said. "It is important." Looking at Yvette, he added, "Alone, if possible."

Princess Tara nodded toward Yvette. "Please, I will get back with you right away."

As soon as Yvette had left the room, the colonel continued, "I sent Lieutenant Jordan this morning to review the area where you were attacked. He found some interesting things. I will allow him to explain."

Lieutenant Jordan was a slender younger man and cut from the same bolt of military cloth as Colonel Lamaze. He stood in front of the princess in a solid, upright position, and spoke with confidence.

"As Colonel Lamaze said, I returned to the point of the attack this morning to review the scene and to gain a better understanding of what happened. Yesterday, we were concerned with your safety and only quickly searched the bodies. Except today, there were no bodies. "

"Animals?"

"No, Your Highness, men had been on the site. Evidence showed tracks leading toward the east and others returning to the castle. Yesterday, I recovered two small daggers and some pieces of cloth, both with the colors and markings of the northern clans. Also, the four bodies did not look like they had been killed at the site."

Colonel Lamaze interjected, "Suggesting they were killed somewhere else and dropped there. The lack of blood on the ground was the clue. Did any of Prince Merryk's men search the bodies?"

"I do not believe so, but I was focused on getting away."

Colonel Lamaze responded, "Understandable. I have been attempting to rationalize the attack and the miraculous appearance of the woodsman. How fortunate he was there, unless it was planned and the whole thing staged."

"Why would anyone fake an attack?"

"The only reason I can think of is to make you fearful, perhaps to push the wedding date forward."

The princess interrupted him, "How many men did we bring, colonel?"

"Ten."

"If we brought ten men and two were killed at the site, and another on the way to the castle, why do we have eight now?"

Lieutenant Jordan quickly responded, "We had ten men and two officers. Now we have the colonel and me and seven soldiers."

"Merryk told me the harbormaster said ten soldiers and one colonel got off of the boat."

Colonel Lamaze said, "He must have missed the Lieutenant. Why do you ask?"

"Not important," Princess Tara said. "You know Prince Merryk does not trust you."

"I do not trust him. Although he is charming enough, I believe the actual force behind him is Chancellor Goldblatt, who has a reputation for plots and schemes. This push for a rapid marriage could be such a scheme. Princess Tarareese, I believe you are still in danger. You must remember you cannot trust these people."

"At least on that issue, both you and Prince Merryk agree. Colonel Lamaze, I appreciate your advice. I will carefully filter everything I hear and remain cautious of Prince Merryk and others. However, the marriage contract is clear, it may not be delayed by more than a few days. The wedding must be this Saturday."

"We wanted you to have all the information. We will continue to serve you in whatever way you think best," Colonel Lamaze said, and Lieutenant Jordan nodded in agreement. Excusing themselves, they left the room, leaving Princess Tara alone.

Standing by the crackling fire, her mind reviewed the discussions of the day. *Colonel Lamaze was not aware of the letter of instruction from the Provost demanding an immediate wedding. He does not know Prince Merryk would have preferred a delay and asked me to consider it. However, because of concern for my life, he made it my decision.*

Colonel Lamaze might believe the attack was staged; except he does not know Prince Merryk was the woodsman. It would be foolish to stage an attack and then be present to be identified as the protector. Prince Merryk has shown no signs of making such a simple error.

The face of the man who hit the door with an ax in his back was filled with surprise. He was not already dead and dropped at the site.

Also, the colonel does not know about the shouted order to kill in our native tongue. The attackers were from my homeland.

However, Colonel Lamaze has been in my father's service virtually all of my life. He is right to suggest I should trust him before Prince Merryk. Perhaps neither of them should be trusted. I am thankful I have Nan to help me.

Princess Tara stepped to the door. Looking for a Teardrop guard, she said, "Please ask the swordmaster to come see me."

"Yes, Your Highness."

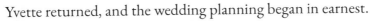

Yvette returned, and the wedding planning began in earnest.

"We should ask Nelly to join us," Yvette suggested. "She will know what is available and how to get what we need."

"I agree." Tara stopped, wrapped her arms around herself to quiet her internal shaking. "This is all happening so fast, so many things moving at the same time. Queen Amanda was right. Getting married is both exciting and frightening."

There was a knock. Yvette opened the door to find the swordmaster.

"Your Highness asked to see me?"

"Yes," replied Princess Tara. "I have a quick question. How long were Lieutenant Jordan and his men outside the castle walls this morning?"

A puzzled look flashed across the swordmaster's face. "I am confused, Your Highness. No member of the Dragoons has been outside the castle wall since they arrived. Prince Merryk, Captain Yonn, and I are all to be told, even if there is a request. I would have known if they had left."

"I must have misunderstood. Thank you, swordmaster."

The swordmaster turned and left the room.

Yvette looked at Tara. "What was that all about?"

"Something my father taught me. Never substitute trust for caution."

CHAPTER FORTY-EIGHT

HORSES AND CHILDREN

The next day, Nelly joined Tara and Yvette to discuss the wedding plans. By late morning, they had made significant progress: the locations for the ceremony and the reception, the menu for the banquet, and a partial guest list. Nan sat on the outskirts of the group, listening intently. She was more congenial than in previous days, but still grumbling about her accommodations.

As the planning continued, Princess Tara asked, "What about the local priest? Should we include him?"

"I am not sure that would be a good idea, Your Highness," Nelly said. "Prince Merryk and Father Aubry have had some difficulties. I would suggest you speak with the prince directly."

"Good idea. Where is he this morning?"

"Probably in the stables. I can check." Nelly replied.

"No need. We will look for him. I could use a break and some fresh air."

Yvette looked at Nelly with a large smile on her face. "The mention of stables was all she needed. Like her father, she loves horses."

Nelly stood. "With your permission, I would like to take care of a few things. The guards will come and get me when you return."

In a matter of moments, Tara and Yvette gathered their coats and, with their guards in tow, headed toward the stables.

"You were looking for a reason to see Prince Merryk anyway," Yvette said confidentially.

"I cannot imagine what you mean," Tara said as both broke into giggles.

Entering the stables, Tara saw it was large and well-designed with neat rows of stalls but held few horses. The smell of fresh hay and animals enveloped her. It brought back wonderful memories. A part of her hoped to find her white mare, Bella, in one stall. *Hopefully father will send her in the summer.*

"Does this not remind you of home? Tara asked.

"Oh yes, one of my favorite parts," Yvette answered with no small amount of sarcasm.

Halfway down the row, a beautiful black stallion attracted her eye. "Well, hello, big boy," Tara said in a smooth and comforting voice.

The stallion moved to hang its head over the rail for attention. Tara moved forward and rubbed the side of his neck.

"You not s'pose to be here," a small voice said, floating in from above Princess Tara's head.

It took a moment for Tara to locate the source. A small sandy-haired girl, not over three or four, was sitting on a stack of hay. "Better be careful," she said. "That horse is Prince Merryk's. Name is Maverick. He not like anyone, 'cept the prince and me."

"I have always believed horses know who they can trust. I think they are smarter than many people."

"Maverick is smarter than most people, but not Prince Merryk. Nobody smarter than him."

Both Yvette and Princess Tara could not help but laugh at the obvious devotion the small waif had for the prince. "My name is Tara, and this is Contessa Yvette."

"I am Maizie. You pretty," she replied.

"Do you know where to find Prince Merryk?"

"Yes, he be right back. He told me to stay put." The word 'put' was said with a crisp tone and the nod of Maizie's head.

Before the conversation could continue, Prince Merryk came into the stable and joined the gathering. "I see you ladies have met."

"This Tara and Tessa," Maizie said.

"She has been warning me about your horse," Princess Tara said, pointing to Maverick, who still stood at the edge of the stall, listening to the conversation.

"Between the horse and this girl, I'm not sure who is the most precocious," Prince Merryk said.

"I have a few questions about the wedding, if you have a moment," Tara asked.

"First, let me show you where Maizie lives." Prince Merryk reached up and plucked the tiny girl from the stack of hay, turned her upside down, spun her around twice and finally settled her on his shoulders. During the entire process of being tussled, the air was filled with a never-ending string of the giggles. Prince Merryk carried Maizie around the end of the stable toward a long row of buildings which lay on the inside of the castle wall.

As they moved closer, Tara saw there were more children of various ages scampering around. The older children appeared focused on tasks. There was a garden patch and a chicken coop. Finally, Prince Merryk stopped and turned into one building.

Princess Tara and Yvette followed into the building. "What am I looking at?" Tara asked as she scanned the large room. An oversized fireplace roared on one side, providing light and warmth. Additional light streamed into the room through open panels on the front wall. The room extended into an eating area filled with a large table and multiple chairs.

Clusters of additional chairs, tables, and cozy sofas filled the space in the large front room. One wall had a large slate surface attached to the wall. The letters of the alphabet ran across the top and numbers one through ten along the side. An aroma of warm bread and soup filled the space. It was busy and populated by clean and tidy children.

"This is the living room and the school," Prince Merryk answered. "This is where Maizie and the other children live." Merryk lifted Maizie off his shoulders. "Go ask Jane if you can ring the bell." Maizie darted like a little rabbit toward the kitchen area, where she greeted an older girl who nodded her head. Returning to Prince Merryk, she yelled, "Pick me up! Pick me up! I ring the bell!"

Prince Merryk again scooped up the little bundle of energy and moved her to a metal triangle hanging just outside the door. Maizie grabbed the metal rod and pounded vigorously. Well, at least as vigorously as possible for a four-year-old.

Tara and Yvette watched in fascination as the children appeared and headed toward a basin.

"This is amazing," Princess Tara said. "What are they doing?"

"All must wash their hands before they can eat," Prince Merryk said.

Yvette commented, "I would have expected chaos, but they seem so well ordered."

"They help grow the food," Prince Merryk said. Pointing to the older one, "Jane, one of them, prepares the food with help from Nelly. They are all very independent and very proud of their home," Prince Merryk explained. "When we found them, the older boys were committing petty crimes to be put in jail. They passed part of their food out the windows in the evening to help feed the others. They were living from place to place, always in danger. All were orphans or abandoned. We simply gave them a protected space, and they have done the rest.

"I helped the older boys to get jobs with long-term professions. We have apprentices that are blacksmiths, stonemasons, and we have our own rat catcher, exterminator. They return in the evenings after their day's work. Everything they earn, they share with the others."

The children, after washing up, went to the table and took their assigned seats. Jane followed with a big bowl of hot soup, whose fragrance they had smelled earlier. There was also warm bread with butter and honey, followed by mugs of milk. Prince Merryk walked around the edge of the table, talking with each child.

Look at him. He knows each one of them and they know him. He has a very special way with these children. He will make a fantastic father.

As Prince Merryk moved around the table, he came to two boys that were approximately the same height. Summoning Tara, Merryk said, "Princess Tarareese, I would like you to meet JoJo and John. Both are seven." Turning to the boys, "See, I told you she was pretty."

JoJo shook his head from side to side. "No, you said she was beautiful."

"Yes, beautiful," agreed John, shaking his head up-and-down. "You said she was beautiful, not pretty."

Princess Tara could not help but smile, and for the first time, she saw Merryk blush. "Very pleased to meet you," she said, extending her hands to both.

Merryk looked at the boys with a stern eye. "Well, which is it: pretty or beautiful?"

Both stopped eating and stared at Princess Tara.

"Well," followed by a pause, "I think beautiful," said JoJo.

"Yes, I agree, beautiful, just like Prince Merryk said," John added.

"I did not," Prince Merryk said.

"Oh yes, you did," both boys replied in unison.

Prince Merryk rubbed the heads of both. "The two of you have caused enough trouble. Now eat your lunch and then get back to your chores." With no further encouragement, the two eagerly returned to their food.

"Children. You can never trust what they say."

Prince Merryk followed Princess Tara and Yvette into the courtyard.

"What you have done with these children," Yvette said, "is amazing, but is this not the duty of the church?"

"In an ideal world perhaps, but as a practical matter, the church does not have the money. They are required to send all the tithes to the Council, who use it for the new cathedral and the Army of Justice. This happens while the local churches fall into disrepair. Nothing is left, not even money for children."

"You do not sound like a believer," Tara said.

"There is a difference between belief and blind obedience to a human organization. Faith is not dependent on money, but organized religion often forgets their primary purpose is to serve the people."

"I intended to ask if the local priest, Father Aubry, should take part in the wedding ceremony."

Prince Merryk emphatically replied, "No! Six months after the children came to the castle, Father Aubry showed up unannounced to review their condition. He became enraged when he saw we were teaching them how to read, write, and count."

"I do not see why that would be a problem," Tara responded.

"In Father Aubry's opinion, it is a problem if you teach girls. Without discussion, he grabbed two children—JoJo and Maizie—to drag them from the castle. Maizie screamed to attract attention. Father Aubry slapped her. Maverick heard her scream. JoJo told me Maverick cleared the top rail of the corral by at least a foot, then blocked Father Aubry's exit. JoJo escaped and went to find Yonn and the guards. Father Aubry held tight to Maizie.

"I also heard the scream. When I arrived, Father Aubry had grabbed a rake to move Maverick out of the way. I told him if he hurt either the girl or the horse, I would kill him. It was probably not the most diplomatic thing to say, but it was how I felt. He said I had no authority over him, and he had a right to take the children if he chose.

"I declared they were my personal wards and, as a result, were my responsibility and none of his concern. Father Aubry did not like this answer. He finally let go of Maizie. I told Maverick to take her into the stables. Father Aubry said I could not touch him. Yonn arrived with guards, and they forcefully 'assisted' him from the castle grounds. So, no. He need not attend the wedding."

"All of this over teaching girls to read. Why not just agree?" Yvette asked.

Prince Merryk turned to her and in a much softer voice said, "Yvette, teaching the girls to read and write ensures they will teach their children. As a kingdom, we will only grow with an educated population. We can't do great things without great people, which means educated people. Small-minded men like Father Aubry will only destroy our future."

Princess Tara watched the exchange between Yvette and Merryk.

"I understand completely," Princess Tara said. "No Father Aubry."

Prince Merryk returned to the stables and the two ladies proceeded back into the castle.

"Do you believe what Prince Merryk said about teaching girls to educate the next generation?" Yvette asked.

"Absolutely. You and I would never let our children grow up without knowing how to read and write. However, some believe education is for the noble families or just for men. They fear education would cause the general people to believe they are more important than they are."

"I find Prince Merryk's accepting children as his personal wards amazing, not a normal thing for a royal man. I wonder, do you think Prince Merryk would allow me to help with the children?"

"I am sure he would," Tara replied. "Just ask."

Chapter Forty-Nine

WEDDING DAY

Princess Tara hugged her robe tightly as she looked out the window toward the floodplain and the distant hills. She acknowledged it would take some time to get used to this bleaker environment. The wedding day had opened brightly, but it had the chill she was coming to expect of a spring day in the Teardrop Kingdom. Sunlight glimmered off the frost, which still lay on the blades of grass. A few early flowers dotted the landscape with small bursts of color. There were fewer flowers at this time of year than she would have seen at home.

A knock on the door interrupted her internal observations. "Enter," she said, without turning to the door.

Colonel Lamaze entered. "Your Highness, I came to check on you this morning."

"I am fine, thank you."

"I want to let you know I still think it is a mistake to be pressured into this marriage. The nature of the attack is very disconcerting. If they staged it to hasten the wedding, you could play into their hands. You cannot trust them. You should wait until you have further instructions from your father."

"Do not worry, I am not blindly trusting anyone. Colonel, the wedding will proceed. Now wait outside. I will advise you when I am ready to go to the chapel."

"Yes, Your Highness."

——— ❈ ———

Nan had been in and out of Tara's room most of the morning, bringing an assortment of items Tara would need for the day, including the special dress her mother had sent. Finally, Nan turned to Tara. "All is working as planned. I have placed a small vial for you in the drawer. Do you know what to do?"

"Yes, after I drop the contents of the vial onto the bridal cloth, I will hand it out the door to the priest. He will show it to Colonel Lamaze and Chancellor Goldblatt to complete the marriage contract."

"Please remember to make it look as realistic as possible. Tell Prince Merryk he needs to help create the illusion of a consummated marriage."

"Then all I have to do," Princess Tara said, "is make it through the two weeks of the honeymoon."

Princess Tara turned and looked at Nan. "I still have concerns about all of this."

Nan placed her hands on Tara's shoulders, as she had done many times in her lifetime. "Tara, please remember this will give you choices. You get to be the one that chooses, not your father or Prince Merryk. Prince Merryk appears to be kind enough, but you cannot trust his family."

"I am not marrying his family. He has been nothing but kind to me, but very well, I understand. Now please get Yvette, so she can help me with my dress."

——— ❈ ———

Yvette entered the room with her normal bouncy flare and a radiant smile. "What an exciting day. Are you nervous?" Without waiting for answers, she continued, "Let us get you into your gown."

"I am glad mother insisted I bring my wedding dress," Tara said. "Mother said. 'you may go to the end of the earth, but you do not have to look like you belong there.'"

Yvette, finishing the last touches on the buttons on the back of the dress, said, "You look amazing."

"Thank you. I just wish my father and mother were here."

"Do not worry, everything will be all right," Yvette said. "You are just having normal bride jitters."

⁂

Princess Tara was not the only one having doubts this morning. Down the hall, Prince Merryk had transferred into the garb selected by Smallfolks. It looked very formal, including a sash that ran across the front, making him look even more regal and military. Merryk thought. *I have had enough military formalities in my past life, but I understand the need for it today.*

"Smallfolks, can you find Nelly for me?" Prince Merryk asked.

"Yes, Your Highness, but I think she is busy getting everything ready for the banquet."

"I need to talk with her before the wedding."

In a few minutes, Nelly scurried in. Her face was flushed. It was clear she had been busy overseeing the wedding details.

"Nelly, you have spent more time with Princess Tara than anyone else. Based on your impressions and, as a woman, what advice can you give me?"

"Prince Merryk, it is not my place to give you advice."

"Nelly, if I don't ask you, all I have left is Maizie. She has already told me we have enough princesses. Please, just tell me your impressions."

"Well, she is very poised, as you know, but she is not as confident as she seems. She decides quickly and relies heavily on the contessa, which is understandable. But Nan also seems to have her ear. While getting settled, I heard references to her father. Both women said he could sometimes be harsh. My guess is she may think all men are the same. I do not believe she will trust quickly. The advice I would give you is simple: be the man I know, and she will be a fool not to fall in love with you."

Merryk reached out and gave Nelly an enormous hug. "Thank you, Nelly. Now, tell me honestly, how do I look?"

❈

Merryk was not aware of the presence of a chapel on the second floor of the main castle until they selected it as the site for the wedding ceremony. Chancellor Goldblatt told him his grandmother had constructed the chapel for the occasions she and Great King Mikael came to visit the Teardrop. It was a relatively small room with two glass windows on each side of the altar. Today, the late afternoon sunlight streamed through the glass, illuminating the entire room, especially the spot where Father Xavier and Merryk were standing.

Chancellor Goldblatt and General Yonn, along with Smallfolks, who stood in the back of the room, represented those on Prince Merryk's behalf. Contessa Yvette and Lieutenant Jordan sat on Princess Tara's side. Nan also stood discreetly in the back. All waited for Princess Tara to arrive.

Colorful bouquets of wildflowers from the surrounding hills filled vases set along the aisle and under each window. The room was filled with the slight fragrance of the spring flowers and a flood of warm sunlight.

Colonel Lamaze and Princess Tara entered the room. They had given the colonel the honor of walking Princess Tara down the aisle. The afternoon light not only caught the place where the prince stood, but also sparkled off the beads and sequins on Princess Tara's gown. Merryk's eyes widened with a bright smile as he stepped forward to greet the colonel and the princess. Colonel Lamaze released Princess Tara's arm but held a glint in his eye that reflected his lack of support for the marriage. Merryk extended his arm to the princess. As she took it, he stopped for a moment and looked directly into her eyes. "I'm sorry we must marry here, rather than the Cathedral in the Capital City. The entire kingdom should see a bride as beautiful as you."

The compliment caught Princess Tara off balance. She felt a bright blush covering her face. *How can this man be so gracious, or is he being something else?*

Prince Merryk then turned and walked with the princess toward the priest. The ceremony continued to the predictable end, when the priest finished and said, "You may kiss your bride."

Princess Tara should have expected this, but she had not. Her eyes widened and her face flashed in fear. *If he kisses me, I will not want him to stop!*

Prince Merryk saw the look on her face. Again, a soft smile appeared on his face. He reached forward and gently kissed the back of her right hand.

Princess Tara felt a sense of relief and some disappointment. *I truly do not know what I want. All this is so I can choose and determine if I can trust him. Yet, I still feel the connection we had when we first met.*

With the ceremony completed, Prince Merryk and Princess Tara walked toward the Great Hall. Before they left the second floor, Tara asked, "May I have a moment with Yvette to freshen up before we go down?"

"Certainly."

Yvette joined Princess Tara as they entered a small study near the chapel.

"Prince Merryk looked fantastic, and the two of you make a beautiful couple," Yvette said.

"I think Prince Merryk attempted to flatter me. He told me a bride as beautiful as I should have been married in the Capital City for all to see."

"I am not sure he was attempting to flatter you. He was telling you the truth. You are exquisite, and he was showing his appreciation for you as his bride. But Tara, you seem more nervous than before the ceremony."

"Maybe it is just the reality of it all. I always knew what everything meant, but now it is real."

"Are you worried about tonight?"

Tara hesitated and stumbled with her voice, "No. But yes."

"How many times have we talked about what you would have to do? In the past, you seemed perfectly all right. Even when your sister taunted you about marrying 'a fat bellied king' or 'a stunted, simpleton prince.' Now you are upset with the 'real' Prince Merryk, who is charming, handsome, and all man."

"The fat bellied king and the stunted prince would have wanted me. I am not sure 'this' Prince Merryk does. He asked me to delay the wedding so we could get to know each other, but the Provost had instructed the priest to perform the wedding ceremony immediately."

Yvette was startled. "He wanted to postpone the wedding?"

Tara bobbed her head up and down in affirmation.

"Really?"

"But what if he never truly wants me?" *Yvette does not know of my and Nan's plan. It seemed like a good idea. Now I am not sure. But Prince Merryk quickly agreed. Maybe he does not want me.*

"Do not worry, I have seen the way he looks at you. I wish I could get General Yonn to look at me like that," she said with a large smile. "Now come on, put a smile back on your face. We have a wedding banquet to attend."

CHAPTER FIFTY

THE BANQUET

P rince Merryk and Princess Tara came down the wide stairwell into
the Great Hall. The Hall had been organized to form a square, with
tables on three sides. The fourth had a raised dais backed by the fireplace.
Candlesticks flickered on the tables. The chatter of guests filled the room.
Then came a momentary silence, followed by a round of applause, as the
prince and princess entered and moved to the head table.

They were joined there by Chancellor Goldblatt and General Yonn on
Merryk's side. Contessa Yvette, Colonel Lamaze, and Father Xavier sat
with the bride.

Merryk had given little thought to the guest list. His focus was on the
problem of protecting the princess. Somehow Princess Tara had, with
the help of Nelly and Smallfolks, identified the people from town who
were the most significant to him. The swordmaster sat at one table with
Smallfolks, who had objected to being seated at all. There were the two
blacksmiths and their wives who had been instrumental in his metal
developments. Marta and her two sons, and the key merchants, all were
included. The orphan children had a place at one corner of the square.
Jane sat close to Maizie and near to JoJo and the others. All were clean,
and Merryk noted, remarkably well behaved.

As the guests settled, Nelly and her assistants served the food. This was
a royal meal with multiple courses: salmon, roast pork, venison, duck, and

an assortment of root vegetables. The addition of the vegetables had been at Merryk's request. The final dessert course was honey cakes, dried fruit, and several types of cheese.

Everything was beautifully presented. Chancellor Goldblatt remarked it was a rare opportunity for the people of the Teardrop Kingdom to celebrate. When the dinner was through, there was a pause for a series of toasts and extensions of congratulations to the bride and groom. Afterward, local musicians arrived with woodwind instruments, a fiddle, and a drum instrument, all of which produced a cornucopia of sound. The added music did not lower the din of the people, who continued in animated speech, perhaps aided by an ample supply of wine.

The music had already started when Yvette turned to the couple. "It is time to dance, but we cannot dance until you and Prince Merryk go first." Merryk heard the words. If fear had flashed across Tara's face at the thought of a kiss, Merryk equally showed fear of having to dance in front of people. His mind filled with thoughts. *Do I do the twist, the robot, the funky chicken, or some form of the hokey pokey?* He decided the best thing to do was fess up. Turning to Princess Tara, "I don't know how to dance. Please show me."

"Very well," she said with a smile as she pulled him into the center of the square. "Hold my hand and put the other one lightly on my waist." As she moved, Merryk recognized a waltz-like movement with side steps and circles. Merryk tried, but without a reference, he was sure he looked like an ugly duckling bobbing around with his beautiful princess. Merryk beckoned to others. "Don't make me dance alone."

Colonel Lamaze quickly rose and turned to Contessa Yvette and asked for the dance. Yvette pushed away his hand. Rising, she went directly to General Yonn. "Will you dance with me?" Yonn needed little encouragement. He immediately extended his arm. The two joined the prince and princess on the dance floor, and soon others joined. Colonel Lamaze was left standing alone at the back of the table.

As the evening went on, Prince Merryk and Princess Tara went to each table to thank the guests for coming. Prince Merryk finally came to the children's table. "Tara, if you don't mind, I see two ladies who need to dance."

Tara replied, "I, also, see two gentlemen."

Merryk went to Jane and Maizie. "Ladies, would you like to dance?"

Jane was a little hesitant until she saw Prince Merryk intended to hold one of Maizie's hands and one of hers so the three of them could bounce in a circle to the beat of the music, or, at least as close to the beat as Maizie could interpret. A similar circumstance was being played out by Tara, JoJo, and John. The music was brisk and, fortunately for Merryk and Tara, relatively short.

There was much laughter and a general feeling of joy filling the room. Tara looked at Prince Merryk. "This is the way I had hoped to feel at my wedding banquet. I am very happy."

Her statement triggered an internal thought. *I still do not know what is right. I enjoy being given the time to choose, but to do it is to create a lie. I know my responsibility is to fulfill the agreements of my father, but I feel something more. I like this man.*

Shortly after the dance, Jane gathered the children and directed them to their home. JoJo grabbed extra honey cakes as he headed out the door. Merryk saw him and gave a big wink.

As the end of the celebrations arrived, Tara and Yvette excused themselves to go upstairs. Other members of the party soon left, while some stayed a little longer to enjoy the wine and music.

After the public rejection by the Contessa, Colonel Lamaze and Lieutenant Jordan had left the banquet. Smallfolks and the swordmaster joined Yonn and Chancellor Goldblatt at the head table. The group of men all moved close to Merryk. Merryk could feel a sense of awkwardness growing. "I know all of you may feel a need to give me some advice. But before you make fools of yourselves, I want you to know I am fine, and I know what I am to do. No advice will be necessary. That is a command," he said with all the authority his voice could produce.

"You are no fun," the swordmaster said, a ribald grin covering his face. "Not even a little advice?"

Merryk looked at the swordmaster. "Certainly not from you. How many wives have you had? Let me think. That would be none."

"I had advice about women, not wives," he replied with a chuckle.

Chancellor Goldblatt interceded, "Your command will be honored, but we all wish the very best for you and the princess. A toast."

As Prince Merryk headed toward the stairwell, Chancellor Goldblatt caught him. "A word, please, Your Highness. The priest, Colonel Lamaze, and I will be just outside the door. I will see the formalities of the marriage contract are completed. Perhaps when we are through, we can return to normal."

"A normal life would be nice. Thank you, Chancellor," replied the prince.

CHAPTER FIFTY-ONE

WEDDING NIGHT

Four guards stood outside the princess's room: two Teardrop Guardsmen, and two Royal Dragoons. Merryk nodded to the swordmaster who had taken up one post.

My people are concerned about my safety, and until the evening is over, there will be danger. 'My people.' An interesting change in my perception.

Merryk gently knocked before entering. The room was lit by the light of small candles and a fire sparkling from the hearth. A slight smell of honey and a touch of perfume flavored the air. It took a few moments for Merryk's eyes to adjust to the dim light and a few more to locate Princess Tara, who stood near the dressing room. She wore a diaphanous nightgown which draped off her shoulders and extended to the floor. Little bursts of light from the fire shot through the fabric, revealing more than Princess Tara may have intended.

"Did the contessa help you pick your gown?"

"Yes. How did you know?"

"Just a guess. It is beautiful." Changing the subject, he continued. "Did you enjoy the banquet?"

"Yes, it was very nice. Everybody seemed to have a good time."

"Tara, thank you for dancing with the children. I know it meant a lot to them."

"They were so excited to be included; they would have bounced around the room without the music."

"I hope I did not embarrass you with my clumsy dancing."

"No, you were good to try. By the end of the evening, you seemed to get better."

"Or you had enough wine to forgive my stumbling."

"I, like you, had very little wine," Princess Tara said as she walked over to the fireplace.

She doesn't understand how her gown is reacting to the light or she would move away from the brighter source, nor does she understand the impact this is having on me, or maybe she does. Being mentally old enough to control myself is one thing, but controlling my younger body's hormones is something else.

"Would you like some wine now?" Merryk said, motioning to the nearby tray.

"Yes," she replied, "wine might be helpful. I am very nervous. Are you still sure about our agreement?"

"I am if you are. I never want you to feel compelled to do anything you do not want."

"There is a risk."

"I understand, but as long as only the two of us know, there should not be a problem."

Tara turned her face away from Merryk and moved to the sofa. Merryk poured the wine and handed it to the princess.

"We need to make this look realistic," Tara said.

"I agree. Your perfect hair does not seem very realistic. If you will allow me." Merryk removed the pins from her hair and allowed it to bounce on Tara's shoulders and then ruffled her hair. "That is better."

"Is there anything else while you are adjusting my appearance?"

"Well, your gown would have some wrinkles."

Without waiting, Tara reached down and grabbed the bottom of the gown and rolled it up to just above her knees, scrunching it as she went along. Dropping back down, the fabric showed the creases. "That should work. Now for you," Tara said, "I am sure you would not still be wearing your jacket and boots."

Merryk responded by removing his sash and coat and, sitting on the armchair, removed his shoes and socks. "Anything else?"

"Your shirt needs to at least be unbuttoned and you would not be so neat."

Prince Merryk untied the string of his trousers to allow him to pull out the shirt. He then unbuttoned the shirt, revealing his broad chest and three neat rows of abdominal muscles.

"Better," she said, "but your hair." She moved over to stand in front of Merryk, reached up to remove the ribbon holding his hair back, and ran her hands through it. She held his head, one hand on each side, and looked into his deep blue eyes. Being so close affected her, she could feel her face turning to a glowing red. Taking a deep breath, "That seems better," she said stepping away.

"Now the bed," Merryk said as he grabbed the top blankets and pulled them toward the foot of the bed. Underneath the blankets was the marriage cloth, placed halfway between the top and bottom of the bed. Tara disappeared into the dressing room, returning in a few moments with a small vial.

"This needs to be in the center of the cloth," she said, handing the vial to Merryk.

Merryk dumped its contents onto the sheet. "That should provide appropriate proof." Turning to look at Tara, Merryk said, "We now have our first shared secret."

Tara did not make eye contact with Merryk, but she grabbed the cloth and folded it to present to the priest. *Our secret and Nan's.*

Tara slipped on a robe and walked over to the door, partially opening it. Father Xavier, Chancellor Goldblatt, and Colonel Lamaze were sitting just down the hall. The priest responded immediately and took the cloth. "Are you all right, my dear?"

The question caught her by surprise. *I am lying to the priest.*

Before she could answer, Merryk stepped up behind her and placed his hand on her shoulder. "Time to come back to bed," he said in a soft voice.

His touch further flustered Tara. Without a word, she shut the door and turned back into the room, and bumped directly into Merryk. For a moment, her head rested on his warm chest. In that moment, her mind raced. *This is not what I want. I do not want to pretend. I want to be married to this man.* Tara moved her arms up to pull Merryk's head down to her.

"Excuse me for a moment," Merryk said, as he stepped past her to reopen the door.

"Swordmaster, advise General Yonn to tell Colonel Lamaze it is time for him and his men to escort the priest back to the Provost. They are no longer needed here."

"Yes, Your Highness." The swordmaster nodded.

The break allowed Tara to regain her composure. *Distance is the only way not to fall into this man's arms.* She moved to the far side of the bed and straightened the blankets.

"So, you will sleep on that side of the bed?" Merryk asked.

"And you will sleep on the sofa," Tara replied.

Merryk laughed. "There is no way I'm sleeping on the sofa for two weeks. We will share the bed."

Sleeping with him in the same bed is not the distance I need.

Merryk looked at the bed. "There are three blankets. You will sleep under all three, and I will sleep under two. There will be a blanket between us. Sufficient to protect your honor and besides, why would I have executed our plan and then attack you in your sleep? You have my word. You will be safe."

Tara's mind wandered. *The one who may not be safe from attack is you.* "I am not a good person to sleep with."

"You must get used to it. Also, do not attempt to steal all the blankets to make me leave."

"I would never do such a thing," Princess Tara said indignantly.

The discussion appeared to be over as Merryk removed his shirt and slid into his side of the bed.

"Are you going to at least wear a nightshirt?"

Merryk glanced back over his shoulder. "I'm wearing more than I normally would."

"What would you normally wear to bed?"

"Nothing," Merryk replied.

This answer was not what the princess expected. *I am glad the light is low. My cheeks are burning from embarrassment or from something else.*

Soon, both of them settled into their sides of the bed and after a few moments of silence, Merryk asked, "Tara, are you awake?"

"Yes."

"I just want you to know you were an exquisite bride. I am pleased to be your husband and looking forward to the opportunity to get to know you." One might have expected a reply, but only silence followed.

After about three or four minutes, there was a response. "Merryk, are you awake?"

"Yes."

"I just wanted you to know I was planning on stealing the blankets."

"I know. Now get some sleep and sweet dreams."

Chapter Fifty-Two

NEXT DAY

I t had been a long time since Merryk woke up with somebody in his bed. Tara had pressed her back against him and lay gently, sleeping. The morning sun broke across the horizon and sent filtered light into the room. Merryk didn't want to wake Tara, but once stirred by the light, Merryk's habits pushed him to the top of the tower for his morning exercises. Quietly, he slipped out of the room. He needed a little extra aggressive exercise to burn off the tension from the previous evening. When finished, he headed down the tower to his own room to freshen up and change. His mind had wandered all morning, making it difficult for him to focus.

Tara is intelligent and beautiful, but so young. For a moment last night, I thought she would abandon the plan. I would not have been able to say 'no.' This younger body has some advantages, but raging hormones is not one of them. I'm glad we will get to know each other, but my younger self has other thoughts and is screaming 'sooner' rather than 'later.'

Princess Tara awoke, still feeling the pressure of Merryk behind her back. She lay quietly, not wanting to wake him, and then she realized he was gone. He had carefully placed his pillow in the exact position so she would believe he was there. *That is funny, but in some ways considerate.*

She stirred from the bed, and within a brief period, there was a knock on the door.

Nan entered and scanned the room to be sure Merryk was nowhere near. "Where is Prince Merryk this morning?"

"I do not know. He was gone when I woke up."

"How did last night go?"

"Everything went according to plan. You are right, Nan, he is a gentleman."

"Gentleman or not, I am sure he will soon start asking questions about your father to gain information. Remember, he cannot be trusted." Nan started to say more, but there was another knock on the door.

This time Yvette came through the door. She had an enormous grin on her face. "How are you this morning?" she said in an exaggerated tone.

"I am just fine," replied Tara in the same exaggerated way. Tara looked at Nan. "That will be all for now."

After Nan left the room Yvette said, "Okay, tell me everything."

"I have no obligation to tell you anything."

"There must be something."

"Yes, I will tell you he is a very warm person to sleep near."

"Warm 'ha.' How did he like your gown?" Yvette asked with a broad smile. "Did he notice at all?"

"Yes, I am sure he noticed my gown. He even asked if you had helped pick it out."

"I knew he would notice."

Both women laughed.

Directly after meeting with Tara, Nan made her way to the barracks. It took a few minutes, but she located Colonel Lamaze sitting with Lieutenant Jordan in the mess hall attached to the barracks.

"I need to speak with you," Nan said.

"You can speak in front of Lieutenant Jordan."

Nan was hesitant, but proceeded. "Very well. My plan is going as I had predicted. I have already contacted the local priest, Father Aubry."

Colonel Lamaze responded, "Good, because we have been ordered to accompany Father Xavier back to the Provost. General Yonn instructed us last night we were no longer needed and should plan on leaving today. We depart with the priest at noon."

"I can get a message to the priest but need to find a way for him to communicate with King Natas," Nan said.

"I expected that," Colonel Lamaze said. "I am leaving Lieutenant Jordan at the port. Here is an additional bag of coins to help Father Aubry get information to the lieutenant."

Lieutenant Jordan looked back at Nan. "I will stay in the port under the pretense of waiting to catch another ship directly to King Natas. I will do this while Colonel Lamaze and the other men escort the priest to the Provost. Father Aubry can find me in the large inn you stayed at when you arrived."

"Very well," said Nan. "I am confident my plan will go forward, but it may be a few days or even weeks before I have the information we need."

"Good luck," Colonel Lamaze said.

Colonel Lamaze and the Royal Dragoons gathered around the carriage, waiting to leave. Chancellor Goldblatt, Princess Tara, and Prince Merryk came out to say goodbye to the priest.

Chancellor Goldblatt said, "I hope you have a pleasant journey home, and one far less eventful than your trip here."

Prince Merryk shook Father Xavier's hand. "Please give my regards to Father Bernard and the Provost."

Colonel Lamaze turned to Princess Tara. "I hope you will be safe here without the presence of your father's dragoons."

"I am confident Prince Merryk will protect me. You need not worry, Colonel Lamaze."

Colonel Lamaze and his men mounted their horses as the priest got into the carriage. Just as they were leaving, a group of ten Teardrop guards, led by the swordmaster, came around the corner. "What is this?" Colonel Lamaze asked.

Prince Merryk looked at him with a wily smile. "We don't want you getting lost on the way to the port, now do we? Have a pleasant journey, Colonel Lamaze."

The colonel sneered, turned his back to the prince, and led the entourage out the castle gate.

As evening came, Prince Merryk joined Princess Tara in the dining room. Princess Tara looked at Prince Merryk. "I know our duties will carry us apart during the daytime. But I would like you to promise, if it is at all possible, we will always have dinner together."

"That should not be a problem," Prince Merryk said.

"No," Princess Tara said. "I want you to promise we will have dinner together, even if we are angry with each other."

"I promise, even though you have not given me cause to be angry with you. Is this something I should worry about from now on?" he said with a grin.

"Only if you give me a good reason," she said, raising her eyebrows in disapproval. Tara softened her face and explained, "When I was little, my mother and father would let their arguments destroy any family dinner. They would go days without being in the same room. I promised myself, if I had a family, we would at least come together for dinner."

"My mother and father would fight," Merryk said, "but they always seemed to understand whatever caused it was less important than the two of them and our family. I completely understand and promise, even if we are angry."

After dinner, they moved back to Tara's room. "What are we going to do for the next two weeks?" Tara asked.

"We should use this opportunity to get to know each other. We should talk about our past, things we would like for the future, and see what things we have in common."

"Do you play cards or chess?" Tara asked.

"Yes, I play chess and, depending on the game, cards."

Tara retrieved a deck of cards and explained a new game to Merryk.

"Do you have questions about me?" Prince Merryk asked as he lost for the third time.

Princess Tara stopped playing. "The one thing I cannot understand is why you are so different from the description they gave us? Most of the time, people make themselves seem better than they are, but you hid who you are. Bluntly, they described you as a simpleton, a bent and stunted individual. You are none of those things. Why did you hide who you really are?"

Prince Merryk thought for a moment. "Prior to my coming to the Teardrop, the description you had of me was, in all honesty, very accurate. There are many things from before my injury I cannot remember. In fact, I remember very little of my childhood, other than what I have been told by Chancellor Goldblatt. I do not remember the faces of my mother, father, or my brother. I know this seems strange. I know their names and who they are, but I don't have a picture of them in my mind."

"Chancellor Goldblatt told me, as a young boy, my older brother and two older cousins bullied me. They made my life a living hell; constantly tormenting, teasing, and doing everything they could to humiliate me. Chancellor Goldblatt said the impact was I became bent over and retreated into myself. I was quiet and shy."

"Smallfolks confirmed I was virtually skin and bones when I arrived. And true to the description you received, I was badly bent over from trying not to attract attention. After I recovered from my injury, I attempted to improve my strength and engaged seriously in my studies. I can say it took almost a year for me to straighten my back. The nutritious food from Nelly, and the warm companionship of those around me, gave me the confidence to become a better student and a stronger person. I have engaged in a series of exercises over the past two years to improve my strength. As a result, I became the man you see today."

"How strange not to remember anything about your youth. Sometimes I think not remembering things could be a blessing," Princess Tara said. "Is there anything that you would like to ask me?"

"I would like to know, were you taught to cheat at cards or are you a natural?"

Fortunately for Merryk, the closest thing for Tara to grab was a sofa pillow.

CHAPTER FIFTY-THREE

HONEYMOON

The next morning, shortly after dawn, Prince Merryk rose for his daily exercises. He was gone for only a few minutes when Tara awakened. She stepped to the door to ask about the prince, but there were no guards. She changed into her clothes and wandered down the hall. Finding Smallfolks, whose eyes were barely open, she asked, "Smallfolks, can you tell me where I can find Prince Merryk?"

"Yes, Your Highness. This time of day, he will be on top of the old tower doing his exercises."

"How do I get there?"

"Well, it is a steep climb. Go to the end of this corridor, then go straight up. You cannot miss it."

"Thank you," Tara said.

Smallfolks was right about the tower. It was narrow and steep, built long before the other parts of the castle. Tara finally made her way to the top and opened the door to the bright spring sunshine. A breeze flashed across the top of the tower, making her shiver, but leaving her invigorated. Wishing she had brought a coat, she gripped tightly to her shawl and looked out across the valley surrounding the castle. The early spring was taking the brown of winter and converting it into a light green. There were patches of flowers, like the ones used in the wedding, popping up across the hills.

The distant mountains were still capped with snow. The entire view was spectacular.

Prince Merryk was near the side of the tower, going through a series of slow movements. "What are you doing?"

Prince Merryk stopped to look at Princess Tara. The morning sun sparkled off her blonde hair and illuminated her smile. "Good morning. I am doing an ancient exercise called 'tai chi.' It is a series of combat motions reduced to the very basic form to allow mastery of each move."

"This looks a lot like fancy dancing," Princess Tara said.

Merryk smiled. "Yes, I guess it looks a little like fancy dancing, but in truth, it is more."

Unbeknownst to Princess Tara, she was not the only one who had ascended the tower steps. Standing just outside the slightly opened door was Nan, who had opened the door just enough to see and hear. She mumbled a single phrase, "Fancy dancing."

The next few days fell into a pattern. Merryk rose early and went upstairs to exercise. Often Tara followed and watched as he performed the tai chi exercises, which were fluid and melodious, followed by other exercises which were more aggressive.

Virtually every day, Prince Merryk and Princess Tara went out for a ride. Prince Merryk had picked a spirited horse for Princess Tara. "I know you are an excellent horsewoman, and I did not want to insult you by giving you a horse that does not match your skills."

"If you want to give me a horse to match my skills, you would let me ride Maverick."

"There are many things I will allow you to do," Prince Merryk said with a broad grin, "but riding my horse is not one. You are *only* my wife." They both laughed.

Princess Tara joined Prince Merryk each day as he anxiously watched as the water built up behind the wooden dam. She had heard his original description but had not focused on the intricacies. Now Prince Merryk described the purpose of the dam, and how it was constructed. "Last spring, the water ran through the gap and up the sides to over twenty feet high. The flow was so massive, it covered the entire floodplain in front of the castle in a brown torrent. This year, because of the dam, the water has moved to the other side of the Finger, to its original riverbed," Prince Merryk explained.

"Why are you concerned about the dam now?" Tara asked.

"The higher the water rises, the greater the pressure on the structure. I have attempted to calculate the amount of pressure, but working with wood differs from stone. I want to be sure it will not break and devastate all in its path. It seems both strong and high enough to shift the water, but I don't know how much water will come. It depends on the amount of snow, and how fast it melts." Prince Merryk said.

While on these visits, Prince Merryk also described another project. He wanted to create what he called *locks;* a series of boxes to lift people and goods above the falls on the other side of the Finger.

"Last year I met members of the Blue-and-White Mountain Clans who had come to the Teardrop to buy salt. They had to transport the salt by mule from here to the mountains. With the locks, we could get the salt to the base of the mountains, saving them almost three days, and opening an opportunity to transport goods or move the point of sale closer. "

"Salt," Princess Tara said, remembering. "You really irritated my father."

"Yes, Chancellor Goldblatt said he was afraid my method of calculating the exact weight of the salt would cause some difficulty."

"Difficulty. Let us just say there will be a new person selling salt this coming year."

"Well, I have been working on a technique for creating our own salt from seawater. It is time consuming, but will give us enough salt that we may not need to buy any from your father, and it may allow us to meet the needs of the mountain clans."

Princess Tara laughed, "I thought you wanted my father to like you."

"I am more concerned about my people," Prince Merryk said.

———⬧———

Tara spent more and more time with Merryk each day: riding, visiting the dam, or, on rainy days, visiting him in his workshop.

Merryk's workshop was an intriguing place filled with unusual items: tools made for surveying, a model of the lock system, prototypes of axes, sketches of plows, boxes for bees.

There was something genuinely interesting about him. He was more than just the nobleman she had expected. He cared about the people of the Teardrop. Tara had never met a man like Prince Merryk. He had the same keen intellect she had seen in her father, but also a commonness which engendered extreme loyalty. Most intriguing were his eyes. They were not just a beautiful blue, but they had a depth, reflecting a sense of understanding. *His eyes see things, not just observe them. I have only seen such intensity once before, in my father. However, there is a kindness in Merryk's eyes I never saw in my father.*

Each night, they had dinner together and then returned to Princess Tara's chambers. Rather than running out of things to talk about, they always seemed to find more. Whether it was the dam, the locks, salt, or horses, there was no end to what they could discuss. Tara knew she would have been captivated by this man even if he were not her husband.

After the first week, as Prince Merryk prepared to go to bed, he discovered Tara had removed one blanket from the bed.

"Tara, why have you removed the extra blanket?"

"I have decided I can trust you. If you have not attempted to take advantage of me to this point, I have no reason to believe that you will.

And if you do so, I know a single blanket will not stop you. In addition, having you trap me under the blanket is uncomfortable."

Two days later, Merryk awakened to find Tara's head lying on his shoulder. She had one arm across his chest and one knee up over his leg. Merryk's younger self was delighted to find Tara so closely attached to him. However, Merryk's older self realized the peril involved in such closeness. He quietly extricated himself from Tara's grasp before she roused.

The days slipped into a familiar pattern of rides and talks. The one other constant was Nan. Every morning she asked, "Did Merryk ask about your father last night?"

"No Nan, he did not ask about my father last night."

"He will. It is just a matter of time."

"Nan, I do not know why you are so leery of Prince Merryk. He has done nothing but take care of us."

"You cannot trust him. His family wanted the dowry, and now they will want political information. The only way they can get it is by Prince Merryk questioning you about your father. If he did not want information, he would have pressed you to become his wife, fully."

"Or," Tara said. "he is honoring the promise he made to not do anything until I was ready."

"That is naïve," Nan said. "He is a man. The only reason he would wait is if he needs something from you or if he does not find you appealing."

"What a terrible thing to say!"

"Nevertheless, it is only a matter of time before he asks about your father."

Chapter Fifty-Four

YVETTE

T he more time Tara spent with Merryk, the less she had with Yvette. Yvette thought she would miss the relationship with her lifelong friend, but new things captured her interest. For some unexplainable reason, educating the girls to teach the children of the future fascinated her. Merryk had given her permission to assist. She helped with letters and simple words with the younger children and reading with the older ones. She left the numbers to Merryk.

As time passed, she grew fond of her students. The little one, Maizie, who called her "Tessa," a form of her title "Contessa," found a special place in her heart, although Yvette knew she would always be second to Maizie's fondness for Prince Merryk. Maizie told Yvette the story about how Prince Merryk had come on his big horse, picked her up from the barn in the middle of a stormy night and brought her to safety. *A tale to remember for a lifetime, being saved by a handsome prince on a stormy night.*

She was a precocious little girl who always had something to say. Sometimes Maizie's opinions would have been best kept to herself, but at four, she was not the slightest bit intimidated. Yvette thought, *perhaps this outspokenness is what I find so appealing.*

The second thing to occupy Yvette was spending more time with Captain Yonn. Yonn had reverted to the title "Captain" after Colonel Lamaze left.

He joked to Yvette, "I guess I had the shortest tenure in history as a general. Nevertheless, it served the purpose of protecting everyone."

Yvette chuckled at Yonn's comments. "Well, you were an excellent general."

"Other than I did not have an army, just the thirty men of the Guard."

"It is not the strength of the army that makes the general, it is the strength of the general," she said, attempting to flatter Yonn.

On their daily rides with Tara and Merryk, riding a discrete distance behind, they could talk. In all of Yvette's life, she had never been with a man where the only thing they did was talk. She found Captain Yonn's history to be very interesting. He was an amazing man. Yonn had lost his mother early, had his father taken away by war, and he had grown from being the stable boy to Captain of the Guard. She had seen how he acted when danger had threatened. He was every bit the captain. And she told him so often.

Captain Yonn found the story of Yvette equally interesting.

"I was born to a noble family and at an early age selected to be a personal companion to the Princess Tarareese. I did not want to leave my family, but soon found Tara to be a wonderful friend. During our early childhoods, we were both left alone by our mothers and fathers. For the first time, I found another person who understood my loneliness. I have told no one that before," she confided in Yonn.

As the days moved on, Yvette grew closer and closer to Yonn. *I want to be more than just friends. Am I just reverting to my old ways? I do not know how Yonn will respond. He feels inferior and that his past indiscretions make it impossible for him to love someone like me or have them love him.* The word *love* in her thoughts caught her by surprise. She never thought about falling in love herself. As she watched the relationship between Tara and Merryk grow, she had to admit she was becoming more infatuated with the captain as each day passed.

———✿———

"They seem to get along nicely," Yvette said as they rode behind the two.

"Yes," Yonn replied. "But there is still something missing between the two of them. I cannot identify it. They are close, but not as close as I would have expected."

"I know what you mean. It is as though they are good friends but have not accepted they are husband and wife."

CHAPTER FIFTY-FIVE
CONFLICT

Tara had become accustomed to Merryk's presence. She looked forward to each night cuddling up beside him and drifting off to sleep. She told Yvette he was very warm, but he was more than warm. He was comfortable and safe. She could not remember the last time she had felt as secure as when tucked in next to Merryk.

The two-week official honeymoon had reached the last night.

"I think we should play chess tonight," Merryk said as they returned to Tara's room.

"Why chess?" Tara asked.

"Because chess gives you less opportunity to cheat."

"I do not cheat," she said indignantly. They both had broad smiles, understanding this playful banter would be ongoing.

As they played, Merryk said, "I have told you after my injury, I cannot remember my childhood. You have said little about your family. I know your father is a powerful king, but when he was not being a king, how was he as a father and husband?"

Tara's mind flashed. *My father is a hurtful man. He beats my mother. They sleep in separate rooms. Father only visits my mother once or twice a month and often leaves her bruised and bloody. Mother defends him as being under pressure, but he is just a brutal man. She says this is just the way we are, or it was her fault for arguing with him. I cannot tell these things to Merryk.*

This is just the information that would hurt my father's reputation. Is this just the first of many questions?

Is this what Nan meant, he would seek information about my father? Was she right all along? He was not to be trusted? Is the reason he has not attempted to touch me because he does not care for me? I was a foolish girl, believing I could find love. I should have remembered he is "royal," and everything will have a purpose.

Tara stiffened as she pushed away from the table. Her tone shifted from playful to abrupt. "Why are you asking about my father? Are you trying to gain political information for your benefit? Does your father want to know our strategic plans? Is that the only reason you have been nice to me for the last two weeks? You just wanted to gain my confidence so I would trust you and now you are trying to ply me for information?"

Merryk had never seen Tara like this. His face filled with surprise, not only by the content of her reply, but by the intensity of her reaction. "I just wanted to know if you wanted a man who treated you like your father treats your mother. I don't care about his politics. That is my father's problem."

"How my father treats my mother is none of your business," her voice crackled with anger.

Merryk took a deep breath and attempted to clarify his question. "Often, the only example a woman has of a husband is her father. I was asking, do you want a man like your father or someone different? I was looking for guidance on how I could be a better husband for you. My affection for you has nothing to do with politics, but everything to do with you."

Tara shook her head from side to side. "I was told I could not trust you." *I cannot tell him I am embarrassed by my father's treatment of my mother, or tell him he hit her often, or that the last thing I want is a man like my father as a husband. Nan was right.* "No," she screamed. "This was never about me. You wanted political information to use against my father. I cannot trust you."

Frustration overcame Merryk. Tara's responses showed he could not reason with her, so Merryk did the only rational thing. He stood up and gathered his jacket.

"I have done nothing to justify your lack of trust, but if this is how you feel, then so be it. I think our honeymoon is over. Tomorrow, I will have my things moved back to my room. Good evening." And with that, Prince Merryk left.

Tara suddenly recognized she had driven Merryk away and may very well have hurt him. *But he deserved it. He just wanted information about my father.* Confusion swept over Tara as she reviewed the conversation over and over.

Unfortunately, Nan was the first to find Tara alone in her bedroom crying.

"I take no joy in being right. I told you, you could not trust him. His willingness to not want a genuine marriage only proved he wanted the dowry and information, and never you. We should let your father know right away so we can save you from this sham marriage." Nan hit all the right points with Tara as she set her trap.

"Yes, we need to tell my father. But how?"

Without hesitation Nan replied, "Do not worry, I will take care of it. I will get the information to him. Where is Prince Merryk now?"

"He went back to his room."

"Good, this will allow you to keep a distance between the two of you so he cannot ask for more information. You should work to keep away from him as much as you can."

It was the following morning before Yvette came to Tara's room. Tara was still crying, as she had done most of the night. Tara explained what happened, as only one could to a best friend. She concluded by saying, "He betrayed me."

"Or," Yvette said, "Merryk was asking what kind of husband you wanted. You and I know you do not want a man like your father. I would not wish that kind of person on anyone. You know what he does to your mother."

"But no one else knows," Tara said.

"Exactly! Maybe Merryk did not care about the politics or the money. He was just trying to please you."

"I thought you were my friend."

"I am your friend," Yvette said, "but he is your husband. You need to talk to him."

"No, I had forgotten he is *royal*. Everything he does has a purpose. I was foolish to believe I could find love in this backwater castle. He is not the handsome woodsman I first saw."

"Of course he is not a woodsman."

"Yes, he *is,* or *was* the woodsman who saved us."

"Prince Merryk was the woodsman! No wonder you did not want me looking to reward him."

"I dreamed he would rescue my life with love. But he never loved me. He just wanted information and money. My father trained me to be smarter. I should have been more cautious, as Nan suggested."

"If Nan suggested it, you know it is wrong. She only does what your father wants, regardless of who gets hurt. What else is Nan telling you?"

"I need to stay away from Merryk and think about what my father would want."

"This is about you and Merryk, not Merryk and your father. You need to fix this."

"I would not know how, and I do not want to. I hate this man. I thought you were my friend," she said again. Her voice was filled with frustration and pain.

"A friend often tells you things you may not want to hear. I think you are treating Merryk too harshly. He has given you every benefit of the doubt and you appear to have given him none."

"I do not want to talk about this anymore," Tara said. The truth Yvette had given her was causing frustration and confusion. "I think it would be best if you went away and left me alone."

Yvette looked at her lifelong friend. "I will go, if you absolutely want me to, but I think it would be better if I just stayed, even if we do not talk."

"Suit yourself," Tara said. And then broke into tears.

Chapter Fifty-Six

FOOD, FIRE AND THOUGHT

Without Prince Merryk to focus on, Princess Tara searched for Yvette. She found her working with the children in their home, teaching the younger children to write their letters with chalk on pieces of slate.

When Maizie saw Tara, she immediately left the table and came to her. "Why mean to Prince Merryk?"

"Have you not been taught it is polite to say good morning first?"

"Good morning. Why you mean to Prince Merryk?"

"Who says I am being mean?"

"Everyone, even Maverick."

"The horse. How does he know?"

"I told him."

"Of course you did."

Before the discussion could spin further out of control, Yvette intervened, "Maizie, leave Princess Tara alone and go back to your letters."

Maizie stomped off, unhappy with the lack of answers from the princess.

"Does everyone know about my dispute with Prince Merryk?"

"This is a small castle."

"Which explains this morning. Everyone was polite, but few smiles."

"What are you going to do?"

"What can I do? I will just ignore them."

"Ignore the only people you will see for the rest of your life?"

"Are you sure you are on my side?"

Changing the subject, Yvette asked, "What are you wearing to dinner tonight?"

"Why?"

"Prince Merryk invited Yonn and me to join the two of you for dinner."

"He did?" Tara said with a sigh of exasperation.

"What is wrong?"

"I made Merryk promise we would have dinner together even if we were angry. I hate this man." She said, rubbing her eyes and shaking her head from side to side.

"You hate him for keeping his promise?"

Tara gave Yvette a look of exasperation. "Are you sure you are on my side?"

Fire is a complex element; in its simplest form, it provides heat and light. However, a sparkling fireplace or gentle campfire is also an excellent vehicle for introspection.

A contemplative Tara sat wrapped in a warm robe, staring into the fireplace—her own personal oracle. Her fingers traced the rim of a hot cup of tea as the fragrance of honey wafted up from the surface of the liquid. She watched the embers shine brightly and flicker out, only to be replaced by others. Only the push of the wind against a shutter interrupted the silence of the castle. She was alone in thought.

Father said whenever faced with a problem, the first step is to break it down into individual parts, test each separately, and then reassemble the distilled

*facts. Nan believes I cannot trust Merryk because he wanted the dowry
and now political information. Yvette believes I rejected Merryk because my
father's treatment of mother embarrassed me and did not want to tell him
the truth. Both Nan and Yvette have my best interests at heart. Can they both
be correct?*

*Merryk wanted the dowry, at least his father did. We had a contract of
marriage exactly for this purpose. Wanting the dowry is not a surprise. It was
expected. Nan says Merryk cannot be trusted because he wants information
about father—political information. But Merryk only asked what kind
of father and husband he was. Even if Merryk had asked about political
matters, would this be unusual? Father told me to gain control of Merryk so
we could use his knowledge against King Michael. Father expects me to gather
information for him. Would it be unrealistic to believe Merryk's father had
not asked him to do the same? We are royal. We will have multiple motives.*

*What information would King Michael want? A better question is, what
kind of information do I have? Father said he raised me to be a queen. Before
they betrothed me to King Hauge, the fat king, father confided in me. I sat in
his meetings, and we talked often. I knew a great deal about his plans. After
the first marriage contract was signed, father became more distant, including
me less and less. When King Hauge died, father immediately looked for
another groom, but he did not invite me into the discussions as before. When I
think of it, I do not have any actual information—apparently by design. I do
not even know why he wanted this marriage. Was it land, access to markets,
money? Father put me in a position to learn, but not to provide facts. At worst,
I can trust Merryk to be royal. He will ask, and so will I.*

*Yvette said my embarrassment caused my reaction. Perhaps all husbands
beat their wives; it is just an unspoken truth. I believe it would take a
harshness I have not seen in Merryk for him to beat me, even if I deserved
it. I saw disappointment in his eyes when I accused him. That hurt me worse
than a blow, although father's slap is something to avoid.*

Yvette was right, I was embarrassed. I was also afraid of what his question meant. Merryk was asking about how to be the husband I wanted. He was thinking about our life together, and now I have pushed him away. Worse, with Nan's help, I have deceived him into placing his trust in me and have put him in real peril. If I can stop the message to my father, perhaps I can fix this.

Dinner was nothing like I had expected. Prince Merryk was talkative and cheerful. He asked about my day and listened to me. He gave an update on the dam and commented about the right time to place the beehives on the floodplain. Having Yonn and Yvette at the table helped smooth the evening. Merryk talked with everyone as though nothing was wrong. Does this mean he is all right with us being distant?

Maybe Nan is right. He never really cared for me.

Could I trust this man with my heart? I may never know.

Why am I so confused? I cannot take my eyes off him when he is near.

Oh, I hate this man!

Chapter Fifty-Seven

MORE QUESTIONS

A light rain—just enough to settle the dust—greeted Willem, the Teardrop courier, as he set out from the port heading to the Teardrop Castle. Although he delivered messages and small packages year-round, this delivery to the castle seemed the most important. Today his pouch carried the first foreign correspondence of the new season. Warmer temperatures and calmer waters had finally opened the port, a little later than usual. Tucked within his weathered leather satchel were foreign letters for the people of the Teardrop Kingdom. However, the largest bundle was always directed to Chancellor Goldblatt. At the end of each season, he carried many letters from the Chancellor directed to distant lands and kingdoms. Today was the day the Chancellor would get his responses.

Three hours into his journey, Willem came across George, the grain merchant's oldest son, traveling fast in the opposite direction.

"Good morning, George," Willem said.

"Good morning, Willem."

"What are you doing so far away from the castle on this fine day?" Willem asked.

"Father Aubry hired me to deliver a message to one of those red caped Dragoons at the inn. He even gave me his horse for the task."

"Not trying to take away my work, are you? I could have delivered it for him."

"Guess it was something kind of important. Said he could not wait for you."

"I will have to watch so you do not steal my job," a smiling Willem said as he tucked his long gray hair back into his big-brimmed hat.

"Do not worry. Just one day on a horse is enough for me. I cannot imagine having to do this every day. I better be going. Father Aubry said not to stop and talk along the way. Good day to you, Willem."

"Good day George."

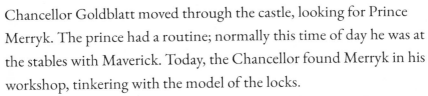

Chancellor Goldblatt moved through the castle, looking for Prince Merryk. The prince had a routine; normally this time of day he was at the stables with Maverick. Today, the Chancellor found Merryk in his workshop, tinkering with the model of the locks.

"How are the locks coming?" Chancellor Goldblatt asked.

"I am pleased with the progress," Merryk said. "What brings you out here?"

"Earlier today," Goldblatt started, "I received the first set of correspondence from abroad. There have been several interesting developments since the port closed last fall. I have not read them all, but I picked some key ones, and they provide some interesting insights."

"What have you learned?" Prince Merryk asked, shifting his attention to the Chancellor.

"First, we caused quite a stir by delivering the tax collector, Jarvis, back to the Capital City in irons. Everyone assumed they would never hold tax collectors accountable for whatever they did in the process of collection. The Lord Commander was furious anyone had interfered with one of his tax collectors. King Michael said it appeared your actions were justified in stopping an assault by the tax collector. The next surprise came when the Lord Commander said he would send a new tax collector right away. King Michael advised him this was unnecessary because he would have you collect the taxes in the Teardrop. Anything encroaching upon the Lord Commander's authority was a direct attack. The two argued, but the king did not relent.

"King Michael said you sent Jarvis back to him for punishment. The Lord Commander asked for permission to punish Jarvis, himself. The king said he will allow him to punish Jarvis, because he was his man. But, if it is determined he stole money, the king would sentence him to death. The Lord Commander asserted there was no sign he had taken money, only abused his power. So, he felt stripping him of his title should be sufficient. It is my understanding the king never shared with anyone he had received taxes from us earlier. "

"What did the Lord Commander do to Jarvis?" Prince Merryk asked.

"It appears he put him on a small stipend and removed him as a tax collector. Other than that, nothing."

"This does not sound like my uncle. He is not a forgiving man. I cannot imagine he would allow a tax collector like Jarvis to continue to live, particularly knowing Jarvis understood he was taking money out of the tax receipts."

"I also find that interesting. Perhaps the Lord Commander was sending a message to the other collectors. He would protect them."

"After the return of Jarvis, the rest of the revenue in the kingdom returned to standard levels. So, after an unusual period of low receipts, suddenly everything went back to normal. As a result, they had enough money to pay off the loans, although just barely. I still believe if required to return the dowry, it will be a problem."

Prince Merryk moved away from the table model. "It seems the Lord Commander was attempting to cover his tracks; not wanting the king to spend any time making inquiries about other tax collectors."

"My assumption also," Chancellor Goldblatt replied.

"The next thing in my correspondence was curious. Ernest, the old scholar who works in the archives in the Capital City, is a friend. I have known him since we were boys. He said the Lord Commander came to ask about an ancient prophecy. This is unusual, because the Lord Commander is not a scholar, nor has he ever shown interest in the archives."

"What did he ask?" Merryk inquired.

"He asked about a rather obscure prophecy, in an old language. Something about a man, coming from a great distance, to unify the world under one kingdom. It is filled with obtuse language and words with multiple meanings. The word for *under* could mean *lead, rule, or direct*. This lore has many versions in many lands. Under the prophecy, this kingdom will *last or grow* for over 1000 years."

"Interesting," Merryk said.

"After the Lord Commander received the information, he, with the aid of a Royal Scribe, sent a letter to King Natas, describing the prophecy and some additional discussion about the power of kings granted by the gods."

"I have heard this described differently as 'the divine right of kings,' an implicit right granted to royalty by God to govern other men. A right given by birth. It is a bunch of bunk," Merryk said.

Merryk returned his attention to the Lord Commander. "I still don't understand my uncle's actions. He is skimming money out of the tax revenues for himself and uses men like Jarvis to do so. He had his tax collectors in place, and they were taking money, possibly for years, without being noticed. Then this year, he reduces the amount of taxes going to the king, putting the new ships in jeopardy. This requires a loan which is sold to King Natas. The second half of the dowry would have been enough to pay the loans for the ships. My death, with lower revenues, would have resulted in a default on the loans and the return of the first half of the dowry; a combination which would put my father in peril. The king would lose the ships and perhaps be required to grant some other kinds of concessions.

"King Natas would gain. But what is in this for my uncle? Could my uncle be working with King Natas to get the ships or access to the Inland Passage? None of this explains the attack on the princess. We still don't have enough information. "

"I have several other facts," Chancellor Goldblatt added. "There was one correspondence from King Natas saying not to worry about the marriage. It was not likely."

"But if revenues were up and they failed to kill me, then the marriage would go through and they would pay the remaining dowry, losing leverage over my father. Still, they attempted to stop the wedding by killing Tara. Perhaps King Natas did not have the money for the dowry? But why would my uncle care? They must have a common purpose we are missing."

"I do not know if this has any impact," Chancellor Goldblatt said, "but the harbormaster talked with the captain of the ship that brought Princess Tara. They gave him double his normal fee, half paid in front and the other half guaranteed to anyone he designated if he did not come back. Suggesting even the trip across the ocean intentionally put Princess Tara's life in danger."

"It implies King Natas was behind the attack on his daughter, but doesn't explain why."

"One more thing. Willem, the courier, crossed paths this morning with George, the son of the grain merchant, who was delivering a message from Father Aubry to a Dragoon. Willem did not get any idea of the content."

"Why don't we ask the older boys and guards to monitor who visits Father Aubry?"

"Someone from the castle, you think?"

"I do not know. However, we need to be watchful."

CHAPTER FIFTY-EIGHT

LIBRARY

Several days later, Yvette entered Tara's room with her standard bouncing step. Tara sat at the desk under the window, working on a piece of paper with a straight edge and quill.

"Good morning. What are you doing?"

"Woman stuff."

"Woman stuff?"

"Yes. Prince Merryk thinks I need something to do, so he asked me to organize the library. Obviously, this is the thing a woman can do."

"Why not give the task to Nelly? She would have it done in no time."

"I have the distinct impression he wants me to do it. At least he seems to acknowledge I am *a woman*."

"Have you figured out how to come to a resolution with him?"

"No, I do not think he even finds me attractive. He makes all our contacts brief."

"Is this what he wants or what you want?"

"At first, I was all right with the distance. But now, I would prefer we acted like friends. I miss him. Intellectually, I miss our discussions."

"I am sure it is all intellectual." Yvette did nothing to hide her mocking grin.

"In any event, I am finished," Tara said, as she looked down at the neatly drawn representation of the room with desks and chairs.

———— ❦ ————

The next morning, Princess Tara joined Prince Merryk and Chancellor Goldblatt in the study to review the plans. Both men sat around the low table in front of the fireplace.

Chancellor Goldblatt's study always impressed Tara. It had the look of a place of learning. Many objects, other than books, filled the shelves. Colored rocks, leaves, and even a butterfly on a thin pedestal were carefully placed among the books. The sun always seemed to fill the room with a special glow. Its position in the castle made it impervious to the constant drafts that haunted the halls.

"You got this done far quicker than I expected," Prince Merryk said.

Princess Tara was a little insulted by his comment. "It was not a grueling task," she said as she placed the diagram on the table in front of the two men.

Prince Merryk looked at the drawing for a moment. He seemed baffled by what he saw. "Tara, I believe I have done you a disservice. My request did not express the task at hand."

Tara's mind raced. *I always do everything well. How could this be insufficient?*

"I wanted you to organize the library. I did not mean tables and chairs. I wanted you to take the lead in organizing the knowledge of the library. We have books on many topics, but we do not have any way to find the information in the books. Chancellor Goldblatt knows the content of many of the books, but how do others find them? How do we find the right book on the right subject?"

Both Princess Tara and Chancellor Goldblatt looked at each other in surprise. "Do you mean you want all the books in one place?" Tara asked.

"Not necessarily. It is important we know how to find them, and their exact content."

"What do you mean by organization?" Tara asked, now unsure of the expected task.

"I was thinking perhaps three cards for each book: the title, the author, the subject. When we have a question, we can search by whichever we believe is best."

"By subject?" Chancellor Goldblatt asked. "How do you suggest we do that when there are so many topics?"

"We organize by major topics and then do subdivisions under each. For example, animals, followed by vertebrates and invertebrates; then by cold blooded or warm blooded. The sciences will be easiest. Take mathematics. It is the major category, then the progressive subcategories: arithmetic—adding and subtracting; algebra—the math of unknown numbers and fixed variables; geometry—the mathematics of shapes; trigonometry—the subject of angles; calculus—the math of derivatives and integrals of functions; then, the more complex math, like quantitative analysis and ultimately physics."

Tara turned to Goldblatt only to see a look of surprise; one she was sure also ran across her face.

Prince Merryk's tone turned serious. "Tara, Chancellor Goldblatt told me you are perhaps the best educated woman in the world. This is an immense project and needs an educated person to see it to completion. You are the very best choice. The Chancellor and I can help, but the task primarily falls to you.

"Why don't I leave you and the Chancellor to discuss how you want to proceed? I promised Maizie I would read her a story this morning."

Silence filled the room as Prince Merryk left, only broken when Chancellor Goldblatt grabbed the diagram, turned it over, and began scribbling intensely.

"What are you doing?" Tara asked.

"I am trying to record what Prince Merryk said before I forget. Have you ever heard of some of the mathematics he described?"

"I thought you instructed him in mathematics."

"Yes, but only for a brief time. After that, his knowledge eclipsed mine. I do not know what some of those were: trigonometry, calculus. I will have to add them to the list."

"What list?"

"The list of things Merryk knows, but has no way to know. It is a lengthy list. Merryk is a most unusual man. Many times, I just nod my head rather than letting him know I do not understand."

"We both have that in common."

"I believe my lack of understanding is a little different from yours. I would remind you he has a big heart, just give him a little time. I will work with you on this project, but he is right. This is an enormous task—organizing human knowledge."

"Picking chairs was much easier."

———— ❧ ————

Tara found Yvette sitting on a bench inside the courtyard, talking with Yonn. Yonn rose as Tara approached.

"Good afternoon, Your Highness," he said as he passed her.

"I hope I did not interrupt your discussion," Tara said.

"No, we were through. How was your meeting with Prince Merryk?" Yvette asked.

"Not what I expected. He wants me to organize the information in the library so we can locate it as needed."

"I thought he was giving you the *womanly* task of arranging the furniture. This sounds like a task for a scholar, not a royal *woman.*"

"Exactly. This makes it more confusing. If he wanted me to select chairs, I knew at least he recognized me as a woman. Now, organizing the library means he recognizes me as a scholar. I do not know which I prefer. I still cannot figure out if he likes me. He rushed off again after the brief meeting."

"Is it possible for him to like you and appreciate your scholarship?"

"I do not know. He is so frustrating," Tara said as she paced around the bench. "I hate this man."

CHAPTER FIFTY-NINE

INFORMATION

The rains of spring had given way to the warm glow of summer. The hills surrounding the castle erupted with a variety of greens. The grass on the floodplain created a verdant carpet, broken only by points of vivid color from the wildflowers. The view outside her window constantly surprised Tara. Each morning, she would hasten to see what new combination of color and light the castle valley would present.

Moving away from the window, Tara turned to Yvette. "I decided I will talk with Merryk."

"It is about time. What exactly are you going to talk about?"

"Nan believes he only acted interested in me because of the dowry and a desire for information about my father. They have the dowry. If Nan is right, now it must be about the information."

"What information is that?" Yvette said as she plopped down on the edge of the bed.

"I do not know, but whatever he wants to know, I will tell him. Then he will not have any reason to flatter me."

"Flatter you?"

"Yes, I am sure he asked me to work on the library to curry favor. He must want something. Rather than just waiting, I will ask," she said with a determined voice.

"Nan may know something about children, but I am sure she does not know much about men. I see the way Merryk looks at you when he thinks no one else is watching. His thoughts are not focused on your political assets."

Giggles flowed from the two women.

"Nevertheless, I will talk with him about politics."

"Are you sure you would not rather talk to him about moving back into your bedroom?"

"I am afraid that may no longer be a possibility."

"Do not be so sure."

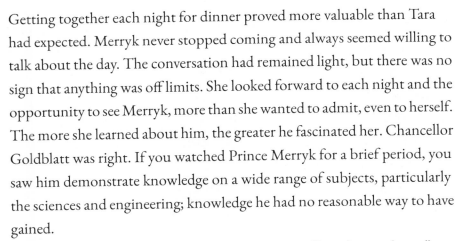

Getting together each night for dinner proved more valuable than Tara had expected. Merryk never stopped coming and always seemed willing to talk about the day. The conversation had remained light, but there was no sign that anything was off limits. She looked forward to each night and the opportunity to see Merryk, more than she wanted to admit, even to herself. The more she learned about him, the greater he fascinated her. Chancellor Goldblatt was right. If you watched Prince Merryk for a brief period, you saw him demonstrate knowledge on a wide range of subjects, particularly the sciences and engineering; knowledge he had no reasonable way to have gained.

"Merryk, there is something serious I want to talk with you about."

"Anything."

"Nan told me I cannot trust you because all you wanted from me was the dowry and information about my father. Is this true?"

"Your question answers much about your outburst several weeks ago."

"It was not an outburst, just a loudly voiced concern," Tara inserted defensively.

A smile crossed Merryk's face, the kind he had shown at the beginning of their marriage. A smile that said he was only a heartbeat away from teasing her unmercifully.

Merryk let the flash of humor pass. "My father wanted the money to pay for some ships. He had a revenue shortfall, so the dowry became the solution. He got all the money, not me."

"But is there any information you want about my father? I promise to answer truthfully as best I can."

"I am sure my father, as king, would have questions, but I do not. I know you and Nan will find this hard to believe, but my only interest is in you. We are a long way from international intrigues and politics, and I like it that way. Our fathers can scheme and plot so long as they leave you and me and the Teardrop Kingdom alone. I really do not care." Merryk paused. "Actually, I would like your input on one topic. I do not know if it relates to your father or not. Chancellor Goldblatt and I have been attempting to determine who is trying to kill you and me and why. Any insight you have might save both of our lives."

The question caught Tara off guard. She expected something about naval strategy or the efforts to dominate surrounding countries, not something as basic as who would want to kill them.

Merryk took the next hour to describe the actions of his uncle, the attacks on him, the tax collection issue, and his thoughts on the attack on her. He shared the latest information received by Chancellor Goldblatt.

"Sometimes I think I understand, but the reason evades me. I believe the Lord Commander is involved in attempting to kill me, but why would he want to kill you? The bigger question is, now that we are married, will it end?"

Tara should have been deeply concerned about the facts Merryk presented. Instead, she felt safer. Tara thought. *He is trying to protect me. I felt like this with my father when I was little, but this was deeper and more sincere.*

"Well, these are not the questions I thought you would have. Perhaps we can continue after I have had time to consider all you have shared. Right now, you left me with more questions than answers. But you have my promise; I will give you my best answers, regardless of where they may lead."

"I would have expected nothing less; both of our futures are at risk."

Merryk has confided in me. He would not have done so unless he trusted me. I can trust him, but I have already betrayed him. This is not the right time to mention my deceit. When he finds out what I have done, it will destroy everything. I could have trusted him with my heart, but now I have ruined it. What am I to do?

CHAPTER SIXTY

CONFESSIONS

S ummer always seems slow to come, then the warm months skip by, too soon, and then little by little, summer's light fades. This late summer's morning, Merryk was at his favorite place—the top of the old tower. Here is where Smallfolks had first described his world. This is where he began his lengthy journey back to physical health. Here is where he exercised every morning and greeted every new day and season.

My workouts are my bridge between my old life and my new. They are constant. They remind me the world around me may change, but I have not. I am the same old Raymond, but also the young Merryk.

I am glad Tara started the discussion about her father. We have broken the chill between us and are communicating again. Tara is a remarkable woman, and I have missed talking with her. Initially, I only saw her as an immature girl. I focused on the age difference between Tara and Raymond, not Tara and Merryk. I remember my life as Raymond, but I live in the world of Merryk. This is my 'real' world.

Now that I have spent time with her, I see her differently. She is a complicated, intelligent, elegant, spirited, and determined woman. Also, my younger self continues to remind me she is also very beautiful. Unfortunately, because of our agreement, I need to keep my contacts with her short to stop my youthful self from acting like a fool. I am glad she has kept her distance. I am not sure how I would react to more physical contact. We had delayed our relationship to get to know each other and married to keep us safe. Both decisions seemed logical then. Now, my mind wishes we were not so logical. But my wishes are not the only ones involved. Tara also gets to choose.

Merryk spoke out loud, although there was no one there to hear, "What was my mother's favorite saying? 'Doing the right thing isn't *always* easy, but it is *always* the right thing.'"

The Queen's Garden lay to the side of the castle. Queen Amanda, during her stay, had planted an assortment of roses and honeysuckle. Ivy covered the exposed rocks surrounding a small pool which collected water from the castle's roof. Several small maple trees, some bright green and others a vibrant red, extended their limbs over the area, sheltering it from the summer's heat and adding an almost mystical glint of filtered light. Songbirds nested above.

Yonn had introduced the spot to Yvette. This is where they came to talk, away from prying eyes and ears. Yonn told her he remembered his mother bringing him here as a child. "I would play on the ground on a blanket while she knitted or sewed. The spot always reminds me of her."

Today, Yvette sat alone on the small bench near the pool reading a book and listening to the birds. Yvette thought of this as her sanctuary, so it surprised her to see Tara rushing into the garden with tears running down her face.

"I am sorry to invade your space," Tara said with a sob. "I just hate her."

"You mean you hate *him?*"

"No, her."

"Who?"

"Maizie. I was just at the school. Merryk picked Maizie up and spun her around, read her a story, and she fell asleep with her head on his chest. I hate her."

"I am confused. You hate Maizie?"

"Yes, that should have been me! Merryk could have picked me up and spun me around. I wanted to fall asleep with my head on his chest."

"Tara, you are jealous. You are jealous of a four-year-old."

"No. Yes. I do not know."

"Merryk is your husband. Just go to his room and stop all this senseless separation."

"No, he is not. He is not really my husband." More tears rolled down Tara's cheeks.

"What can that possibly mean?"

"We never consummated the marriage."

"Why in the world?" Yvette asked.

"Because I made him promise not to touch me until I chose."

"But how did you provide proof?"

"Nan helped me. She said the little treachery would allow me time to determine if I could trust him."

"Nan! When are you going to understand? She only does what your father wants. If she suggests something, it is not in your interest. It is in his."

"It does not matter now. Merryk does not find me attractive at all. He is friendly and courteous, but he never attempted to touch me, even when I intentionally wrapped myself around him."

"You did not. Do you have any idea how hard you made it for him to keep his promise? Yonn said Merryk was acting agitated and exercising more than usual. He is trying to do what he thinks you want, trying to please you. Have you told him you changed your mind and want to be his wife?"

"No. I am not sure how that conversation would go or how to even start it."

"Words will be your downfall. What you need is a little action. Just go to his room tonight or be waiting for him when he comes in. You do not have to say, 'I have changed my mind.' He is a smart man. He will figure it out."

"I cannot do that. What if he does not find me attractive? I would make a fool of myself."

"Being jealous of a four-year-old is making a fool of yourself."

"I cannot do that until he knows the entire truth."

"What truth?"

"When I was first angry with him, Nan convinced me to send a letter to my father saying the wedding was a sham. I tried to stop it, but by the time I asked, it was already gone. Merryk needs to know what kind of woman I am before he accepts me as his wife."

"Nan again! Tara, I will help you, but only if you promise me never to trust Nan again. Do you not see a sham wedding gives your father leverage over Merryk and King Michael? The letter was for King Natas' benefit, not yours."

"I was angry and not thinking."

"I know you are in love. Are you sure you do not want to just wait for him in his bed? In the morning, you can tell him about the letter. It would surprise you how simple things are to resolve when both of your heads are on the same pillow."

"No, I cannot do that without knowing if he is attracted to me. He also needs to know what I did, so he can choose."

"Okay, here is the plan. First, we prove he is attracted to you. When you know he is, you can tell him about the letter. But you need to tell him before he learns from someone else."

"He will never trust me again."

"I think he will. Prince Merryk is not like other men. He will understand and forgive you. You just need to explain it to him."

"How do we verify if he likes me?"

"First, I will talk to Yonn to get his impression. Then you need to interject yourself into direct contact with the prince. Go to the roof to watch him exercise; go on rides with him; stay close to him. Whenever you can, touch him. Fall often, so he must catch you. We need to adjust what you are wearing to be more relaxed, open, more revealing."

"Does that stuff work?"

"Trust me. Finally, my years of indiscretion will be valuable," Yvette said with pride.

"Tara, Nan will see what we are doing and attempt to stop you. She is not to be trusted. Believe nothing she says. Remember, she is the one that got you into this total mess."

Chapter Sixty-One

CONTACT

The morning sun had broken above the eastern horizon when Merryk emerged from the stairs at the top of the old tower. His eyes swept across an azure sky, unmarred by even a sliver of white. The early birds scattered and chirped as they searched for worms. The pair of golden eagles, who claimed the valley as their own, soared in the cool air looking for careless rabbits.

A perfect morning for my exercises. Merryk thought.

Merryk began, as always, with gentle warm-up exercises. The first was a simple turning at the waist, propelled by moving the arms from side to side. His head turned as he heard the door to the stair opening. Tara emerged. Her hair was pulled into a casual knot. She wore a shawl over her shoulders and riding pants rather than her customary long dress. The morning light reflected the same deep blue of the sky in her eyes.

Now, it really is a perfect morning.

"Good morning. What a beautiful day," Tara said as she surveyed the unbroken sky. "I thought this might be an excellent time for me to learn *tai chi.*"

"What a pleasant surprise. I see you came dressed appropriately."

"I hope so. Is this all right?" Tara asked as she removed her shawl, revealing a short sleeve low necked blouse which hung gently over each shoulder.

"Perfect," Merryk said as his eyes locked with hers. "I don't think I have told you how beautiful you look in the morning sun."

Tara shifted her eyes down, her cheeks slightly flushing. "You have said nothing like that since our wedding day."

"I know. Forgive me, I am a fool."

"Do not be silly," she said as her eyes reached out to his and she gently touched his arm. "Now show me how to do this."

Yvette continued to pace between the fireplace and the window. She had come to Tara's room early to help her get ready to join Merryk on the roof. Now all she could do was wait and walk.

Yonn agreed with me. Prince Merryk is attracted to Tara. Yonn said Merryk was having difficulty getting the physical part of their relationship going. When I explained to him Tara had made Merryk promise not to touch her, he replied, 'Now things make sense.'

Funny, I did not hesitate to tell Yonn everything. I know I should have maintained Tara's confidence, but I know I can trust Yonn. He would never break our confidence, even to Merryk.

It is hard to understand why Tara pushed Merryk away. Compared to a fat bellied king or a stunted and twisted prince, he is fantastic. Compared to most anyone, he is fantastic. She should have known he would honor his word, no matter how hard it was.

If all this blows up, we would have to leave the Teardrop. I do not want to leave. I have a new life here. I like these people. I like Yonn. Yonn may have been a scoundrel in the past, but he is my scoundrel. When we get through this mess, I will tell him I do not want to just be friends, no matter what the difference is in our stations.

Tara entered the room, interrupting Yvette's internal thoughts.

Before Tara could even settle, Yvette asked, "How did it go?"

Tara ignored her for a moment as she sat on the edge of the bed and then threw her arms back up over her head to lie on the bed. "He said I was beautiful, and he was a fool."

"Really? Tell me everything."

Tara's voice was full of excitement and joy as she recounted the exchange with Merryk. "I guess he could find me beautiful and still not be attracted to me," she said.

"You will drive me to insanity," Yvette said in exasperation. "Finding someone beautiful and telling them is the definition of being attracted. Sometimes I think you would be happier if you were not so smart." Yvette grabbed a pillow and hit Tara directly in the head.

A short flurry of pillows and laughter erupted.

"What is next?" Yvette asked.

"He and I will ride out this morning to see the progress on the locks. I will ask Nelly to make some lunch for us."

"Perhaps I can come too. After the attack on us, Yonn swore he would never allow Merryk to be alone outside the walls."

"Great, what should I wear?" Tara asked.

"Your standard riding attire will be fine, nothing too revealing. You want to keep him guessing about what you will wear, and remember, more touching."

"Yvette, you really are good at this."

Tara joined Merryk the next week for virtually everything. She touched him every time she could. She held onto his arm when they walked to the village and readily accepted his hand.

"I think you need to back off on the falling," Yvette said. "Prince Merryk told Yonn he is concerned about your balance." A broad smile covered both their faces.

"He seems to enjoy my company and does not shy away from my touch. He has told me several times about how nice I look and when he talks to me, his eyes reach out to mine. I think he may find me attractive."

"Do I need to hit you again? I told you, it was your stupid request not to be touched that held him back. Now is the time to tell him what you have done, ask for his forgiveness, and then go to his bedroom."

"You always make it sound so easy."

"Because it is. But, whatever you do, do not let the separation return."

CHAPTER SIXTY-TWO

JOURNEYS

The last days of summer passed quickly. Prince Merryk, after another ride with Tara, returned to his room to find Smallfolks. "Smallfolks, Jamaal ZooWalter said the Blue-and-White Mountain Clans come south in the fall to hunt. Do you know when exactly?"

The diminutive man scratched his beard. "If I remember, it was around now, a couple weeks before the Harvest Moon. Why are you asking?"

"I was thinking Yonn and I might go north for a little exploring. I thought we might run into some more people from the Blue-and-White Mountain Clans. How did you and my grandfather contact them?"

"You do not contact them. They find you. Tricky ones, especially their leader Gaspar ZooWalt, Jamaal's father. Yes, they come south this time of year. Not a good idea to go north, although it is not as dangerous as when I joined your grandfather. In those days, the northern savages often came south in raiding parties. The clans have stopped that now."

"Was it a raiding party who killed your family?"

"Yes, I was just nine." Smallfolk's eyes became teary as he remembered. "My father told me to hide in a pile of sticks behind the barn and not to come out until he came for me. My father never came, but your grandfather did; pulled me out and wrapped me in the big black leather coat you still wear and brought me back to the castle.

"Without your grandfather, I would still be under that pile of sticks. It was the next year we went north, just the two of us. It was just foolish, but your grandfather was always willing to take risks. Only thing about him I never really liked. But I was young and did not know any better. Besides, I would have followed him anywhere."

"Still would I am sure," Merryk inserted.

Nodding his head in agreement, Smallfolks continued, "We went up the river until we came to a great rockslide. We found a path around the loose rocks. I think this must be the same path the Blue-and-White Mountain Clans use today when they come to trade. From there, it was a two or three-day ride until we broke into a deep, wide valley with a beautiful blue lake with a grassland plain beside it. We stopped for the evening. Your grandfather caught two large trout from the lake. I remember the smell of them cooking over the open fire. It was that night they came."

"The Blue-and-White Mountain Clans?"

"Yes, a big band of twenty to thirty men and women. I will never forget the clanswomen. Not soft and gentle, like Nelly or Princess Tara, but warriors dressed in rough cloth and skins. They carried swords and long knives. They say they are more dangerous and vicious than the northern savages themselves. Some of them were beautiful; fierce and beautiful."

"Smallfolks, it sounds like you fell in love," Merryk said with a chuckle.

"If I had grown to be a real sized man, I admit it would have crossed my mind to search one out. Thank goodness I did not grow. Most likely, they would have killed me."

"Is this when you and grandfather first met Gaspar ZooWalt?"

"Yes, but in those days, I think he was just called 'Gaspar ZooWalter.' He was a big burly man with muscular arms, a bushy beard, and fire burning in his eyes. They call them the 'Bear of the North,' but not to his face. The savages had killed his oldest son and daughter-in-law. Gaspar and his wife took their child to raise. Gaspar's wife died the next year from an illness, leaving him to raise the child alone. Gaspar was on a quest to destroy all savages. Your grandfather and Gaspar took to each other. I never really understood the connection. Great King Mikael went back several times to fight with Gaspar and the Blue-and-White Mountain Clans. He would not take me with him again, said it was too dangerous."

"Finally, Gaspar united the clans and drove the savages north. Then they made him the Walt."

"You said you never trusted Gaspar. Why?"

"He always seemed to take your grandfather into danger. Every time he left, I did not know if he would be returning. You cannot trust a man who leads others into trouble."

Merryk nodded, "Especially if it was Prince Mikael."

"I always felt better when your grandfather returned," Smallfolks added.

"Chancellor Goldblatt said it was those ventures north that moved the Blue-and-White Mountain Clans to join the High Kingdom and support King Mikael."

"I suppose it had some good, but always at substantial risk."

"Well, Yonn and I will retrace your journey. I will survey the areas as we go, perhaps get some rock samples and a new map out of the trip."

"You have no reason to go north, and you might find a lot of trouble, particularly if you come across Gaspar ZooWalt. You should not go."

"I will be all right, don't worry," Merryk said as he placed his hand on Smallfolks' shoulder.

Smallfolks shook his head as he moved toward the door. "Same thing your grandfather used to say." Mumbling as he went out the door, "Nobody ever listens to me."

Yonn and Yvette joined the prince and princess for dinner. The four had established personal places to eat at the long dining room table. Merryk had suggested the couples sit facing each other at the end of the table with no one at the head. However, no matter how many times Merryk made this request, either Nelly, Smallfolks, or one of the other attendants always reorganized it, so Merryk sat at the head. Merryk had complained to Tara, who said, "They are just doing what they have been taught out of respect for you. Where we sit is not important to us, but it is important to them." Eventually, he gave up. Merryk sat at the head, Tara on his left with Yvette beside her, and Yonn on his right.

As dinner ended, Merryk said, "I spoke with Smallfolks today. He said now is the time he and grandfather went north to meet with the Blue-and-White Mountain Clans. So tomorrow morning, Yonn and I will head north for seven to ten days. I want to expand our maps and hopefully come in contact with the clans' hunting parties."

Tara's face showed surprise at the announcement.

"It is a three-day ride to the big lake and valley where the Blue-and-White Mountain Clans hunt. If we don't find them there, we will then proceed further north. If we connect, I want to stay a few days to learn more about them."

"This will be the last good meal in a while, unless Merryk is a better cook than me," Yonn said with a laugh.

"It would not surprise me to learn that Prince Merryk is an excellent cook," Yvette added.

"I have not been away from you since I arrived nearly six months ago. I want—," Tara stopped and corrected herself, "We want to go."

Yvette's head reacted with an involuntary negative shake.

"That would not be a good idea," Prince Merryk replied. "We will ride in rough terrain for multiple days and sleep under the stars on the ground."

"Sounds like an adventure," Tara said. Looking at Yvette, "Remember the last time we slept under the stars? It was years ago, just one night, but I remember watching stars fall across the sky. We want to go."

Yvette's head now was moving even more violently.

"Tara, this is a hard trip. It will have no luxuries or softness. The ground will put rocks in your back regardless of your station. After a couple of days, we will smell like the horses with only the streams of melted snow water to wash, and it will be dangerous."

Yvette's head now bobbed up and down in agreement with Merryk.

"I am concerned about the danger of being left alone. Do you think we should be separated when we do not know if the peril has passed? Besides, if I survived the stormy seas to get here, I can handle a horse and a rocky bed for a few days. I might prove myself to be tougher than you think," Tara said.

Merryk saw the determination in Tara's eyes.

"Yonn, what do you think? Should we take them with us?"

"If there is to be danger, I would prefer the four of us were together." He looked at Yvette as he spoke.

"If you are serious, we will leave at first light. We take what we can carry on one pack horse. Ladies, riding clothes and only essentials; pack for hot days at first and cold nights. As we move north, the weather will get cooler. Chancellor Goldblatt said the weather should hold for the next couple of weeks, but we should prepare for rain."

"That went well," Tara said as she and Yvette moved to their rooms.

"How *exactly* did that go well? We are about to travel on horseback into the mountains for at least a week, with nothing that looks like comfort."

"I thought you would be pleased. I did *exactly* what you told me to do, 'not let separation occur.'"

Yvette shook her head. "I meant here in the castle. I did not mean following him on a trek into the wilds. Have you told him yet about the letter?"

"No, but this will be a perfect opportunity."

"Or he will get angry and leave you tied to a tree for the wolves."

"I thought you said Merryk would forgive me."

"That was before you included me in your *adventure*."

CHAPTER SIXTY-THREE

NORTH

The mid-September morning rose into the crisp air with a golden glow.

"It is going to be a beautiful day," Merryk said to Yonn as the two readied the horses outside the doors of the Great Hall.

"It will be hot this afternoon with no clouds to block the heat. I am glad we are moving north into the mountains."

"By tonight, we will be thankful for the fire," Merryk said.

Moments later, Princess Tara and Contessa Yvette came through the doors. Merryk saw the ladies had taken his advice and wore utilitarian riding clothes: long pants with tunics and jackets. They also were carrying reasonably sized bags. Smallfolks, Nelly, and Chancellor Goldblatt came to say goodbye.

Smallfolks came to Prince Merryk holding an oaken stick with metal bands around the tips. "The blacksmith brought this walking stick last night. He said you wanted it for your trip."

"Thank you, Smallfolks. I do."

Prince Merryk turned to Chancellor Goldblatt. "We will follow the path I described last night. We should be back in seven to ten days."

"Be cautious, I am uncertain of your reception," the Chancellor replied.

Merryk nodded. "Ready to go, Maverick?" The big black horse stomped his front foot and, with a shake of his head, led the others out the gate.

The trail moved along the castle wall to the back, past the lake, then north along the side of the stream. It was wide enough for two or three to ride abreast. Princess Tara and Prince Merryk had ridden this section of the route many times. Soon, Tara moved up next to Prince Merryk.

"What did the Chancellor mean when he said, 'uncertain reception'?"

"The Lord Commander, a couple of years ago, sought conscripts from the Blue-and-White Mountain Clans. He arrived unannounced and was met with armed resistance, then summarily escorted south. Gaspar ZooWalt sent a message to King Michael that the clans would come to the aid of the High Kingdom only in times of need. They would not support sending men to be slaughtered by the Lord Commander."

"The Lord Commander must have loved that," Tara replied.

"The Chancellor also said my father has not been as gracious to the clans as my grandfather. There is a general feeling in the south the clans are somehow lesser people. King Michael may not believe this, but he has allowed the slurs to continue. As a result, one more royal family visitor may not be well received."

"You might have mentioned this before we left," Tara said.

"Would it have mattered?" Merryk asked with a smile.

"Not in the least, but why is it you want to go?"

"The clans are buying more salt every year from your father. They are coming south more often with furs to trade. They are a potential trading partner for the Teardrop, one not across the sea."

"Why do you think they are buying more salt?" Tara asked.

"My guess is the population is growing. The truth is, we know little about the clans or their size. I believe they need to reach out for trade just as we do."

"Just when I thought you were an adventurer, I discover you really were a merchant at heart."

"Kingdoms grow and prosper with trade. The best way forward for the Teardrop is to be a good merchant. It will lift all our people," Merryk said.

"My father says trade is good to support armies, but conquest is the best way to expand kingdoms."

"Conquest comes in many forms. The least costly and most effective is trade."

Tara nodded her head in agreement. "Your push to create salt now makes more sense. Losing the market will weaken my father and strengthen the Teardrop."

"Your father can still compete, but he will need to match the local prices and he must move the salt across the sea. We have the advantage. Even if he beats the price, the people of the Teardrop will pay less for salt. Either way, we win."

"He is really not going to like you," Tara replied with a shake of her head.

"I'm not sure he likes me now."

The land undulated under the worn path heading north. By midday, the group had made it above where Merryk and Marta's boys had cut the lumber for the dam. At sunset, they stopped on the riverbank. The great rockslide could be seen ahead. Behind them, the whole of the Teardrop Valley lay gentle rolls of land with a meandering stream merging into the horizon.

Merryk patted Maverick as he looked back. "Magnificent place to call home, isn't it?"

The horse bobbed his neck in agreement.

"Tomorrow we will start to climb," Yonn said, pointing to where the path turned from the river and moved into the forest.

"Why don't you see if you can find us something to eat?" Merryk asked Yonn. "I will get a fire started."

"I saw some pheasant a little way back," Yonn said, grabbing his bow and moving off to hunt.

The first evening was uneventful. The pheasant was excellent. Deep grass near the stream made a soft cushion for their bedrolls, with a star-filled sky offering a canopy for their beds.

The trail the next day was nothing like the path from the castle to the slide. At first it seemed to climb around the edge of the rock slippage. However, to Merryk's engineering eye, it was carefully designed. The switchbacks in the many steep sections moved away from the slide, never toward it. This insured the predictable seasonal shifts would not affect the trail.

The trail also disappeared periodically into the surrounding firs at just the right places to find springs which sprang from the mountain side. At each spring, an area had been cleared and leveled to allow space for breaks. On the path itself, brush and debris had been carefully removed to avoid impaired travel.

After six hours of steady climbing, they breached the first range.

Everyone stopped to take in the view back toward the castle.

"It is so clear, I think I can see the ocean," Yonn exclaimed. "I have lived here all my life and never made this trip. I would not have believed this unless I saw it myself."

Tara and Yvette said nothing, but their eyes scanned the view in appreciation.

"Nature always surprises," Merryk said, as he prodded Maverick to continue.

The path dropped over the crest and moved into the stunted trees of pine and firs. Inside the forest's edge was a small alpine lake. Around the edge lay a clearing with a fire pit and a place for horses and people to rest.

"This must be where we spend the night," Merryk said. No one objected.

"Thank goodness," Yvette said. "When you said a tough trip, I thought you meant long. I do not know who needs to stop more, me or the horse." She quickly dismounted, but uncharacteristically began to care for her horse.

"I would have thought she would have left that for Yonn," Merryk whispered to Tara.

"Yvette has been my friend since we were ten. To be my friend means you must know how to handle horses, if not love them. Also, do not let her gentle exterior fool you. She has a much tougher core. You never know when she will surprise you."

The second evening, the ladies opted for cheese and bread brought from the castle rather than the squirrel suggested by Merryk and Yonn.

A lumpy rock mattress replaced the thick grass of the first night. Merryk used piles of leaves to soften the ground, but there is only so much that can be done to soften rocks. Nature placed at least one inconvenient rock beneath each traveler.

The third day, the steep ascent leveled off and was replaced by a path moving repeatedly over one hill, then down a small gully and then up another hill.

"I know we are going up and down over these ridges, but I have the feeling that we are going down overall," Merryk said.

Around the next bend in the trail, they came to an overlook exposing a valley with a large crystal blue lake. Velvet grass skirted the lake on three sides while a fir and pine forest hugged the fourth. The teeth of the northern mountain ranges lay across the horizon.

"This is amazing," Tara said.

"I am not sure I have ever seen anything this beautiful, not just the lake, but the rows of mountains," Yvette added as she looked beyond the valley.

"The path works its way down the hillside to the valley floor," Yonn said, pointing to the broad switchbacks carved in the mountainside.

"It will take an hour or more to get to the bottom," Merryk said. "This must be the place Smallfolks described. Tonight, I think we should have trout."

"Do you think we might swim in the lake? It would feel good to remove some of this trail dust," Tara asked. "It might ease some of the stiffness from the ride."

"Expect it will be a chilly dip in pure melted snow," Merryk answered. "We will set up camp for a couple of days. Smallfolks said you do not find the clan as much as they find you. Perhaps this will give them the opportunity."

It was mid-afternoon when the four made their way to the edge of the lake. After agreeing on an appropriate campsite, Yonn unpacked the horses and tied them on long ropes to allow them to graze freely in the long grass. Merryk went to his backpack and retrieved a thin line and several shiny hooks he had brought for this exact occasion.

Tara and Yvette gathered a change of clothes and sought a sheltered cove in which to bathe.

"Don't go too far afield," Merryk warned. "We all need to stay alert."

It was clear they had heeded his guidance as screams of shock returned to the camp from just around the corner. "That won't be a long bath," Merryk chuckled to himself as he moved off to fish.

Yonn had a fire going when Merryk returned. He had organized a place for the horses for the evening. The ladies were drying their hair by the fire.

"Did you enjoy your swim?" Merryk asked with a smile.

"You were right about the melted snow," Yvette said. "It was frigid, but also quite invigorating."

"How did your fishing go?" Tara asked.

"Not bad," said Merryk as he lifted two sixteen-inch brown trout.

"They look good," Yvette said. "What are we going to fix with them?"

"I brought a few potatoes from the castle, which we will fry."

"I found some blackberries for dessert," Yonn added, as he returned to the campsite with the large berries held in a cloth.

Merryk retrieved two utensils from the pack. One was a large pot for boiling water and the other was what he called a frying pan: a twelve-inch cast skillet of his own design.

It was no time before the thinly sliced potatoes were sizzling in the skillet and the fish filets were on sticks cooking over the fire.

As the dinner concluded, Yvette said, "I knew Prince Merryk would be an excellent cook."

"Perhaps tomorrow you ladies can cook," Merryk said with as straight a face as he could muster.

Tara replied, "Only if you want burned water and some more berries."

Everyone laughed.

After dinner, Yonn gathered the horses from the glade and staked them close to the campfire. Yvette volunteered, with Yonn's help, of course, to clean the utensils.

Merryk extended his hand to Tara. "Are you up for a walk by the lake?"

"Absolutely," she said as she grabbed his hand and then his arm to pull him close to her.

A round orb of light now reflected off the glasslike surface of the lake. The near full moon illuminated the surroundings like midday.

Coming to a log lying on the bank, Tara said, "We should sit for a moment." Still staying close to Merryk, she added, "This is so beautiful."

"But still not as beautiful as you," Merryk said in the voice she had heard when she first met her woodsman. The voice was the combination of strength and gentleness, which only appeared when he talked with her.

As before, he reached up and swept the loose hairs from Tara's forehead and pushed them back over her ear. Unlike the first time, he did not drop his hand from her face, but captured it gently in his hand. His eyes were locked on hers as he gently pulled her forward for a kiss. Just before their lips met, Yonn's muted voice interrupted, "Merryk, we have guests."

"Guests with bad timing," Merryk said with a big sigh.

CHAPTER SIXTY-FOUR

GASPAR

Merryk had selected the campsite with a rock outcropping to its back. The warmth of the fire would radiate from the stone and provide additional warmth in the cool evening. It now fulfilled a secondary purpose as a defensive rear to the camp. Merryk asked both Tara and Yvette to move in the space between the campfire and the stone. Yonn positioned himself on one side of the ladies, and Merryk on the other. Merryk moved his grandfather's sword near and placed the new walking stick next to him.

Maverick became unsettled and started shaking his head, as he had done when Merryk was attacked in the stable. "We know, Maverick. We know they are here," Prince Merryk said in a voice directed at the black stallion.

Merryk turned to Yonn. "How many do you think there are?"

"I saw at least four. They all appeared to be from the clans, or at least they are dressed that way."

Merryk rose from where he sat to add a log to the fire and then returned to his place. The log caught fire and expanded the circle of light around the camp.

In a few moments from the shadows, a voice came, "Hello in the camp. May we come in?"

"Yes," Merryk replied.

Three men and one woman moved into the halo of light cast by the campfire. All were dressed in the garb of the Blue-and-White Mountain Clans with characteristic plaid cloth and tied in either a sash or a belt.

"We were hunting and smelled your fire from up the valley. We came to check. Fire can get out of control in these mountains and cause plenty of trouble. What brings you this far out?"

"We are just on an excursion from the South. We heard of this lake and thought we would come and see it before the winter snows made it impossible."

"Who exactly are you?" the man asked.

"Just simple people with an interest in exploring."

"Simple people do not travel with fine horses or with women who look more suited for warm houses. Are not you worried about bandits?"

Merryk dropped his hand to grasp the walking stick by his side. "Bandits normally go where people can be expected. You did not expect us."

Suddenly, another dozen men and women appeared in the light around the fire.

"There are more of you out there. Show yourselves," Merryk said in a loud voice. The balance of the group appeared, perhaps twenty or twenty-five. Merryk reached his hand out to touch Tara's hand. "It's all right," he whispered.

Turning his attention back to the group, Merryk continued. "We are simple people. The other gentleman is my assistant. The ladies, as you noticed, are more comfortable in different surroundings, but wanted to come. In truth, they have not complained as much as I had thought. And I am just a simple merchant."

A deep voice cut over the crackle of the fire. "Enough with this farce." The entire group parted as one man stepped through. He was older, with graying hair and a gray shaggy beard, fiery eyes, broad shoulders, and immense arms. "There is nothing simple about any of you. The young man is Captain Yonn, commander of the Teardrop guard. The auburn-haired

lady is the Contessa Yvette D'Campin, Lady-in-Waiting to her Highness
Princess Tarareese, daughter of King Natas, and wife to Prince Merryk
Raymouth, firstborn son of the Inland Queen and the grandson to Great
King Mikael, our liege lord."

Upon the announcement of Merryk's title, the entire group dropped
to one knee. This action surprised Merryk. He preferred to be treated
as an ordinary person. Moving around the fire to face the spokesperson,
Merryk said, "And you are Gaspar ZooWalt, leader of the Blue-and-White
Mountain Clans and the Walt to the council of Walters." Merryk made a
motion for all to rise and extended his hand to the older man.

Gaspar's face scowled. "I do not need your hand to rise, young man," he
said as he came firmly to his feet.

Merryk was undaunted. He did not withdraw his hand at the rebuff, but
merely left it outstretched. "Walt, if my hand is needed for you to rise, then
it is there for you, but I extended it hoping we would be friends as you were
to my grandfather."

Gaspar gazed intently at the young man and then shook his hand. "I see
Chancellor Goldblatt has done an excellent job with your education."

Merryk shook his head. "No. Actually, the information was not from
Chancellor Goldblatt, who knows a great deal about the world, but
unfortunately, not very much about our northern allies. I had to rely on
smaller folks."

"Smallfolks! Is that old bastard still alive? You cannot believe anything he
says," Gaspar said in a grumpy tone.

Merryk's face expanded with an enormous smile. "You understand that
is exactly what he said about you."

Gaspar allowed a smile to crack his face. Then he turned to the group.
"We will spend the night here."

It sounded like a simple statement, but his words had the impact
of an order. Immediately, all the people sought spaces for the evening.
Additional fires were started and within a short time, everyone had a place.

"We will post guards," Gaspar said.

"Surely you are not expecting bandits?" Yonn asked.

"As the young prince guessed, there are no bandits out here, but," Gaspar replied, "there are wolves." Turning to Prince Merryk, Gaspar said, "I think you and I have much to talk about."

Merryk nodded.

Gaspar looked back across the group. "Now, we should all get some sleep. We will leave at first light."

———— ✺ ————

Merryk noticed Tara seemed upset over the events of the evening. Her eyes were focused on the women of the group. They were much as Smallfolks described them: some were older, some younger, all had a rugged look, and all carried weapons. Seeing them, Merryk understood Smallfolks' attraction. They were both fierce and beautiful.

"What is bothering you?" Merryk asked Tara.

"The women cannot seem to keep their eyes off me," Tara said.

"Well, they get little opportunity to see princesses in this part of the world and you have blonde hair. As you notice, blonde hair is a rarity. But if you are concerned, just stay close to me and you will be fine." Merryk adjusted his sleeping blanket so Tara could move to the far side between him and the rock.

Tara thought. *Staying close to Merryk is always a good idea.*

———— ✺ ————

Gaspar ZooWalt prided himself on his ability to judge men, but this young man, Prince Merryk, had caught him by surprise. There was something different about him. Gaspar found few men surprised him anymore. *I cannot remember whether King Mikael, Merryk's grandfather, had the same presence. I was a young man when Prince Mikael came north with his young squire, who was barely ten. I immediately trusted the strong young man with the black horse and long black coat. Merryk reminds me of him in almost every way. If I did not know better, I would say I was looking at the young Prince Mikael, down to his horse and sword.*

Gaspar let his mind wander. *Could he be the one?*

CHAPTER SIXTY-FIVE

BASE CAMP

The morning sunlight had just hit the valley when the clan members began to move. Merryk's night was sleepless because Tara had rolled and fidgeted constantly.

As soon as Merryk stirred, an older woman appeared with a cup of steaming hot broth, which reminded him of bone marrow soup. Soon, another brought warm flat bread. Neither woman spoke but merely delivered the food before going to the others who were rising.

Yonn returned to the fire and sat next to Merryk. "How long have you been awake?" Merryk asked.

"Not long. I got up to check the horses. Everything is fine. Do you really think there are wolves?"

"I am sure there are wolves, but what motivated Gaspar were years of war against the northern savages. Old habits die slowly."

"We need to rouse the ladies. This group looks like it will be ready to move soon."

Yonn woke Yvette, who shook Tara. As soon as both had moved to a sitting position, another younger woman appeared. After a brief exchange, both stood to follow the woman.

"We will be right back," Tara said.

Merryk and Yonn stood and gathered their weapons. Merryk started to fold his bedroll when a woman stopped him. She shook her head and pointed to where Gaspar and several other older men had gathered.

"I do not think we are supposed to do that," Yonn said.

———— ❧ ————

"Good morning, Prince Merryk," Gaspar said. "I heard you had a restless night."

"I would have slept fine, but others made it difficult," Merryk said with a smile. "How long to the base camp?"

"About four hours. We should be there by midday."

A young, frustrated clan member interrupted the discussion. "Excuse me, Your Highness, but your horse refuses to allow anyone to saddle him. I tried, but he is so strong and scary."

The older men in the group all chuckled.

"Maverick has a mind of his own. I will take care of him after I gather my bedroll."

"We will get your bedroll," Gaspar said. "Your grandfather had a black horse: big, scary, and only loyal to the king."

By the time Merryk was done with Maverick, everything was picked up. Tara and Yvette had returned and were gulping down the soup and bread.

"Good morning. You both look a little harried," Prince Merryk said with a smile.

"We were told the Walt waits for no one," Tara said as she rolled her eyes and finished her bread.

It was less than three quarters of an hour from the time Merryk had opened his eyes until the group moved up the valley. The camp was dismantled and steam from the water doused on the campfires rose from the pits.

At the head of the valley, the trail moved into the deep wood. Early morning sunlight shot rays through the canopy, illuminating random sections of the woodland floor. The rich smell of pine filled the air. The moss and ferns naturally suppressed sounds. Only the occasional chirp of a bird or the drops of moisture on leaves broke the silence.

This forest reminds me of the Olympic National Park. Merryk thought. *I wish we had time to explore.*

The group moved efficiently through the forest. Gaspar was near the front, following a small group of men that had gone on ahead. *Scouts, again an old habit.*

Near the top of the ridge at the end of the valley, the path broke into three paths: one continued north; another west; and a third started east and then dropped into another valley to the south.

"Some are going to the valley to the west. A big herd of elk has been spotted and they will hunt the area," Gaspar explained as half of the group broke off onto the alternate path. "Our base camp is south."

"How many came on the hunt?" Merryk asked.

"About one hundred fifty," Gaspar said, "the biggest hunt in several years. The omens said it would be a productive hunt. I hope they meant game, as well as finding you."

The remaining group made its way along the ridge line until it broke free of the forest. Out from under the trees, the whole of the landscape was exposed; the many rows of blue and white mountains lying on all sides. Most were in defined ripples of the earth's crust, but a few looked like volcanic cones dipped in perpetual snow. The horizon held two such peaks close to each other.

"Those mountains are impressive," Merryk said. "Do they have a name?"

Gaspar replied, "They are called 'Leden Grubi.'"

Yvette, hearing the exchange, responded, "Tara, that is the name several of the women called you."

Tara nodded and turned to Gaspar. "Walt, does it have a meaning in common language?"

Gaspar thought for a second, scratching his beard, and said, "It means icy tits."

Yvette's attempt to suppress her laughter only resulted in several loud snorts. Yonn had the good sense to pull up on his horse to avoid joining in Yvette's laughter.

Only Merryk appeared to be unshaken. He looked at the mountains, then back at Tara. "They certainly are beautiful," he said with a grin and a twinkle in his eyes.

The princess' face went bright red from embarrassment. For once in her life, she could not think of a thing to say.

———— ❧ ————

Merryk smelled the campfires before he saw the camp. His first glimpse came as they stepped out from the forest into a large glade. There were several circles of tents around one large circular tent set in the center.

"Each clan has their own group of tents," Gaspar said. "Mine is in the center."

"How many clans are there?" Merryk asked.

"The Council of Walters has eight members, not counting me. One clan has two Walters, twins, but they only get one vote. So, seven clans."

Racks of meat hung toward the side of the encampment, with smoke fires beneath them. "We slightly smoke the meat and then pack it in salt to take it home," Gaspar said. "The hunts used to be critical for survival in the winter, but now, they are reason to come together and for younger people to meet. Tonight, for dinner, we will have fresh elk."

Notice of the return of the Walt and his guests rippled through the camp. Soon, people were standing along the route to the center tent in greeting. Merryk saw Tara gripping her saddle tightly. "They are just curious."

Tara nodded, but did not relax the stiffness in her body.

Upon reaching the center of the encampment, men appeared to take care of the horses. The same lad from the morning appeared near the prince. Hesitation marked his every move as he neared Maverick.

"What is your name?" Merryk asked.

"I am Arras Gorg, the youngest son of Gorg Walter," he said with pride.

Prince Merryk turned to the big stallion. "Maverick, this is Arras. He is a friend and would like to care for you." Maverick's head turned to the lad as he spoke his name. "Can you cooperate with him? I will be fine and not far away."

Maverick hesitated for a second, then bobbed his head up and down in agreement.

Arras's mouth opened wide in surprise.

"He will be more cooperative now, but you keep your eyes open. He is a trickster."

Maverick shifted his head as if to deny the accusation. Finally, he allowed Arras to lead him away.

———— ❖ ————

Jamaal Zoo Walter came from the pavilion. First, he greeted his father, then came to the prince. "Prince Merryk, welcome."

"Good to see you again, Jamaal."

"We prepared tents for you in my group. The ladies are already being escorted. May I show you? After you are settled, please join the Walt for a late lunch. His tent is behind the pavilion."

Merryk found Tara standing alone by the fire in front of their tent. "How are the accommodations?"

"Fine," Tara snapped without turning, but continued to seethe, staring into the fire.

"What's wrong?"

Tara lashed out at Merryk, hitting him squarely in the arm. "*Certainly beautiful*. No defense just, *certainly beautiful*." Tara hit him again.

"I assume you know all of my other honest responses would have been more embarrassing and stop hitting me."

Tara let out a deep sigh. "Why do they have that impression of me?"

"Perhaps it is your rigid back and lack of smiles."

"I do not know how to respond to their stares. They look so judgmental."

"Relax, be yourself. Smile. Talk to the women. They are as uncertain of you as you are about them. We are among friends."

Merryk turned to go to the Walt. When he was safely out of reach, he added, "Oh Tara, they are beautiful."

Chapter Sixty-Six

OOLADA

Merryk made his way through the orderly rows of tents toward the central path leading to the large pavilion. The camp was well organized. Although people were scurrying around, everyone appeared to have a purpose. They looked up from their tasks to watch the young prince walk by, but rapidly returned to their work.

Merryk held his new walking stick in his hand as he moved forward. *You look like a walking stick, but you are too heavy and short to be a good one. Carrying my grandfather's sword seems too aggressive, but a walking stick should be all right. Besides, everyone else is armed.*

Jamaal said the Walt's tent was behind the central tent. As Merryk proceeded to the rear, he discovered another large tent connected directly to the pavilion. A single guard stood at the entrance.

Posted guards, old habits.

The guard was a woman, not much younger than Merryk. Her hair was midnight black and shined in the light. She was a lean, but full-figured woman. She wore the sash of the Zoo clan across her tunic and a pair of soft hide pants. As he approached, the muscles in her arms rippled as she gripped the hilt of her sword.

"Good afternoon, I would like to see the Walt."

"The Walt is not to be disturbed."

"I am sure he will see me. I am—"

"I do not care who you are, my instructions are the Walt is not to be disturbed."

"I understand, but if you will please tell him Prin—"

"I do not care who you are. The Walt is not seeing anyone." The guard started to pull her sword from its sheath, showing a willingness to use weapons to enforce her directions.

"That will not be necessary, but I must insist." Merryk changed his casual tone to a commanding voice.

The impulsive guard withdrew her blade. "I am the one who will insist."

"Gaspar, some help," Merryk said in a loud voice. With the flick of his walking stick, he hit the back of the guard's hand, forcing her to drop her sword. Startled and filled with rage, she attacked him barehanded. Merryk grasped her oncoming right hand, pulled it up and around her head, causing an unpracticed pirouette. The guard's spinning feet tangled, so the slight bump of Merryk's foot to her backside sent her tumbling forward into the only visible mud puddle in the glade.

The call and the commotion brought both Gaspar and Jamaal from the tent.

"Oh, I see you have already met," Gaspar said, in obvious understatement.

"Not really," Prince Merryk replied.

"Very well, Prince Merryk Raymouth, please meet my granddaughter, Oolada Zoo."

"Oh no, I am so sorry Lady Zoo. I should have introduced myself," Merryk said as he extended his hand to help Oolada to her feet.

Oolada swiped her hand across her face to remove the mud. "I should have allowed you, Your Highness." Only the mud hid the bright red covering her face.

"Now come inside Prince Merryk, it is time for lunch," Gaspar said matter-of-factly.

Jamaal hung back. A mocking grin covered his face as he looked at his niece. "Two things I thought I would never see. The great Oolada Zoo disarmed by a Southerner with a stick and someone who calls you, Lady Zoo. I do not know which is the greater surprise, Lady Zoo." Laughing to himself, he entered the tent to join the Walt and the prince.

"Please excuse my granddaughter," Gaspar said. "I am not sure I have raised her properly. She was just a toddler when she came to live with me. My wife died soon after."

"She is the daughter of your older son who was killed by the savages?" Prince Merryk asked.

"Yes, she played with dolls at my feet in the Council chamber; except her dolls played war and carried swords."

"Father attempted to get her to spend time with other children, but she only seemed secure around him or Helga," Jamaal added. "Memories of the loss of her parents always brought her back to her grandfather's feet."

"As she got older, she developed an aptitude for weapons and strategy, particularly on domestic-clan matters," Gaspar said. "I should have discouraged her, but in truth, I am proud of her."

"As you should be. Her only mistake today was using the wrong size weapon and underestimating her opponent," Merryk replied.

"Underestimating, yes indeed," Gaspar chuckled. "Now," pointing to the table, "let us have lunch."

The lunch lasted over two hours. By the time it was complete, Oolada had recovered her sword, and removed the mud, but was still working on recovering her dignity.

How could I have been so foolish? All everyone was talking about was the prince. When a stranger shows up asking for grandfather, my first thought is an outsider to be stopped. I thought our liege lord would be much older, not so tall, and certainly not so strong. He has amazing blue eyes. Shaking her head. *Oolada, he made a fool of you. Then, just to add insult to injury, he called me Lady Zoo. But the way he said it did not sound like an insult.*

The flap of the tent opened to allow the Walt and prince to exit.

"Thank you for lunch, Walt. I appreciate the food and the conversation. Until this evening," Merryk said as he excused himself from Gaspar.

As he walked by Oolada, he stopped. "Please accept my apology again, Lady Zoo." Then, with a nod of his head, he proceeded toward his tent.

Gaspar ZooWalt stepped up to place his hand on Oolada's shoulder. They watched as the tall, young prince departed. "That, my granddaughter, is what the blood of kings looks like."

CHAPTER SIXTY-SEVEN

HELGA

Lowering himself to the cushions on the tent floor, Gaspar groaned as old men do, sounds he never uttered when anybody else was present.

I cannot be weak or old. I need to stay strong until the clans can take their proper place among the High Kingdom, then another can lead.

"What do you think?" Gaspar said aloud to the empty tent.

Stepping from behind the animal hide partition, Helga joined the Walt in the main room. "What do I think, or what do I know?"

"Both."

"What I think is easiest," Helga said, as she moved to a low table to prepare cups of tea for herself and Gaspar. "I think you had very low expectations for this simpleton prince."

Gaspar nodded his head. "Of one thing I am certain, he is not a simpleton. He is well educated and articulate, although his lack of an accent is interesting."

"A result of his injury. And you should have believed Jamaal's evaluation."

"I like to see a man for myself," Gaspar said in an independent tone.

"So, what did you see?"

"Except for the accent, I had to remind myself I was not talking to Great King Mikael. I wanted to share a story to see if we shared a memory."

Helga delivered their tea. "He is not King Mikael, although a large streak of compassion runs through him like the king. My impression is he is very intelligent. A man's knowledge can come from education or experience. Prince Merryk has an abundance of each, way more than his short years can explain."

"I do not understand," Gaspar said. "Chancellor Goldblatt is a brilliant teacher. If anyone could educate the prince, it would be him."

"Perhaps the Chancellor explains the education, but his answers were based on experience which cannot be taught. He listened and thought before speaking, an interesting quality in a royal. When he first entered the tent, he was still thinking about Oolada. He was concerned he had hurt or embarrassed her. As he talked with you, I felt a much older man, which makes no sense," Helga said, shaking her head.

"Is he the one?" Gaspar asked.

"I will need to see him directly, not just hear him. Perhaps I can see how his energy connects with others."

"This evening at dinner will give you an opportunity."

"There is something else," Helga added. "The prince frightened Oolada."

"No, she was just caught off guard. It was a good lesson."

"It was not losing her sword which frightened her. Prince Merryk called her, 'Lady Zoo.'"

"That was nothing."

"To you perhaps, but for Oolada, it was the first time a man had treated her as a woman. The prince reminded her of what she is not."

"How about the suitor a little while back?"

"It was almost two years ago and Oolada broke his nose and sword. Since then, there have been no others.

"Gaspar, this is serious. Finding the man in the prophecy is only one part. There must be a 'daughter of the clans.' I know you hoped this would be Oolada. A woman, not a warrior, must fill this role, a noblewoman.

"Oolada does not understand what that even looks like, much less how to act noble or be Lady Zoo."

"How hard can it be?" Gaspar asked.

Helga shook her head from side to side. "Men judge other men by strength; women are far more critical and even cruel. Look at the women's comments about Princess Tara."

"What do you suggest we do?"

"We have two ladies with us: one noble and one royal. Ask Oolada to act as their host. It will not be enough, but at least she can see what it means to be Lady Zoo. Also, no more guard duties and no sword."

"All of that will be easy, except the 'no sword,'" Gaspar grumbled.

"Oolada, will you come in here?" Gaspar asked as he stood at the open flap of the tent.

"Yes, grandfather," Oolada replied. She only called him grandfather when they were alone or with immediate family.

"I have a new task for you. I want you to be the host for the two women with Prince Merryk."

"Surely someone else is better suited."

"Jamaal's wife is not here. You are the only female member of the Zoo clan, so the task falls to you."

"How about Helga?"

"She is not a Zoo. I want you to go now, see if they need anything and if they are comfortable. You will sit with them this evening at dinner, so you may talk. I want you to observe them. You can learn much from their visit."

"But I have nothing in common with them. They do not treat their men as women should. The princess did not share a blanket with the prince. Neither of them got up early to be sure their men had food," Oolada said.

Ignoring Oolada's comments, Gaspar continued, "While they are here, you will have no more guard duties, and you are not to carry a sword."

"No sword! You said it was irresponsible to not have a weapon."

"Noble women do not carry swords. You may carry a small blade, but no sword. Also, talk with Helga about what you should wear."

With her shoulders drooped, she shook her head from side to side as she left the tent. Just before she reached the opening, Gaspar said, "Oh yes, please tell Princess Tarareese Helga would like to talk with her privately tomorrow morning. You will escort her."

"Yes, grandfather."

Chapter Sixty-Eight

TARA & HELGA

The sun had already pressed into the sky when Yvette opened the flap to Tara's tent. Yvette shook Tara slightly to rouse her. "Tara, time to wake up."

Tara's hand crept across the bed, looking for Merryk.

"He and Yonn have gone hunting with Gaspar and Jamaal. They left two hours ago. You need to get ready to see Helga. Oolada will be here soon. You should get something to eat."

Tara stretched again, pulling Merryk's pillow over her head. "This was one of the best night's sleep I have had in a long time."

"Since your honeymoon?"

"Perhaps, yes. I cannot lie. I really have missed him being near."

"Does this mean you finally talked with him about what you did?"

"I was going to, but we got sidetracked."

"Sidetracked is good. I heard you laughing last night." A smirk covered Yvette's face.

"Not that kind of sidetracked," Tara said as she hit Yvette with a pillow. "He tickled me, made me laugh, and told me the women of the clan could never think of a woman as 'Leden-Grubi' who laughs with her husband at night."

"So true," Yvette nodded in confirmation. "Tara, you must talk with Merryk before somebody else tells him."

"I know. The other night at the lake I was ready to tell him, but he almost kissed me, and then the clan came. You know how things have been since we got here. I will do it before we go back."

"Almost kissed you. Do you still wonder if he finds you attractive?"

"No, I am now sure he does."

"Then you have no reason not to tell him. I would do it while we are still near all these people. He will be less likely to leave you tied to a tree for the wolves."

"You and the wolves!" Another pillow.

"Seriously, you must do it before he hears from someone else."

"I know."

"I have food outside by the fire. Now hurry," Yvette said as she left Tara to get dressed.

Tara thought the fall seemed to come quicker in the mountains. The shadows were longer despite the bright sunlight. Many deciduous trees had begun their annual migration from green to gold. The morning air was crisp, laced with the smell of fresh pine and camp smoke. Yvette interrupted Tara's internal thoughts.

"Are you ready for your meeting this morning?" she asked.

"As well as I can be. I must admit, meeting the 'Oracle of the North' is a little intimidating. It surprised me to see Helga last night. I do not know what I was expecting."

"More chicken bones and runes, and less gentle face and gray bun?"

"Exactly. I do not know if her gentle nature makes her more or less threatening."

"You should ask Oolada about her. Did Merryk tell you what happened yesterday between Oolada and him?"

"No, what?"

"I overheard some of the women this morning. Evidently, Oolada was on guard duty outside her grandfather's tent when Merryk came. She did not recognize him and drew her sword to stop him."

"What happened?"

"Merryk disarmed her and pushed her. She landed in a mud puddle. Evidently, Oolada being disarmed is an unusual event. She is a serious warrior."

"Was she hurt?"

"Was who hurt?" Oolada's voice broke into the conversation.

"You," Tara replied. "Yvette said you had an encounter with Prince Merryk. Are you all right? He is very strong."

Oolada's face turned red. "I am afraid the biggest injury is to my reputation. I am also sure Prince Merryk thinks I am a complete fool."

"The one thing I can assure you of is Prince Merryk does not think like that. My guess is he is still concerned about any harm he may have caused you," Tara said. "You will find he is a most forgiving man."

"Listen to yourself," Yvette mumbled to Tara.

"I can hope," Oolada added. "Now, are you ready to go see Helga?"

The two women said goodbye to Yvette and walked through the rows of tents to the central path. The smiles of other women greeted both of them along the way.

Tara asked, "Oolada, I am a little frightened about speaking to Helga. Do you know her well?"

"Grandfather likes to say he raised me, but it was Helga. After my parents were killed and my grandmother died, she was the only woman in my life. I can tell you; she is as kind as she seems. The only unusual thing about her is when her gift happens. One minute it is 'tomorrow will be better' and then, 'TOMORROW WILL BE BETTER.' Oolada tried to make the second phrase sound ominous by lowering the tone of her voice.

Both Tara and Oolada laughed.

"Thank you for sharing. I feel better about talking with her now," Tara said.

Oolada stopped and looked to the southern sky. "That is unusual. There are storm clouds forming over the mountains to the south. Normally, this does not happen until winter. We will probably get some rain this afternoon."

As their walk concluded, Oolada announced, "We are here."

The tent for the "Oracle of the North" was just like all the others. Nothing outwardly showed any difference in the status of one of the clan's most valued members.

As they arrived, Helga stepped from the tent. She was just as Tara remembered her from the previous night: shorter than Oolada; dark brown eyes that seemed to look into you, rather than at you; a smooth complexion which hid her age; gray hair tied into a neat bun; and she wore a long tunic over the traditional hide pants. She looked just like any other older woman of the clan. Absolutely nothing about her screamed *unusual*.

"Good morning," Helga said. "Oolada, if you would stay outside, I would like to talk with Princess Tarareese alone."

Oolada nodded and moved to a log near the fire which burned outside the tent. "I will be right here if you need me."

Helga raised the flap of the tent to allow the taller Tara to duck inside. "Thank you," Tara said. The inside of the tent was orderly. In the center, pillows encircled a low table. A sleeping pallet was against the rear wall.

"I have prepared some tea," Helga said as she motioned for Tara to sit.

An awkward silence lingered in the tent until Helga had finished pouring the tea. "May I see your hand?" she asked, extending hers to accept it.

Tara placed her hand in Helga's.

Helga's eyes grew wide in surprise. "You are a virgin! This explains much. What have you done, my child? Do you know the danger you have placed on Prince Merryk, yourself, and countless others?"

The revelation of her secret in such a sudden fashion sent Tara directly into tears. She was overcome and sobbed uncontrollably.

Helga moved around the low table to place her arm around Tara. "I am sorry I was so abrupt, but I was so surprised. Now tell me everything. We must fix this quickly."

For the next hour, Tara explained everything. Something about the gentle lady pulled each fact and emotion from Tara. Helga listened, asking few questions, until Tara had exhausted her story and her tears.

"Men can be foolish, but women cannot. You knew your duty even if the prince, out of honor, would forsake his. Your wedding and genuine marriage were not about either of you, but about the fate of nations. A fate which now hangs in the balance. You have put forces in motion, which I fear only you can change."

Then Tara saw what Oolada had described. Helga's eyes seemed to look beyond the tent as she continued in a flat tone.

"If Prince Merryk still lives, a time will come soon, when only you can resolve this problem. It will require you to use all your courage to do something you never imagined. If you do, nations will be saved and your mother's prayer that 'you find a man to love who loves you' will both occur."

A roll of thunder shook the tent. Helga's eyes refocused in an instant. She stood and dashed to the tent's flap. Opening it, she looked out toward the churning storm clouds which boiled over the southern mountains and cascaded into the valley. Helga yelled, "Oolada, send somebody immediately to find Gaspar and the prince! Riders are coming from the south."

Helga turned back to Tara, who sat frozen by the revelations. "Go pack, you will need to leave immediately. I will have Oolada get you and Yvette some hide pants for the trip. They will make the ride easier on you."

"What has happened?" Tara asked, still in a daze.

"The things you set in motion are here."

CHAPTER SIXTY-NINE

STORM CLOUDS

It was a beautiful morning to be hunting. The air was crisp and the sky clear. Merryk had jumped at the opportunity to go hunting with Gaspar, Jamaal, and Yonn, along with two of Jamaal's nephews. The six had moved through the woods north of the camp into a smaller valley, where they discovered another glade.

Heavy dew lay on the long grass covering the open space. After tying the horses in the forest, the group slowly moved around the edge of the opening. They hoped to find deer grazing in the early morning.

Merryk's mind wandered, remembering other hunts. *Since he was ten, he had joined his grandfather and dad every year to hunt deer in the Blue Mountains of Oregon. The trip was always just after the harvest, this time of year. For the first couple of years, Raymond only watched and learned. A new rifle for his thirteenth birthday brought him his first kill—a small two-point buck. Success was always the goal, but secretly, Raymond just liked time with the men of his family. Sitting around the campfire was when he first heard the stories of Vietnam and Korea. None of the stories glorified war, but they always emphasized the importance of friends and duty.*

Jamaal raised his hand for all to stop. Near the edge of the forest stood a magnificent buck with four tips on each antler. Merryk and the others froze in place as Jamaal moved forward slowly.

A modern hunter would have already taken the shot, but bow hunting requires being closer and takes more skill.

Jamaal's arrow struck just behind the shoulder blade and sank to the feathers. The shot had punctured the lungs and the heart. The buck immediately fell to the ground.

The entire group broke the silence with a cheer.

"A great shot, Jamaal," Merryk said in admiration. "I had forgotten the skill bow hunting takes."

"What other kind of hunting is there?" Gaspar asked as he patted his son on the back.

A clap of thunder rolled through the valley. Turning to look south to the source of the sound, Gaspar said, "It is unusual to have thunder this time of the day. It normally happens only on sultry afternoons."

"Clouds are forming in the south," Jamaal added. "We should head back. If we are quiet, we can hunt along the way. I do not want to get caught in the rain."

The two nephews volunteered to take care of the kill, allowing the others to move off to hunt.

Under his breath, Yonn quietly said to Merryk, "I think Jamaal wants to be sure Gaspar is not caught in the rain."

Merryk nodded.

After a few minutes, more thunder rippled among the surrounding peaks. "I think we should forgo hunting and just head back," Merryk suggested.

"The thunder has already frightened the game," Gaspar said. "Everything will be on edge."

"At least Jamaal was successful. This has been an exceptional experience. Thank you for letting us come along," Merryk said.

"It is our privilege, Your Highness. Next time you need to hunt," Jamaal answered.

"If I hunt, you will see my skills as an archer and learn it is not safe to hunt with me. Who knows what I might hit?"

Everyone laughed.

After moving an hour back toward the camp, a rider met them.

"ZooWalt, Helga says you and the prince must return at once. Riders are coming from the south, and she said to tell you not to delay."

Merryk saw Gaspar's face turn grim, as if remembering other times. "Helga has not sent such a message in many years and has never sent one without need. We ride!" With a kick of his heel, his horse quickened its pace.

Princess Tara returned to her tent and began gathering her and Merryk's things.

"What is going on?" Yvette asked as she entered the tent.

"You need to pack right now. And pack for Yonn. We are to return to the castle today."

"Why?"

"All I know is Helga has seen messengers coming. They will require we head back to the castle today, immediately."

"Tara, you are not being very clear. What happened with Helga?"

A deep sigh came from Tara. "Helga knew everything at the touch of my hand. She said I have been foolish but may be able to fix it if I am brave."

"You did not need a seer to hear that. I have been telling you for months," Yvette said as she sat on the edge of the bed. "Why the hurry to return to the castle?"

"Something in the message," Tara said as she frantically gathered her belongings.

"Stop for a moment. Stop!" Only the sharpness of Yvette's voice reached her. Tara crumpled onto the bed and sobbed.

"There is something you are not telling me."

"Helga said much more. She said I knew better, and I should have done my duty. But all I wanted was a choice. Now everything may be lost. Many may die, including Merryk." Tara continued to sob.

"This seems extreme. How can your mistake place so many and Merryk in peril?"

"I do not know, but she seemed certain."

"Please remind me not to ask Helga about my future," Yvette said.

"Yvette, this is serious."

"Before we panic, we should wait to see what the message says. After we know exactly what we are facing, then we can decide on a course of action. With facts, you can think your way through, like you always do. You are Princess Tarareese. You are not alone."

Tara reached up and gave her friend a hug. "I do not know what I would do without you."

"One last thing, whatever you do, do not tell Prince Merryk he is going to die."

Two blue-cloaked Teardrop guards and the clansmen who guided them stood beside their still steaming horses at the edge of the camp. Prince Merryk, with Gaspar and the others, emerged from the forest and went immediately to the men.

Both guards looked exhausted and were covered in dust. The senior stepped forward, "Your Highness, we have an urgent message from Chancellor Goldblatt."

Prince Merryk accepted the letter and tore open the seal.

Your Highness, Prince Merryk,

Within the last hour, I have received word from the harbormaster that your father's flagship lays at anchor in the port. The king, queen, the Lord Commander, and cousins were aboard. They have asked for accommodations for the evening and are arranging transportation to the Teardrop. They should arrive at the castle on the day of the full moon. The harbormaster reported their mood seemed serious, not lighthearted as one might expect from a surprise visit of pleasure.

Two things concern me about their presence: First, the king goes nowhere without advance notice to ensure accommodations are prepared. We have received none. Second, I have never known the Lord Commander to travel with the king. The two have reached a comfortable balance, but only if they remain apart.

Something is unusual; something serious enough to get them to travel together. It may be the question of tax collection has come to a head, and the king needs your testimony to confront the Lord Commander. My sources say conflict has recently erupted between the two.

Having them together is not good. The sooner you can get back, the better. Your protection of the king may be needed.

Remember, he has few he can trust.

Sincerely,
Chancellor Geoffrey Goldblatt

When Merryk finished, he handed the letter to Gaspar.

"Yonn, we need to leave as soon as possible. It will still take three days for us to get back."

Gaspar interrupted, "Not if Jamaal takes you over the pass of Leden Grubi. The path will cut south far quicker and lead to the castle from the east rather than the north. This route will take two days."

"We could travel at night under the nearly full moon. If we are lucky, this would remove at least half a day, if not more," Jamaal added. "But we will have to walk the horses over the pass. It is too treacherous to ride at night, even with moonlight."

Princess Tara and Yvette joined the group. Gaspar handed Tara the note. After reading, she said, "I think we should go over Leden Grubi and try traveling at night. If it works, we will gain time. If not, we will still be there in two days."

"I would suggest you and Yvette stay and come back with the guardsmen after they rest," Merryk said, looking at Tara.

"Yvette can stay, but I am not leaving you," Tara said with the most determined tone her voice could muster.

"You are not leaving me here. Besides, I got these new hide pants to wear," Yvette said as she placed one hand on each hip.

"Ladies, I appreciate your enthusiasm, but this is a grueling path. Traveling at night is far harder than in the daytime. We would have only brief breaks if we are to gain time," Jamaal said. "We may walk as much as we ride."

Gaspar listened to everyone. "If the ladies want to go, they should. Prince Merryk, it is important for you to get back to the castle. A conflict between your father and your uncle is a serious issue. Strife between the two of them threatens the kingdom. Chancellor Goldblatt was an excellent advisor to your grandfather. Heed his advice."

CHAPTER SEVENTY

ROAD TO THE CASTLE

T he initial wave of storm clouds which flowed into the valley had rolled on. Although filled with angry thunder, the clouds never shed a drop of rain. "A good omen," Gaspar had said.

Despite the preparations made by the women, it was still two hours before the group headed out. Gaspar made everyone sit down and eat. "Prince Merryk's and Jamaal's horses need a few moments to rest before they begin the journey and you need to eat," Gaspar said.

Jamaal had made one more attempt to dissuade the women from coming. He seemed to make progress until Helga said, "This is their path as much as Prince Merryk's."

Just before they left, Helga called Yvette to her side. "You are a good friend. The princess will need your support." Grabbing Yvette's hand, her eyes seemed to look beyond. "You have found your sheepherder. Do not let your past deny your future." Just as sudden as the look appeared, it vanished. "Have a safe trip. Expect it will be hard," Helga said, then she left to say goodbye to the others.

Finally, just after noon, the party left the camp. Jamaal and two other Zoo clan members joined the original group—Merryk, Yonn, Tara, and Yvette.

Gaspar and Helga watched as the group moved into the forest. "Now that you have met him, is he the one?"

Helga paused and then drifted into a deep stare. A flat voice replied, "If he lives at the rising of the full moon, he will be a man of destiny."

The first part of the trip retraced the descent into the valley of the campsite. When they had reached the ridge, the peaks of Leden-Grubi shined in the distant sunlight.

"They look a long way off," Tara said.

"They will get much larger as we get closer," Jamaal commented.

Just after they entered the forest again, a path broke left and dropped to the south. *I'm surprised I didn't see that path as we passed*, Merryk thought. *I'm glad the clouds didn't reduce this trail to mud.*

Half an hour down the path, 'dropped to the south,' became a literal description.

"We need to lead the horses for the next section and watch for loose rocks as we go," Jamaal warned.

The rocky path made a steep descent into what looked like a ravine. The sound of flowing water soon rippled through the air.

"I am glad we did not get rain out of the storm," Yonn said, as they came to the edge of the swiftly flowing stream.

"We should stop for a while," Jamaal said. "And let the horses drink and rest."

Soon after, Jamaal mustered the group. "We need to keep moving. We need to be out of the valleys to take advantage of the moonlight."

Moving up the side of the stream, they came to a place where it widened. "We will cross here. You can still ride," Jamaal advised.

Yvette looked at Tara. "It never occurred to me we would not ride. This water is freezing."

After crossing, the path rose out of the ravine to a broad ridge.

"If we turned east at this point, we would come to the hills behind the Capital City. We will go west to the Teardrop," Jamaal said.

The space afforded one of the few opportunities for Tara and Yvette to ride side-by-side.

"What did Helga say to you?" Tara asked.

Yvette smiled. "Oh, just something about sheep in my future. It was like she had talked to my mother."

"She quoted my mother, too," Tara replied flatly.

As the afternoon sun touched the surrounding peaks, more and more they rode in shadows. Mostly, the group moved in silence. Jamaal pressed on; only twice did he stop. Finally, they were forced to stop to wait for the moon to rise higher in the sky.

"We should make a small fire and heat some food. This may be our last chance," Jamaal said. "It will be at least an hour before we can start again. Get some rest and hope for a cloudless night."

Sooner than everyone wished, Jamaal pushed them on. "We need to lead the horses out from under these trees. The next section will be more climbing, but the area is open, and we can ride slowly."

"We must be on the side of the volcano," Merryk said. "I'm glad this area is not covered with snow."

"Further up, we will pass some caves which go back into the mountains. A few years ago, Oolada and I, with some other clansmen, got caught in a sudden snowstorm. We took shelter in the caves for a day."

"How did you get down?" Tara asked.

"Early snow comes and goes quickly. By noon the next day, it was gone. However, I would not want to cross this pass any later in the year than now. You never know when it will snow."

Jamaal continued up the slope. The group's hope for a cloudless night came true. On the exposed side of the mountain, moonlight lit the path. It was like traveling in daylight, but without colors, just combinations of black and white.

About an hour beyond the trees, Jamaal stopped the group again. "We should lead the horses for the next section. Watch your footing. It will drop off on the side and be steep."

Sliding off Maverick, Merryk looked out from their perch at the surrounding rows of mountains. "Amazing view," he said to no one in particular. Patting Maverick's neck, he asked, "How are you doing, old friend?

Characteristically, Maverick bobbed his head up and down.

The path, true to the prediction, grew steeper and narrower, slowing the passage. Soon both man and horse were puffing for air.

The elevation is as much a problem as the slope. Merryk thought.

The assent continued for another three quarters of an hour. Coming around the side of the mountain, a section of basaltic palisades rose to the side of the trail. Uniquely stacked vertical rows of rock, one by another, seemed to hold back the side of the mountain.

"At the far end of these rocks are the caves," Jamaal said as he continued to move forward. Breaking out over the crest, he added, "The path will go down from here. We will plan to stop at the tree line. It will be warmer and easier to breathe. We will need to stay there until the first light."

The moon had fallen from its apex and moved toward the horizon. As it fell, the stars popped out of the blackness in countless numbers. *At any other time, it would be great to just sit and watch*. Merryk thought.

The descent seemed less steep than the other side. After thirty minutes of walking, Jamaal announced they could ride. After an hour, as the moon finally escaped the sky, they came to the tree line.

"Even if we wanted to keep going, there is no light," Yonn said. "Honestly, I am okay with stopping."

The women, who had not complained, simply removed their saddles and rubbed down their horses. The clansmen made a fire and offered flatbread and jerky. Tara moved next to Merryk, who had laid his head on his saddle and stretched out on the ground. Placing her head on his chest, she said, "Merryk, there is something important I need to tell you."

"You can tell me later, Tara." In an instant, he drifted off to sleep.

It was still dark within the forest cover, but the sky now glowed as the early rays of the sun appeared. Jamaal nudged Merryk.

"Did you sleep at all?" Merryk asked Jamaal.

"Yes, but I seem to feel the sun and I cannot sleep after dawn. Even as a boy, I woke up before the others."

"Where are we this morning?"

"We made more progress than I had hoped. I was fearful the women would hold us back, but not a word of complaint or delay."

"They're both pretty tough. How long to the castle?"

"If we catch the light in the next half hour, I think we may make it to the castle by late afternoon." Jamaal continued, "From here it is all downhill, other than the ridge to the immediate east of the castle. Compared with what we have covered, the eastern ridge is nothing."

"I do not know how to thank you, Jamaal. I know this was a risk and I will not forget," Prince Merryk said, grasping Jamaal on the shoulder.

"You are my liege Lord, Your Highness. Helping you is my honor."

Even if it were all downhill, six more hours on a horse with only two or three hours of sleep was wearing everyone down, including the horses. Jamaal stopped more frequently as they crossed small streams to allow the group to splash cold water on their faces. A clansman prompted another break, almost falling from his horse. The focus which had marked yesterday's trip was replaced with the need to push through their fatigue.

Deep sighs of appreciation came from all as the Teardrop Castle appeared from the crest of the eastern ridge.

"We are about three quarters of an hour away," Yonn said confidently, now that he was firmly in familiar territory.

"Now all we need to do is find our smiley faces to greet the king and queen," Tara said with a hint of irony.

"How bad can it be?" Merryk asked as a smile covered his face.

CHAPTER SEVENTY-ONE

COURTYARD

With the goal in sight, everyone's spirits lifted. Even the horses sensed the end of their ride and a return to the stables.

After fifteen minutes of descent, the group came to a small stream which marked the eastern edge of the valley. Before they crossed to the castle, Merryk asked everyone to stop.

"Jamaal, can your men water the horses so we may talk?"

Yonn, Tara, Yvette, and Jamaal gathered near Merryk on the stream bank.

"I have given the arrival of the king's entourage some thought. Chancellor Goldblatt believes this is about the missing tax revenue and confronting the Lord Commander. However, asking the princess and me to visit the Capital City would have achieved the same thing. It would not have required a trip by the Lord Commander and the king. Also, a visit from the king would have been announced, if nothing else, to ensure we prepared accommodations. A simple visit would not require the attendance of both men. I believe there is something else.

"I do not know what will greet us at the castle. If this is about tax collections and my uncle perceives he is in danger or feels trapped, it would not be inconsistent with his character for him to strike out before I can talk with the king.

"If the king is in peril or already a captive to my uncle, both the princess and I will be in peril and may need to escape.

"Yonn, I need you to promise not to intervene if I am attacked. I need to know you will be alive to protect Tara and Yvette. If something happens to me, they will have no one.

"Jamaal, I would ask one thing. Regardless of what happens to me, assist Yonn in getting the ladies to safety. Take them back north, but do not intervene. Your aid would place the Blue-and-White Mountain Clans in peril."

"I would act only for myself," Jamaal replied.

"But you are a Zoo. They would interpret any action on your part as an act of the Walt. No, promise not to help me. Caring for the women's safety is enough."

Both men nodded in agreement. Then the group prepared for the last portion of the journey. Merryk followed Tara toward her horse.

"What should we do?" Tara asked, her voice soft with concern.

"You need to carry my walking stick. If I lose my grandfather's sword or cannot get to it, I will need the stick. Besides, they are less likely to remove a walking stick from a princess than a sword from a prince."

"Surely there is something more."

Merryk placed his hands on both of Tara's shoulders and looked deep into her eyes. "I need you to be brave and promise you will go with Yonn and Jamaal if anything happens. Most important, I want you to know if I could have chosen, I would have chosen you." He then pulled her closer and gently placed a soft kiss on her lips. Breaking the kiss, he said, "I have wanted to do that since the first time I saw you."

Tara melted into Merryk's arms. He could feel her heart pounding against his. "We must go," he whispered, then helped her onto her horse.

"Merryk, I need to tell you something."

"We will have plenty of time later."

He turned to the group. "I am hopeful my fears are unfounded, caused by a lack of sleep. If so, after a bath, we can have a laugh and a splendid meal."

Coming from the east meant they were not visible to anyone at the main gate until they had passed through and were in the courtyard. People filled the courtyard. Many were local and others Merryk recognized as being from the port. Carts containing food and beverages were scattered across the space.

Yonn broke from the group to address the guard at the gate. One guard moved immediately to the castle, and another joined Yonn as he returned to the group. "I have sent notice to the king and the Chancellor of our arrival."

"Your Highness, everyone will be pleased you have arrived so quickly," the guard said.

"What is going on?" Merryk asked.

"With so many visitors, it required services to come from all around."

"Many visitors?"

"It is not every day we have two kings, an arbitrator, and Judges."

Merryk caught sight of the red cloaks of Natas' Dragoons mixed among the crowd. Merryk turned and looked at Princess Tara. "Two kings and Judges?"

Tara's face lost all its color.

Finally, they reached the doors of the Great Hall and dismounted.

Smallfolks came scurrying out the door and down the steps. "My prince, I have water for you." Under his breath, he warned, "There is great danger and conflict. Your uncle is here."

Merryk drank a large mug of water in a single gulp and dumped another over his head, shaking off the excess. Smallfolks offered water to the princess and contessa.

Merryk moved to Maverick. "No matter what, do not get involved. Do you understand?" Maverick shook his head, but not in agreement.

A deep, ominous voice broke over the din of the crowd. "Still cannot manage that horse, I see."

Without turning to look, Merryk asked, "Do you recognize that voice?"

Maverick emphatically shook his head and flared his nostrils.

"Protect the women," Merryk whispered to the great stallion.

"Would the Lord Commander like some water?" Smallfolks asked as he stepped between the two men.

The Lord Commander backhanded Smallfolks across the face. "Out of my way, you old fool!"

Smallfolks fell to the pavement, dropping the tray and pitcher, which shattered on the ground.

Merryk, ignoring his uncle, went directly to the fallen Smallfolks. "Are you all right, my friend?"

"Yes, my lord," Smallfolks said, lying about his condition.

As Merryk was bending down to help Smallfolks, the Lord Commander reached out and grabbed Merryk's right arm from the rear. Merryk stood, spun his right arm around backwards, circling his uncle's. The uncle's grip failed and slipped. Merryk caught his uncle's right hand with his left and turned the thumb down, locking the elbow of the Lord Commander. Using the uncle's rigid arm as a stick, he pushed his uncle away.

"Do you want me out of the way so you can hit the old man again?"

With the push, he released his uncle's arm. Merryk filled his lungs and stretched himself to his full height, at least one half-foot taller than his uncle.

"They said he had gained weight," a voice said to Merryk's right.

"And it looks like you finally learned to stand straight," replied another voice to his left.

The voices of his two cousins echoed in his memory from their first attack.

"I do not care how straight and tall he becomes. He is still a drooling, half-blood fool and he will not push me," his uncle replied.

Moving toward Merryk, the Lord Commander grabbed Merryk's tunic
with both hands, as if to shake him. Merryk sagged a little, shot his arms
between his uncle's hands, breaking the grip, then circled his arms around
to settle them at his chest. Finally, his palms exploded upward, hitting his
uncle's riding armor in the breast. The result was a loud bang, followed
by his uncle leaving the ground and being sent backward half a dozen feet
before landing unceremoniously on his rump.

The human noises which had dominated the courtyard became silent.
No one paid attention to anything except the Lord Commander and
Prince Merryk.

"You will die for that boy," the Lord Commander's voice dripped with
malice.

"You will have to do better than you did last time," Merryk replied.

"We will not make that mistake twice, will we boys?" The Lord
Commander said as he looked at his sons. They stood, one to the left
and one to the right of Merryk, younger copies of their father. Both drew
their swords. The brother on the left struck first. A sideways slash, Merryk
avoided only by jumping backwards. Still, the tip of his blade cut Merryk's
tunic across the chest.

Merryk stepped back to Tara. "The stick."

Tara tossed the heavy piece of wood to Merryk.

"He may be taller, but he is not any smarter. Be careful brother, Merryk
has a stick," mocked the second cousin.

The same brother as before lashed outward with his broadsword in a
diagonal across Merryk's body. Merryk's stick caught the blade and drove
it to the ground, holding it there momentarily.

There was an audible click as Merryk slightly twisted the top of the
wooden stick. From inside came a sliver of shining Damascus steel. Merryk
laid the tip on the left shoulder of his cousin and effortlessly slid it directly
across to the right. For a moment, the attacker did not know what had

happened, until a look of terror crossed his face, as blood sprang from his throat.

The second cousin now pressed his attack, swinging his sword directly downward toward Merryk. All training said moving away from the blade was the correct answer, but before the blade could drop, Merryk stepped into his cousin. The blade came down, but behind Merryk without damage. Merryk pushed his cousin away. The cousin again raised both hands over his head for another downward strike. With his hands held high in the air, the bottom of the riding armor rose, fully exposing a gap at the belly. Merryk dropped to a knee and struck upward. The tip of the blade slid into the exposed gap to pass unimpeded into the heart and left lung.

The upheld sword fell to the side. The man hung on Merryk's sword until Merryk removed it, allowing him to crumple to the ground.

With a bellow like a wounded bull, his uncle charged at Merryk. Rage overcame wisdom as he held his arm outstretched. Merryk easily sidestepped the oncoming blow and brought his blade around in an arc, catching his uncle's arm at the wrist. The Lord Commander's sword fell to the ground, his hand still attached.

Merryk then lashed at the back of his uncle's legs, forcing him to his knees. Laying the blade on his uncle's shoulder he said, "Don't worry about your hand uncle; it was the one that was stealing money from my father."

"I stole nothing. I was entitled to the money as much as he was. I just took what was mine. I should have had it all."

"I understand your feeling of entitlement," Merryk said. "But why did you try to kill me?"

"You are the bastard spawn of the slut Inland Queen. You are what happens when the blood of animals mixes with royal blood. My attempt to kill you was an act of mercy. I was putting a twisted animal out of its misery."

Merryk's eyes spotted a stately man with a crown standing on the stairs. His complexion and hair color matched his own.

King Michael and Queen Amanda had come outside as soon as they heard Prince Merryk had arrived.

The king had reached the top of the steps just as the Lord Commander bellowed his promise to kill Merryk. A shout of the king's voice could have stopped everything, but surprise momentarily held him. Prince Merryk was the youthful vision of his father.

The speed at which Prince Merryk had dispatched the three seasoned warriors left no other time to speak. By the time the king had overcome his astonishment, the two nephews were dead, and his brother was on his knees admitting theft of royal taxes and an attempt on Merryk's life.

Prince Merryk, in a loud clear voice, called out. "Father, the Lord Commander has admitted to theft of the royal taxes, an attempt on the life of a member of the royal family and insulted the queen. I think treason also lurks in his heart. What is your judgment?"

The king took two steps forward to look at his brother. "Show him the same mercy he intended to show you."

Merryk nodded. In a loud voice, he proclaimed, "In the king's name, I sentence you to death."

The sliver of shining steel whipped through the air one last time, severing the Lord Commander's head from his body.

CHAPTER SEVENTY-TWO

TRIBUNAL

The silence of the crowd held for only a few moments. Soon the people broke into small groups, and murmurs filled the courtyard. Prince Merryk saw the conflict had drawn many of the Teardrop's guardsmen. Turning to Captain Yonn, Prince Merryk directed, "Please see the bodies are cared for properly. Regardless of what they may have done, they were still members of the royal family."

"Yes, Your Highness. Immediately," Yonn replied.

"Thank you for taking care of them," King Michael said as he approached his son. "Are you all right?"

"Yes, father. I am sorry I had to do that," he said, looking back over his shoulder as his men gently gathered the bodies. "They left me no choice."

"I saw everything. You were defending yourself, and the last stroke was at my command."

A woman, whom Merryk assumed was his mother, laid a gentle hand on his shoulder to get his attention. "You have changed much in the last two years, my son."

"Just nutritious food and fresh air," Merryk replied with a smile.

"It appears Chancellor Goldblatt has not been completely honest about your recovery," his father, the king, said. "Unfortunately, we have more to attend to this day before we can talk. King Natas has a complaint to present to the Provost's arbitrator."

"What complaint?" Merryk asked.

"First, wash and change your tunic, then join us in the Great Hall," King Michael said as he and the queen returned to the hall.

"Prince Merryk, I have seen many battles, but never one like that," Jamaal said as he came to congratulate Merryk. "You have the most interesting walking stick."

"Just a little something I have been working on," Merryk added with a smile.

Merryk excused himself from Jamaal and moved through the crowd to Tara, who had remained near the horses.

"Are you unharmed?" Tara asked, placing her hand on his chest.

"Only winded and in need of a new tunic," he said, pointing to the rip across his chest. "My father says your father is here and we need to join them in the Great Hall."

To no one in particular, Merryk asked, "Can somebody find me a new tunic?"

Yvette, standing beside Tara, whispered, "You never told him."

"There was never a right time."

"Now you have no time. What are you going to do?"

"I do not know."

Smallfolks, who was near, heard the request and searched Merryk's pack for an extra tunic. "Here, my prince," he said as he handed it to him. "We should move to the gatehouse so you can change."

The ubiquitous Nelly appeared with a basin of water. "Are you okay?" She said, looking at the droplets of blood splattered on Merryk's arms.

"I am fine. These spots are not mine."

Princess Tara followed Merryk to the gatehouse. When she arrived, he had replaced his tunic and was drying his hands. "We need to talk."

Before Merryk could respond, a Teardrop guard interrupted, "Your Highness, the king has requested your presence in the Great Hall immediately."

Merryk nodded in affirmation.

"Merryk, I am afraid," Tara started, but Merryk interrupted. "You have nothing to fear. We will be fine. Now we must go."

Merryk grabbed Tara's hand and gently pulled her toward the Great Hall.

———※———

Tara's mind seemed to stall. *I see the people. I hear the noise and feel the heat coming off the pavement. I just cannot feel myself. I am being pulled to my fate. What have I done? What things have I put in motion? Merryk is alive. Now whatever happens depends on me.*

Merryk looked over and saw Tara staring blankly ahead. "Tara, are you all right?"

Tara only nodded.

Entering the Great Hall was different today. As the great oak doors shut, so did all the outside sounds. They had reorganized the Great Hall. Three separate daises sat across the front of the room. The one on the right held King Michael and Queen Amanda. The one on the left held King Natas and Queen Stephanie. A simple table occupied the center dais where Father Xavier quietly sat.

Each platform also held two fully armored Judges, one to the left and the other to the right. Their polished armor gleamed in the light. Each held a full-length shield embossed with the Golden Crest of the Provost. All had their broadswords drawn with the tips touching the ground.

Another table was sitting in front of the raised platforms. Two more Judges stood near, waiting for Prince Merryk and Princess Tara.

Captain Yonn, Contessa Yvette, Chancellor Goldblatt, along with Colonel Lamaze, and Nan sat in the rows behind the empty table. Their expressions ran the gamut of emotions, from the concern of Yvette and the Chancellor to the smirk of Colonel Lamaze.

Only the sound of their footsteps on the cold stone broke the silence of the room as they walked to the small table. Tara could feel her heart straining against her chest. Only squeezing Merryk's hand helped.

"Breathe," Merryk whispered as they came to the table. His blue eyes seemed to reach out to comfort her.

After sitting down, Merryk looked up. "Why are we here, Father Xavier?"

Before the priest could answer, King Natas interrupted. His voice was sharp, cutting at each word. "We are here to review the fraud you perpetuated on the church and my kingdom. We seek the return of the dowry, damages for the insult to my kingdom, and to rescue my daughter from a sham marriage."

Father always seeks to intimidate those around him.

"Is that all?" Merryk replied. His eyes focused on King Natas.

Father does not intimidate Merryk.

"This is not a joke, boy," Natas' answer was tinged with anger.

"We have evidence they never consummated the marriage. It was a fraud just to gain the dowry. A plot designed to steal from me and to embarrass the church."

"You will need more than the guesses of servants to support this claim," Merryk said as he looked back over his shoulder at Nan.

"I do not base my claim on guesses or servants, but on the statement of my daughter. She knows the truth."

Tara saw Merryk's face go blank, his shoulders slumped. She had done what three experienced warriors could not do. She had defeated him. *If I saw hatred, it would be better than the disappointment I see.*

"They warned me," was all Merryk said, shaking his head from side to side.

King Natas began to speak, but Father Xavier interrupted him. "There is no reason to delay with useless arguing. We have Princess Tarareese here. She can give her own testimony." Looking at Tara, "It is all right, my dear, you have nothing to fear. Please tell us the truth of this matter. Is your marriage a sham?"

Can I be brave? Tara took a deep breath and stood to address the tribunal. "It is true we have not consummated the marriage, but this was at my request, not Prince Merryk's. I was attacked on the way to the Teardrop, and I feared, if we did not marry immediately, my life would be in peril. Prince Merryk wanted to wait. He promised to protect me, but I insisted we go forward with the ceremony. I made him promise, on his honor, we would not be intimate until I chose. As a man of true honor, he has kept his promise. Failing to consummate this marriage falls on me. There was no plot to deceive or to commit fraud, just a silly girl wanting to be safe and make choices for herself."

For a moment King Natas' face showed surprise at his daughter's answer, then in a flash, it hardened as he pursued his attack. "Regardless of the motivation, the truth is there is no marriage. The marriage contract has not been fulfilled, and I am entitled to damages, the recovery of the dowry, and the return of my daughter."

"No, father, I love this man. He is honorable, strong, brave, compassionate, and gentle. I cannot imagine my life without him," Tara shouted.

"She is clearly fearful of him. Father Xavier, declare this marriage void and we can go home," Natas pressed.

"I can promise you, Father Xavier, this will be a genuine marriage, at least if Merryk still wants me." Tara turned to Merryk. "I choose you."

King Natas now attacked his daughter. "So, you promise proof again. No, you had your chance. We cannot believe anything you say. There is no future proof you can provide that we will trust. At this moment, the marriage is a sham, and that is the only truth."

Helga's words rippled through Tara's mind. *Something you never imagined.*

"Then your proof will be presented. Mother, Queen Amanda, and Father Xavier please, come with us?"

"Tara, what are you doing?" a confused Merryk asked.

"Please, Merryk, I beg you, trust me one more time."

King Natas started to complain, but Father Xavier had already risen to follow the two queens. All three followed Tara as she pulled Merryk into the anteroom just off the Great Hall.

"What is going on?" King Natas demanded.

King Michael, who had only listened to this point, replied, "I am afraid we have no choice but to wait. Kings or not, the women will have their due."

Chancellor Goldblatt did not know how long the group was gone. The click of the doors to the anteroom broke the silence of the hall. A befuddled priest scurried out. Father Xavier, a man of pale complexion, was now stark white. Shaking his head and talking to himself, he returned to his place on the dais. The priest was not a worldly man, and whatever he had witnessed rattled him.

"Do you want us to stay until you are ready?" Queen Amanda asked as she looked back at Prince Merryk and Princess Tara, who were adjusting their clothing.

"No mother, please go ahead. Tell the tribunal we are right behind you," Merryk replied.

Queen Stephanie and Queen Amanda moved out the door of the anteroom, which Father Xavier had left open in his hasty exit. They chatted as they exited the room.

"Our mothers seem to get along nicely," Tara said as she moved next to Merryk.

"Are you all right?" he said, extending his arms to envelop her.

She snuggled into his chest, "Yes, I am all right. How about you?"

"This was not how I imagined—"

Tara cut him off by placing a single finger on his lips. "I propose you show me later what you had imagined, and then I will show you what I had imagined."

"A proposal I can accept," Merryk said playfully. "But first, we need to find out the judgment of the arbitrator." Merryk's voice turned serious. "We have chosen each other; now, we must trust each other, no matter what. I want you to know, regardless of the decision, I will not let them take you away from me."

"Nor will I go," she said, reaching up for another kiss.

"Okay, we must go now," Breaking away from the kiss and pulling Tara toward the door.

Just outside the door, Merryk stopped. "Do you still have the nightgown from our wedding night?"

"Yes," she smiled.

❦

Queen Stephanie came forward to the dais and dropped a soiled cloth at the feet of her husband. "We owe the Father a new shawl," she said as she joined Queen Amanda in returning to their seats.

Goldblatt recognized immediately what had transpired. Before Natas could recover and begin another attack, he stood. "Father Xavier, if I may speak on behalf of the prince and princess." He did not wait for approval, but began.

"King Natas asked for immediate proof of the marriage. It is hard to conceive of proof more immediate or better witnessed. Each kingdom was represented by their queen and you representing the Provost. This is a genuine marriage. A fact to which you can now testify.

"Although King Natas seems focused on the dowry and its return, the church's purpose for wedding contracts is to establish viable families. Families which help join nations together to prevent strife. The dowry is secondary to this purpose, in fact incidental.

"King Natas may argue, because of the fraud, it cannot so easily be cured. But the testimony is his own daughter was the driver of the incident. There is no justice in rewarding King Natas for the fraud of his own daughter. The Council of Justice cannot allow a person to benefit from the fraudulent action of their own representative. The long-term ramifications of such a decision on future agreements would be devastating.

"The conduct of the two young people is not to be approved, but they are young. Passion fills their decisions more than logic. Both should acknowledge their lies and ask the church for forgiveness.

"Beyond question, they fulfilled the marriage contract today and the most King Natas can say is he prematurely paid the dowry. A slight matter now that he is required to pay it.

"I know your superiors have given you instructions to verify the evidence and end this agreement. However, when you received those instructions, no one could have expected the heroic act of Princess Tarareese. I am not aware of any royal princess proving her marriage with such courage.

"Based upon all you have heard, and especially upon what you have witnessed, declare this a completed contract and a viable marriage. Then, we can enjoy a glass of sherry."

"It is not that easy," King Natas responded.

Father Xavier raised his hand to interrupt. "King Natas, I believe it is just that simple. You complained they had not consummated the marriage. The couple has given indisputable proof of what you wanted. The marriage contract is complete, and the marriage is viable. We have nothing further to do."

Upon hearing the pronouncement, all the Judges moved to escort the priest from the room. There was no doubt the proceeding was over.

King Michael and Queen Amanda left the dais to talk with Chancellor Goldblatt. Queen Stephanie went to the back of the room to find her daughter. King Natas began to argue but found no one to listen.

By the time Merryk and Tara returned to the Great Hall, the priest was standing to leave. King Michael and Queen Amanda met Merryk and Tara as they reached the front of the room.

"What is happening?" Merryk asked.

"Nothing, thanks to the ingenuity and courage of your wife," King Michael said with a broad smile on his face. "The contract is fulfilled, and all is right with the world. Except the two of you need to apologize for lying to the church."

"I think a letter of contrition to the Provost will do," Chancellor Goldblatt said as he joined the two couples. "I will draft it so we can send it back with Father Xavier."

Seeing her mother approaching, Tara said, "If you will excuse me, your majesties, I would like to speak with my mother."

"Father does not look happy," Tara said, pointing to King Natas as he stormed out of the room.

"He was dealt an unforeseen loss."

"I am sorry, mother, but I just knew I needed to hold on to Merryk. He is the man I love, and who I believe can love me."

"My prayer answered," Queen Stephanie replied.

"I hope so," Tara said. "The Oracle of the North said if I were brave, all might be saved. Is there still a chance of war?"

"There is always a chance of war, but without the sanction of the Council of Justice, no one would aid your father. Political forces dictate the time for war, and your decision disrupted those forces. I do not believe there will be a war, but conflict will continue between the High Kingdom and your father."

"Merryk wants the Teardrop to stay out of any conflicts. He says we are not interested in our fathers' issues so long as they do not affect the Teardrop."

"Your father may take solace from Prince Merryk's neutrality. No more about politics. Now tell me all about your handsome prince."

Chapter Seventy-Three

AFTER

Three sharp knocks rang at the door to Merryk's room. "Your Highness, please, it is late. The king is looking for you, and Queen Amanda and Queen Stephanie want Princess Tara to join them for morning tea."

Sliding out of bed and into his robe, Merryk went to let in Smallfolks.

The lump of blankets on the bed slowly reacted to a stretch by the hidden occupant.

"I have tea and something for you to eat; but you both must hurry. I have run out of excuses for your absence," Smallfolks said in desperation.

"All right, we will hurry. Now please leave and let us get dressed," Merryk replied.

The lump spoke, "Master Smallfolks, please ask the contessa to get me an appropriate dress and bring it here."

"Yes, Your Highness," Smallfolks said as he scurried from the room.

Merryk pushed the heavy curtains away from the windows, allowing the bright sun to cascade into the room. "It is later than I thought."

Tara's head emerged from the blankets for only a moment and then retreated like a small child, hoping for more hours of sleep.

"Tara, get up. Everybody is missing us. Smallfolks brought boiled eggs and bacon."

"Would not you rather just come back to bed?"

"What I would rather do is not important. We must get going."

There was another knock at the door. This one lacked the urgency of the first.

"Good morning Yvette," Merryk said to the contessa as he opened the door to let her into the room.

"I will get dressed in the other room," Merryk said as he exited to his closet.

Yvette laid the dress over a chair and then mercilessly began poking at the lump. "Get up! Get up! Get up!" It was a familiar chant she had used many times over the past decade.

Knowing it would not cease, Tara emerged from the blankets.

"The queens are in the garden. We need to hurry. Your mother and father are leaving tomorrow morning with Father Xavier and the Judges. This is your chance to see her alone."

Merryk was amazed at how fast Yvette had gotten Tara moving. By the time he had returned to the room, they were already working on her hair. He grabbed a boiled egg and some bacon while they finished.

"Not perfect, but it will have to do," Yvette said.

"Okay ladies, let's go."

Entering the Great Hall, Merryk saw Chancellor Goldblatt. "I need to talk with the Chancellor. Please go ahead. I will find you later."

Tara and Yvette moved about halfway across the Great Hall when King Natas came through the front doors, followed by Colonel Lamaze.

"He does not look any happier today than yesterday," Tara whispered to Yvette.

"Good morning, father."

With no acknowledgment, he began, "I expect betrayal from everyone else, but never from you." King Natas moved his hand upward to slap Tara.

Mother said, 'do not turn your head. The slap will hit your ear and that is worse.' Tara shut her eyes, expecting the blow.

The sickening sound of flesh against flesh rang through Tara's head. Except there was none of the accompanying sting of the blow or the jerking of her head.

Opening her eyes, she saw her father's hand suspended in the tight grip of Merryk's. The two men's eyes locked without blinking.

Merryk spoke first. "We do not hit women."

"She is my daughter."

"She is now my wife."

"I am a king."

"You are a visitor in another man's castle."

King Natas shook Merryk's grip from his arm as he lowered his hand. Colonel Lamaze moved near King Natas. The king, for a second, looked like he would direct the colonel to act.

Merryk saw the look. "A waste of a soldier and the breach of the terms of arbitration," he said, motioning over his shoulder to where two Judges stood.

Before King Natas could walk away, Merryk asked, "I was hoping you and I could speak alone for a moment. Tara, please go to our mothers. Everything here is all right."

"We can go into the anteroom," Merryk said to King Natas.

"Why not?" King Natas responded. "You seem to use it for everything."

Merryk laughed, "Perhaps we should call it the multipurpose room."

King Natas smiled despite himself.

"Colonel Lamaze can wait outside the door," Merryk said. Once inside the room, Merryk motioned for the two to sit on opposite couches.

"I am uncertain why you violently object to me as a groom, and I do not expect you will tell me. However, your attack on your daughter is a concern. As of *now*, she does not know you tried to kill her on the way to the Teardrop."

"You have no proof," King Natas said emphatically.

"Your daughter told me you are a very logical man. If you will indulge me, I will explain my proof; both inferred and direct."

King Natas replied, "You are very wrong, but I am interested in how you came to such a ridiculous conclusion."

Merryk started. "Three simple reasons: First, you sent her early in stormy seas on a boat ill-suited for the trip, hoping for it to be lost."

"How would you know this?"

"You paid the captain double the normal fee; half up front and the second half to whoever he picked, even if he did not return. The ship you selected lay at anchor with two new ships, both better suited than the flat-bottom boat you chose. You also demanded they take a direct route for speed, one that increased the peril."

Natas replied, "At a dangerous time of year and with important passengers, an extra fee just made sense."

"Very well. Second is a bit of a love story. It involves a lady of noble birth and a lieutenant in the Royal Dragoons, one of your men. The lady's father refused to give permission for them to marry, unless the man had reached the rank of captain. So, he undertook a dangerous and secretive mission, with a guarantee of promotion upon completion. I am sure he was told to strip all indications of his origin, but the order could not stop his love from giving him a token—a special necklace with a simple medallion and an intricate silver chain worn under his shirt.

"Your country is known for the skills of your silversmiths. They are very proud of their work and strive for uniqueness. Each craftsman can readily identify their work.

"The leader of the men who attacked your daughter wore such a token."

"Interesting story, but I do not see how this attaches the man to me. How do I know such a chain exists or if it came from the attacker? Attackers were killed by a mysterious woodsman who was never found."

"I know it came from the attacker, because I tore it from his neck after I killed him," Merryk said matter-of-factly.

King Natas tried to disguise his surprise by remaining silent.

"I also watched as Colonel Lamaze instructed his men to hide the bodies, so when my men came to examine them, they were gone."

King Natas had no further response. After a few moments, he said, "You said you had three reasons."

"I think the last is the most compelling. You refused to send Tara's horse with her. Throughout all the kingdoms, it is said if you had to choose between a horse and a member of your family, you would choose the horse. If Tara had been killed, either at sea or by the attack, you would never get the mare back. A loss you were unwilling to accept."

"This story explains why Tara would betray me."

"Except," Merryk added, "she does not know. I thought you and I might come to an understanding, which would make this revelation unnecessary."

King Natas stood and walked to the cold fireplace. "What do you want?"

"Four simple things: First, upon your return home, in a good ship, send Tara's horse to her.

"Second, I have control of the taxes for the Teardrop Kingdom. I propose an agreement, with a five-year term, to remove all taxes on trade between our countries and guarantee standard docking fees. You have many items to sell. We have a few. The agreement would open markets for both. Chancellor Goldblatt has prepared the document for your signature. We can execute it in front of the priest before you leave. Consider it a sign of good faith.

"Third, Tara told me you have some large horses from the Vale of Clyde. We would like a small breeding herd—a stallion and five mares. We will pay a reasonable price."

King Natas returned from the fireplace back to where he had been sitting. "My daughter will not be told of your speculation?"

"I will not share 'my speculation' with your daughter. You have my word of honor."

"You said there were four things."

"Yes, I want you to promise you will stop trying to kill us."

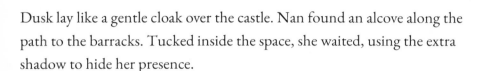

Dusk lay like a gentle cloak over the castle. Nan found an alcove along the path to the barracks. Tucked inside the space, she waited, using the extra shadow to hide her presence.

Colonel Lamaze was punctual, arriving shortly after Nan.

"Did you speak with the king? Can I come home?" Nan asked the questions in rapid succession.

"Calm down," the colonel said. "The king needs a method to communicate with the princess and receive updates."

"It has been only six months, but this place makes it seem like forever. There is nothing here. I do not know how these people survive. Even if I wanted to stay, I am not sure that Prince Merryk will allow me."

"King Natas wanted me to tell you how much he admires your support but believes the next year will be critical. If you can stay that long, then you can come home," Colonel Lamaze said with the most sincerity his lie could muster. "You must stay to protect the princess and for the king.

"Here is more coin. Continue to cultivate Father Aubry as an ally. The king is not through with this young prince or his father."

CHAPTER SEVENTY-FOUR

BEFORE WE LEAVE

"My mother and father want to meet with me tomorrow morning before they leave," Tara said.

"Going to see your father alone is not a good idea, particularly after his attack yesterday, and the swollen face your mother tried to hide this morning at breakfast. I will not allow him to hurt you."

"With my mother there, I believe I will be all right. Also, an attack on me would violate the terms of arbitration. You can send the swordmaster and another guard to escort me. If they hear any disturbances, they can come in, but I do not think it will be necessary."

⁂

The next morning, the castle was buzzing with activity as the guests prepared to return to the port. King Natas, Queen Stephanie, Father Xavier and all the Judges, even the ones assigned to protect King Michael, were departing. "I should not need the protection of Judges in my own kingdom," King Michael had said.

Amidst the turmoil, Princess Tara made her way with the swordmaster and three guardsmen to the suite of King Natas.

Two Royal Dragoons, along with two Judges, were standing outside the door.

"The princess is here to see King Natas," the swordmaster announced.

"Very well, we have been expecting her," the senior dragoon said as he stepped aside to open the door for Tara.

Before stepping through the door, Tara turned to one of the Judges. "I am entering as a representative of my husband and King Michael. I assume I have your protection."

"Absolutely, Your Highness."

"Good morning, mother and father," Tara said as she entered the room.

"I am glad Prince Merryk allowed you to come," King Natas said as he rose to greet his daughter.

"We have tea," Tara's mother said from the small round table in the corner. Queen Stephanie had selected her seat to hide the darkening bruise on her face.

"First, yesterday's encounter was unfortunate. I know you can appreciate my frustration. I believed my help was requested and you can always count on me to come to your aid. The letter I received painted a dire picture. I was doing what any father would do.

"Your mother and I both spoke with you before you left. We believe nothing we have seen has changed those instructions. The young prince seems quite enthralled with you, just as we had planned."

"I love him," Tara replied defiantly.

"Of course," Natas replied, furrowing his brow in sincerity.

Tara looked at her mother, who was listening but not engaging in the conversation. She kept her eyes cast down.

This will be father's talk. Tara thought.

"I know, as my daughter, you will do the right thing when the time comes.

"I also wanted you to know I am sending your horse to you as soon as I return. Having something from home will remind you of your country and should reduce the tedium. Now that I have seen the Teardrop Kingdom, I am surprised anyone can live here."

"Thank you, father. I have missed Bella and it will seem more like home if she is with me."

"Now, if you will excuse me, I must join Prince Merryk and Father Xavier to sign a document. As a token of my good faith and to show there is no ill will, I asked Prince Merryk to accept an agreement to waive taxes and duties on all goods between the Teardrop and my kingdom. This will help tie you closer to your true home."

Standing, he gave Tara a perfunctory hug before leaving the room.

Tara sat down with her mother. "How magnanimous of him to accept the proposal Merryk submitted to him yesterday. Prince Merryk and I discussed the mutual relationship before he presented it," said Tara sarcastically.

"It is your father's nature to claim victory in the face of loss, and he has never been shy about taking credit for the ideas of others."

Changing the subject, Tara's mother reached across the table and grabbed her daughter's hand. "I am so proud of you. Your courage at the tribunal was remarkable. I am sure future noble mothers will tell the story of Princess Tarareese.

"You need to remember what motivated this courage was not the purposes of your father, but your genuine desire to find happiness with Prince Merryk. As I get older, I recognize how rare this is. I support your father, as is my duty, and I will never work at cross purposes to him; unless it is necessary to protect you."

"Even when he beats you?"

"Yes."

"I have never seen rage like father's in Prince Merryk. All I have ever observed was disappointment. Merryk's look of disappointment is worse than being hit."

"That is because you love him, and his opinion matters above all else. I have never seen you happier. You have completed your duty to our kingdom. Now it is your duty to support your husband; not follow the directions of your father. I believe supporting Merryk will not be difficult.

"I do not know the brother, Prince Merreg, but after meeting Prince Merryk, I think you can still be a queen."

"Merryk does not want to be king. He is content with what he has and what he can do for the Teardrop Kingdom and its people."

"Exactly the type of man who should be a king."

"Perhaps, although I think Prince Merryk as the king would be a challenge for father."

The two stood and moved toward the door. Queen Stephanie stopped. "One last thing, Yvette asked me to tell her mother she had found a sheepherder. A strange message. Do you know what it means?" she asked.

Tara smiled.

At midmorning, the assembled group: Father Xavier, King Natas, Queen Stephanie, and the Judges—all rode out the castle gate. At the rear, a bruised and black-eyed Colonel Lamaze led the group of Dragoons.

As the last person went through the gate, Captain Yonn joined Merryk on the steps of the Great Hall. "They should set sail in three days. Not soon enough for me," Yonn said.

"Yonn, this morning the swordmaster told me there was some kind of altercation last night in the training arena. Do you know anything?"

"It was nothing. Colonel Lamaze asked for a lesson in hand-to-hand combat. No weapons—just hands. I was showing him some of the techniques you and I use."

"How did the lesson go?"

"I tried to teach the Colonel not to lead with his face. He is a slow learner. In the end, he got the message."

Before walking away, Merryk patted Yonn on the shoulder.

CHAPTER SEVENTY-FIVE

KING'S ISSUES

The ambient sound within the castle had dropped with the departure of the tribunal participants. The vendors and extra servants who came to help gathered their belongings to return to their normal lives; further reducing the din. It had only been three hours, and already the castle was moving toward normality. The only remaining guests were King Michael, Queen Amanda, and their guards.

Jamaal ZooWalter and his men had left at the break of light, hours before the main group.

"I see you are getting an early start," Merryk said, finding Jamaal and his men in the stables.

"As I said, something about the sun just wakes me up," Jamaal replied. "Thank you for your hospitality and for introducing me to the king."

"I owe you the thanks. I am not sure we would be in the same place if you had not gotten us here when you did. Tara and I owe you a debt of gratitude. If there is ever anything you need, please let us know. Also, extend my thanks to Gaspar."

"I will. I will also be sure Oolada gets your present."

"I just hope Lady Zoo doesn't use them on me."

"Not to worry, My Lord, she seldom attacks friends." Jamaal's face reflected his natural sense of humor.

"Have a safe trip. Until we meet again." Merryk shook Jamaal's hand. Within minutes, the Blue-and-White Clansmen vanished into the north.

Merryk used the lull in activity to visit Maverick. Picking up a brush and running it along the side of the stallion's neck relaxed Merryk as much as the horse. "My old friend, how are you today? Things have been crazy since we returned. Have you rested from our journey?"

As always, the horse responded to each question with a nod of his head or a shake of his mane.

"Any other woman would be jealous of your horse," Tara said as she joined Merryk in the stables.

"I'm sure Maverick would tell you your jealousy is justified because I love him the most."

The stallion bobbed his head in agreement.

Tara moved next to Merryk, adding her hand to the side of Maverick's neck. "I know the love of a horse is different and I am not threatened. Soon Bella will join us. My guess is after Maverick sees her, he will have someone else to love."

"Excuse me, Your Highnesses," Smallfolks politely interrupted. "The king would like Prince Merryk to join him in the Chancellor's study."

"Go ahead, I will finish here," Tara said, taking the brush from Merryk.

Merryk bent down to give Tara a kiss on the cheek and followed Smallfolks to the study.

Merryk entered the study to join King Michael and Chancellor Goldblatt. The two older men sat around the low table in front of the fireplace. A pitcher and three cups of tea rested in the middle.

"Good, Smallfolks found you," King Michael said, pointing to offer Merryk his grandfather's empty chair. "I was pleased to see my father's chair had been returned to this room. The Chancellor said it seemed to fit you. I see he was right.

"Merryk, Geoffrey and I have been talking. Under normal circumstances, your mother and I would stay a week or so to get reacquainted with you. However, these are not normal times. The death of my brother will set in motion several things within the kingdom."

"Father, I'm sorry for causing so much trouble," Merryk said.

"On the contrary, you were able to do what I had found impossible. You exposed a thief and a traitor in a manner which shielded me from any responsibility. In some circles, it will make you unpopular, but for me, it was the removal of a difficult political problem. Having the sons meet their fate at the same time also stopped any revenge from the family. The three men had many women, but never wives. There are no recognized heirs.

"My current problems are both financial and military. Chancellor Goldblatt, would you explain the financial?"

"Merryk, as you know, the information we received described the shock caused by returning the tax collector to the Capital City. The amount of money returned did not surprise the Lord Commander. I believe he thought we brought everything we had found. He never knew we had delivered money to the king earlier in the year. Quickly taking care of Jarvis reassured the other tax collectors. Returning the revenues to normal levels was intended to stop the king from further inquiry, just as we had concluded."

"Nevertheless, I believe every tax collector has two sets of books," the king interjected. "We need to get to the records before they are destroyed and collect the extra money. My guess is the money is in the Lord Commander's palace. I need to seize both the money and the books."

Chancellor Goldblatt continued, "Which means the king must appoint a new Master of Revenue and new tax collectors. We have identified a potential candidate, the son of Duke Blountsymth. He is in his early forties, knows the workings and perils of the court, and his family has been loyal to the throne for over 300 years."

"My next problem is military," the king said as he stood and moved toward the window.

"The Lord Commander and his sons were the top three military officers. Their loss will shake the ranks. Every officer was hand selected by the Lord Commander and loyalty was everything to him."

"That explains the looks of contempt I've been receiving from your guards," Prince Merryk added.

The king continued, "The only person with a chance to keep control is your brother, Prince Merreg. He has been with the Lord Commander for many years and is the natural replacement to command, not only because of his title, but because of his previous support for the Lord Commander.

"The problem is, I cannot do these things away from the Capital City. I need to be there when notice of the Lord Commander's death is announced."

Chancellor Goldblatt added, "The king believes this will send some rats scurrying for safety and others for power; both of which he needs to observe."

"As a result, we need to leave in the morning. I asked your mother if she would like to stay for a visit, but she recognizes the challenges I face, and did not want to be away from me. Although she would be safer here."

"Father, until Prince Merreg can control the military, you may be in personal danger."

"As I am sure the Chancellor has explained to you, a royal is always in danger."

"I would like to send ten Teardrop Guardsmen to escort you, mother, and the bodies of our family members back to the Capital City, as an 'honor guard.' They can also act as your personal guard until you have trusted people around you," Merryk said.

"Most astute," the king said, "My compliments to you, Chancellor Goldblatt, for educating my son to think like a member of the royal family."

"In time, Your Majesty, you will come to understand Merryk needed little guidance; he has superior instincts."

"Geoffrey and I have not always agreed. The last events have reminded me of how much I value his opinion. I want you to know I have asked him to return with me to resume his duties as Chancellor. Before you object, he respectfully declined, unless I commanded it. The Chancellor said he is still concerned about King Natas' role in these events and potential revenge against you. He asked to stay with you, and I agreed, so long as we continue our correspondence."

"The Chancellor is correct," Merryk added. "King Natas played a bigger role in everything than we can explain. Did the Chancellor tell you we believe he tried to kill Princess Tara? We still don't understand the reason."

"Yes, I would like to say I am shocked, but King Natas is a driven man. If he felt it would forward his objectives, he would not hesitate."

"Princess Tara does not know of our suspicions," Prince Merryk added. "I don't want to affect her relationship with her father."

"Again, my son, remember to be careful where you place your trust. Be assured, I respect your opinions and I will keep your confidence."

"Now go find your mother and spend the rest of the afternoon with her. Take your bride with you. She is really a remarkable young woman."

The last dinner with the king, unlike the two previous, was a small family event, just the king, queen, Merryk, and Tara. The conversation was light.

The physical changes in her son amazed Queen Amanda. King Michael commented several times about Merryk's resemblance to his father. It amused King Michael that Merryk had a big black horse and wore the same long black coat, just like his father.

Shortly after the last course, Tara whispered to Merryk. "Tara just reminded me tomorrow will be a long day for you, and she is tired from our trek across the mountains. If you wouldn't mind, we would like to retire."

"An excellent idea," King Michael said. "I would not mind having a good night's sleep before we face the road and the sea."

Merryk held Tara's hand as they walked to their room. After reaching the top of the stairs, Merryk said, "I'm a little surprised you're still tired from our journey."

Tara released Merryk's hand, stepped ahead of him, and turned to walk backwards for a moment. "*You* said I was tired; *I* said it was time to go to bed." With a broad grin and a slight skip, she hastened ahead of him toward their room.

Merryk stopped, but only for a second.

CHAPTER SEVENTY-SIX

GOODBYE

The top of the old tower was always the best place to start a new day. The passing of the full moon seemed to open the door for cooler weather. A crisp sky kissed with a slight blush of red filled the morning horizon. Waifs of gray clouds hung in the distance.

Merryk's thoughts were as mixed as the colliding colors.

It has only been two years since I first stood here. I am not sure anything has changed, except me. Two years ago, I thought of myself as a person stranded in a strange place looking for a way home. Today, I stand looking out over my home. I remember what it was to be Raymond, but now, as Merryk, I have found my place in this world. This is a world with a future. I feel like Merryk can make a difference here; more than Raymond could in his world.

The sounds of people scurrying below making the last preparations for the king's departure brought Merryk's attention back to the present. *I must go see everyone off.*

The efforts of many had the carriages loaded quickly. Within an hour after breakfast, the king and his entourage were ready to depart.

Prince Merryk approached the swordmaster who was cinching his saddle for the ride. "Thank you for leading our group. I know Captain Yonn warned you. This could be dangerous. The king is unsure of who he can trust, so your presence is important. Protect the king, but be careful. I want everyone back as soon as possible. My father promised a ship for your return. I pray it will be before the storms of December."

"Not to worry, my prince. This reminds me of going away as a young lad, except I know what can happen. All who are coming are veterans and single, except for Jason, who said his wife was glad to be rid of him."

Merryk and the swordmaster laughed.

"Goodbye, my son," King Michael said as he gave Merryk an awkward hug.

Merryk's mother gave a quick hug to Tara and then grasped Merryk tightly. "I am so proud of the man you have become," she said. "I asked Tara to convince you to come see us in the spring."

"I will see if we can make that happen," Merryk said, releasing his mother. "Now, I hope you have a safe trip."

Then, without additional fanfare, the caravan left. The swordmaster spread the Teardrop's men to match the king's own guard, one for one. *The swordmaster is not taking any chances.* Merryk thought.

CHAPTER SEVENTY-SEVEN

GIFTS

The warm fall days continued into October. The deciduous trees covering the low hills surrounding the castle turned every imaginable color; shades of gold only overshadowed by rusts and reds.

In the evenings, Merryk and Tara often stood on the top of the old tower, looking out at the sky. The nights were clear, and the stars erupted with the subtle shadows of the Milky Way. The air grew colder with each passing day, but Tara seemed perfectly warm wrapped in Merryk's arms.

"I saw Yvette with Yonn today," Tara commented.

"That is not unusual," Merryk replied.

"But they were holding hands. I think Yvette may have convinced Yonn they are more alike than he knows."

A full month after Tara's father had left the castle, she and Chancellor Goldblatt sat in the new library space working on the categorization of the castle's books. The task, which had originally seemed like punishment, had become a joy to Tara. She thrived on the complicated problem. *Chancellor Goldblatt has become a good friend. I had forgotten how rewarding intellectual challenges can be. This is important work, and I truly enjoy working with the Chancellor and Merryk.*

"Tara! Tara!" Prince Merryk yelled as he hastily came into the library. "You must come now!" Without waiting for a reply, he grabbed her hand and almost dragged her down the stairs and out the front doors.

Coming through the main gate were half a dozen monstrous horses. The reddish-brown animals were marked with bold splashes of white across their chests, white manes, and socks on each leg.

"Our horses are here," Merryk said in excitement.

"Horses? Where is Bella?" Tara asked as she hurried down the steps toward the oncoming herd. Bringing up the rear was a white mare covered in a royal red blanket. The horse's long, slender features were a stark contrast to the raw strength of the Clydesdales. While the larger horses moved with strength, Bella held her head high and her normal stride was more of a prance, the embodiment of elegance.

"Bella!" Tara shouted as she ran past the other horses to the mare, wrapping her arms around the horse's neck. The white mare's reaction was a mirror of Tara's joy. The horse nuzzled Tara and pressed her neck against her in a virtual hug.

A young man stepped forward to Prince Merryk. "Your Highness, I am Petri and this is my brother Paulo. We escorted the horses from King Natas. If you choose, we have been given permission to stay and serve you as stable attendants. We have worked with the big horses all our lives and know their temperaments. We also have this letter for Princess Tara and all the bloodline books for each horse."

"Welcome Petri and Paulo. I am sure we can find a place for you in our stables. I had forgotten how magnificent these animals truly are. We will be glad to have your expertise in dealing with them."

Merryk took the letter to Tara, who was still talking to Bella. "Tara, from your father," Merryk said as he handed her the letter.

While Tara read the note, Prince Merryk reached out to pat the white mare. "Bella, I am Merryk. I have a friend you will like."

After reading the letter, Tara turned to Merryk. "My father sends his regards. He says although you offered to pay for the big horses, he is going to give them to us as a wedding present. He also said before you thank him, we should feed them for a while. He said he hopes that Bella and we will be happy. There is also a note from my mother, which I will read later."

The warm days could not last. Ultimately, they were overcome by the grayness and chill of early winter skies. Sun occasionally broke through the cover, but only in small fits and never with an intensity to generate warmth.

The second week of November, Captain Yonn sought the prince, finding him with Chancellor Goldblatt in the study.

"Prince Merryk, the swordmaster and our men have returned."

"Your Highness," the swordmaster said as he bowed his head.

Merryk ignored his formality and gave him a hug. "Welcome back. I was afraid you decided to stay forever."

"Not to worry. All of us were eager to come home, except maybe Jason, who was not looking forward to seeing his wife." The swordmaster continued, "Prince Merryk, the king said to assure you he is fine and to deliver these letters and documents to you and the Chancellor."

Merryk turned to see one of the guardsman's arms filled with a large bundle carefully wrapped in both canvas and leather. "Thank you," Prince Merryk said.

When everyone except the Chancellor had left, Merryk turned his attention to the bundle. Opening the package, he discovered a bound volume with multiple ribbons coming from beneath its cover. "What is this?"

"It is a wedding present from the king," Chancellor Goldblatt said. "Your father and I discussed it before he left. These are the title documents to the whole of the Teardrop Kingdom, together with all documents necessary to pass total control to you. You are now the sovereign of the Teardrop Kingdom."

Merryk's hand reached out to open the tome. "But why?"

The Chancellor explained. "You solved an impossible problem for the king when you killed your uncle. There was no practical way for the king to confront the Lord Commander and maintain control of the Army without risking a breakup of the kingdom. Your fight was not the actions of the king, so his death was not the king's doing. Getting your uncle to admit to his theft, in front of his own men, cleared the way for the king to seize money others might have claimed and silenced opposition.

"Finally, your father gave you the Teardrop Kingdom because he hoped to avoid future conflict between you and your brother. Now each of you has your own kingdom. Although the bulk may go to your brother, you and your family will always have a place."

Later that evening, Merryk held onto Tara's hand as they returned from the stable. As they crossed the courtyard to the main castle, Merryk looked up. The short days of winter had already dropped the castle into darkness. Pops of early stars were scattered across the sky.

"This has been an amazing few weeks," Merryk said as he scanned the sky. "You have Bella, we have our men back, and I don't know what to say about the present from my father."

Before Tara could respond, Merryk lifted Tara's hand over her head, spun her around, and then dipped her in his arms to give her a kiss.

As he pulled her back into a standing position, she caught her breath and asked, "What was that for?"

"It is just good to be young again."

EPILOGUE

On a stone balcony in Crag d'Zoo, the ancestral fortress of the Zoo Clan, Helga stood looking toward the jagged peaks which lay on the horizon. After a few minutes, she returned to the warmth of the fire.

Gaspar ZooWalt sat in his chair looking into the fire.

"Before you ask, I have seen nothing. Everything feels like it is in balance."

"I *so* wanted Prince Merryk to be the one," he replied.

"Prince Merryk is a 'man of destiny,' but it is unclear if he is the 'man of prophecy.' I believe he is a force for good, but my experience is, good never goes unchallenged. How he responds will decide. All we can do is wait."

ACKNOWLEDGMENTS

It is an overused expression that writing is a journey, but it is true. My records indicate I wrote the first outline of this trilogy in July 2017, nearly six years before the publishing date. How long the ideas had bounced in my head before then, I truly do not know.

Like all first-time authors. I was reluctant to begin. Finally, my forty-year friend, Ken Olsen, gave me the last push. "Are you going to talk about a book or write one?"

Once I decided to go forward, a group of people came alongside me with comments, criticism, and, most of all, encouragement. These books would never have happened without each of their contributions.

My books were molded by these early readers: Ken Olsen, Bob Cramer, Teresa Hooker, Eugene and Robin Walker, Steve and Patti Davis, Michael Pratt, Dwayne and Sue Mattson, Hilary Barnes, Sarah Gruhler, Russ and Emily Boardman, and A.J. Sousa. Each provided a unique point-of-view, and I can say without a doubt, the book is better because of each of their contributions. Two played additional roles. Eugene Walker provided the technical editing for books one and two, and Steve Davis consulted on the martial arts. I will always be thankful to this group of individuals.

I dedicate this book to my wife, Tricia. She has affected the book more than any other person. Dedicating the book to her seems too little for her hours of reading and editing. This is as much her book as mine. Thank you for believing in me and pushing when needed.

There are three reasons people write books—you have a story you want to tell; you want to make money; or you want to be famous. The reality is the only thing you can do is tell your story. Everything else is beyond your control.

So here is my story. It is about the importance of being true to yourself and to your guiding principles, regardless of the circumstances. The question is, *how would you respond to this circumstance?* My hope is you will like the story. If so, please tell others.

Thanks,

J. R. Clemons

ABOUT THE AUTHOR

J R Clemons is a retired business executive and life-long resident of the Pacific Northwest. His family consists of his wife, their four daughters and nine grandchildren. All live within a fifteen minute drive of his home. J R grew up on classic science fiction, Dune and Foundation, although nothing impacted his view of storytelling more than Tolkien.

Books in **The Raymouth Saga**:
The Shell – *Book 1*
God's Tears – *Book 2*
Destiny's Choice – *Book 3*

Made in the USA
Columbia, SC
20 February 2023